ALSO BY EDWARD KELSEY MOORE

The Supremes at
Earl's All-You-Can-Eat

The
Supremes
SING
the Happy
Heartache
BLUES

The Supremes SING the Happy Heartache BLUES

EDWARD KELSEY MOORE

HENRY HOLT AND COMPANY NEW YORK

Henry Holt and Company
Publishers since 1866
175 Fifth Avenue
New York, New York 10010
www.henryholt.com

Henry Holt® and 🛡® are registered trademarks of
Macmillan Publishing Group, LLC.

Copyright © 2017 by Edward Kelsey Moore
All rights reserved.
Distributed in Canada by Raincoast Book Distribution Limited

Library of Congress Cataloging-in-Publication Data

Names: Moore, Edward Kelsey, author.
Title: The Supremes sing the happy heartache blues : a novel / Edward Kelsey Moore.
Description: First Edition. | New York : Henry Holt and Company, 2017.
Identifiers: LCCN 2016048172 | ISBN 9781250107947 (hardback) |
ISBN 9781250107923 (electronic book)
Subjects: | BISAC: FICTION / Sagas. | FICTION / African American / General. |
FICTION / Cultural Heritage.
Classification: LCC PS3613.O556 S88 2017 | DDC 813/.6—dc23
LC record available at https://lccn.loc.gov/2016048172

Our books may be purchased in bulk for promotional, educational, or business use. Please contact your
local bookseller or the Macmillan Corporate and Premium Sales Department at (800) 221-7945, extension
5442, or by e-mail at MacmillanSpecialMarkets@macmillan.com.

First Edition 2017

Designed by Kelly S. Too

Printed in the United States of America

1 3 5 7 9 10 8 6 4 2

This is a work of fiction. All of the characters, organizations, and events portrayed in
this novel either are products of the author's imagination or are used fictitiously.

For my father,
Reverend Edward K. Moore Sr.

The
Supremes
SING
the Happy
Heartache
BLUES

CHAPTER 1

*I*t was a love song. At least it started out that way. The lyrics told the tale of a romance between a man and the woman who made his life worth living. Being a blues song, it was also about how that woman repeatedly broke the man's heart and then repaid his forgiving ways by bringing a world of suffering down on him. The beautiful melody soared and plunged, each verse proclaiming rapturous happiness and gut-wrenching pain. Here, in a church, this piece of music couldn't have been further outside its natural habitat. But the tune's lovely mournfulness echoed from the back wall to the baptismal pool and from the marble floor to the vaulted ceiling and settled in as if the forlorn cry had always lived here.

As the song continued and grew sadder with every line, I thought of my parents, Dora and Wilbur Jackson. The blues was Mama and Daddy's music. Nearly every weekend of my childhood, they spent their evenings in our living room, listening to scratchy recordings of old-timey blues songs on the hi-fi. One of those might have been as sorrowful as the dirge ringing through the church, but I couldn't recall hearing anything that touched this song for sheer misery.

Mama preferred her blues on the cheerier and dirtier side—nasty tunes loaded with crude jokes about hot dogs, jelly rolls, and pink Cadillacs. The gloomy ballads, like this one, were Daddy's favorites. I never saw him happier than when he was huddled up with Mama on the sofa, humming along with an ode to agony. He would bob his head to the pulse of the music, like he was offering encouragement to a down-in-the-mouth singer who was sitting right next to him, croaking out his hard luck.

Sometimes, before sending me to bed, my parents would allow me to squeeze in between them. They've both been dead for years now, but their bad singing lingers in my memory. And, because I inherited their tuneless voices, I remind myself of my parents every time I rip into some unfortunate melody. Whenever I hear a melancholy blues, I feel the roughness of Daddy's fingertips, callused by years of carpentry work, sliding over my arm like he was playing a soulful riff on imaginary strings that ran from my elbow to my wrist.

I'd be ordered off to bed when Mama'd had enough of the dreariness and wanted to listen to a record about rocking and rolling and loving that was too grown-up for my young ears.

Even though the song rumbling through the sanctuary would have been a bit dark for Mama's taste, she'd have loved the singer's wailing voice and the roller-coaster ride of the melody. And she wouldn't have let this song go unnoted. If she had been in the church with me, she'd have turned to me and declared, "Odette, your daddy would've loved this song. Every single word of it makes you wanna die. I've gotta write this in my book."

My mother's "book" was a calendar from Stewart's Funeral Home that she kept in her pocketbook. The cover of the calendar showed a gray-and-white spotted colt and a small boy in blue overalls. They were in a meadow, both of them jumping off the ground in an expression of unrestrained bliss. Above the picture were the words "Jump for Joy," and below, "Happy thoughts to you and yours from Stewart's Funeral Home." Whenever Mama ran into something that she felt was remarkable enough to merit celebration, she wrote a note on that day's date so she'd never forget it.

Mama's book first appeared on a Sunday afternoon about ten years before she passed. We'd just walked out of our church, Holy Family Baptist, and Reverend Brown stood at the bottom of the front steps saying good-bye to his flock. Mama strode up to him and said, "Reverend, you're the best preacher I've ever heard. I've been thinkin' about your Easter sermon all spring. It was truly a wonder; really opened my eyes. I want you to know that you can consider this here soul a hundred percent saved."

Reverend Brown, who was more than a foot taller than Mama, bent over and took her hand. "That's so kind of you, Dora," he said. "I'm just doing what I can for the Kingdom."

"I mean it," Mama said. "You've won this battle for the Lord. And I wanted to make sure to thank you, since I won't be comin' back."

Reverend Brown hung on to Mama's hand and waited for her to deliver the punch line to what he assumed was one of the peculiar jokes she was known to tell. But Mama wasn't kidding. She explained, "Remember how you preached that if we really wanted to be closer to God, we should look at the world around us and write down a little thank-you to Him for all the things He gave us? Well, I took your words to heart and I've been doin' that ever since."

Mama opened her pocketbook then and pulled out a rolled-up wall calendar. She flipped three pages back to Easter and showed the pastor where she had written, "Best Sermon Ever" in the little square for that date. Then she showed him how she had jotted brief notes on each day of the calendar since then.

"Reverend, you truly preached your ass off this mornin'. But, just like you said, it was nothin' compared to the way I feel when I'm sittin' alone, thankin' God directly. So I'm takin' your advice and skippin' the middleman." She waved her calendar in the air. "From now on, I'm goin' straight to the source."

She pulled a pen from her pocketbook and wrote an entry on that day's date in her book that read, "Second-best sermon ever." Then she patted Reverend Brown on his cheek and walked away from Holy Family Baptist forever.

Stewart's Funeral Home came out with a new calendar each year. Since Mr. Stewart was notoriously cheap, he reused the same cover. Mama had a fresh "Jump for Joy" book every January.

Her habit of hauling that calendar out, scribbling on it, and reciting her observations to anyone nearby was just one of many odd behaviors Mama was content to display in public. I was uncomfortable with the additional stares and whispers that followed her newest eccentricity, but Mama was immune to embarrassment. She told me, "Folks can laugh at me all they want. But when the blues comes lookin' for me, I'm gonna wave my little book at it and tell it to move along, 'cause I know how to jump for joy."

She wrote in her book until her last morning on this earth.

As the sanctuary reverberated with the howling third verse of the astonishing blues singer's lament, I imagined Mama beside me in the pew, writing, "Bluest blues in all creation." With Mama in mind, I leaned toward my husband, James, and shared my evaluation of the music filling Calvary Baptist Church: "This is the saddest song I have ever heard."

James said, "Your old man would've loved it."

The singer who sat hunched over his guitar in a dark corner, crooning and roaring about loving and forgiving his cruel woman, looked to be about seventy. He was tall and skinny, and he had a white beard that swallowed his face from nose to neck. James was right. Daddy would have loved the way the blues man bent the pitches of the tune in such a bleak way that you knew love had brought him trouble and that there would be more bad news coming in the days ahead.

"The blues is what a love song turns into after the singer's had his teeth kicked out," Daddy once said. What kind of beating had life given to this bearded man, who stared at the floor and filled the room with gorgeous sorrow? How did he end up here, curled around his guitar, letting loose a heartbreaking cry for all the world to hear? Every line of this song brought to mind Daddy's definition of the blues. There was no way this man had a single unbroken tooth left in his mouth.

Full of love, loss, passion, and bitterness, the song was made even more pitiful by the occasion. It accompanied a radiant bride as she made her stately procession down the center aisle toward her groom. She moved toward the altar with an ease and grace that were quite impressive, considering the character of the music and the fact that she had recently celebrated her eighty-second birthday.

The bride, Beatrice Jordan, was the mother of my best friend, Clarice. Miss Beatrice was a leading member of Calvary Baptist, the most nononsense church in Plainview, Indiana. She was a good Christian woman whose greatest source of pride came from being a better Christian than anybody else.

I loved Miss Beatrice, but she was so extravagantly and annoyingly devoted to the Lord and to making sure that everybody else was, too, that being around her for too long had a way of shattering my resolve to keep His Commandments. Over the years, she'd pushed me to take the Lord's name in vain more times than I'd like to recall. And Miss Beatrice had driven everyone I knew to think about murder at least once.

The groom was Mr. Forrest Payne, the owner of the Pink Slipper Gentlemen's Club, the only legally operating business in Plainview that had ever been called scandalous. The club had been known for on-site gambling, prostitution, and a flagrant disregard for all liquor laws. There was a time when reputations were ruined and marriages destroyed just because previously respectable men had been seen walking near the Pink Slipper's door.

The club's unsavory public image scared away many potential

customers but served as effective advertising for just as many others. My aunt Marjorie swore that the Pink Slipper was the only place in town to hear the blues done right, as well as the only place to find corn liquor as potent as the killer brew she concocted at home. She was a Pink Slipper regular till the day she died.

And when I say "till the day she died," I mean it. Aunt Marjorie had a fatal heart attack while disarming a man who'd pulled a knife on her during a fight at the club. At her funeral, Forrest Payne comforted Mama by telling her that her sister had passed with her opponent's knife clutched in her fist and a satisfied grin on her face.

The brawls, overt prostitution, and gambling were now history, or so I'd been told. These days, the club was more likely to be spoken of as a respected music venue than as a low dive. Forrest had been rehabilitated, and his business had been purified along with him. The major reason for his rise from social pariah to elder statesman and philanthropist was, at that moment, serenely gliding his way, clutching a bouquet of pale peach roses and silvery-white chrysanthemums.

This love match had taken everyone by surprise. Over the years, Miss Beatrice had become famous around town as the nutty old woman who regularly stationed herself on a hillock at the edge of the Pink Slipper's parking lot and yelled warnings of eternal damnation at arriving and departing patrons through a bullhorn. She blamed Forrest for facilitating the repeated infidelities of her first husband, my friend Clarice's father. And it had become her life's mission to keep other men from following that same sinful path. In spite of her softened feelings toward Forrest Payne, even nowadays she showed up at the parking lot occasionally to shout at patrons on evenings when the dancers stripped. She'd left the bachelorette party Clarice had put together for her the night before her wedding to do just that. But since romance had warmed her heart, instead of yelling, "The fires of hell await you, sinner!" at departing customers the way she used to, Miss Beatrice now hollered, "God bless you, fornicator! Drive carefully!"

Several times during the ceremony, I glanced over my shoulder and searched for Mama. The idea that I might see her wasn't just wishful thinking on my part. In addition to a wide mouth, a round frame, and a tendency to talk too damn much, I have also inherited my mother's ability to see dead people. Mama was the first of the departed to seek out my company. She surprised me in the middle of the night several years after her passing, and she visits me regularly. Dead, Mama can be as much of a handful as she was when she was alive. But she's easier to take than a number of the spirits I've had to contend with.

Events that defy explanation draw my mother to them like magnets, so I found it hard to believe that she could stay away from the union of Beatrice Jordan and Forrest Payne. Mama's spirit was nowhere in sight, though. So I paid close attention and took note of every detail around me. It's not easy to astound a ghost, but the next time she stopped by, I intended to give Mama a description of the day's festivities that would knock her socks off.

Looking as perfectly put together as always, my friend Barbara Jean Carlson sat on my left side in the pew, adjusting her pearl necklace and smoothing nonexistent wrinkles from her skirt. Back in the 1960s, our schoolmates had started calling Barbara Jean, Clarice, and me "the Supremes" after the singing group. The more widely known Supremes had been separated by fame, acrimony, and death. But more than forty years after our trio was formed, the Plainview Supremes stood united.

Barbara Jean cozied up to her husband, Ray. But she and I had our eyes on Clarice, to the preacher's right, waiting for her mother to finish her journey down the aisle. That day, it was our job to remind Clarice, who was still in shock over her mother's change of heart regarding Forrest Payne, to smile. To that end, each time Clarice looked our way, we grinned and gestured toward our faces as if we were presenting brand-new refrigerators to contestants on a TV game show.

Poor Clarice. Whenever she forgot to smile, she took on the astonished expression that had first crossed her face a few months ago when she'd learned of her pious mother's romance with the owner of the Pink Slipper Gentlemen's Club.

Miss Beatrice had told her daughter that her love affair with Forrest began the night she was stranded at his club by a sudden snowstorm that blew in during one of her bullhorn protests. He had insisted that she wait out the storm in his office, and they'd chatted for hours over tea. After that, they'd become inseparable.

What Clarice said to me was, "Mother claims that saving Mr. Payne's soul is like climbing a spiritual Mount Everest. She can't resist the challenge." Miss Beatrice had also told Clarice that Forrest Payne had served her loose-leaf Earl Grey from a bone china tea service. Though her mother had gone to the Pink Slipper to do her version of God's work, it was the tea service that had won her over. Clarice had said, "I tell you, Odette, fine china is like opium to that woman. The moment that Wedgwood cup hit her lips, Mother was a goner."

We may never learn whether it was the Good Book or the china that brought Miss Beatrice and Forrest Payne together. But as his bride marched toward him, Mr. Payne looked as happy as a kid on Christmas morning. And Miss Beatrice seemed overjoyed to be marrying the man she'd spent decades denouncing as a servant of Satan.

The silver-embossed wedding program identified the saddest processional music ever heard as "The Happy Heartache Blues." When the song came to an end, the bearded blues man disconnected his guitar from the amplifier and limped away from the altar with an awkward gait that made me think he might be older than I'd guessed.

Calvary Baptist wasn't the sort of church where people applauded music, religious or secular. Such a display would be considered tacky at best, damnable at worst. But when the singer finished, everyone on the groom's side of the sanctuary and plenty of folks on the bride's side clapped in ovation. The blues man shuffled off without acknowledging the applause.

The pastor then began a loud and harsh homily, full of accusations and dire predictions. This was in keeping with Calvary Baptist's reputation as the church most likely to tell its members that weekly attendance was the only thing keeping them from heading straight to hell. It was a sermon right up Miss Beatrice's alley. With every mention of damnation, she turned toward the wedding guests and nodded her head in agreement so we wouldn't get the impression that she was going to allow the joyfulness of the occasion to stand in the way of her efforts to save our unworthy souls.

Despite the gloomy music and the brimstone-heavy sermon, the wedding was lovely. Clarice and her mother had planned it to perfection. Miss Beatrice wore an exquisitely embroidered ivory-colored suit with an ankle-length skirt. The groom wore a gorgeously tailored black suit, which was a shock for everyone in attendance; few in Plainview could recall seeing Forrest Payne in anything other than his signature canary-yellow tuxedo. According to Clarice, there had been a compromise between her mother and her soon-to-be stepfather, granting Mr. Payne the right to choose the wedding march and Miss Beatrice the right to banish the yellow tuxedo for one afternoon.

Calvary Baptist Church is the prettiest house of worship in Plainview. It might not be what most people would call a friendly or inviting place, but the altar is made of ornately carved oak with, as its centerpiece, a magnificent pastor's chair that would have been right at home in a medieval castle. The towering stained-glass windows paint every surface in the sanctuary with color and make you feel as if you are at the center of a rainbow. At Calvary Baptist, you can't help but contemplate the Divine.

Behind the baptismal pool, there is a mural of the Crucifixion that makes the angry shouting of the pastor in front of it fade from your mind. The depiction of the bare-chested, muscular Jesus in the painting is so sexy that it's hard to take your eyes off it. Sunday services at Calvary tend to go on forever. By the second hour, the majority of the congregation's ladies, and a fair number of the men, start taking a mental break from their weekly browbeating to stare up at the beefy Lord and Savior on the wall. The Redeemer's charms are so potent that most congregants can't recall the sermon's topic by the time of the benediction.

In this setting, two unlikely people proclaimed their everlasting love for each other in front of an amazed assemblage.

With a few reminders from Barbara Jean and me, Clarice managed to hold on to her smile, even as she played the piano during the blessing of the rings. Clarice is an extraordinary musician. She had already begun winning ribbons and praise for her piano playing when we met as five-year-olds. But after a midlife resurgence, she was no longer Plainview, Indiana's secret. She was making recordings and traveling the country, performing for bigger audiences every year.

Clarice's handsome husband, Richmond Baker, served as Forrest Payne's best man. As always, Richmond radiated charm and goodwill. But it was hard to know if he was genuinely happy about having a role in the proceedings or was putting up a front for the sake of his wife.

In the fifth year of a separation, Clarice and Richmond's marriage had finally hit smooth sailing. For Clarice, anyway. Life as a semi-single woman fit Clarice better than marriage. She was happy living in her own house and entertaining Richmond only when she saw fit. For nearly all the years they'd been together, Richmond had been as proficient an adulterer as Clarice's father had. Yet Richmond was still trying to comprehend why Clarice had decided she couldn't stand living with him anymore.

Decades of watching him break Clarice's heart had seen me alternating between fantasies of taking a hammer to his head and visions of using a cleaver on his private parts. But even I had to admire the hard work he'd put in to demonstrate to Clarice how much he'd changed since she'd left him.

It was especially tough for Richmond to show that he'd given up his old ways on the day of Miss Beatrice's wedding. The groom's side of the sanctuary was populated with women who knew Richmond from a time before he became enlightened. Five years into his non-promiscuous existence, these ladies still remembered him quite fondly. From the front to the back of the church, top-heavy dancers from the Pink Slipper Gentlemen's Club and other extravagantly dolled-up women waggled their fingertips at Richmond and mimed phones at their ears, mouthing, "Call me." Even as he did his best to ignore them, I was certain that Richmond's already oversized ego was expanding every second that he stood alongside Mr. Payne up at the altar.

After Clarice finished playing—the wedding program said the piano piece was "Clair de Lune," by Debussy—she took her place beside her mother again. Miss Beatrice gave her daughter a kiss on the cheek, and the pastor gave the assembled guests one more warning to repent from our evil ways before moving on to the vows.

If Richmond didn't take notice of the behavior and appearance of the folks on the groom's side of the room, the Calvary Baptist regulars filling up the bride's side certainly did. Miss Beatrice's family and friends reacted to the exposed cleavage, gaudy jewelry, body piercings, and general raucousness of the Pink Slipper folks with a combination of open-jawed gawking and loud clucks of disapproval. Miss Beatrice's grandchildren seemed to be the only members of her family having a truly good time. Clarice's daughter and three sons, who had all come from their homes out of town to witness their grandmother's surprising coupling, could barely contain their amusement. Clarice's children were all over thirty, but the occasion had them giggling and whispering into each other's ears like schoolkids. They stopped only when Clarice gave them the stink eye from the altar.

After Miss Beatrice and Forrest Payne were pronounced man and wife, their guests stepped outside into brilliant sunlight. In another week or so, the weather would be hot and humid, but on this day, the skies were cloud-free and there was just enough of a breeze to make the men feel comfortable in their suits and ties. The air smelled faintly of freshly mown grass and of smoke from charcoal fires in nearby backyards.

Mama would have adored everything about this day. She'd have witnessed an infamous purveyor of indecency and a woman who had devoted herself to stomping out, or at least *pointing* out, sinfulness profess their love for each other. She'd have seen the upstanding members of Calvary Baptist Church looking like their heads were going to explode as they played host to a crowd of people they'd have preferred to burn at the stake. And Mama would have had herself an annoyingly gleeful time, humming along in her wandering pitch with "The Happy Heartache Blues."

As the guests tossed rice on the newly married couple, the flower girl, Clarice's seven-year-old granddaughter, excited and happy in her lilac taffeta dress, ran circles around her ring-bearer cousin, leaping up into the air and trying to touch that glorious blue sky. Mama, never one to restrain herself in the presence of wild exuberance, would likely have shared in the rejoicing by jumping right along with the flower girl, and then scrawling an entry into her book.

Weeks after the wedding, I would look back and wonder if things might have turned out differently if Mama had seen or heard the old blues man that afternoon. Just a few words from her might have changed the outcome, or at least given James and me a chance to brace ourselves. But that's how this journey works. We can't prepare for the calamity heading our way, because it never looks dangerous until it's right on top of us. We're always too busy singing our sweet love songs and jumping for joy to realize that our teeth are about to get kicked out.

CHAPTER 2

*E*l Walker told himself that once he was back at home, even though he wasn't certain where home was anymore, he would see the humor in the latest turn his life had taken. He would cash his check, buy a bottle of whiskey, and have a good laugh about having spent two weeks in Plainview, Indiana, the one town on earth he'd sworn he would never visit again. But right now, his only laughs came from watching the ongoing slapstick routine performed by the patrons as they walked past him. One after another, they stumbled over a deep dip in the floor a little more than an arm's length from El's barstool. When he'd walked into the Pink Slipper Gentlemen's Club earlier that day, he had surprised himself by smoothly sidestepping that depression in the slatted wood as if it had been just a few days, instead of decades, since he'd last entered the place.

He'd warned Forrest not to let Leroy build that floor back in 1949. Leroy was a hell of a bass player, but he had already disappeared into the heroin hole by then. He was the first of the bandmates to get hooked, and he couldn't be trusted to do anything other than bang out a bass line. But Leroy's father was a local handyman with a good reputation, and Leroy had looked like such a natural when swinging a hammer that Forrest had foolishly let him loose on the floorboards of his new emporium, where Leroy did just the kind of job a junkie could be expected to do. The floor he constructed rose and fell drastically every few yards. Now three generations of the club's patrons owed twisted ankles and spilled drinks to that strung-out mess of a bass slapper.

El, along with Leroy and the rest of his bandmates, had helped build the club in '49. Forrest had run out of funds halfway through construction, so he'd promised El's band a regular weekend gig if they would pitch in to finish the place. They'd been children, most of them too young to legally enter the club. And they'd had no idea what they were doing. But together they'd scavenged, begged, or stolen every stick of lumber and each nail, and they had assembled something that still stood.

The juke joint they'd cobbled together as teenagers had been repurposed a number of times and had become the cornerstone of Forrest's ten-acre complex of spectacularly lucrative enterprises. Now the rickety shack had been declared fashionable by a new generation. Restored to its original mission as a haven for blues lovers and drunken fools, it was more popular than ever.

El thanked the bartender for his second whiskey. All those years of traveling and playing at clubs small and large—well, mostly small— and the best thing about the traveling life remained the free drinks. Alcohol calmed his nerves. Nearly seven decades of performing, and El still felt a tingle of fear each time he moved toward a stage. That was a fact the boy who had helped build this place would never have believed.

Booze also dulled the pain in his foot. Numbness had been the problem before El had lost two toes to complications from diabetes a year before. Now sensation had returned with a vengeance. The discomfort had grown worse over the last couple of months and had spread past his ankle. He turned on his stool and faced the stage on the opposite side of the room. With his back pressed against the bar, he swung his right leg back and forth several times, hoping that improved circulation might rush the healing alcohol to his sore foot.

The ache had subsided somewhat since he'd performed at Forrest's wedding one day earlier. And now the whiskey had begun to warm his spirit as it anesthetized his foot. With each sip, El silently thanked Jim Beam for his infinite mercy.

The band onstage was a five-piece group, just like El's had been in the early days. Sax, keyboard, string bass, guitar, drummer. They weren't half bad for a bunch of college kids. Most of them were classical players from the state university on Plainview's east side. Like a lot of the young ones El ran into, they had gravitated to the blues because they wanted to wear fedoras and talk like hepcats from a 1950s movie. The kids could play their instruments, though. They had chops to burn. It wasn't their fault that having chops wasn't enough. And, of course, they didn't have Lily. Nobody sang or pounded those piano keys like Lily.

El was astounded to see that the sax player was sipping from a bottle of water. *Water.* Who ever heard of a blues man drinking water? Blues men drank whiskey and, occasionally, coffee or Coca-Cola to recover from the booze they'd consumed the night before. But never water. After the show, the kids would surround him as they always did nowadays, seeking advice and asking questions about every cut on El's one album, bootleg copies of which they all seemed to own. El would tell them that the first step to being blues men was to spit out any drink that wasn't some shade of brown.

Bubba, the sax player with whom El had shared the stage across the room half a century earlier, wouldn't have been caught dead drinking water. At thirty, Bubba had been the only real adult in the band at the beginning. He had claimed to have been playing with the same reed since he was twelve years old, a feat made possible because both he and that thin slice of bamboo had been preserved by repeated soakings in cheap liquor. El knew that Bubba had been exaggerating. But the man's saxophone had sounded great, and at thirty, Bubba looked like a school-boy. So maybe there was something to it.

Bubba had a long face that reminded El of the large and exception-ally ornery horse El's foster mother had owned. And Bubba had been nearly as brawny and tough as that horse. El had seen Bubba put away two fifths of Old Crow in a single evening and still have enough coor-dination and confidence to ask the finest women in the joint for a dance. It was Bubba who was usually left with the job of picking up the less experienced drinkers from wherever they'd collapsed at the end of the night. The sight of Bubba hauling limp drunks, draped over his wide shoulders, two at a time, through the club's doors was something El would never forget.

Bubba was long gone now. Done in by his unquenchable passion for quick-tempered and well-armed women. Unfortunately, they had loved him right back. He'd died in 1972 in a hospital bed, where he'd been recuperating from a gunshot wound inflicted by his final poorly chosen girlfriend. The bullet wound had been a minor injury, and he'd been due to leave the hospital the day he died. But then he got caught in the crossfire of a gunfight that broke out between his girlfriend, who had come to apologize for shooting him, and his wife, who had been keep-ing a vigil at his bedside. At his memorial service, the police had to be summoned to contain the brawl that broke out among a dozen of Bubba's women. El knew of at least six blues songs that had been com-posed about Bubba's funeral. He'd written one himself.

Tonight, there was one more act before El was supposed to go on. The emcee, a round little man in a maroon sharkskin suit, trotted up to the microphone and asked the audience to show their appreciation for the band. Then he announced the next performer. "Our man El Walker is back at the Pink Slipper after a long absence, folks. And he'll be taking the stage in just a minute. But first, we'll see some dancing and get the Good News from sweet Charmina. Y'all put your hands together for our favorite servant of the Lord. And dig deep in your pockets to help this little lady put a new organ in her church's loft. Here she is, the Pink Slipper's own pole dancer for Christ, Miss Charmina."

An attractive young woman strode onto the stage. Charmina had a lovely face. She had full lips, large brown eyes, and round cheeks. Her black hair fell onto her shoulders in glistening ringlets that bounced with each step she took. Her Kewpie-doll dimples gave her an air of innocence even as she strutted in front of the band toward the pole at the end of the runway at center stage.

El liked that she had some meat on her. Most dancers were so skinny these days, but not her. Back when he was part of the original house band, the girls were bigger. Much bigger. No one talked about firm abs or well-defined arms back then. Any woman who took the stage without jiggling a little couldn't hope to be handed any real money. More likely, she'd be handed a ham sandwich.

Charmina was in no danger of wasting away. Her generous curves were outfitted with, and accentuated by, a bodysuit that perfectly matched her skin tone, making it appear from a distance as if she were nearly naked. Over her bodysuit, she wore a bikini made of dozens of green felt fig leaves. In one hand, she carried a large white wicker basket.

With her free hand, Charmina flung aside a curtain that covered an easel. Her grandly theatrical gesture revealed a sign that read, "Eve's Expulsion from the Garden of Eden." When she thrust a hip toward the band, they began to play "What a Friend We Have in Jesus."

Charmina had already been working for Forrest for several years when, after leaving the club one night, she had staggered, drunk, into a revival meeting. Once saved, she immediately ceased performing most of the services that had made her the most popular dancer at the Pink Slipper, opting instead to hand out Scripture verses and to interpret biblical scenes through pole dancing. At first, her new act didn't go over well with the club's regulars, and Forrest came close to firing her. But her sincerity and her polite reminders to Forrest that, being an elderly man, he should get right with the Lord while he still had the opportunity moved him to allow her to dance for the glory of Jesus on Sundays, his slowest night.

To Forrest's surprise, the faithful began flocking in to see Charmina. Her Sunday Gospel Dance soon rivaled Saturday nights in popularity. And Charmina's fund-raising proved so successful that her pastor's wife, who had once been among her most vehement critics, was now her biggest supporter. The first lady of Calvary Baptist Church had converted from foe to fan the moment the tally of Charmina's donations from her opening month at the Pink Slipper was announced. It was a habit of the pastor's wife to jot down multiple money-raising suggestions on Post-it notes during the church finance committee's meeting and pass them along to her husband. When she learned the amount of money Charmina's theological pole dancing had brought in, her only note to the pastor read, "Recruit more whores."

The Scripture-based stripping paid off in ways Forrest hadn't imagined. Charmina got to spread her message. Forrest developed a new customer base and inched nearer to heaven. Calvary Baptist Church acquired a new roof and was on its way to a new pipe organ. And when the nature of Forrest's relationship with Beatrice took its dramatic turn, he was able to offer up Charmina's performances as evidence that he was redeemable. Everybody won.

Now Charmina moved fully into the lights of the stage and set down the basket. She reached inside and extracted a snake. Six feet long, El guessed. A pale yellow-and-ivory albino python. Draping it across her shoulders and down the length of both arms, she began to dance. The snake's name, El would later learn, was Percy.

El couldn't abide snakes. It was a lingering effect, he believed, of the years he'd spent with a foster mother who was as nutty as hell and obsessed with snakes. When she was angry with him or any of the other kids, she would force them all to assemble in the kitchen. She would plant herself at the head of the table and, opening her Bible, tell them just what happened to misbehaving children when they received their punishment in hell.

"First, you get cast into a pit," she'd say. "Then the snakes come for you. Big snakes. And you can yell all you want. Just gonna be more snakes comin'. Squeezin' and bitin' to beat the band. Then you'll know the wages of sin for sure." After she'd made her point, she would use her Bible to deliver a slap to the backside of whomever she was angriest at that day. Then she would leave them in the kitchen to contemplate their penitence.

El had been his foster mother's favorite, so he hadn't gotten the closed fist, the hickory switch, or the extension cord as often as the other children. Still, she had regularly whacked him with her Bible until he was fourteen and had grown so big that she worried he might hit her back. From that point on, she would simply touch her index finger to the corner of one eye to let him know that she was watching him. "Snakes, you little bastard," she would say. "Snakes."

El took another swig of whiskey to drive away thoughts of that foul woman, but Charmina didn't make it easy. She and her snake were slithering toward him through the crowd. As the band played, Charmina strolled from table to table. Whenever she received a tip, she exchanged the bills for one of her fig leaves, so her felt-foliage bikini disappeared as she collected donations. By the time she worked her way over to El, the top of her bodysuit was uncovered. Not wanting to be any closer to Percy than he had to be, El practically tossed two dollar bills at her to get her to go away. When he looked at the fig leaf she'd left with him, he saw that it had an inscription on it. He held it up high where the light was a little better. When El read the words on the foliage—"His Forgiveness Awaits You"—he shook his head and muttered to himself, "Tell me God ain't got a sense of humor."

El's attention was drawn back to the music. The kid playing the string bass was engaged in a flirtatious back-and-forth with Charmina, who made her way toward the band, her fists bulging with bills. She climbed onstage, shaking her hips in perfect time to his thumping beat. The band began "Jesus on the Mainline." To the roaring approval of the audience, Charmina playfully tucked her last fig leaf into the bassist's shirt pocket. Then she and Percy returned to the pole to finish their dance.

The bass player was a healthy-looking red-haired kid. Studying his sweet young face and his permanent blush, El imagined that the boy's cheeks had been pinched by a doting grandmother just before he took the stage. Poor messed-up Leroy had been around the same age as this youngster when he'd ruined the bar floor in 1949, and they were both good musicians. But Leroy, who had been as scary and strung out as the redhead was angelic, switched his addictions every season or so and could never have been accused of looking healthy. When Leroy was doing cocaine, he would rush the tempo so aggressively that they had to add an extra song to each set to fill the remaining time. On heroin, he stretched everything out so long that Bubba would turn gray from lack of oxygen as he tried to hold the ever-lengthening notes on his sax.

Leroy outlived Bubba, but not by much. The band was in Memphis recording their one album, the one that was supposed to make them all rich and famous, when Leroy announced that he was done. Done with dope. Done with alcohol. Done with loose women. Done with the band. He said that Bubba's death had shown him the error of his ways. As he packed up his bass, Leroy told his bandmates that they were heathens in his path. Then he raised his middle finger to them and stomped off to seek God. They never saw him again.

El never learned if Leroy found God. But God found Leroy for sure. Just a week after leaving the band, Leroy was struck dead by a bolt of lightning while walking down a busy Memphis street. He had his wallet in his hand and was exactly halfway between a Christian bookstore and a massage parlor when the lightning got him. Whether he died a righteous man or a sinner depended on who was telling the story.

"It's a sweet, sweet day to be alive, ain't it, El?" someone said.

The mixture of rasp, sibilance, and singsong was unmistakable. One of the many remarkable things about Forrest Payne was that what you heard coming out of him didn't match what you saw, not even a little bit. He had the off-center nose and hulking build of a boxer, though he'd never been in the ring. His hands were checkered with faded jail-house tattoos. But when he spoke, he sounded like a twelve-year-old bully performing a mean-spirited imitation of a young girl with a lisp.

Forrest, like El, was a tall man. Both of them had once been six-three. Neither towered over the crowd the way they once had. But wasn't every-thing smaller now that they were old men? The music, the people, the entire world. El was months shy of his eightieth birthday. And Forrest . . . El didn't know for sure how old Forrest was, but he knew that Forrest was every bit as close to the grave as he was.

Forrest wore a canary-yellow tuxedo with a white silk shirt. Lacy ruffles poked out of the cuffs of his jacket sleeves. It was the uniform he had worn since he'd opened the Pink Slipper in 1949. El had been along when Forrest bought his first yellow tux at a shop in Evansville the night before the club opened. Five minutes after they'd walked into the store, a slick salesman had the two country boys convinced that the yellow tux was practically a necessity for any young business owner. "This suit announces, 'I'm lively and classy, too,'" he'd said. And they'd been naïve enough to believe him.

By the time Forrest realized he'd been taken, he had grown to like the way he looked in yellow. Six decades later, he owned twenty garish yellow tuxedos. Few people had ever seen him wearing anything else.

Forrest placed a manicured hand on El's shoulder. "It's a sweet, sweet day to be alive," he said again.

"I wasn't expectin' to see you around today," El said. He watched a slightly drunk young couple crash into each other as they negotiated the crater in the floor. Then he asked, "Your wife here, too?"

"Bea won't come in a place that sells liquor." Boasting of his respect-able bride's virtue caused Forrest to puff out his chest and straighten his spine. "She might show up out in the parking lot and do a little protestin' later. She's determined to steer me over to the right path. God love her."

"That oughta keep her busy," El said. He brought his hand to the breast pocket of his jacket before remembering that he had given up cigarettes after a bout with pneumonia a few years ago. Besides, by law, there was no smoking in the Pink Slipper now. Clean air and blues men drinking water in public. What had the world come to?

"Gonna have a honeymoon?"

"Oh, we'll take a trip sometime soon. But I'm not about to miss my man El."

The band launched into an up-tempo anthem, and the crowd responded by clapping along with the drumbeat. El swung and flexed his aching foot in time with the music. "They're good," Forrest said. "But y'all had the hunger."

"We had the hunger, all right." El chuckled and tossed back the rest of his drink. "We were damn near starvin'. Remember that time Lily passed out in the second show, nothin' in her stomach?"

"Yeah." Forrest hummed along with a few lines of the tune the band was roaring through. Then he said, "Speakin' of Lily, a customer from the old days came through last week and told me he'd run into her in Chicago."

"Don't know anything about that," El grunted. He regretted having mentioned her name. Being here was bad enough.

Forrest pointed at El's empty glass, and the bartender rushed over with a refill. "James was at the wedding," Forrest said. "Did you see him?"

El waved his whiskey beneath his nose like smelling salts. Setting his drink on the bar, he used his index finger to push an ice cube to the bottom of his glass. He brought his finger to his mouth and let a drop of whiskey, far better liquor than he could afford these days, roll across his tongue. "No, I didn't see him."

"I'm not tryin' to meddle in your business, but you might wanna go talk to James. Your son is a good man, and I bet he'd be glad to see you."

Careful not to put weight on his aching leg, El turned on his bar-stool until he was facing the band. "I'll take that under consideration," he mumbled.

Understanding that it was time to change the topic of their conversation, Forrest said, "So you gonna sing my song tonight?"

"I figured you'd probably had enough of it."

"I'll never get sick of that song. I want you to play it every night you're here. And record it. We got the latest equipment."

"Whatever you want. It's your club."

After months of searching, Forrest had tracked El down in Missouri. The job El had been working, a week at a hole-in-the-wall in St. Louis, didn't pay much. But it was the best gig he'd landed since Hurricane Katrina had run him out of New Orleans and put him on the road for the first time in years.

El'd had two nights left in St. Louis when he'd gotten the phone call. The manager of the club, standing just offstage, had waved him over between sets. "Some guy's on the phone for you. He's been calling all day."

The manager, who was used to cops on the hunt for his employees, leaned toward El. He whispered, "Listen, if something bad is about to go down, don't let it happen here. Okay, man?"

There was a time when hearing from a club manager that he'd received a mysterious phone call would have sent El running out the back entrance, into the alley. But those days were gone. Anybody he'd owed money to had either died or long since given up trying to get it back. Old age, lack of energy, and a sometimey prostate meant that there had been no serious woman trouble in his life for years. Any lawmen looking for him had given him up for dead decades ago.

The caller hadn't been a lawman, a bill collector, or an angry husband. When El picked up the receiver in the manager's office, he heard a melodic, hissing voice that he recognized immediately. Forrest Payne said, "Hey, El. I need you to come to Plainview and play for my wedding."

El hadn't been back to Indiana since the 1970s. He had been born there and raised there. But he never owned up to that anymore. If asked, he claimed New Orleans as his home. Now here was Forrest Payne, the man who had given him his first paying job, more than sixty years ago, asking him to return to the scene of so many early triumphs—and crimes.

Forrest said, "I've had five marriages, and only the first two were worth a damn. I've been trying to figure out what went wrong with the last three before I do it again. And you know what the difference was?"

El heard the snick-snick of a cigarette lighter and listened as Forrest sucked in two scratchy inhalations. When he understood that Forrest was waiting for a response, El said, "I don't know. What was the difference?"

"You, man. You're the difference. You played for those first two weddings and brought me good luck. I need that luck again."

"You don't need any luck from me," El said. "No rich man needs to borrow luck from somebody as broke as me. You got all the luck, gettin' married at your age. Seriously, I'm damn near eighty. You must be what, ninety?"

Forrest said, "Don't worry about how old I am. I'm older than twenty-one and younger than dirt. All you need to know is that I want you here bad enough that I hunted you down."

"I appreciate the offer." El turned his back to the club manager, who sat across the room at his desk, pretending not to listen in on El's phone conversation. Speaking more quietly, he said, "I had trouble in Plain-view. I'm not lookin' to start it up again."

"I'm the only person above ground here who remembers you or the troubles you had, and I need you next weekend. And listen, I know you're the best, so I'm prepared to treat you that way. I'll pay you what that dump is paying for a week, if you'll sing one song at my wedding. You know which one I want. On top of that, I'm offering a week of shows here at the club, two weeks if you got the time. I've got a good young band to back you up. Listen, work the two weeks and I'll pay you for three."

A two-week gig was tempting, especially for three weeks' pay. But hell, he'd once crossed his heart and promised he wouldn't return to Plainview. And he'd been proud that he'd kept that one promise. There had been some good things in his life in Plainview, four to be exact. And the only one he still had was his guitar. He'd destroyed the other three, with youthful selfishness, cruelty, and violence. The thought of a day in that town made El feel as if a hand were squeezing his throat.

"Look," he said, "I appreciate the thought, but Plainview ain't the place for me. Besides, what would I do in a titty bar for two weeks?"

"First, old friend, that is the saddest question I have ever heard a grown man ask," Forrest said in a mock-sympathetic whine. "Second, the Slipper's gone respectable. It's a music club now, like the old days. Hell, the mayor's in the front row listening to the band as we speak. And his wife's there with him." Forrest released a hoarse cackle so loud that El had an impulse to pull the phone away from his ear.

"I'm offering you good money. Come to town and bring me some luck," Forrest said. Then he quoted a dollar figure that made all the bad times El had experienced in Plainview seem slightly less awful. El's more positive feelings about Indiana lasted until he had accepted Forrest's offer and hung up the phone. After that, fear rushed in. He was certain he'd just made a dreadful mistake.

THE SNAKE DANCER took her final bows. She exited the stage with the wicker basket that had once held Percy and was now overflowing with cash. The emcee told the audience to prepare themselves for some great old-time blues. El took his guitar from the case that was stretched across the two barstools next to him. It was the same leopard-spotted instrument he'd played since 1949. Folks might forget El's name, but they always remembered Ruthie, his gold, black, and white beauty, his guitar.

El hobbled to his place in front of the band. He thanked the audience, acknowledged the young men behind him, and sat on his stool.

This set would be a long one, alternating between his solo numbers and some tunes with the band. Throughout the first two songs, El struggled to forget where he was, to block out images of Lily and his former life. All the other old folks he knew lived in terror that their memories would fail them, but El felt cursed with total recall.

During the third song in the set, he finally slid into that sweet place. The guitar became a part of him, the music pouring directly out of his body. He began to improvise more extravagantly, stretching the key and leading the bass player on a chase that the young man had difficulty keeping up with. The kids on the stage were excited by the challenge, though. They soon let go of their nerves.

Near the end of the set, El hit his stride. Tonight would be special for the youngsters and for him, too. Then his numb foot came alive again, the pain sharper than it had ever been. His leg was on fire from his knee to the arch of his foot. He was singing when the pain interrupted. He was at the peak of a phrase, floating a high note over the bass line with Ruthie and with his voice. Discomfort forced him to take a quick inhalation of breath and let loose a sharp gasp. El kept going. A few seconds later, he was back in sync with the music. But the throbbing continued.

He managed to get through another twelve bars. Then he signaled the band to take a round of solos. The college boys rose to the occasion, and by the end of the tune, El felt slightly better. He blocked the sensation of nails pounding increasingly deeper into his foot by singing and playing louder. By the time he got to the last song, each of the kids in the band believed that this gig was the best experience of his life, and the audience was in a frenzy.

El finished the set with the song Forrest had requested, "The Happy Heartache Blues." By the final verse, more than a few listeners, including El's old friend, were in tears. The audience stood in ovation.

Unfortunately, when El tried to stand, everything around him shifted, as if the entire room were plunging through the hole that Leroy had built into the floor. He was falling, twisting, toppling sideways to avoid landing on Ruthie. Had there been an earthquake? *First that damn hurricane, now an earthquake. I am one cursed son of a bitch.* But even as he thought this, the recognition came to him that no one else had moved and that the quake was entirely within him.

The audience's applause ended in a communal gasp. And the sound of one old man hitting the floor.

The band members reached El first. The redheaded bass player was pre-med and began checking for injuries. El argued that he was fine. The boy insisted that El not try to get up. The emcee came to the stage. He took the microphone and calmed the crowd, saying, "Everything's under control, folks. We'll have the show going in just a minute." He launched into some tired jokes. More people gathered around El.

Forrest Payne, his yellow tuxedo glaringly bright beneath the stage lights, appeared beside El just as he was sitting up. Charmina dropped to her knees to El's right and began to pray.

"I'm all right," El said. "Just help me up."

Charmina and the musicians began to lift him. They managed to bring him to his feet, but one step was all it took to prove that he couldn't put the slightest bit of weight on his leg. And he was cold, wet with perspiration, and beginning to shiver.

"Don't worry," Forrest said. "There's an ambulance on the way."

El was about to argue that he just needed a little help getting back to his barstool and his therapeutic whiskey when the sensation of being weighed down forced him toward the floor again. Once more, Charmina knelt beside him. When El realized he was laden with the bulky python, which had slid from Charmina's shoulders to his as she'd helped lift him, he understood the reason for his feeling of overwhelming heaviness. Briefly, he felt relieved. Then the snake gave El's chest a squeeze.

"Percy really likes you," Charmina said.

El sat, bathed in the dazzle of Forrest's tux and the glow of the stage lights, as the python wrapped him up from waist to neck. Outside, the sirens grew louder.

What a fool he'd been to come back to Plainview. Leaving this place and staying away had been the only smart things he'd ever done. Now he would be punished for breaking his vow never to return. And, as if all the bad memories weren't enough, it turned out that his foster mother had been right all those years ago. The Day of Judgment was upon him, and it had come with a big snake.

CHAPTER 3

*T*he same moment El Walker hit the floor at the Pink Slipper Gentlemen's Club in Plainview, a performer who had recently begun calling herself "Audrey Crawford" sat down at a piano onstage at the Simon Theater in Chicago. Even before the welcoming applause had faded, she wished she had chosen different attire for this venue. Her gown was silver lamé—vintage, more than fifty years old. Its long, clinging sleeves had looked great in her mirror at home and just as good in the dressing room here at the theater. But the damn thing was hot. Sweat ran along Audrey's hairline beneath the blond wig she wished she could rip from her head. No, she'd been taught as a youngster that horses sweat, men perspire, and ladies glow. She wasn't sweating; she was glowing her ass off. As soon as she returned home, she would take a pair of scissors to those silver sleeves, if not to prepare the dress for the next time she wore it, then at least to exact revenge on it.

The gown and wig did make her look glamorous in an old-movie-star way—from a distance, at least. She knew how to move elegantly onstage and, hot or not, the silver dress was flattering. Both her look and her name—a combination of Audrey Hepburn and Joan Crawford—were perfect fits for the Simon Theater, a former neighborhood movie house that had been renovated in the style of a 1950s supper club.

The Simon Theater had been a movie palace in the 1920s and then a burlesque house, a dirty-movie joint, a foreign-film venue, and an eyesore slated for demolition. But it had managed to survive urban decay and gentrification to live again in its latest form, having kept, all along, the surname of its original owner, Mr. Arthur Simon. The attractive and well-constructed neon sign that bore Mr. Simon's name had proved to be more expensive to remove or replace than to repair. And so, with each incarnation, the place remained the Simon Theater.

Audrey's stage name had come to her in a flash of inspiration when she'd arrived at the theater to audition. Well, it hadn't exactly been a formal audition. She had been walking past the theater on a hot day and had seen that the front doors of the establishment were propped open, allowing a cool, air-conditioned breeze to escape onto the sidewalk. The promise of relief from the heat had summoned her. She hadn't even noticed the piano onstage until she was inside, fanning herself in front of a magnificent oak bar. Once Audrey had seen the piano, black and lustrous under the lights, what else was she supposed to do but the thing she had always done? She'd made her way through half-moon-shaped tables ringed by repurposed movie theater seats, stepped onto the stage, and begun to play and sing.

The current owner of the theater, and the person who had given Audrey her job, was a young man with a taste for the music and aesthetics of his parents' and grandparents' generations. He was also an ambitious real estate hustler who had leveled historic buildings in a five-block radius around the theater to build unsightly, overpriced condominiums. He had left the Simon and its neon sign in place so he could save a few dollars and proclaim himself a preservationist. The day Audrey had wandered in, he had been in the theater to oversee the final stages of the renovation, not to audition lounge singers. When he'd climbed up to the main floor from the storeroom to discover Audrey—the third neighborhood eccentric to sneak inside that day—he hadn't had the energy to yell at her as he'd yelled at the previous intruders. He had walked behind the bar and poured himself a club soda, intending to simply wait her out.

He'd listened to two old ballads, followed by a salty blues song, and then he'd offered her a job. When he'd asked her name, she had looked around at the red velvet curtains, the cushioned theater seats, and the film posters—all remnants of a more gracious era—and renamed herself Audrey Crawford, after her two favorite movie stars.

She performed most weeknights and did the early shows on Fridays, Saturdays, and Sundays. Her style was too low-key for the late-night weekend audiences. What Audrey did well was what she was doing now. She played the piano. She sang. She talked.

She specialized in themed evenings. She picked a topic and gathered songs from her vast repertoire to go with it, though she never planned out exactly what she was going to play. Often she just talked and let the themes come to her. She ended her sets when her voice gave out or the bartender signaled for her to take a break, whichever came first.

That evening, perspiring under the lights in her silver lamé, she quietly rolled chords and tinkled tunes on the piano, speaking to about one hundred people, a good turnout for the Sunday after-dinner set.

"I was born in a little town called Plainview, Indiana," Audrey said.

A young man in the audience yelled, "Woo-hoo! State U!" The woman sitting with him woo-hooed back at him.

Audrey said, "Proud alumni in the house tonight." She played a snippet of State U's fight song, and the young man howled again.

"I don't know much about the university side of town. I grew up on the side where the drunks weren't young or cute, and showing off your smarts was more likely to get you beat down than get you laid."

She talked about Plainview that night because her hometown had been on her mind. She had awakened with a picture in her head of fire-flies in the summer evening sky. Plainview sat in a valley, and from June to August, legions of lightning bugs flashed on and off in the surrounding hills, like a continuous, distant fireworks display. That image was so clear she was sure she must have been dreaming of home during the night. At breakfast, she had found herself thinking of how the trees on those hills appeared to absorb the fog just after dawn. Like magic. Had the place really been that beautiful? The morning's memories almost made her want to return to Indiana to have another look. Almost.

Around lunchtime, Audrey recalled the smell of southern Indiana air on the first warm afternoons of spring—mossy, green, and alive. As she walked along the Chicago pavement on her way to the theater, her mind leapt back to the elastic quality of the earth beneath her bare feet when she'd strolled the Indiana woods after a light rain shower. Plain-view lacked so much, but that day she remembered the qualities that had made her hometown wonderful for short bursts of time.

"Plainview wasn't such a good place for me. You've heard the story. Bad daddy, dead mama, poor innocent waif facing the nasty old world on her own." Audrey played the opening phrase of "Nobody Knows the Trouble I've Seen." "But one day a voice whispered in my ear. It said, 'Child, you better put a swing in your hips and march your fine ass on away from here if you wanna live.' So I left Plainview and I made a new home here.

"Tonight, folks, I'll be performing songs about home." She surprised herself with that one. She had thought she was going to sing about friendship. But now that she'd changed course, songs about home it would be. She said, "Home is where the hate is, right?"

"Heart!" the State U graduate yelled back at her.

Audrey winked at him. "Like I said, college boy, we knew totally different sides of town."

She crescendoed through a series of arpeggios, intending to make her way toward the opening of "Green, Green Grass of Home." Instead, she surprised herself again by launching into the introduction to the unofficial state song of Indiana, a tune she hadn't sung since the year her fourth-grade music teacher had drummed it into her head.

Well, this is as good a place to start as any.

She pursed her lips to blow away the droplet of perspiration that dangled from the tip of her nose. Then she crooned, *"Back home again, in Indiana . . ."*

CHAPTER 4

Clarice and Richmond Baker were no more than two feet inside Earl's All-You-Can-Eat when Richmond placed a hand on Clarice's arm and, after a slow, deep inhalation, gasped, "Oh, sweet Lord, it's cherry pie."

Clarice sniffed the air. "That's cherry pie, all right."

Recently, pies of any sort had been in short supply at Earl's, where the Supremes and their spouses had met for after-church supper for more than forty years. Concerned about her husband Little Earl's hypertension and dangerously high cholesterol, Earl's co-owner and the primary baker at the diner, Erma Mae McIntyre, had taken up the cause of healthier eating. She had revamped the restaurant's menu, expanding the vegetarian offerings and preparing lighter desserts. These days, she rarely made the rich treats for which she had become widely known since she and Little Earl had taken over the restaurant from its founder, Big Earl McIntyre.

In spite of Erma Mae's efforts, Little Earl maintained every ounce of his three-hundred-pound frame through frequent excursions to Donut

Heaven, just down the block. However, without the extra calories from testing batter and gobbling up the last bits of leftover cobblers, cakes, and puddings, Erma Mae had shed fifty pounds. The short supply of her popular baked goods had created a demand that bordered on hysteria. Once word circulated that there was cherry pie at Earl's, the place was likely to be mobbed. Even now, as churchgoers trickled in, Clarice could hear patrons excitedly whispering into their phones, "Get here now."

From the cash register, Little Earl called out to Richmond, "How 'bout those Reds?" Eager to talk sports, even though he'd be talking about little else once James Henry and Ray Carlson arrived, Richmond began walking toward the register.

Clarice waved hello to Little Earl and called out to Richmond, "I'm going to head for the dessert table." She rushed past the steam tables that held meat and side dishes to claim her place in the line that was already forming around the sweets. She wanted to be sure to get pie for Odette and Barbara Jean, in case they were late.

Once she had acquired her slices of pie, she wove her way through the diner, pausing along the way to say hello to several acquaintances. Congratulating herself for not having dropped one morsel of flaky crust from the three plates she held, Clarice sat at her usual spot at one end of the window table. From this vantage point, she watched Richmond as he moved through the crowded diner. As always, he was a pleasure to behold, slapping old friends on their backs and charming women with his Barry White basso voice and his fluorescent smile.

Clarice knew that she had aged well. She'd always been an attractive woman, and nightly applications of face cream had helped her to maintain the illusion of youthful skin tone. Though she had never achieved a level of thinness that satisfied her mother, regular exercise and periodic starvation had enabled her to hold on to her shapely figure. But Richmond was something special. At sixty-two, he was in better shape than most thirty-year-olds. His once-black hair had evolved into a glistening silver-white mane that demanded to be caressed. He had a square jaw and sharp cheekbones. Today he was dressed in a tan suit and a mauve shirt. With his broad chest and narrow waist, he looked like a G.I. Joe action figure masquerading as a Ken doll.

It was Richmond who had restarted Clarice's abandoned piano career. She had been a child prodigy, winning contests and performing with symphony orchestras throughout the Midwest, but she had waved good-bye to all of that when she'd married Richmond. Then, decades later, after she had finally tired of his cheating and walked out on him, Richmond had surprised her by secretly sending recordings of her playing to the man who had offered to manage her career when she was young. To Clarice's further amazement, that manager, Wendell Albertson, had remembered her and was still interested in working with her. Now Clarice was enjoying the career she had dreamed of as a young woman. She was traveling, giving concerts around the country. If Wendell Albertson had his way, she'd soon be performing around the world.

The musical life Richmond had engineered for her was just one of the wonderful things about him. She loved him. She always had. She supposed that she always would. He'd been a wonderful father to their four children, and he was an even better grandfather. He was unfailingly charming and capable of great kindness. Of course, during the same years when Richmond had been demonstrating his talents as a good father, a reliable provider, and an amusing and consistently presentable dinner companion, he had also repeatedly humiliated her and broken her heart.

Now, with his wife living across town in a house she rented from Odette, it seemed that Richmond had actually grown up. He was finally ready to be the husband Clarice had spent their entire marriage hoping for.

The problem was that Clarice didn't want a husband. What she wanted was a little bit of amicable companionship and a lot of great sex. Richmond was brilliantly adept at both of those jobs. Conversations with Richmond didn't tend to be deep, but they were pleasant. And Richmond had honed his lovemaking skills to a fine edge through years of scandalous behavior. Whenever Clarice's new life onstage became overwhelming, it was a godsend to know that he was ready and able to provide stress relief.

Clarice, lost in her thoughts of Richmond, didn't notice when her cousin Veronica sidled up to the table. When she felt the table jerk from something being slapped down beside her plate and heard Veronica squeal, "Isn't he gorgeous," Clarice snapped out of her reverie and let out a startled yelp. And when she beheld the photograph that her cousin had flung in front of her, she yelped again.

"Honestly, have you ever seen a baby this beautiful?" Veronica said.

Clarice didn't want to lie on a Sunday, so she searched hard for something nice to say about Veronica's grandson, Apollo, the ugliest baby she had ever seen. She turned her head sideways to get a new perspective on the infant's teapot ears, his blotchy skin, and the oddly shaped mouth, which seemed to be impossibly far from his porcine nose. *Don't worry, he'll grow out of it* didn't feel like the right response. Clarice's late aunt Glory had charitably described her daughter, Veronica, as "touchy," and Clarice knew that she would have to choose her words carefully if she wanted to be even remotely truthful and also have her cousin act civilly toward her at the next few family gatherings.

Veronica's tendency to take quick offense and to lose control of her anger had steadily grown over the thirty-seven years since a member of the Temptations had broken her heart. In 1973, Veronica and Clarice had gone to see the Temptations perform in Louisville. Clarice had come back to Plainview alone and informed Veronica's parents that their daughter had fallen in love with one of the band members and would be traveling for the next year as part of the group's entourage.

After about two weeks, Veronica's singer boyfriend got tired of her and called her father to tell him where he could pick her up.

For months, Veronica blamed her father for separating her from her one true love, and she refused to speak to him. Then her next-door neighbors' son, Clement Swanson, started dropping by. Clement had a reputation for being both lecherous and stupid. But even those who disparaged his morals and mocked his intelligence admitted that he was good-looking. So the moment Veronica's father saw Clement sniffing around, he built a six-foot-high picket fence on the line that divided his property from the Swansons'. He decreed that any interaction between Veronica and Clement would happen from opposite sides of that fence.

Clement liked a challenge, and he wasn't about to let a fence stop him. Knowing that Veronica was still pining for her Motown man, he showed up for one of their chats through the pickets wearing a pale lavender three-piece suit and sang "My Girl" while performing a few Detroit-flavored dance moves. Veronica's resistance caved in right on the spot.

Their first daughter was born nine months to the day after Clement did that dance. At Veronica and Clement's wedding reception, her father, who never did warm to Clement, spent most of the evening slumped in a corner, crying about how he should have nailed the pickets close enough to provide effective contraception.

Clarice turned the picture of Apollo in her hands, hoping to find a side of him that she could enthusiastically compliment. She decided to comment on the baby's extraordinary hair. It was shiny and black, and there was a tremendous amount of it. Hair sprouted from his wide forehead, nearly merging with the thick eyebrows that accented his squinty eyes.

Clarice said, "He's got quite a head of hair on him."

Veronica, who seemed to have forgotten about the existence of her three granddaughters since the birth of her first grandson, gushed, "He's a beauty, all right. I've got a hundred new pictures of him to show you.

Sorry, I can't do it now, though. I need to consult with Madame Minnie, and I want to make sure I'm first in line when she gets here."

Minnie McIntyre, the widow of Big Earl, ran a fortune-telling business from a table in the corner. Those who swore by her gift listed the few instances when the messages she'd received from the spirit world had proved accurate as evidence of her psychic ability. Nonbelievers maintained that anyone who issued dozens of predictions a day over the course of fifty years had to strike it lucky occasionally.

Veronica had been on both the devoted and the disgruntled customer sides of the Minnie McIntyre argument. Their warm relationship had soured after Minnie's prediction that Veronica's daughter Sharon would be swept off her feet by a tall, handsome stranger motivated Veronica to push Sharon into an ill-advised engagement. That whirlwind romance had ended abruptly when police officers interrupted the wedding ceremony to arrest the groom, who turned out to be a fugitive felon.

In the weeks following the wedding disaster, brokenhearted Sharon had comforted herself by working her way through nearly a third of the three hundred servings of uneaten wedding cake in her mother's deep freezer. With every pound Sharon gained from her mostly cake diet, Veronica grew angrier with Minnie. All was forgiven, though, after Sharon attempted to swallow the head and torso of the marzipan groom from her cake topper and was literally swept off her feet by a good-looking, lanky paramedic who performed the Heimlich maneuver on her to save her from choking to death. The young hero turned out to have quite a sweet tooth and, with the promise of all the cake he could eat, began visiting Sharon regularly. The young people were married the following summer.

Seeing then that Minnie had been spot-on in every aspect of her prediction, except for properly identifying the groom, Veronica's faith in her psychic was restored.

"I'll come by the house with more pictures later," Veronica said to Clarice, snatching up the photo of Apollo and hurrying across the room to the corner to wait for Minnie. Clarice heard a series of squeaks and gasps just after Veronica walked away and she knew her cousin was showing off her picture of her shockingly piglike grandbaby on her way to the fortune-telling table. She thought, *What on earth am I going to say when I have to look at a whole stack of those things?*

Through the diner window, Clarice saw Odette and James Henry crossing the street, heading toward Earl's. They were far enough down the block that she couldn't see their faces, but their silhouettes were unmistakable. James was slender and a foot taller than his round wife. Clarice's mother, always one for pointing out traits she found aesthetically displeasing, had taken note of the disparity in Odette's and James's physiques even before they'd married. Beatrice had said, "I'm not saying that they shouldn't be together. I'm just saying that you might be doing your friend a favor by telling her that they look like a giant number ten when they stand next to each other. I wouldn't want to go through life like that."

Odette and James paused on the sidewalk and waved at someone as they approached the diner's entrance. Barbara Jean and Ray Carlson soon came into view. Barbara Jean had been the prettiest girl in Plainview when they were growing up. At sixty, she was the wealthiest woman in town and still possessed the type of beauty men wrote songs about and acted like fools over. Today, dressed up and made up for church, she was a vision of elegance and perfection. Ray was just as eye-catching. Behind his back, Clarice, Barbara Jean, and Odette sometimes called him "the King of the Pretty White Boys," a nickname Clarice had given him as a teenager. Though he was no longer a boy, Ray was headed toward old age just as pretty as he'd ever been. Almost a year after their long-delayed wedding, these two former teenage lovers inspired admiration, lust, and envy simply by walking down the street.

Clarice rose to greet her friends and walk through the buffet line with them. Minutes later, they were seated at the window table that had been permanently reserved for them since 1967, in recognition of Richmond's status as a football hero, Clarice's renown as a local music celebrity, and Barbara Jean's breathtaking beauty. Barbara Jean and Odette sat at Clarice's right and left. Ray and James took their places at the opposite end of the table on either side of Richmond.

Odette lifted the plate that held her slice of cherry pie and waved it beneath her nose. "This smells incredible," she said. "Clarice, you are an angel. You know, there's not a single piece left. Ladies, I'm warning you now that you'll want to avert your eyes when I get to work on this. It won't be attractive."

Clarice laughed and said, "I'd expect nothing less."

As Odette quickly and loudly devoured her pie, Barbara Jean asked Clarice about preparations for the recital Clarice would be performing in two weeks to benefit the pediatric unit at University Hospital. In recognition of Barbara Jean's philanthropy, the children's wing bore the name of Barbara Jean's late son, Adam. In addition to raising money for the hospital, the performance would serve as a run-through for a program Clarice would play in Chicago in July. The Chicago concert, outside in a downtown park, would put Clarice before the largest audience of her career.

"I'm still trying to decide about one piece," Clarice said. "I've got to make up my mind soon. The Chicago organizers want to know what I'm playing so they can advertise, and the hospital recital programs have to go to the print shop this week."

Having finished her pie, Odette began working on the other items of food she'd taken from the buffet line. Between bites, she asked Clarice, "Are you nervous?"

Clarice glanced at Richmond. He was tossing an imaginary football in the air, entertaining Ray and James as he held court on his favorite subject. Not long after Clarice had left Calvary Baptist for the local Unitarian congregation, she and Richmond had fallen into a routine of him picking her up every Sunday morning and driving her to her new church on his way to Calvary, where he was still a deacon. But today she'd awoken feeling antsy. So as soon as Richmond had pulled into her driveway, she'd waved him inside and then dragged him to her bedroom to enjoy a fast tussle that had made them both late for their respective services.

"I've been a little edgy," Clarice said. She carefully trimmed a narrow strip of fat from a slice of roast beef, chewed, and swallowed. "But I'm finding ways to handle the strain."

The sound of rustling cloth and the tinkling of a bell announced the entrance of Minnie McIntyre. She had on a loose white robe with a gold belt. As she always did when she was on the job, she wore a white turban with a small silver bell jutting out from its top. The bell rang, Minnie said, whenever she received a message from her spirit guide, a dead magician named Charlemagne the Magnificent. In her right hand, she held a rhinestone-encrusted cane. She'd needed the cane to steady her since an accident that had resulted in a broken ankle. Minnie blamed Clarice for causing her injury. She claimed to have no memory of having taken the tumble that broke her ankle after losing her balance as she reached out to grab Clarice's throat in a fit of anger. What she did remember was that Clarice was at fault and that, in spite of her own willingness to pardon Clarice's transgressions, she was duty-bound to deny Clarice her forgiveness until Charlemagne told her it was time to move on. So far, she said, the spirits were not in a forgiving mood.

On her way to her station, Minnie stopped at the window table. Bowing her head so that the bell atop her turban rang, Minnie said to Clarice, "Charlemagne has been talking about your big Chicago concert, but I don't want to upset you by telling you what he said." She patted Clarice's shoulder. "You have my sympathy."

Erma Mae stepped through the kitchen door just in time to hear the tail end of what her mother-in-law was saying to Clarice. Moving far more quickly than she ever could have before healthy eating trimmed her figure back to her high school weight, Erma Mae rushed to reach the window table before things got out of hand. She knew that Clarice was likely to ignore any provocation, but she'd seen what Odette was capable of doing and saying when she went into protector mode.

Erma Mae placed a hand on her mother-in-law's arm and said, "Miss Minnie, Veronica Swanson is waiting for you." Escorting the fortune-teller toward her table in the corner, Erma Mae turned toward Clarice and mouthed, "Sorry."

Clarice was struck by the urge to run home and practice. After keeping company with Veronica and Minnie, it would feel good to work out some frustration on the piano. Besides, even though the hospital concert wasn't important in comparison to most of the recitals she'd played recently, she wanted it to be a success. The concert was for a good cause, and it would be her last performance before Chicago.

Clarice's pulse quickened as she silently counted down the days until the journey north to Chicago. The anxiety she'd temporarily banished that morning with Richmond returned as she thought of just how close she was to the date of the big show. Her neck stiffened and her temples began to throb.

She considered running to the other end of the table and dragging Richmond home for their second stress-relieving go-round of the day. Why not? He wasn't likely to say no. Also, she had just read an article by a doctor who maintained that sex was good for lowering blood pressure. It wasn't just that she'd be alleviating stress; she could be preventing a stroke. It would be like filling a prescription, really. She could be saving her life and Richmond's, too.

"Clarice, are you all right?" Odette asked. "You look a little flushed."

"I'm fine," Clarice said. Her eyes were on Richmond as, all dimples and good humor, he expelled his loud bass bark of a laugh in response to something Ray had said. "I've got a bit of a headache, but I plan to take something for it just as soon as I get home."

Clarice ate one more bite of roast beef and set her knife and fork on her plate. "I'm sorry to take off so soon," she said. "But I've got practicing to do, and it would probably be best if I took that medicine before my headache gets any worse." She pushed her plate of cherry pie toward Odette and, rising from her chair, called out, "Richmond!"

CHAPTER 5

A hospital is a crowded place when you're a woman who sees ghosts. The minute James and I stepped through the doors of University Hospital, I met up with a slew of dead folks. The recently dead, the long dead, and the nearly dead strolled the hallways in varying states of joy and sorrow. People who were thrilled beyond measure to be released from the bonds of the physical world glided along next to others who were pissed off beyond consolation to be parted from their bodies. Most of them ignored me. Some, aware that I could see them when others couldn't, nodded my way as James and I passed by. A few even waved and called out, "Hey, Odette!"

I've never figured out how the dead know that I can see them. It could be that my mother tells them about me. When Mama was living, she had the same gift. Unlike me, she saw no reason to keep quiet about it. In fact, she took considerable pleasure in passing on messages from the other side. As soon as Mama's special ability made its appearance, the departed began showing up on her doorstep, asking her to play interpreter between them and their survivors. Feeling that it was her duty to help people and possessing an affinity for putting her nose in other folks' business, Mama eagerly cooperated.

Unfortunately, her assistance was rarely appreciated. It turns out that dead folks are just like live ones. The biggest fools are the ones with the most to say. The deceased with good sense are usually too busy leading their afterlives to bother chitchatting with living friends and relations, but the dead buffoons can't shut the hell up. Mama's ghost acquaintances wanted to confess their long-ago extramarital affairs, gossip about nonsense that everyone they knew had stopped caring about, and criticize their surviving spouses' home-decorating choices. They rarely conveyed any useful information. To my knowledge, they never once shared winning lottery numbers, passed on a decent recipe, or even helped someone find their lost car keys. So, because Mama wasn't telling the living anything they wanted to hear, she gained a reputation as a crackpot and a nuisance, instead of as a psychic.

Of course, there was evidence supporting the notion that Mama wasn't quite right in the head before she started seeing ghosts—her well-known passion for marijuana smoking, for instance. Mama put the most glassy-eyed college boys to shame. And I gave her a hard time about her habit, until my months of chemotherapy. Though my Indiana State Police captain husband prefers not to notice, I still regularly tote my weed and rolling papers off to our backyard to sing my changed tune.

On the advice of a witch, Mama had once hauled her heavily pregnant body up into the branches of a sycamore tree. The witch had told her that climbing the tree and singing a hymn there would get her overdue baby to come. Sixty years later, people still walk up to me and ask, "Is it true that you were born in a sycamore?"

Yes, I was born in a sycamore tree. And because of the circumstances of my birth and an old superstition that a child born off the ground will wind up fearless for his or her entire life, I continue to face the rumor that I'm not afraid of anything. Truth is, plenty of things scare me. When

I was growing up, though, all the adults in my life believed that my birth in the tree had made me endlessly brave. And when the people you love and trust tell you as a child that nothing frightens you, part of you believes them even after life has proved them wrong. So while I'm not fearless, I'm no scaredy-cat.

The elevator doors opened with a quiet squeak, and James and I stepped out onto the brightly lit fourth floor of University Hospital. Barbara Jean was at the nurses' station there, talking with two women. The nurses' pale blue surgical scrubs contrasted sharply with Barbara Jean's magenta tea dress. She wore a pair of matching high-heeled shoes that made my feet ache just to look at them. If I'd ever been reckless enough to try on those shoes, I'd have made it about three steps before either the four-inch heels or my ankles would've collapsed.

Nearly everyone on the hospital staff knew Barbara Jean. Her first husband, Lester Maxberry, was quite a bit older than she was, and during his last twenty years, every organ in poor Lester's body operated on a part-time basis. As soon as the doctors would get one part up and running, something else would go on strike. When he died, in 2005, the only shocking thing was that an illness didn't get him; an accident did. His death was caused by plain old bad luck.

Lester died with a bigger pile of money in the bank than anyone in Plainview, including Barbara Jean, had imagined. When she sold his business, the stack of cash grew higher. These days, Barbara Jean occupies her time with giving that money away. The staff members who'd arrived too recently to know Barbara Jean from the many trips she made to the hospital with Lester know her as a benefactress and a volunteer.

The consultation James and I were headed to was taking place in the Lester Maxberry Women's Health Center at University Hospital. If you turned left after walking through the visitors' entrance to the building, you'd be facing the children's wing and the Adam Maxberry Auditorium, named after Barbara Jean's son, who died as a little boy. Our friend Clarice would be performing a piano recital in that auditorium in a week and a half. Barbara Jean also ran a charity that brought free flower arrangements to hospital patients. If you had no family or if your people were needy, the Maxberry Foundation made sure your room was filled with as many blooms as you wanted.

At the nurses' desk, Barbara Jean gave each of us a quick hug. "What a happy coincidence," she said. "I wasn't expecting to see you."

She said she just happened to be on the same floor as my doctor's office, delivering a vase of flowers to a patient in a connecting ward. But I wasn't buying it.

Barbara Jean is kind. She has lived through great suffering and managed to come out on the other side without bitterness. But she's no actress. She was there to see me.

I was about to receive the results of tests I'd had a few days earlier to mark five years since I'd been treated for non-Hodgkin's lymphoma. I wasn't keeping the tests secret. Barbara Jean and Clarice had been with me through every step of my illness, and they knew the dates as well as I did. But I also didn't want to make a big deal of it. My husband and my friends weren't what you'd call easygoing when it came to matters of health, not *my* health at least. I thought that downplaying the five-year anniversary might save us all some stress.

I should have known better.

Barbara Jean said, "I was just about to head over to the surgical wing and drop off these flowers." She picked up a milky-green glass vase from the counter of the nurses' station. The vase contained an arrangement of roses that matched Barbara Jean's ensemble so perfectly you'd have sworn she'd had the cloth of her dress woven to match the flowers, or maybe had the roses bred to coordinate with her dress. Considering her devotion to fashion and her unlimited resources, either seemed a real possibility.

"They're for Mr. Walker, the man who sang at Miss Beatrice's wedding. Poor thing has diabetes real bad, and they had to take part of his foot this morning. Apparently, he's got no family. And the nurses say he's depressed."

The blues man had seemed in bad shape when he'd limped off into the shadows after his performance at the wedding. I wondered for a moment if maybe Barbara Jean really was at the hospital to deliver flowers. But just as I began to think I might have been flattering myself that she was there to check on me, I heard another familiar voice repeating the same line I'd just heard. Behind me, Clarice said, "What a happy coincidence. I didn't expect to see you."

Clarice hugged me and gave me a peck on the cheek. She did the same with James and Barbara Jean. After the hugs, she said, "I was checking out the piano for my recital."

The auditorium was on the first floor, and we were on the fourth.

James studied the carpet rather than look at Clarice as she performed an acting job even worse than Barbara Jean's. As soon as I glanced his way, I knew that he'd called them to let them know when and where to find me. I couldn't help but feel a little happy about it. Like having good friends who will risk annoying you to show their support, having a husband who will ignore your wishes to make sure he fulfills your needs is too damn good to be upset about.

"Let's cut the crap, ladies," I said. "I'm glad to see you. Quit your lying and come along with us."

Barbara Jean pressed her hand to her chest and put on a fake offended expression. She said, "I'll have you know I wasn't lying. Not entirely. The man who sang at the wedding *is* here, and the flowers really are for him." To Clarice, she said, "Isn't it a shame that our friend has such a suspicious nature?" She placed the vase back on the counter. Then she hooked one arm around my elbow and the other around Clarice's and said, "Shall we go, Supremes?"

With James trailing behind, we marched for my doctor's office, arm in arm, just the way we had strolled the halls of our high school more than forty years earlier.

My doctor was running late, so we sat talking in the waiting room outside her door. James hardly said a word. With one hand he grasped my fingers, squeezing them until they went numb. With his other hand, he rubbed his jawline. James has a dark, raised scar that runs from his right earlobe to the tip of his chin, a souvenir from the lowlife father he barely knew. When James was fretful, he massaged his scar as if it had become inflamed.

Meanwhile, Clarice and Barbara Jean couldn't stop chattering. Barbara Jean gave us the details about the bird conservation project that had taken her husband, Ray, to the West Coast for the week.

When we met Ray, he was a dirt-poor and drop-dead gorgeous teenager who raised and sold chickens for a living. He was so often covered with chicken feathers that, in addition to "King of the Pretty White Boys," we called him "Chick." That nickname faded from use, but Ray's obsession with birds never went away. He now worked at the university, studying hawks. Years after he'd stopped sharing his living quarters with chickens, it was still rare to find him without a stray feather on his shoulder.

Clarice rattled off a list of events she had in mind for our families to enjoy when her children and mine gathered in Plainview after her Chicago recital. Our two daughters were best friends who spoke every few days, but the July reunion would mark one of those increasingly rare occasions when her four kids and my three, along with their spouses and children, would all be in Plainview together. I gave my wholehearted approval to her plans for a week of nonstop eating and endless spoiling of grandbabies.

Talk of grandchildren led to some good-natured competition between Clarice and me over my two grandkids and hers. That opened the conversation to the pictures of Veronica's grandson, Apollo, that she had been showing around town. At the mention of that child, we all went quiet. That way, we let it be known that we had witnessed the unique horrors of that poor baby but, because we'd been raised right, weren't going to discuss them out loud.

The door to my oncologist's office opened and my doctor, Catherine

Reese, stepped out. The cheerful look on her face when she greeted us set everyone in my little entourage at ease. James and I followed her into her office feeling good.

Sure enough, Dr. Reese had nothing but positive news. No cancer. All systems in balance. Everything functioning as well as a sixty-year-old woman who was fifty pounds overweight could hope for. James released the painfully tight grip he'd had on my right hand so he could turn in my direction to kiss me. My mother appeared behind Dr. Reese then, clapping her hands with happiness. She wore an orange dress that was the shade of a shiny new traffic cone. The color bounced off every reflective surface around us, and the entire room filled with sunlight. The brightness was so intense that it was hard to believe that James and Dr. Reese couldn't see it. Almost a dozen years dead, and my mother still shone more brilliantly than anybody I knew.

"Wonderful, wonderful!" Mama sang out. She did a celebratory dance beside the doctor's desk. She shimmied and shook. Her wide hips gyrated in one direction while her heavy bosom spun in another. My mother and I were built identically, and I made a mental note to never allow myself to do Mama's unflattering little dance in public. I was thrilled to see her, though.

Mama followed James and me back into the waiting room after my appointment. Unseen by Barbara Jean and Clarice, Mama joined in with them when they surrounded me, leaping up and down in celebration after getting the thumbs-up sign from James.

I enjoyed sharing the happiness with my friends, but I hadn't seen Mama in months and I was eager to talk with her. She'd been with me from the start of my struggle with cancer. She'd kept me company and advised me. She'd stood beside me through the worst of it.

I said, "I'm going to go to the bathroom. You can decide where to take me out for lunch while I'm gone."

The one time I'd discussed seeing ghosts with my friends and family was when I thought I was dying and would never be talking with them again. Since then I'd kept my mouth shut about it. The only reason James knew I was still associating with the departed was that Mama liked to keep me company while I did household chores and I tended to forget myself then and speak out loud to her. Otherwise, I kept my conversations with spirits private. At the end of the hallway, in the small one-seater ladies' room, I said to Mama, "Good to see you. It's been a while."

"Has it?" she said.

"Three months."

"Really? The days get away from me now. I'd have sworn I saw you yesterday."

"I love your dress. I don't believe I've ever seen it before," I said. Depending on what Mama said about her dress, I might have to break my rule about not passing on what the dead had to say. If there was shopping after death, Barbara Jean would want to know.

Mama twirled so that the hem of her dress flared out around her, practically filling up the cramped room. When she stopped spinning she said, "I'm glad you like it. Your daddy bought it for me years ago. Before you were born. Before your brother even. I used to wear it night-clubbin' when I was a hot young thing. It seemed like the perfect dress to get good news in."

She snapped her fingers. "That reminds me. I gotta write this down." She reached into her pocketbook and pulled out a pen and her "Jump for Joy" calendar from Stewart's Funeral Home.

I hadn't seen that calendar for years. "You still write in that thing?" I asked.

"Of course I do." As she wrote, she said, "This is the fifth-happiest day I've ever had. It's got to go in my book."

"Fifth-happiest day? I'm flattered."

"You should be. I had good stuff in here before I died, but since then the competition's been stiffer than ever."

Mama put away her book. "How's Eleanor," I asked.

The former first lady Eleanor Roosevelt first started visiting Mama in the 1970s. Apparently Mrs. Roosevelt had sensed a kindred spirit in Mama. The two were now having a well-deserved good time in the after-life, carousing the way marital and parental responsibilities hadn't allowed them to when they were living. Together, they put on quite a perfor-mance, but the Dora Jackson and Eleanor Roosevelt show was best observed from a safe distance.

"I'm not sure where Eleanor is," Mama said. "She was with me earlier, but your aunt Marjorie popped up and invited her to go shoot craps. They were gone before you could blink an eye. They could be anywhere, those two wild women."

"Pot calling the kettle black," I said.

"Thank you much." Mama performed a curtsy.

Mama asked about my children, and I was happy to brag on them. I told her about Jimmy's new business, something he and his wife did with computers and money that I didn't fully understand. I gushed about Eric, finally happy with a partner who seemed to appreciate him. And I told her about Denise going back to college now that her children were in school all day. We didn't talk about my brother, Rudy. She'd been watching him as closely as she'd been watching me, even if he didn't know it.

When I told her about Forrest Payne marrying Beatrice Jordan, Mama let out a squawk. "Now, ain't that some shit," she said. "I hope he remem-bered to bring a hammer and chisel along on the wedding night. 'Cause it's a sure bet Beatrice had a few layers of rust down there." Then she got the giggles over her nasty joke and howled until she doubled over.

When Mama straightened up, I said, "I should get going before James comes looking for me." Then, from force of habit, I flushed the toilet and I washed my hands.

Mama and I left the bathroom and headed back toward the ele-vators. We were halfway there when I saw Wayne Robinson. He was mumbling and grinding his teeth on the unlit cigar in his mouth as if he were softening it up to eat it later. He ran his fingers through the sparse gray hair on the top of his head and shuffled along beside a young nurse. When the nurse turned and stepped into a room, walking right through him, I understood that he wasn't among the living, at least not entirely.

Wayne Robinson kept coming toward me, still talking to himself. When he was just a couple of feet away from Mama and me, I said, "Hello, Mr. Robinson."

He dragged himself past me and entered an open door to my right.

He sat in a chair beside an occupied bed and buried his face in his hands. In the bed lay Wayne Robinson, in physical form. The patient was older, thinner, and sicklier than the man in the chair. His breathing was shallow but steady. His eyes were shut. There were no visitors present aside from the near ghost who grieved hard for himself a few feet away from his own body.

"Friend of yours?" Mama asked.

"I knew his wife and his son," I said. "You met his son, too. Terry Robinson. Cute kid with the soft voice who used to come by my house four or five years back."

Mama said, "I remember. Sad little boy."

"Well, that's who made him so sad. He gave Terry a rough time."

"Like James's daddy?" Mama said.

"Kind of. But there's more ways to cut a child than with a blade."

A nurse named Darlene Lloyd appeared next to me at the door to Wayne Robinson's room. Darlene had been one of my favorite nurses during my time in intensive care five years back. A nonstop source of gossip, she had kept me entertained between visitors. She said hello and asked about my health. Then she asked if I knew Wayne Robinson. When I told her I was a friend of his son's, she could hardly contain herself.

"Just between you and me, it's a waiting game now," Darlene whispered. "Does Terry know? I can't imagine his sister or brother told him."

"It's a safe bet they haven't," I said.

Calling Terry about this was my job. I'd promised him that I'd call if this happened. Considering what that notification might set in motion, it wasn't a vow I particularly wanted to keep. The thing was, at the time I'd told Terry that I'd be sure to let him know if his father died, Wayne Robinson had been an energetic, barrel-chested, athletic man, several years younger than I was. I never thought I'd have to follow through on that promise.

Darlene did her best not to sound excited, but she couldn't keep the gleam out of her eye. "Of course I'm sorry to see the gentleman in this condition. But I can't help but wonder what Terry's going to do when his father passes," she said, not sounding very sorry at all.

You and almost everybody in town, I thought.

A buzzing noise came out of a nearby room, and Darlene excused herself.

Mama said, "Wait a minute. I remember the whole story about that boy and his father now." She chuckled and leaned into Wayne Robinson's room for another look. "This could get real good."

"Oh, grow up, Mama. There's nothing funny about this."

"You have to admit, though, there's high entertainment potential," she said.

When we turned down the hallway that led back to James and my friends, I said good-bye to Mama. She said, "I'll come by later this week."

Then we blew kisses each other's way, and she vanished.

The moment Mama was gone, my stomach growled and my mind returned to food. My friends and I met at Earl's nearly every Sunday and often once or twice during the week as well. I'd stopped in just a day earlier. But in my mood—a mixture of happy, relieved, and nostalgic— Earl's was where I wanted to be.

When I reached James and the Supremes, who were waiting for me by the elevator, I said, "Pork chops. I'd like to go to Earl's for fried pork chops and celebrate my good health by eating something that'll kill me."

As we entered the elevator, I reached behind my husband and pinched his skinny butt cheek. He wrapped one of his long arms around my shoulders and gave me a squeeze. I had an impulse to say something to mark the occasion, maybe take a cue from Mama and tell James, Barbara Jean, and Clarice that their sweetness and loyalty made me want to jump for joy. But that wasn't my style. I hugged James back and I sighed, "Pork chops."

CHAPTER 6

*B*arbara Jean was nosing the front end of her pearl-gray Mercedes into her driveway when she realized that she had forgotten to deliver the flower arrangement to El's hospital room. Talking with Odette, Clarice, and James in the waiting room, celebrating Odette's positive test results, and then the raucous three-hour lunch at Earl's had driven the errand from her mind. Rather than leave the delivery for another volunteer or another day, she backed her car onto the street and returned to the hospital.

He lay asleep when Barbara Jean entered room 426. A low-pitched snore that sounded like a distant drum roll escaped from him with every breath. His white beard, bushier than she remembered from the wedding, quivered when he exhaled. His right leg was elevated, and his heavily bandaged foot was visible. She tiptoed in and placed the flowers on a stand beside his bed, hoping not to wake him.

His eyes opened just after she set the vase down. Barbara Jean was about to say hello when, blinking, El rasped, "Loretta Perdue, you are a sight for sore eyes. What are you doin' here?"

It was a shock to hear her mother's name. Gone for forty-three years, Loretta was remembered by very few people. And, for propriety's sake, many of those who had known her best now claimed never to have met her. Even Barbara Jean rarely spoke of her. She had only recently stopped dreaming of her mother's final days and the bad things that had happened when they'd lived together in the shabbiest house in the poorest neighborhood in town.

Loretta had died in that run-down house in Leaning Tree, decades before the neighborhood was transformed from the poor, black area of Plainview into a fashionable outer suburb of nearby Louisville, filled with overpriced boutiques and specialty food shops. Liver disease robbed Loretta of the loveliness that had brought a stream of men to her door. By the end, she had the sunken eyes and loose jowls of a poorly preserved seventy-year-old. She was thirty-four.

El rubbed his forearm across his face, trying to shake off the pain-killer haze. "Loretta?" he said, less certain this time.

"Hello, Mr. Walker. My name is Barbara Jean Carlson. Loretta Perdue was my mother. I'm afraid she passed some time ago."

He reached for a pair of silver wire-rimmed eyeglasses that sat on the meal table next to his bed. After putting them on, he stared at her for several seconds. "You're Loretta's child, all right. She was one fine-lookin' woman."

The few conversations Barbara Jean had about her mother these days followed a similar pattern. Someone would mention that they had known her mother in the distant past. Then they'd go on for a while about how pretty she had been. And then the man—it was always a man—would abruptly stop speaking when he remembered, possibly from intimate knowledge, that Loretta had ended her days trading her diminishing beauty for enough cash to buy the liquor that kept the shakes and hallucinations at bay.

Barbara Jean regretted having said anything at all about Loretta. She wished she had crept out of the room when he'd called her by her mother's name. What harm would it have done to let him think that he'd had an especially vivid dream of a night with Loretta in the 1950s?

Barbara Jean was about to say good-bye and wish El a speedy recovery when he said, "I used to live with your mama."

So this old man had been one of the low characters who'd shared the Leaning Tree dump with her mother. Barbara Jean remembered the ones who had caused the most trouble—the hoods who had used and beaten her mother and the vile characters who had made her own life hell by sneaking into her tiny room off the kitchen after Loretta had passed out. But the faces of the men who had stayed for shorter periods of time had blurred together long ago. She didn't want to know where this man fit in to all of that.

She edged toward the door, making a mental note to ask another of the volunteers to deliver the next arrangement to El's room. "I'll be going now. I hope you feel better soon," she said.

Then he surprised her again. "Me and your mama were in the same foster home."

"What?"

"Yeah, we were in the home together for about four years."

Loretta had been stingy with the details of her early life. She said she'd been raised in a Louisville orphanage and that she had come to Plainview for a job when she was a teenager. A foster home had never figured into the tale she'd told of her past. If there were holes in her history, Loretta had made it clear to Barbara Jean that she wasn't interested in filling them. And it wasn't safe to pester her once she'd told you that she didn't want to be bothered.

Part of Barbara Jean thought it wiser to leave, but curiosity and the memory of the exquisite sounds that had poured from El at Miss Beatrice's wedding tugged at her to stay. Barbara Jean found herself stepping toward the chair beside the bed. "You knew my mother when she was a little girl?" she asked as she sat.

El let out a quick snort of a laugh. "I knew Loretta when she was young, but I don't think you could ever call her a 'little girl.' It was like she was already grown the day she walked into that foster home. She was as tough as they come, and she got tougher every year. But that's how most of the kids in that house were. All a bunch of sad, beat-up babies tryin' our best to act big."

Barbara Jean recalled Loretta's sadness and how she had tried to defeat it by endlessly scheming to capture the miracle man who would bring love and money raining down on her. But every failed affair brought more depression. Each downturn resulted in more drinking.

"I never knew Loretta was in foster care. She never said a word about it."

"That doesn't surprise me. Nobody ended up there because of somethin' they'd wanna talk about. There were five kids there while I was at the house. Three turned out messed up and two died young. As I recall, your poor mama didn't make it to fifty."

Actually, Loretta hadn't lived to see forty.

"I've got pictures from back then, if you wanna see 'em," El said.

"Yes, thank you, Mr. Walker. I'd like that."

"Call me El. It'll do me good to hear a beautiful woman say my name."

He pointed at his guitar case, which was leaning against the wall beneath the television set. "The pictures are in there with Ruthie. Could you bring it over?"

Barbara Jean fetched the case. She set it beside El, who undid the latches and lifted the lid. "That's Ruthie?" Barbara Jean asked as he pulled the shiny, leopard-spotted guitar from the case.

"Yeah, that's my girl." He dragged his fingertips across the strings, stroking the instrument with the tenderness of a newly reunited lover. As he laid the guitar next to him on the bed, Barbara Jean noticed the scarring on the insides of both of his arms. Some of the damage was

new, as if his nurses had been forced to make multiple attempts at finding viable veins for his IVs. But most of the marks were the faded tracks
of amateur needle punctures. She'd seen the same patterns lined up on
the arms, legs, and even the feet of some of her mother's friends, and
she understood what those dark tattoos testified to.

El picked up a plastic grocery bag from where it had been squeezed
in beside the guitar. He pulled a large manila envelope from the bag
and opened it. A stack of photographs spilled out onto the pale blue hospital sheet. He removed two pictures from the pile and slid one of them
toward his visitor.

The photographer had captured Loretta in mid-spin, standing on one
foot. Her mouth was open, as if she were howling with joy. Her teeth
sparkled as brightly as the rhinestone-encrusted harem costume that
clung to her shapely figure. Barbara Jean knew that high forehead, the
broad cheekbones, and the round lips that always seemed puckered for
a kiss. This was the face she had nearly forgotten. Her mother was in
her early twenties in the picture, and so full of strength and energy that
she looked as if she were about to become airborne.

"Wow," Barbara Jean said. "She looks so happy."

"That was your mama, only happy when she was dancin'."

In the foreground of the photograph, several men stood with their
faces tilted upward, gazing at Loretta. Their arms were raised high,
dollar bills clutched in their fists.

"I used to have thousands of pictures. But I lost most of 'em in
Katrina, along with my camera. I've got a lot more than these, though.
I just keep pictures of family in the case with Ruthie." El pushed the
second photograph closer to her. "This is at the foster home."

Five adolescent children and a middle-aged woman posed on a lawn
in front of a two-story brick house. Three boys and two girls stared at
the camera with toothy smiles, and angry eyes. They looked as if they
were dressed for church, the boys in suits and ties, the girls in floral

patterned dresses and shiny Mary Janes. Barbara Jean recognized one child in line immediately. Loretta must have been around twelve or thirteen years old. She had never seen a picture of her mother this young.

"There they are. My brothers and sisters," El said of the row of white and black faces in the photo.

"Your foster home was integrated way back then?"

"Sure was." El turned toward her as he spoke, and the movement jostled his bandaged foot. He let out a long hiss between pursed lips. But when Barbara Jean asked if he wanted her to call for the nurse and request more pain medication, he said no.

"For a long time, that house was the only place in Plainview that was mixed. The second was the Pink Slipper. Folks nobody gave a damn about were always left to mingle as they pleased, long as they didn't try to associate with decent people."

With a slightly trembling hand, El dragged his index finger beneath the faces of the people in the photo. "That's me at the far end. The chubby white kid next to me is Harold, the foster mother's real son. The short, light-skinned boy is Bert. He was the original drummer in the band. He died in a car crash on his eighteenth birthday. The tiny blond girl is Lily. Man, could she sing. Blue-eyed soul twenty years before anybody called it that."

El's finger landed below the face in the photograph that Barbara Jean knew well. "That's Loretta, of course. The foster mother, Mrs. Taylor, is there in the middle. She was truly a piece of work. Batshit crazy and mean.

"They took this picture right before Easter. I think that was the second year your mama was at the house. Mr. Clancy himself from Clancy's Department Store came to the house to hand out new Sunday clothes. They lined us up in the yard and took a picture of us looking grateful for what he'd done. The picture ended up on the front page of the newspaper on Easter morning. There was also a picture of Mr. Clancy and a quote from him that said, 'It does my heart good to visit these poor, desperate children and give them these small gifts to help them celebrate the resurrection of our Lord and Savior.'

"They couldn't take pictures of us on Easter morning, 'cause the clothes were back at the store by then, or they were at church on the backs of some kids whose mamas and daddies could actually pay for 'em. That was how Mrs. Taylor worked it. Every Christmas and Easter, we got toys and clothes in front of cameras. Then, when the picture takin' was done, every bit of it went back to Clancy's. Mrs. Taylor was the only one who got to keep her clothes. I don't think she even cut her own son in on the deal."

"That's horrible," Barbara Jean said.

"That's the way it was. I'll tell you what, it taught us a lesson that none of us forgot. Ain't nothin' fair in this life, and ain't nobody gonna help you but you. Bein' Loretta's child, you surely heard that before."

Barbara Jean had, indeed, learned that philosophy from her mother. Lessons in facing the realities of a hard world came nearly every day. "There's only so much to go around in this world, and nobody gives anything away unless something's in it for them," Loretta had often said. "You gotta take what you can before somebody else beats you to it." If Barbara Jean rolled up her sleeves for El or exposed her back to him, she could show him the faint, crisscrossed scars from the belt buckles and extension cords Loretta had employed as teaching aids during her drunken training sessions. Barbara Jean had accepted her mother's view as the truth, until Odette, Clarice, and Ray—especially Ray—had come along and proven Loretta wrong.

El said, "I'll tell you what, Loretta sure shook things up the next spring. Your mama liked that next year's Easter dress, and she decided to keep it. I'll never forget the look on Mrs. Taylor's face when Loretta strutted down the stairs wearin' that lace dress and new patent leather shoes on Easter morning. Mrs. Taylor hollered, 'Where'd you get that? Where'd you get that?' And then down came Lily, wearin' the dress she'd had to pull off and send back to the store the week before. So Mrs. Taylor screamed at her, too.

"Lily started cryin' and she looked over at Loretta. Then Mrs. Taylor turned back to your mama. She grabbed her by the arm and said, 'Dammit, where did you get those dresses?'

"Loretta was only thirteen years old, and already tough as an old leather boot. She looked Mrs. Taylor dead in the face and said, 'I got 'em from Clancy's Department Store. They took one look at my poor, desperate ass and wouldn't let me leave without takin' these small gifts to help celebrate the resurrection of our Lord and Savior.'

"Mrs. Taylor hauled off and slapped Loretta so hard she hit the floor. But your mama got up and slapped her right back. She was the first one to ever fight back, and it shocked the shit out of us kids and Mrs. Taylor, too. We all just stood there, frozen, watchin' it. The whole morning went that way, Loretta and that woman slappin' each other back and forth till neither of 'em could lift their arms anymore.

"That was just the beginning of the two of them goin' at it. They fought and cussed each other till the day your mama left the house to come and work at the Pink Slipper with Lily and me.

"Loretta stole herself a new dress every month after that." El laughed so hard that he began to cough. When he recovered, he said, "Loretta was somethin' else. That girl would steal just about anything that wasn't nailed down."

El stopped suddenly, the way most men did at some point when they spoke to Barbara Jean about her mother. He'd reached that inevitable point in a Loretta story when he realized he was about to say something that shouldn't be said in the presence of the woman's daughter.

There was a light rap on the door, and a nurse walked into the room. She announced that it was time for El's pain medication and then placed a small white paper cup containing two pills next to the water pitcher on the table beside his bed.

After the nurse left, El said, "Sorry, I didn't mean to call your mama a thief. We all did whatever we had to do back then."

"You don't need to apologize to me. Loretta raised me. Whatever nasty story you could tell me about her, I could tell you a nastier one. My mother was a thief and a drunk and a whore. It's not pretty, but it's reality."

"There's reality and there's truth," El said. "Truth is, there was more to her."

"Maybe," Barbara Jean said.

She picked up both photos and looked back and forth between them, taking in the sight of Loretta, first as a child and then as an object of desire. El was slowing down, and she knew that she should leave and let him rest, but she was enjoying their talk and she didn't want it to end just yet. She said, "They told me at the nurses' station that you don't have a next of kin in your file. Are you sure there isn't anybody they should call to let them know you're here?"

"My wife's dead. I had a son. But I lost him."

Barbara Jean said, "I'm sorry. I lost my boy, too." She reached out and rested her hand on El's shoulder.

"Don't feel sorry for me. Everything and everybody I lost, I didn't deserve to keep." El reached for his guitar and pulled it across his lap. Instead of playing, he placed his palms flat on the body of the instrument and held still, as if he were feeling for the lingering vibrations of an old song. He said, "Loretta and Bert were the lucky ones. Goin' young is the way to do it." His remaining energy drained out of him then. He fixed his rheumy eyes on his gauze-wrapped foot. Speaking in a voice so low that it sounded almost as if he were humming, he said, "You understand, don't you, Loretta? It's better to be in the grave than to end up like this, hacked up and just waitin' to die."

Barbara Jean stood from the chair. She took the guitar from El's lap and returned it to the case. Then she put the photos in their plastic bag.

She placed the bag alongside some loose sheet music that had been wedged in next to the spotted instrument, snapped the case shut, and leaned it against the wall below the television.

Before leaving, she went to El's bedside and whispered, "I'll be going now. I'll come by again tomorrow. Thank you for showing me those pictures. I really appreciate it." She laid her hand softly on his shoulder and said, "You're a good man."

El mumbled, "Mrs. Taylor's gonna whoop your ass if you keep lyin' like that."

Barbara Jean made a quick stop at the nurses' station on her way out to tell them how El had been talking. It was never a good thing when a patient mentioned being better off dead. Then she went out to her car and headed for home.

During her drive, Barbara Jean thought about her chat with El and how she'd nearly fled the room when he'd first called her Loretta. The memory of his music had slowed her down. Escaping his hospital room had lost its urgency after that melancholy wedding march that had made everyone in the church want to cry or kiss, or both, had come to mind. And now Barbara Jean had actually had a conversation about Loretta that hadn't left her wanting to hide her face in shame, break down in tears, or drink herself into darkness.

When she walked into the kitchen of her home, Barbara Jean was surprised to find Ray standing beside the breakfast table. He hadn't been due to return for another day. But there he was, sorting through the mail and smiling at her.

He said, "Hey, sweetheart. Did you miss me?"

They were both past their sixtieth birthdays, but they were still newlyweds—newlyweds who had lived out a love story that contained forbidden youthful passion, a tragic parting, a decades-long separation, and a joyous reunion. Theirs was the sort of affair that blues songs, even entire operas, were written about. Barbara Jean ran to her husband and threw her arms around him. She kissed his mouth and cupped his stubbly cheeks in her hands. When they separated, she ran her fingers through his unruly salt-and-pepper hair and said, "You need a haircut." But as she said it, she thought, *All these years and you're still the King of the Pretty White Boys.*

CHAPTER 7

*T*erry Robinson and I became friends in the gazebo that James had built in our backyard as a present for me during my illness. My gazebo is the exact size and shape of the one my father put together for Mama behind our house in Leaning Tree, the neighborhood where I—and every other black Plainview resident over forty—grew up. Inside Mama's gazebo, Clarice, Barbara Jean, and I shared our deepest girlhood secrets, and James and I first got up to no good as hormone-crazed teenagers.

One of my gazebo's eight sides is open, forming an arched entranceway that admits the morning sun. The other seven sides are made of solid cedar on the bottom and latticework that starts about waist-high and continues to the ceiling for the honeysuckle, trumpet vine, and clematis to climb. Built-in benches ring the interior. James and I pretended that the gazebo was constructed purely so that I could relax outdoors during my recovery and relive memories of happy times in Mama's garden. But James built the gazebo so I would have a place to smoke marijuana to ease my chemotherapy side effects.

I came into a large store of marijuana as a sort of inheritance from Mama, whose formidable gardening skills had resulted in some very potent and hardy new strains. For years, right in her own backyard, she grew varieties of hemp that weren't supposed to survive anywhere near Plainview. If Mama had been born in another time and place, or had been more academically inclined, she could have been a prize-winning horticulturalist. She was every bit as much of a plant expert as any of the professors over at the university.

But Mama was just a country girl from southern Indiana who liked seeing the world through the haze of a sweet buzz. When I was sick, she and Mrs. Roosevelt guided me to a treasure trove of her perfectly preserved goods. Now that I no longer need marijuana for strictly recuperative purposes, like my mother before me, I explore cannabis's preventative properties. Using Mama's seeds, I grow my own plants in a secluded spot in my garden. And as Mama used to say, "I'm headin' glaucoma off at the pass."

James, an Indiana state trooper for four decades, feigns ignorance of everything that grows or is consumed in our backyard.

It was chilly out that morning five years ago when Terry Robinson and I first talked. The grass was wet with dew, and the temperature was frosty enough that I could faintly see my breath. Before heading out the back door that morning, I had slipped into a jacket, put on a pair of red galoshes, and wrapped my head, bald from the medication, in a bath-towel turban to guard against the cold. I wondered if I should go back inside for a heavier coat, but I decided to tough it out for at least a few minutes to see if I got used to the crisp air. I tromped out across the damp grass, carrying my rolling machine and a metal TV tray table to set the machine on. It was my habit to take my machine, papers, and pot out to the gazebo every Monday and roll a week's worth of joints. I could never hand-roll worth a damn, in spite of having seen Mama do it at her kitchen table thousands of times. I'd purchased a little red cigarette-rolling machine that just required loading and cranking to get the job done.

Mama was with me that morning, as she often was during that time. She followed me out my kitchen door and sat beside me in a sunny spot opposite the open wall of the gazebo. She watched as I picked the seeds and stems out of the marijuana she had grown in her garden years earlier.

"They say it'll be near seventy degrees today, but it's nippy this morning," I commented, arranging the first paper in the cigarette roller.

From a few feet away, someone who wasn't Mama said, "Yeah, it is kind of cold." Even though I had grown accustomed to strangers calling out to me, I was startled by this unexpected voice.

From my seat in the sun, my middle-aged eyes could barely see the boy who sat in the shadowy corner of the gazebo farthest from Mama and me, his feet on the bench, his arms wrapped around his shins. I wouldn't have noticed him at all if he hadn't spoken up.

I pulled a handkerchief from my pocket, laid it over the pile of marijuana on the tray, and said, "Good morning."

"Good morning," he replied.

He brought his feet to the floor, stood, and took a couple of tentative steps toward me. He was a thin child of fifteen or so, with a narrow face and deep-set eyes. He looked familiar.

I was on medical leave at the time, but I've worked in the cafeteria of James Whitcomb Riley Elementary School for decades. There are only three grade schools in all of Plainview, so a third of the kids in town pass through my workplace. I searched my memory, trying to locate a younger version of this boy's face among the Riley Elementary students. I came up empty.

I said, "I know you, don't I?"

"Yes, ma'am." He had a girl's voice. It wasn't particularly high-pitched, but it was airy and soft. "My mother gets her treatments at the hospital at the same time as you. I'm Terry. My mother is Gail Robinson."

I remembered him then. I saw his mother nearly every time I went in for chemotherapy. I'd gotten the impression that she was on a tougher regimen and was there more frequently than I was. The boy was often in the infusion room with her, and I'd seen her husband, Wayne Robinson, once or twice.

"It's nice to meet you, Terry," I said. "I'm Odette."

"Odette Henry," he said. "Mrs. Baker introduced us once. She's my piano teacher. At least she used to be before Mom got sick. I remember your jacket. I was at the hospital when Mrs. Baker gave it to you."

I'd thrown on my leopard-spotted coat before leaving the house. Clarice had bought animal-print jackets for herself, Barbara Jean, and me. "Because nothing can stand in the way of a wild woman," she'd said when she'd unveiled them during one of my chemo sessions. Her jacket was a zebra print. Barbara Jean's was tiger-striped. My leopard-spotted blazer had immediately become my favorite item of clothing. The three of us got more of a kick out of parading around town together in our animal jackets than was altogether healthy for women our age, but we didn't much care.

Terry said, "All of the fashion magazines say that animal prints are an important component of the modern woman's wardrobe." Then Mama and I listened as he named several magazines and fashion experts that he was certain would approve of my jacket.

I interrupted his list of periodicals and trendsetters by asking, "Terry, what brought you by here?"

He said, "I was just stopping for a rest on my way to school."

When he saw that I wasn't buying that tale, he lifted his backpack from the bench behind him and said, "I guess I'd better get going now."

He moved toward the open side of the gazebo. In the sunlight, I saw his face more clearly. I saw his delicate, pretty mother in him. I could also see his red eyes and an expression on his face that was a mixture of fear and sadness.

"Hold up," I said. An obedient boy, he stopped and turned toward me. "Is your mother okay?" She'd been weak the last couple of times I'd seen her. And I braced myself to hear that she was gone.

"She's about the same," Terry said. "She's getting better, I think. But right now, she's the same."

"Then what's going on? And don't tell me you decided to stop here and take a nap. I know where the high school is, and I know this isn't on your way."

Terry looked like he was trying to come up with something to say, and then he dropped down onto the bench beside Mama. He crossed his legs and let his foot bob in the air as if he were tapping the brakes of a skidding car. After all my years working at Riley Elementary and raising children of my own, I recognized the look of a child who wanted to talk but hated what he had to say.

"There are these guys who started teasing me back in grade school because of my name."

"What's wrong with Terry?" I asked.

"My real name is Tercel, like the car. My father owns a repair shop, and he says he didn't see the point of having kids if they couldn't advertise for him. My brother's Seville, and my sister's name is Cherokee."

Though I'd never been formally introduced to Terry's older sister, I had seen a lot of her. I'd once walked in on Cherokee Robinson buck naked with another woman's fiancé in the gazebo behind Mama and Daddy's house. I'd only known who she was because of the affair she was also having with Richmond Baker at the time. Clarice and I had laughed our asses off when we learned about the automobile-themed names Wayne Robinson had given his children. Of course, I wouldn't mention any of that to Terry.

What is it with the Robinson family and gazebos?

Terry said, "They stopped with the car jokes. But if they catch me on the way to school when nobody's around, they punch me and call me names."

Looking at this soft-spoken boy with his girlish face and feminine movements, I could easily imagine the kinds of names the other boys were calling him.

Terry rubbed one of his hands over a short, military-style haircut that didn't match his face or his personality. "A couple months ago, they started waiting at the end of my street almost every day. I've been leaving the house early and going a few blocks out of my way so I don't run into them."

From talking to Terry's mother at the hospital, I had a vague sense of where the Robinsons lived. Terry's morning detour was more than "a few blocks." By swinging through my backyard, he was adding at least forty minutes to his walk every day.

"Have you hidden out here before?" I asked.

He began tracing the toe of his shoe over the floorboards and wouldn't make eye contact with me.

"Have you hidden here before?" I asked again.

He muttered, "A couple times."

Mama, who had been uncharacteristically quiet as I talked with Terry, finally put in her two cents. She rose from her seat on the bench. Then she turned toward Terry and me and began to preach the Gospel According to Mama.

"He needs to learn to fight. Tell him he's gonna have to fight or those bullies'll think they can whoop his ass whenever they want to. He's skinny, but there's still stuff he can do. Your daddy was a little guy, and the bigger boys liked to mess with him when we were kids. He couldn't really fight worth a damn, but he wouldn't stop swingin' and punchin' even if they had him on the ground. It finally dawned on those bad boys that if your daddy ever caught one of 'em alone, he was gonna beat 'im half dead. So they left him alone. They went lookin' for somebody who wouldn't fight back.

"Also he should start carryin' a knife. Or I could get your aunt Marjorie to come over and demonstrate how to make a shiv out of a sharpened spoon and some duct tape. A good homemade shiv is some scary-lookin' shit."

Mama meant well. But her advice often involved doing things that can lead to injury or imprisonment. And Aunt Marjorie was even more dangerous. Mama had a point about the boy learning to fight, though. The first time James and I noticed that our son Eric stared up at the mural of hot, bare-chested Jesus at Clarice's church the same way his sister did, we saw to it that he could hit back hard at anybody who messed with him. Plainview isn't New York City. Some kids have a much tougher time here than others.

I thought Terry should try other solutions before he armed himself. "Maybe we should talk to your father about this," I said.

Terry jumped up from the bench. He walked through Mama and shouted, "No!" as if I had just suggested that he set his hair on fire. "You can't tell my father!"

I held up my open palms and spoke slowly and quietly. "I'm not going to tell him. But this is the kind of thing fathers can be good at fixing."

He came back to the bench and sat down again. "I can't talk to him," he said. "Things'll get a lot worse if my father knows."

"Does he hit you?"

"He doesn't hit me. He just hates me."

I doubted that Terry's father hated him, but I didn't argue. Whether what Terry had said was true or not, I could tell by the look in his eyes that he believed it. In light of what happened later, I'm glad I didn't try to tell him that he was wrong about Wayne Robinson.

"My dad hates me," Terry repeated. "But my mother likes me. So it's okay."

"Sweetheart," I said, "there's not a single thing okay about that, either it being true or just you believing it. That's not how it's supposed to work."

I could feel myself inching toward matters that were none of my business, as has always been my habit. So I changed the subject.

"You used to take piano with Clarice, huh?"

"Until last winter," Terry said.

"Hopefully, you can start again when your mother gets well," I said, though I didn't think his mother would recover. When Mama had accompanied me to the infusion room at the hospital, Mrs. Roosevelt had tagged along. The former first lady was still driven to comfort the dying, and Gail Robinson's weak condition never failed to draw her attention.

The sun's angle had changed enough that more light came into the gazebo through the lattice on the eastern walls. The shadows softened, and there was less glare pouring in from the open archway. "They've probably stopped looking for me," Terry said.

"I'm in no rush," I said. "Since you're late anyway, why don't you come on inside and have a snack? Maybe we can find a way to make the situation with those boys a little better." Terry looked so relieved that I thought he might throw his arms around me.

"Good," Mama said. She was still standing in front of me and still in the mood for battle. "While you're eatin', give this boy some tips. If you want, I can show you how he can take care of those boys with a bicycle chain and a rock."

Instead of advising this sweet boy to commit a felony, I began covertly packing away the accessories of my own misdemeanor. The last thing I needed was for a teenager to start spreading the word that I had a supply of weed. As nonchalantly as I could, I pushed the marijuana back into the glass jar and tucked the rolling machine beneath my arm.

As he followed Mama and me toward the house, Terry said, "I saw what you were doing."

His words gave me a jolt, but I kept walking. I thought of my policeman husband, totally sympathetic to my situation but still a cop. Cancer or no, word getting out about his wife smoking pot would mean trouble for James.

But Terry Robinson saw me through the eyes of a kid, a perspective that didn't allow for a chubby old woman like me to have more marijuana on hand than the most glassy-eyed of the young stoners at his high school. "Tobacco kills almost half a million Americans a year, Mrs. Henry," Terry said. "You really shouldn't go near that stuff."

With my hand resting on the little jar of marijuana in my pocket, I said, "You're right, Terry. And I appreciate your concern. You have my solemn promise that I will never touch tobacco as long as I live."

Having guided my feet to the straight, narrow, and tobacco-free path, Terry expanded his chest like a proud soldier displaying his medals. I liked that my promise seemed to make him happy. The next vow I made to Terry proved to be more troublesome.

CHAPTER 8

Clarice lifted her hands from the keyboard and allowed the sound of the final chord of Beethoven's *Waldstein* Sonata to echo in the room and reverberate through her body. *That* had been good. More than good. Every phrase, every note had been shaped just the way she'd wanted it to be. She'd luxuriated in the sensation that came over her when she was playing extraordinarily well, the feeling that she was making it up as she played, rather than interpreting the notation.

Here in her living room at seven in the morning, everything came so easily. But lately, her great performances traveled no farther. In front of a live, listening audience, the risk taking and experimentation that had always made the experience of playing the piano so thrilling deserted her.

Even if some special moments occurred during the overly careful music making she presented to the public, she wasn't likely to be aware of them. These days, when she sat down in front of an audience to play, nearly all she heard was the pounding of her heart.

Over the years, she'd been hounded by worries over her parenting skills, her religious devotion, and her value as a wife. None of those insecurities had ever taunted her when she played, though. The outside world had gone silent and all doubts had vanished the moment her fingers touched ivory. Until recently. Irrational fear had taken root in her brain, and no amount of common sense could quiet the sharp-tongued critic in her head. After years of fantasizing about a performing career, she had one. Now the voice in her head was determined to force her to admit that she didn't deserve it.

Worse, Clarice had to wonder if the story she had told herself most of her life—that it was her mother and then her husband who had kept her feeling trapped and frightened all those years—might have been false. Between her mother's constant criticism and Richmond's unceasingly maddening behavior, they had made it easy for her to blame them for every twinge of anxiety she felt. But it wasn't Beatrice or Richmond who tormented her with the question "Who do you think you are?" Clarice listened to the taunting words in her head with a musician's keen ear, and she knew her own voice when she heard it.

Just as Clarice had begun discovering that Richmond might have been miscast as the villain in her inner drama, she had recognized a better role for him. With the Chicago concert looming, she had developed a habit of calling Richmond late at night and inviting him over. And when he arrived at her door, Richmond could barely say hello before she was on him, insisting that he get to work. She'd done just that last night. Richmond, who could sleep through the most thunderous sonata, lay snoozing upstairs in her bed.

Clarice understood that her solution to the stresses of her new life was fraught with potential complications. Richmond saw each night he spent with her as a step toward reunion. She knew that allowing him to continue believing that would likely lead to trouble. But every time that mean little orator in her head enumerated the reasons she should doubt herself, it was followed up by a louder voice that hollered, "Get Richmond over here, right now!"

Richmond had proved better at calming her nerves than any pill. So she'd decided to worry about the potential side effects from her remedy later.

Clarice turned away from the piano and stood. She thought about going back upstairs and returning to bed, but instead she walked to the couch. The distance was short, since her grand piano, the one piece of furniture she had added to the house after she'd rented it from Odette, dominated the space. Two long strides brought her to the overstuffed sofa and the coffee table that had been there since Clarice had visited Odette in this room when they were girls.

When Clarice had first rented the house, Odette had told her that she was free to redecorate as she chose. But Clarice's needs were simple, and she liked keeping things the way they had been when Miss Dora and Mr. Jackson had lived here. She also supposed that she hadn't really believed at the time that she was in the house to stay. Certainly Richmond had expected her to come home. As it turned out, though, living on her own for the first time in her life had proved to be much more fulfilling than she had anticipated. Now she couldn't imagine leaving.

Odette's father had built the house himself, and he'd had a good time putting it together. The house looked as if Mr. Jackson had made his construction decisions by flipping coins and rolling dice. Rooms were circular, triangular, trapezoidal, and pentagonal. Some doorways were delicately arched, while others were pointed on top like dunce caps. As a consequence, Clarice supposed, of the strangely shaped and seemingly randomly placed windows with their multicolored glass, sunrise brought spectacular splashes of color inside every morning.

Clarice remembered how her own parents had laughed about this place. "Good Lord, the man has built a carnival funhouse over there," her mother had once said.

She had been partly right. The house was designed to delight. But it was also built solidly. Never a leak or a draft, whatever the weather. Perhaps if Beatrice could see the rainbow that the sun had painted on the ceiling above Clarice's head, she might understand how magical this home was.

From the moment Clarice had come to live here, the house had seemed to cry out for music. Between her own practicing and the playing of her students, the rooms were regularly filled with classical melodies. But what the house demanded was the heat and abandon of the blues, the music that had poured from the stereo or the radio every time Clarice had come by the house to see Odette when they were girls. Maybe that was what she should do to celebrate this morning's Beethoven: put one of the blues recordings she'd bought after moving in on the stereo or return to the keyboard and play one of the two blues songs in her repertoire.

The phone rang before she could make a decision. When she answered, her cousin Veronica skipped over any exchange of greetings and said, "You're talking to one of the four new associate pastors of First Baptist Church."

Plainview's fertile Baptist rumor mill had spoiled Veronica's surprise before Clarice had gone to bed the previous night. Several members of her cousin's church had called with the story of how, at a poorly attended deacons' meeting, Veronica and three other deacons had promoted themselves to the ceremonial post of associate pastor. Rather than tell her prickly cousin that she already knew about her new title or that she'd heard that the church's congregation was reacting to the elevation of their new associate pastors with a mixture of amusement and mockery, Clarice said, "Congratulations."

"If this doesn't prove to you that Madame Minnie has the gift, I don't know what will. She predicted this," Veronica said.

A year ago, Minnie had lost patience with Veronica for using her fortune-telling appointments to complain that her church didn't appreciate her unique spiritual insights. Minnie had shouted, "If you can't shut the hell up, then get your own damn church."

Having interpreted Minnie's outburst as a prophecy that she would soon lead her own flock, Veronica had promptly enrolled in an online divinity school. Now, degree in hand, she was ready to save souls at First Baptist. The congregation's continued resistance to her efforts to facilitate their salvation was, she believed, a clear indication of how badly they needed saving.

"I've got all kinds of ideas for the church. I'll show you my list when I come over later."

With each word Veronica spoke, Clarice's Beethoven buzz faded further. She said, "Today's not the best time for me. I've got a lot of practicing to do for the hospital recital next week."

"Oh *please*, Clarice, it's not like you've got a real job. You can play the piano anytime. I'll bring you the pictures of Apollo that Sharon sent the other day. They're the cutest ones yet. You will just die."

Clarice's free hand tapped imaginary piano keys on her knee. *She's my blood and I love her. She's my blood and I love her.*

"Veronica, today isn't good for me."

"I'll bring Aunt Beatrice with me, and we can look at the pictures together. It'll be fun. I'll be there around four."

Veronica and Mother. Veronica hung up before Clarice could speak another word.

The tension Clarice had shaken off with the aid of the *Waldstein* Sonata took hold of her again. Back to the piano for more Beethoven? Or maybe blaring some Mississippi blues from the stereo might relax her. Rejecting those options, she rose from the sofa and headed up the stairs to the bedroom where Richmond lay.

He was sleeping on his side. The bedcovers were bunched at his waist, and his bare chest was exposed. There was no mistaking that he had once been an athlete. Even though he was asleep, the musculature of his body suggested that he might at any second leap from the bed in some thrilling acrobatic motion.

This was her Richmond. The only man she had ever loved, though that hadn't always seemed like the brightest idea. She would never know the total number of affairs he'd had. Hell, maybe he didn't know, either. There had been decades filled with nights when he didn't bother to come home, countless calls from strange women, rumors that made their way to her ears, anonymous letters from writers who claimed to be concerned friends.

Still, she had stayed with him. When she'd finally left, it'd had relatively little to do with Richmond. She had walked out because she just couldn't stand herself anymore.

She'd felt a cold rage toward Richmond for years by the time she left him. But her ire had inspired more exhaustion than histrionics. And anger wasn't the reason she continued to refuse to return home. She stayed in her Leaning Tree rental because she could no longer picture herself in her old house and her old life. She had left home just the way her children had—first Ricky, then Abe, then the twins, Carolyn and Carl. They had matured and stepped out into the world just the way they were supposed to. When Clarice's turn came, she had taken off, too.

Looking down at Richmond with the red and orange light from one of Mr. Jackson's prism windows painting his face, it was difficult for Clarice to think of anything but the good times and easy to imagine that more of them lay ahead. But the indications were that Richmond was about to ruin everything.

Suddenly he needed to know how she felt all the time. And he wouldn't accept "fine" as an answer. "No, really, Clarice, I want to know what you're thinking. I want to know how you feel." It was like being cross-examined by a dogged, lovesick hippie.

Then, after almost forty years of having half the bed to herself every night, Richmond suddenly wanted to cuddle. As soon as she got comfortable, there he was, enveloping her in a wrestling hold. With his hot breath against her neck, his stubble scratching her shoulder, newly sensitive Richmond was a chore to sleep with.

Even though she had assured him that it was unnecessary, Richmond seemed determined to demonstrate to her that he had become more caring and enlightened. It was sweet, she supposed. But she had grown tired of wading through Richmond's deluge of chitchat and embraces to get to the thing he was truly good at. If she wanted scintillating conversation and hugs, she could call Barbara Jean or Odette.

After giving it a rest for more than a year, Richmond had begun pestering her about moving in with him again. Just last week, he'd hinted that the two of them should renew their marriage vows on the occasion of their upcoming wedding anniversary. "It would be like a fresh start," he had said.

Twice during the past month, Richmond had unexpectedly dropped to one knee in front of her and then looked up at her as if he were about to say something. The first time, she had silenced him with a passionate kiss that developed into a breathless encounter on the piano bench. The second time, she had interrupted him to express her admiration for the flexibility he had gained since the knee replacement surgeries he'd had a year earlier, dwelling on the more gruesome details of his operations until the last vestiges of romance had been excised from the situation.

Thinking about marriage made Clarice feel even more jittery. She climbed into the bed alongside Richmond. Though she didn't always want him around for the entire night, it was convenient to have him available for sunrise relaxation. Any amount of morning physical contact tended to put ideas in his mind, and she was eager to get those thoughts in place before he felt the need to show her how modern he had become by inquiring about her mood or pulling her into a platonic hug. She rested her right hand on Richmond's hip. Without opening his eyes, he stretched and yawned. Then he rolled over and grunted.

Now that he was on his back, Clarice placed her hand on his flat belly. Richmond, a true morning man, responded to the invitation of the hand on his stomach as she had hoped he would. He snuggled in close to her and pressed his lips against her neck. He mumbled, "Good morning, baby," and moved a hand beneath the T-shirt she had worn to bed. Richmond flashed his dimples and whitened teeth at her, then began kissing her along her collarbone.

It's so cute when he thinks he's seducing me.

CHAPTER 9

The two women in the photograph posed in front of a jukebox. Bodies in profile, faces turned toward the camera, they stood with their backs arched and with their hands on their hips, parodying fashion models. Because the picture was in black and white, Barbara Jean couldn't tell the color of the tight dresses Loretta and Lily wore. But she could see that the dresses were sequined from the tiny stars of light created by the reflection of the flash of the camera.

Barbara Jean said, "Loretta always liked her clothes loud and shiny. When we went shopping together, everything we brought home looked like it had been pulled out of a comic book. She wanted to know that every eye was on her, and she brought me up to be the same way. To tell the truth, I kind of miss those loud clothes. It made dressing up fun."

El, who was sitting up in his bed facing Barbara Jean, agreed. "The poorer the kid, the more they want to shine. Boy or girl, it doesn't matter. Saturday night at the Pink Slipper back then was a sight to see—all of us broke-ass kids, wearing our finest. It just about blinded you to look around the room."

"Were Loretta and Lily close?"

"All of us kids from the foster home were tight for a while. Harold was my main runnin' buddy for a long time, and Loretta and Lily were like twins. Your mother was a good friend to have. She wouldn't back down to anybody. If there was serious trouble, Loretta was somebody you wanted on your side."

Barbara Jean laughed. "If there was serious trouble, Loretta probably caused it."

"You might be right about that," El said. "But your mother was good to Lily. Loretta looked after her like a big sister. It was hard not to be that way about Lily. She was cute and sweet-natured. Looked like a grown up doll-baby. Loretta and me both tried to look out for her. But before long, I was puttin' that shit in my veins and couldn't look after anybody."

"And Loretta became a drunk," Barbara Jean added.

"Like I told you before, none of us made it out of Mrs. Taylor's house okay."

El let out a groan, and Barbara Jean offered to fetch the two untouched painkillers that sat on the table next to his bed. He declined the pills but accepted a cup of water.

He said, "Lily couldn't stand to be alone, and that kept gettin' her in trouble. Did Loretta ever tell you the story about her and Lily in Louisville?"

"She never mentioned Lily at all, not that I remember."

"That's hard to believe, the way the two of 'em hung together in the old days."

"What happened in Louisville?" Barbara Jean asked.

El took another sip of water and said, "About a year after we left the foster home, Lily met this man at the Pink Slipper. He bought her some jewelry and took her shoppin'. She'd never had a man spend any real money on her before, so she decided she was in love. Of course, this guy was trouble. He used to mess with another girl your mama ran with, and he slapped that girl around so bad she moved halfway across the state to get away from him. Everybody warned Lily. But she was stubborn. She told us all to kiss her ass, and she took off for Louisville with that lowlife. Not even a week later, we heard that this dude had beat her bloody when she figured out he was a pimp and tried to leave him.

"I still remember how Loretta carried on when she found out what had happened. She cussed and screamed and spat like she'd lost her mind. Forrest Payne told her to calm down and let the police deal with it, but Loretta wasn't havin' it. She said she was gonna take care of it herself. She took off for Louisville that same day, with a tough woman who was one of the regulars at the club for backup. They were in Plainview with Lily before the Pink Slipper closed that night. Lily was bruised and bandaged, but she got up onstage and sang our second set with us.

"None of 'em would talk about what happened in Kentucky, but pretty soon word got around that the guy who'd beat up Lily had been found inside a corner mailbox. *Three-hundred-pound man, jammed into a mailbox.* He lived, but he was majorly screwed up. It was a year before he could talk again and another six months before he could walk.

"One night when we were all drinkin' at the club, I asked your mama about it. I said, 'Loretta, I gotta know. How the hell did you get that fat man in that box? That's gotta be against some laws of physics.'

"Loretta took a long drag off her cigarette and said, 'I'm not admittin' to anything, but I will tell you that there ain't a force on this earth strong enough to overcome two truly pissed-off women if they've got a couple crowbars and enough time to put 'em to proper use.'"

Barbara Jean laughed so hard that tears came to her eyes. "My mother being a good friend to anyone is news to me. But the crowbar part, that sounds like Loretta."

Barbara Jean pulled a handkerchief from her purse and wiped her cheeks. Then she set the photograph of Loretta and Lily on the bedspread and said, "Look, El, your doctor wanted me to talk to you about something. He told me that you're refusing to have the surgery he needs to perform."

El said, "I see. They got you on their side and sent you in to do their dirty work."

"I'm on your side, El. I just think you should get the operation. He said it won't be nearly as invasive as that first surgery. They just need to clean things up."

"That's what they say. But I've seen it before with the sugar. They start cuttin' and cuttin'. Next thing you know, there's hardly anything left of you. They took a couple toes a year back and half my foot two weeks ago."

"Your doctor says if you don't do it, you'll get sicker, and maybe even die." She twisted her monogrammed handkerchief between her fingers and then put it away inside her purse. She said, "We haven't known each other long, but I think of you as a friend. So I want you to be healthy. I'm also being selfish. I want you to live long enough to show me more pictures."

She picked up the photo of Loretta and Lily again and turned it toward El. "I'm an alcoholic, like my mother. I haven't had a drink in years, but it's still a part of me. When I'm with you, talking about Loretta, I don't want to drink. And that's amazing, because I always want to drink. So I want you to stay alive because it helps me." The corners of her mouth turned upward slightly. "Listen. I've got a deal for you. Loretta never told me about Lily and Louisville. She did tell me how to shove a big man into a little mailbox, though. You have the surgery and I'll clue you in."

"That's the trouble with you fine women. You turn those pretty eyes on a man and make promises and the next thing he knows, he can't think for himself anymore."

"So you'll have the surgery?"

"Hell, why not?"

Barbara Jean leaned forward and kissed the center of his forehead, leaving a blood-red lip print behind. She said, "You're doing the right thing."

"And you don't play fair," he said. "Just like your mama."

Barbara Jean was astounded to hear herself say, "Thank you."

CHAPTER 10

After the young surgeon who would be operating on him left his room, El lay with his eyes closed. He thought about music and tried to block out the rest of the world. Maybe there was a song in all of this, his very last one. If "The Happy Heartache Blues" had brought them to tears, wait till folks heard the one about the lame old man.

The doctor had said, "I'm almost certain I'll be able to save a significant portion of the foot," congratulating himself in advance for his fine work. It was clear to El that the surgeon believed he was doing El a great favor. But the truth was, half a foot, no foot, no leg—it was all the same.

While he'd had the club gig in New Orleans, El had been able to take a long break from the heavy lifting that was a regular feature of his younger life. But the hurricane had stripped away the blues club and his little house. Then he'd gone back on the road again, hauling his guitar, his satchel of clothes, the arrangements for the other musicians, and his bulky, ancient amplifier from job to job.

He was too old for life as a traveling man. His arms, legs, and back had let him know about it every day. Even with all of his possessions inside luggage on wheels or strapped to lightweight carts, he had needed the assistance of helpful strangers. At first, he'd resented the offers of aid. *Do they think I'm decrepit?* But by his second week of traveling, his aching body had announced its limits, and El had been reduced to standing helplessly at bus stations and on train platforms, waiting for someone to offer to assist him. And that was when he still had two feet.

When Forrest had called and offered the wedding gig and two weeks of work, El had allowed himself to fantasize that he could slip into a small corner of his old life and then escape again. As an old man, he would return to where it had all begun and launch a new, final chapter. With his pockets full, he might even get back to Europe, where a good blues man could still find work and respect. But Plainview had slapped him down again. No Paris. No London. No Berlin. Instead, an indefinite sentence here in this bed for his ancient crimes.

El had wanted to tell that smug doctor that he wouldn't just be slicing on a man. He would be operating on a performing pack mule. The man couldn't exist without the beast of burden. Now that the mule had been hobbled, the remaining piece could only wither away.

It had been Ruthie—his wife, not his guitar—who had first called him a pack mule. El was still with her then; he hadn't blown that all to hell yet. He was still acting the part of a decent man. The band had their first tour. Well, they'd called it a tour. It was a weekend in Indianapolis followed by one night in Memphis. He had waddled into the living room loaded down with over a hundred pounds of what he thought were the bare necessities.

Ruthie had taken in the sight of him, both hands full, bags hanging from his shoulders, guitar strapped to his back. She'd clamped her hand over her mouth to keep from laughing out loud and waking James, who was asleep on her lap, and said, "Good Lord, you look like my grandmama's pack mule." For the rest of their time together, she would send him off to gigs by swatting his hip and saying, "Giddyup, old boy."

The night it all fell apart with Ruthie, El had ended up on a barstool at the Pink Slipper talking to Marjorie Davis, the club's unofficial security guard. It had been late, and Marjorie had finished helping Forrest clear out the last of the patrons. Forrest was an imposing presence on his own, but Marjorie was scarier. When she informed a nuisance customer that he had overstayed his welcome, he was wise to leave immediately. If he didn't, she would tell him he had till the count of five to start moving toward the door. Then she'd begin to count out loud.

No one ever heard her get to five. On four, she would grab the troublemaker by his neck and lift him a few inches in the air with one of her muscular arms, and jerk him from side to side as the toes of his shoes skidded across the floor. That move came to be known as "the Marjorie shake."

She was a kind woman most of the time, and she was known to have a friendly and unshockable ear. But she also had an old-fashioned Baptist's clear-cut sense of morality. And she was comfortable with the role of protector of the weak. If El hadn't been so drunk and so high, he would never have chosen Marjorie as a confidante. But between gulps of whiskey, El had shown her the bloodstain on the arm of his white cotton shirt and confessed what he had done to James earlier that night.

Marjorie toyed with the whiskers on her chin and sloshed a heavy gulp of whiskey around in her mouth. He'd half-expected her to grab him by the throat, but she didn't. She looked at him then and said, "I always felt sorry for you, 'cause I know you kids didn't have it easy with that crazy bitch Taylor. Even after you started shootin' that mess in your arm, I believed you might turn out all right. But you don't get forgiven for some things—not by me. And I think you understand that no matter how many times you wash that shirt, there ain't a man or woman in this place who's gonna look at you the same after today.

"Right now, I'm tryin' to think about how much I love your music, so I don't kill you. But my goodwill ain't gonna last forever. I'm gonna do you a favor and think about that sweet blues of yours for the next few minutes. You'd be smart to be out the door when I'm done thinkin'."

Marjorie closed her eyes and started to sing in her crackling, coyote-howl voice: *"Come back to me and break it, love. Break my happy heart."* El stood then and staggered out of the Pink Slipper for what he thought would be the final time.

CHAPTER 11

*A*udrey Crawford quietly played "At Seventeen" as she spoke to her audience. "I got kicked out of the house two weeks before the end of my senior year. I came in from school and heard Daddy and my big sister, Cherokee—yes, that's her real name—talking upstairs. I couldn't understand every word they said, but I could make out that I was the topic of their conversation and that Daddy was cussing like a maniac. Hearing Daddy going off like that threw a fright into me, because that wasn't his way. Even though my father had a temper that sent people running in the opposite direction, he couldn't abide foul language. If he caught one of his kids whispering so much as a gosh darnit, we'd get a slap that shut us up quick. But that day, I decided that I'd had enough of being scared of my old man. So I marched up the stairs and into battle."

Audrey pounded through the opening bars of "The Marines' Hymn" as an inebriated woman at a rear table howled out, "From the Halls of Montezuma!"

"Daddy and Cherokee were in my bedroom. Daddy was pulling

clothes out of my closet while Cherokee paced in front of my dresser. She waved her arms in the air and said, 'See, I told you what you'd find if you looked in there. This is why I can't get anywhere. I can hardly show my face in this town, the way people talk about him.'

"They saw me when I walked in the room, but neither of them missed a beat. Cherokee kept wailing about what an embarrassment I was, and Daddy went searching through my closet for the dresses I'd made on Mom's sewing machine.

"When he was done, Daddy turned my way, and I saw that he was crying. He said, 'All I done for you . . . all I done for you, and you turn out like this.'"

Audrey traveled the length of the keyboard with a glissando and launched into a bit of "Cry Me a River."

Had she said too much? After all, there were always a few people in each crowd who didn't know that Audrey was also Terry. Even her boss, who'd met her in what Audrey thought were her male clothes, didn't figure things out until she'd been working at the theater for a week.

Audrey had spent over an hour on the phone with her old friend Odette Henry that morning. As soon as they'd exchanged hellos, Odette had said, "Terry, your father's in the hospital." After an afternoon and an evening spent thinking about her childhood and those final, ugly days in the Robinson home, Audrey hadn't been able to muster much concern for images and illusions. What was it Odette had said to Terry during one of their backyard talks all those years ago? "It's your truth. Go on and speak it."

"Daddy called me a punk and a few other choice names," Audrey told her audience. "Then he took two quick steps in my direction and raised his fist like he was going to hit me. I wasn't worried, though. My friend Odette had taught me to fight by then. And she'd done a good job. I might not have looked it, but I was the toughest sissy in southern Indiana. Daddy backed down when he saw my Odette Henry stare."

Audrey furrowed her brow and curled her upper lip, giving the crowd a taste of the fierce look that had made her father step away that day. "Instead of trying anything with me, Daddy took his anger out on my clothes. One by one, he picked up blouses and dresses and used his hands to rip them into shreds.

"While I watched Daddy rip my beautiful creations apart, I kept wondering how he could be so surprised. Wasn't I the same boy who requested a pair of white vinyl go-go boots for his sixth birthday so I could do a Nancy Sinatra impression in the church talent show? Didn't I use wood glue, aluminum foil, and silver glitter to transform my Batman lunchbox into a beaded clutch purse when I was eight? And wasn't I the kid who caused his fifth-grade class picture to have to be re-photographed after I managed to clip on a pair of homemade rhinestone-and-fake-pearl chandelier earrings just before the photographer snapped the picture? What were they expecting to find in my closet? Power tools and stacks of dog-eared *Playboy* magazines?"

As the audience chuckled, Audrey played "Macho Man." "I thought it was funny, too. I had this image of myself lying facedown on my bed, one hand stroking a radial saw, the other paging through images of Miss February as I humped away at my pillow in a fit of youthful heterosexual passion. The picture in my head was so absurd that I laughed out loud.

"And that was it. Daddy saw me giggling and said, 'I won't have a goddamn sissy livin' under my roof. You'll never spend another night in this house.'"

"Macho Man" faded into "So Long, Farewell."

"My father was one of those people who never went to church but talked a good game about how tight he was with the Lord. He used to say, 'What makes us Christians superior to everybody else is our God-given mandate to forgive.' I held out a little hope that Daddy might demonstrate some of that superior Christian forgiveness he bragged about. Even when I was dragging my duffel bag down the stairs, I thought he might stop me and tell me to come back. I kept looking over my shoulder for him to stomp up to me, yelling about how I was grounded till I graduated high school and that the sewing machine was off-limits forever. But he never said another word to me.

"My sister didn't say anything either, even while she was holding the front door open for me. That bugged me almost as much as what my father had done, because Cherokee and I both knew that the show she'd put on in my room hadn't really been about my dresses or me being who I am. The problem between Cherokee and me was Mr. Andre Bailey."

Audrey played "Mad About the Boy."

"Andre Bailey was gorgeous. Six and a half feet of muscle with a square Dudley Do-Right chin. Andre had hands the size of Virginia hams and golden-brown eyes that made you want to fall out on the floor every time he looked your way. He also didn't have a brain cell in that beautiful head of his. He was perfect.

"Cherokee thought he was perfect, too. His parents owned a successful laundry and dry-cleaning business in downtown Plainview, and with his good looks and prospects for an inheritance, Andre was something she had to have. She did everything but dance naked in front of him to capture his attention. Cherokee worked for months, and never got anywhere with him.

"Well, at Andre's request, I *did* dance for him—not naked, but in some of the dresses I made on Mom's sewing machine. Andre and I saw each other on the down low for almost a year before Cherokee caught me hopping out of his car in a black cocktail dress late one night. A day later, I was homeless.

"While I lugged my possessions down the sidewalk in front of my house, I had a talk with my personal savior, Miss Joan Crawford. In her movies, there always came a point when Joan was scorned and abandoned and she realized that she'd have to take on the world alone, armed with nothing but pluck and extraordinary cheekbones. I turned to Joan for advice, and she told me that getting kicked out was the best thing that could've happened. Joan said I should be glad to escape Plainview before the town crushed my spirit forever. She said I should go to my mother's cousin in Louisville before I lost my nerve and went back to my father, begging.

"As always, Joan Crawford was right. However, I should have asked her for more complete instructions, because I'm certain she would have told me not to do what I did next. I went to see Andre."

Several audience members groaned in unison. Audrey played "Why Do Fools Fall in Love?"

"Besides Andre, there were four people in his father's dry-cleaning store. Mrs. Carmel Handy, a skinny old lady with big hair who used to come by the house and pray over my mother before she died, two ditzy teenage girls who were there to giggle and flirt with Andre, and Andre's father, Mr. Bailey. Andre's dad was snoring in a chair in the corner. He was always drunk, but everyone politely referred to him as being 'under the weather,' since he had money.

"I strutted past all of them until I was face-to-face with Andre. Then, as only a seventeen-year-old in love could do, I leaned across the Formica counter and said, 'Andre, I love you and I want you to come to Louisville with me. I've got a little money saved up and I'm leaving tonight.'

"Andre whispered that I should keep my voice down. Then, just loud enough for the other people in the store to hear, he said, 'Mr. Robinson, please wait until I have attended to the other customers' and 'I'm afraid your articles are not ready for pickup just yet, sir.'

"He looked past me and said, 'Mrs. Handy, if you've got your receipt, I'll be happy to fetch your jacket for you.'

"It finally hit me that Andre wasn't going anywhere with me, so I turned to leave. Between the counter and the door, I called on my personal savior again. *What would Joan Crawford do?* Of course, Joan had the right answer.

"I pivoted around in the doorway of Bailey's Laundry and Dry Cleaning and pointed my right index finger at Andre. (Oh, how I wish I'd had time to paint my fingernails. This was truly a moment that cried out for fire-engine-red nail polish.) I said, 'When you see my father, tell him I'll be back. Tell that motherfucker I'll be back for his funeral. And as soon as they lay him in the ground, I'm gonna piss on his grave. Tell him that when I do it, I'm gonna squat like a woman.'

"The other people in the store stared at me like I had just escaped from the zoo. Just for dramatic effect, I trained my should've-been-red fingernail on the members of the crowd like it was a gun and added, 'God help anybody who tries to stop me.' Then I made my grand exit.

"The story of the scene I'd made had traveled from one end of Plainview to the other before I left town that evening. I was so excited by the fuss I created that I got on the wrong bus. I meant to go to Louisville, but, by mistake, I got on a bus bound for Chicago. I was halfway to Illinois before I realized what I'd done. But that little mix-up kept me from living with another relative who didn't really want to be bothered with me and brought me here to you fine folks. So it turned out for the best."

As Audrey began to sing "My Kind of Town," she wondered again if she had said too much. No, Terry might hesitate. Audrey, with her fire-engine-red nails, wouldn't be quieted.

CHAPTER 12

I met Lily in the woods behind Mrs. Taylor's place," El said. "I used to go there a lot to play my guitar. There was noise twenty-four hours a day in the house, and the forest was the only place I could get a little bit of quiet. As long as I came back with firewood, Mrs. Taylor didn't much care where I went."

Perched on the edge of his hospital bed, Barbara Jean held a picture of El's band. He and Lily stood, front and center, on a small stage. He clutched his spotted guitar. Lily's hip was thrust toward the camera. Singing, they leaned in toward each other with their mouths wide open. They looked like two children delighting in making mischief.

"I told you I was Mrs. Taylor's favorite, right? Well, the thing that made me her favorite was my guitar. I could play her a tune and get her out of a bad humor pretty quick. That was how I made my first money as a musician. If one of the other kids was in trouble, they'd run to me and say, 'Get downstairs fast. I need you to play something for her.' I'd say, 'Sure thing. For a nickel.' Made a nice little piece of change for myself that way."

El reached for the plastic cup on the table next to his bed. He took a long sip of water, and after Barbara Jean refilled the cup for him, he took another.

"I couldn't read music then. I used to hear songs on the radio and go out into the woods to learn 'em. I couldn't really sing, still can't. But I was loud. I'd set up shop under a tree and just let 'er rip.

"One day while I was singin', I heard footsteps comin' up on me. I turned around and saw a girl walkin' my way. White girl, about my age, with a round, pink face and dirty blond hair. She stopped ten paces away from me and just stood there starin'. She didn't say a word, just kept her big gray eyes on me. So I went back to singin'.

" 'Blues in the Night' was Mrs. Taylor's favorite song that year. I was stoppin' and startin', trying to get it right. I was about fourteen then and I thought I was a hotshot. So as soon as I had the chords down, I started showin' off for the cute girl. I sat on a stump, singin' about love and two-faced women—like I knew what any of that meant—thinkin' I sounded pretty damn good.

"About halfway through the song, she joined in. I'm tellin' you it was somethin' else when that girl sang. She was a year younger than me, I found out later. She probably weighed about seventy-five pounds. But when she opened her mouth, she sounded like a big-boned blues shouter. Shut your eyes and you heard the bayou and smelled moonshine. It was crazy."

El picked up his guitar and strummed a few chords. He sang, *"Take my word, the mockingbird'll sing the saddest kinda song."* Then he positioned the guitar on the sheets beside him. "Believe me, she sounded a hell of a lot better than that.

"I started back at the beginning of the song, and she showed me what she could do. When we were done, she turned around and ran. I started wondering if maybe I had dreamed the whole thing. But when I got back to the house with my guitar and the firewood, she was there, standin' in the kitchen.

"Mrs. Taylor turned to me and said, 'This here is Lily. She's gonna be living with us.'

"Harold Taylor was in the kitchen, too. Even then, he stared at Lily like a starving man lookin' at a platter of steaks. His mother must have noticed it, too, 'cause then she said, 'And I don't want any of you boys gettin' any ideas. You'll keep a good distance from her, if you wanna keep your balls.' While she was talkin', she picked up a kitchen knife from the counter and waved it at us so we could tell she was serious.

"That was how it all began. After that, Lily would follow me out into the woods to sing almost every day. Harold would trail along after her and clap and whistle after every song she sang. Those days with the two of them out under the trees were the first good times I can remember havin'."

In the three days since his second surgery, Barbara Jean had become a constant presence in El's room, spending almost every minute of the hospital's visiting hours with him. As El had foreseen, his second operation had resulted in the loss of more of his foot than the surgeon had expected. The pack mule was lame, for sure.

Decay was easier to take now that he had a plan in mind for how this would all end. The previous surgery had caught him unaware. This time around, all he had to do was bide his time till the day he could leave this place and escape watchful eyes. Until then, he had a beautiful woman to make him feel useful and allow him to pretend that he was a better man than he knew himself to be.

There were dangers to talking about the old days. After he'd slipped and told her that he'd once had a son, he'd worried that she might hound him for information until he slipped again and maybe even said James's name out loud for the first time in years. But Barbara Jean never pushed him to tell more than he wanted to, even when it was obvious that he was leaving out names or fudging on dates so he wouldn't give away too much of his history. He liked that about her. She was curious, but she understood that there were stories, or parts of stories, that were better left untold. Loretta's child would have had to learn the importance of keeping secrets early on.

Barbara Jean said, "So how did another woman's name end up on your guitar? You were in love with Lily, right?"

"No, plenty of folks thought there was something goin' on between us, even those who should have known better. But it was never like that with me and Lily. She was good-lookin' enough. I wasn't half bad myself in my youth, but back then, even the dumbest black boy kept his distance from white girls if he valued his life. Besides, we were like brother and sister. Since I was the favorite, I ran interference to keep Mrs. Taylor off of her. When that didn't work and both of us got whooped, we'd haul our bruised behinds out to the woods and sing up a storm. Me and Lily had something better than a romance."

Barbara Jean said, "So that song you sang at the wedding wasn't about Lily?"

"No, 'Happy Heartache' is about another lady altogether. She was a real killer."

It was just past Memorial Day. The grass outside was lush, and the trees were fully leafed. Every afternoon, the sun brought that late-spring green into El's room. He knew from the tint of the light on the walls that a nurse would soon arrive with a dose of the all-important pain pills. He enjoyed Barbara Jean's company, but the delivery of those little white pills was the true highlight of his day. Those junkie ways never fully left, no matter how long a man stayed clean.

Barbara Jean asked, "Do you have any pictures of your parents?"

"My mother died when I was a week old. Daddy is the only family I ever had."

He sifted through his bag of photographs and removed one. "That's him."

Barbara Jean took the picture from him. The man in the photo was tall and thin, like El. He wore a striped vest and a bowler hat, and he stood next to what appeared to be a very tall leopard.

"Daddy's name was Joe. The leopard was called Raja."

Barbara Jean held the photo at arm's length to try to bring it into clearer focus. After studying the picture, she said, "Is he petting that thing?"

"Yep, Daddy and Raja were close. Daddy worked on a riverboat. That was before I was born, so I'm just repeatin' the little I remember him sayin' and what Mrs. Taylor told me later. It was a gamblin' boat with shows and girls. The usual stuff. Totally low-rent, except the boat also had a circus. They had a boa constrictor, a couple of chimps, and a leopard. The leopard was so vicious that it wore a muzzle twenty-four/seven. The customers had to stay a long ways away from the cage or Raja would get edgy and tear up the trainer who went into the cage with him for every show. At least, that's what the guy who ran the attraction said.

"My father told me how he and the other guys who worked on the boat used to get drunk and dare each other to sneak into Raja's cage. The closest they ever got was pulling back the curtain the animal trainer used to throw over it at night. Somebody would get brave enough to lift that tarp, but as soon as the leopard turned his head, the guy would lose his nerve and take off runnin'.

"Anyway, the boat sank during a storm one night. My old man had to swim for shore. Daddy said that as soon as his feet touched land, he decided he was done workin' on the river. While everyone else from the boat stood by in the mud waitin' for the rescuers, he started walkin'. He'd heard there was quarry work in Plainview, so he headed here."

Barbara Jean said, "It's a long way from the river to Plainview."

"Sure is. And it was worse because the whole time he was walkin', he kept hearing somebody or something walkin' along with him in the trees beside the road. He'd planned to bed down somewhere out of the rain that night, but the thought of whatever was stalkin' him made him keep goin'.

"Around dawn, Daddy was cold and wet and could hardly get his legs to move. And he knew he was still bein' followed. He was just outside Plainview when he heard a rustling in the brush right to his side and he knew something was comin' his way real fast. Before he could get his tired legs in motion, he saw it. It was the leopard from the riverboat. A second later, the leopard was on him. It rammed Daddy with its head and knocked him to the ground. Then it went straight for his throat."

Barbara Jean reflexively brought her hand to her neck. "Oh my God."

El said, "It didn't bite him, though. Raja got a mouthful of Daddy's collar and started to chew. And the whole time, its leopard spots were drippin' off. Raja the leopard turned out to be a big-ass goat that the circus owner had painted spots on."

Barbara Jean said, "You're telling me that people believed a painted goat was a leopard?"

"My hand to God," El said, lifting his palm. "As soon as Daddy found a place to stay, he painted the goat's leopard spots on again and took to the road with his own wild animal act. That's what he did for the rest of his life."

Barbara Jean looked at the picture of El's father and the leopard again. She squinted and then smiled. "I'll be darned."

El said, "I traveled with Daddy, too, but I barely recall it. He taught me how to play the guitar, though."

"This guitar?" Barbara Jean asked, pointing at Ruthie.

"No, the one my father had was an acoustic. He won it in a poker game. He couldn't play it, but he helped me to pluck out a couple tunes, and I was playin' pretty good a few months later. Daddy and Raja were both dead by the next year. Nobody ever told me exactly what happened to 'em. Not too long after that, I was in the foster home. All I got from my old man was this picture, a guitar he couldn't play, and a story about a leopard that was really a goat."

Barbara Jean looked at the guitar in the case that lay open beside El on the bed. She said, "So your father is why you play a leopard-spotted guitar?"

El touched the tip of his nose with his index finger. "Exactly. I saw that guitar in a pawnshop and knew it had to be mine. I was there to sell the guitar Daddy gave me. See, I'd found out I was gonna be a father myself, and I decided it was time I got a real job. I was good with my hands, and one of my buddies said he could hook me up with a job in construction. But then I saw this guitar. I'd never seen another one like it. Still haven't.

"It probably got painted that way to cover up some bad wood. But that didn't matter to me. I laid eyes on those leopard spots and knew it was a message from my old man that I was headed down the wrong track. I ended up givin' the pawnshop my old guitar and the last money I had in the world for this baby. Thought my wife was gonna kill me. But she forgave me when I spent the first money I made with the guitar putting her name on it."

"So Ruthie was your wife?"

"Yeah," El said. He squinted down at the picture of himself and Lily that rested in his lap as if he might see something new in it. Then he said, "What junkies know that other folks don't is that reality is a mean little mirror. That mirror will show you every nasty thing you ever did to yourself and anybody else, unless you break it."

Barbara Jean said, "You told me once that there's reality and there's truth. The truth is, everybody makes mistakes. When I went to AA, I learned to forgive myself. I think you should forgive yourself, too."

"You've got a tender heart. I hope you don't mind my sayin' so, but you didn't get that from Loretta. You must have a lot of your daddy in you."

Barbara Jean let out a quick snort. "That might be the case, but I wouldn't know. I've never laid eyes on my father, and Loretta wasn't what you'd call forthcoming in regard to him."

Darlene Lloyd, the nurse on duty that afternoon, entered the room.

Her white sneakers squeaked on the tile floor as she walked to El's bedside with his afternoon pain medication. She said, "Mr. Walker, I've got
to take a look at your bandage." She turned to Barbara Jean and added,
"Mrs. Carlson, you're welcome to come back a little later."

Barbara Jean said, "It's time for me to go, anyway." Then to El: "I'll
see you tomorrow at my friend Clarice's recital."

"We'll see. I might go, if I'm feelin' okay."

"You'll go," Barbara Jean said. "Clarice is incredible, and it'll do you
good to get out of this room. Besides, it's just downstairs."

"I'll make sure he gets there," Darlene said.

Barbara Jean thanked her and waved good-bye.

As Darlene began to unwrap the bandage on El's foot, he tossed one
of his pills into his mouth and chewed it to hurry the effects. Then
he pulled his guitar into his lap.

El picked out a melody and felt the beginnings of the opiate tingle.
Hell, maybe he would go to the concert.

CHAPTER 13

*T*he recital hall shared an atrium entrance with the children's wing of the hospital. That afternoon, the space was filled with well-dressed people chatting and helping themselves to the food and beverages that had been supplied for the crowd by the benefit's organizers. Barbara Jean and Ray stood in the center of a group of hospital board members whose bowing and scraping around the handsome, wealthy couple made them look like the court of the queen and king of a high school prom. I was deciding whether to walk over to Barbara Jean or make my way toward the mountain of shrimp on a nearby table when Wayne Robinson approached me.

He wasn't dead yet, I knew. His death would be big news in Plainview, and I was certain that when he passed, word would get to me within minutes. Also, it was my experience that the spirits of the fully departed appeared more substantial than he looked that day. The man before me was still sketchy at the edges.

It would be a great exaggeration to say that Wayne Robinson looked happy, but he wore the first smile I'd ever seen on his face as he stood in front of me and said, "Hello, I was hoping we could have a talk."

Because James was beside me and several other people were within earshot, I didn't respond. But right then, James caught Barbara Jean's eye. They acknowledged each other with a wave, and my husband took a step in Barbara Jean and Ray's direction. I gestured to James that I was going to head toward the hors d'oeuvres. I made my way to a table and filled a plate with as many shrimp as it would hold. Then I moved to a vacant corner of the atrium where Wayne Robinson and I could speak unobserved.

He was a short man, just a little taller than me, with a square face and a wide jaw. He was making an effort to be charming, but it didn't come naturally to him. His strained grin and unblinking eyes made me think of a crocodile. He said, "I recall that you were friends with my son Terry. I was hoping that perhaps you might be able to talk to him. I know how he respected your opinion. You probably know that he and I had a falling-out before he ran away. We both said things we didn't mean. I'd appreciate it if you could suggest to him that he let bygones be bygones, in case he's thinking about dredging up the past. It would be better for Terry that way. Don't you agree, Mrs. Henry?"

I was surprised that he knew my name. Our only previous conversation had come almost five years earlier, when I'd gone to see him about Terry. His son had shown up on my doorstep with a duffel bag and a sad tale that he was trying to paste a happy face on. When I went to see Wayne Robinson on behalf of his son that day, I got as far as saying, "Hi, Mr. Robinson, you probably don't remember me, but I knew your wife and I'm a friend of your son Terry."

He frowned at me through his front screen and said, "I don't have a son named Terry." That was the end of our talk. He didn't shout or slam the door on me. He just denied that his youngest child existed and walked away. Now he was making nice, wanting to chat with me about that same boy.

"Mr. Robinson . . ." I said.

"Wayne," he interrupted, still trying to be friendly.

"Mr. Robinson, I was sorry to hear about your health problems. I'm sure this hasn't been easy for you or your children, especially since your wife passed not too long ago. But I don't think it's my place to tell Terry what to do." I popped a shrimp into my mouth and wondered if I had time to reload my plate before the recital. I said, "I'm a believer in the power of prayer, and I promise I'll ask the Lord to heal you so you can talk to Terry yourself."

The smile that he was trying to maintain faltered a bit as he said, "That's the problem, Mrs. Henry. There won't be a recovery for me. I've heard what the doctors are saying. They're just waiting for my daughter to get back to town and make the final decision."

I said, "You never know. They'd given me up for dead five years back, and I'm still here."

He raised his voice as he began losing patience with me. "I don't see why you can't just have a talk with him. You've heard about that nasty thing he said he was going to do. You can't believe that's right."

I said, "If you were hoping for someone to support the most peaceful and polite way of settling a fight, I'm afraid you've got the wrong member of the Henry family. My husband is the dove in our house. Unfortunately for you, James doesn't see ghosts, so you're stuck with the hawk. And I believe Terry deserves to sort this out whatever way he sees fit."

Ray and James walked up to me then. I turned away from Wayne Robinson, who had completely given up on charming me and was now pouting and cussing. I hugged Ray and then I oohed and aahed over the way he looked in his blue pin-striped suit. "Ray," I said, "you're a lovely sight in a pair of jeans and a T-shirt. But in a suit, you are truly a sweet blessing from God." We both laughed like I was kidding, but I was dead serious. If I'd kept a "Jump for Joy" calendar like Mama did to write down everyday wonders, I'd have penciled in a note about how beautiful blue-eyed Ray Carlson looked that day.

Wayne Robinson kept jabbering at me about how unfair I was being. I ignored him while I talked to my husband and my friend. I suppose I could have been nicer, but my spirit-coddling days were done. Besides, he had started off on the wrong foot by telling that lie about Terry running away. A better person might have had more sympathy for this man's hardship, but it galled me that he would expect any favors from me.

A chime rang to signal that the auditorium was open and that everyone should move inside. I told James and Ray that I would be right behind them and asked that they save me a seat. Once I was alone, I turned again to Wayne Robinson. I wanted to end my conversation with him on a warmer note than I'd left it earlier, considering his present situation.

"I really am sorry that I can't help you. It might be a good thing for you to go back upstairs and fight to stay in that body of yours so maybe you can make peace with your son. Or you might find that it's time to let go and move on. Sometimes it's good to know when to walk away from a fight."

Wayne Robinson scowled at me and showed me the sour, angry face I remembered from our brief talk through his screen door. He said, "You're just gonna let him shame me when I'm dead the same way he shamed me when I was living?" He was getting louder and more excited as he spoke. "I deserve better! This isn't right!" shouted the man who had put his own child out on the street over a few dresses.

I said, "I'm sorry, Mr. Robinson." I enjoyed the last shrimp on my plate and walked into the auditorium.

CHAPTER 14

Clarice peeked out from behind a maroon velvet curtain and watched her audience assemble. Barbara Jean, Ray, and James sat in the reserved front row, along with several men and women from the hospital board. Odette soon arrived and took the empty seat next to James. Beatrice swept in with Richmond on one arm and Forrest Payne on the other. They were followed by Veronica and her husband, Clement. In an elegant knee-length, pale taupe evening dress, Clarice's mother was the best-dressed woman in the room. Veronica was a close second. She'd shown up in a floor-length beaded gown that was inappropriate for the occasion, but—Clarice had to admit—beautifully made. Even Beatrice and Veronica couldn't draw anyone's gaze away from Forrest Payne's perfectly fitted yellow tuxedo, though. As usual, Forrest's only possible competitor was the sun.

The rest of the seats filled quickly with ticket holders. A dozen or so students from the university's music school stood against the far wall.

Near a ramp connected to the side entrance, Clarice saw Darlene Lloyd pushing in a wheelchair carrying El Walker.

Until an hour before the performance was scheduled to begin, Clarice had felt more relaxed than she'd been for her other recent concerts. But then her manager, Wendell Albertson, had walked onto the stage as she was warming up. He claimed that he had flown in from New York for business nearby and decided to take in her concert. She thanked him for coming and pretended to be pleased to see him. Yet she couldn't help but feel that he was there to check in on his investment. The critics had been decidedly less enthusiastic about her more recent performances than they had been about the concerts that had immediately followed her first recordings. Whether Wendell would admit it or not, she was sure he had traveled to the Midwest to see for himself what was happening with her.

Now, with just a few minutes to go before the start of the program, Clarice felt her pulse begin to race as she watched Wendell talking to her mother in the audience. It crossed her mind that she might send a message to Richmond that he should come backstage for some private time in her dressing room. Then she thought that might be a bit much. It was a Sunday, after all.

She took a few deep breaths and attempted to calm down. She told herself that she was prepared and she had nothing to worry about. She tried to convince herself that Wendell's presence was a good thing. She could show him that the last review, in which the critic had described her as an "empty technician," had been the product of a prickly journalist's bad mood and not an accurate assessment of her current playing.

Someone tapped Clarice on her shoulder, and she turned to see the president of the hospital board standing beside her. He said, "I'm about to introduce you. Is there anything you need before we start? Water, maybe?"

Clarice wanted to say, *See that muscular guy sitting between the two*

overdressed women? Tell him to get backstage and drop his pants right now!
Instead she replied, "A bottle of water would be nice."

The board president's introduction was a bit long-winded, but smoothly done. He recounted her childhood musical achievements, making them sound, Clarice thought, more impressive than they had been. Then he quoted the brilliant reviews of her recordings and cherry-picked positive comments from the reviews of her recent live performances. When she took the stage, the audience was primed for something special.

She was performing three Beethoven sonatas, the same three she would be playing in Chicago. The trouble began almost immediately. She played the first note. Then she couldn't remember the second. She had learned this piece—opus 23, the *Appassionata*—when she was a teenager, and she had performed and taught it more times than she could count. But the second note of the piece was gone from her memory.

For what felt like several seconds—but was, in reality, only two—she waited for the second note to come to her. It didn't, so she jumped to the third note. Now the know-it-all music students in the back of the auditorium were probably whispering to each other about the colossal mistake they'd just heard from a soloist who should know better. Though she couldn't see Wendell Albertson's face, she knew that he must be grimacing.

The rest of the sonata flew by as Clarice closed her eyes and shut down her brain. When she reached the end, she was breathless and jittery, but there had been no more major missteps. The audience's applause was loud and immediate—the blessing of having friends and family in attendance. When she glanced up at the clock offstage as she rose to take her bow, she realized that she had rushed the tempos so much that she had shaved a full two minutes from the performance time. No wonder they were impressed, she thought. Panic had caused her to perform a miracle of velocity.

The next two pieces, which comprised the rest of the program, went slightly better. She wasn't as flustered, and she was occasionally able to make music. When she struck the final chord of the last sonata, she could actually remember having played the piece, and she believed she had created one or two nice sounds along the way. But the *Appassionata* had been a disaster, remarkable only in its speed. Clarice knew that she didn't deserve the standing ovation the crowd gave her. She could tell from her manager's wrinkled brow and pinched mouth that he knew it, too.

The audience hushed as she sat at the piano for her encore. Clarice announced, "Variations on 'The Happy Heartache Blues,' by El Walker." Then she began to play.

When Barbara Jean had asked her to perform El's song as her encore, Clarice had planned to play only a straightforward transcription. As she'd worked on it, though, the melody had climbed beneath her skin and stayed. From the sheet music Barbara Jean had slipped out of El's hospital room, Clarice had created a set of variations based on the haunting tune. The arrangement was simple and just under four minutes long, but the effect was powerful. The most appreciative clapping of the afternoon came after the encore.

Above the noise of the crowd's response, Clarice acknowledged the composer. "Mr. El Walker," she called out.

Darlene Lloyd pushed El's wheelchair forward and brought him to the front of the hall. Clarice was relieved when he raised his head to look up at her on the stage and mouthed, "Thank you." His chair was turned so that he faced the applauding crowd, and then Darlene helped him rise from the wheelchair to acknowledge the audience. With clear discomfort and effort, El stood on one foot and executed a movement that somewhat resembled a bow.

Led by Barbara Jean and Ray, then quickly followed by Odette and James, the audience stood again to honor both Clarice and the old man in hospital scrubs.

Clarice saw El change as if a switch had been flipped. He went from flashing his tobacco-stained teeth at the appreciative crowd to squeezing his eyes shut against pain that had suddenly become overwhelming. He fell back into his wheelchair and growled, "Get me out of here, dammit," at the nurse behind him.

Only Clarice and those in the front couple of rows noticed the quick shift in El's demeanor, and they weren't able to observe him for long. Clarice watched the nurse rush El toward the exit. Soon the two of them had disappeared.

Health crises, large and small, were commonplace here. Once El was taken away, the focus quickly shifted back to Clarice, who bowed and smiled as her heart rate, at last, began to slow.

Soon she was standing before a long line of people, each of whom wanted to personally congratulate her. The president of the hospital board embraced her and said that between donations and ticket sales, they'd made far more money for the hospital than they'd hoped to. Old friends kissed her and raved about how proud of her they were. Strangers who'd come to see her after hearing or reading the tale of the resurrected piano prodigy gripped her hand and told her that she was an inspiration.

As well-wishers moved forward to deliver their compliments, Clarice began to remember scattered moments of the recital that hadn't been total failures. The afternoon had been successful as a fund-raiser, so it had succeeded in at least one way. Also, she had performed three major pieces of the piano repertoire. Stunt programming, maybe. But just getting through those three warhorses was worth something, wasn't it? She would have to meet a higher standard in the weeks to come, but there might be some small part of this day that she could count as a victory.

Then a group of music professors from the university, with several of their students in tow, stepped up to shake her hand. Each of the students expressed admiration for her dexterity. Did she detect sarcasm? It was hard to tell with young people these days. The *Appassionata* must have been every bit the trainwreck she'd feared it was.

Wendell Albertson said, "There were some really lovely moments."

That was no compliment. That was how you described diamonds scattered over a pile of manure.

Her mother followed Wendell Albertson in the line. Beatrice Jordan Payne congratulated her daughter and reiterated her disappointment that Clarice had chosen to perform on a Sunday, a day reserved for religious contemplation. Then she embraced Clarice and whispered, "Let's drive to Louisville this week and find you a more flattering dress."

I am a terrible musician. My own mother says I am hell-bound. And I am fat.

After she had shaken the hundredth hand and her throat was dry from repeating, "Thank you," Clarice stood inside a circle of appreciative hospital board members. They yapped at her like overly stimulated Chihuahuas, excited by the event and the private reception that would occur later at Ballard House, the Queen Anne mansion Barbara Jean owned in downtown Plainview.

Just beyond the ring of well-heeled admirers, Richmond stood waiting. Broad-shouldered and bursting with virility, he made everything around him, even Forrest Payne's yellow tuxedo, seem dim.

Clarice crossed her arms and drummed her fingertips against her elbows. As the guest of honor, she had to put in an appearance at the reception. But she would duck out early. There was practicing to do. And, praise Jesus, there was Richmond.

CHAPTER 15

*A*fter giving their congratulations to Clarice, Odette and James moved toward the back of the auditorium to join the cluster of guests preparing to walk to the reception at Ballard House. Before they reached the other members of the procession, the staticky scratch of the hospital intercom drifted into the hospital auditorium. James inclined an ear toward the open door, listening. Then he said to Odette, "I should go check that out."

"Check what out?" Odette asked.

"That announcement. It's the code they use when somebody needs security to come fast."

The announcement filled the air again. "Dr. Strong needed in room 426, stat."

Odette said, "You're off duty today, you know."

"I know. I'll just see if I can help. Then I'll be right back," he said, already turning toward the hallway.

Outside room 426, Darlene Lloyd was slumped against the doorjamb.

She grimaced as a doctor probed her arm. As he approached, James heard Darlene say, "I don't know what got into him. He was always such a sweet old guy. Maybe he's having a reaction to one of his meds."

James stepped into the room and saw El, red-eyed and perspiring, standing in front of an open closet door. El leaned on a metal crutch as he swung its mate at one of the two security guards who stood between El and James.

"I'm goin', dammit! You can't keep me here!" El yelled.

The security guard who had just dodged the crutch said, "Mr. Walker, nobody is trying to keep you prisoner, but you still need help."

The other guard said, "Yeah, old fella, we're just trying to help you." When El swung the crutch again, the guard nearest to him backed off. Then the guard used a hand gesture to signal his colleague that it was time to move in and put an end to El's tantrum.

James recognized one of the guards as a moonlighting state trooper. "Can I help?" he asked.

The guard answered, "I think we've got it, Captain Henry. Something upset Mr. Walker here and he pushed a nurse against the wall. We're just going to get him under control so the doctor can administer a sedative."

El turned and looked at the newcomer in the room. Then dropped his crutches to the floor. His defiance drained away, and he fell back onto his bed with his arm flung across his face. The security guards moved in and placed El in restraints, and the doctor stepped forward to administer an injection.

El groaned, "This damn town. I never should've come back to this shit hole."

Now that the old man was under control, James stepped into the hallway. A small crowd of familiar faces greeted him just outside the door.

Downstairs in the auditorium, Odette had mentioned to Barbara Jean that James had run off to room 426 to help attend to an emergency. Knowing that the room number was El's, Barbara Jean had decided to go to the fourth floor to find out what had happened. On her way, she'd asked Forrest Payne to come with her, thinking that, whatever was going on with El, he would be comforted by the presence of two friends. Odette had come along because James was already there, and because it was her nature to be where trouble was percolating.

Now Odette, Barbara Jean, and Forrest stood blocking James's way. "Is he okay?" Barbara Jean asked.

James said, "He's all right, I think. Something got him agitated, and he gave his nurse a shove. The doctor's in there with him now."

Forrest placed his hand on James's arm. "I'm so glad you're here," he said in his sweet, whispery voice. "I told El you were a good man. I told him, no matter what happened way back when, you'd want to see your daddy."

James blinked and tilted his head slightly as he tried to comprehend what Forrest was telling him. "What?" he said. But it was becoming clear then, and he didn't wait for Forrest to say more.

James entered room 426 again and walked over to the side of El's bed. The doctor and the security guards stepped aside as James moved in close and leaned over the patient.

El turned away from James with a quick, almost spasmodic motion. He didn't fight, though, when James placed a hand on his jaw and brought the older man's face around so that their eyes met. The hand that wasn't on El's beard came up suddenly and landed on the metal railing of the hospital bed with such a loud clank that everyone in the room jumped.

Odette entered the crowded room and went to James's side. When she placed her hand at the center of his back, she could feel his heart racing beneath his suit jacket. James released El and, in a gesture Odette had seen thousands of times, brought his hand to his own jawline and rubbed the long scar there.

El let out a moan and muttered another curse about the "damn town" that had done him wrong again.

James bent down and brought his lips close to El's ear. Speaking in a tight, halting voice just loud enough for Odette to make out, James snarled, "I forgive you."

Odette heard her husband speak of forgiveness, but no absolution was offered in his angry growl. When he straightened and glared down at the man in the bed, she placed a hand on James's arm. She was that sure he was going to strike El. But James turned around and walked stiffly toward the doorway. He stopped when he stood beside Forrest. He said, "Thank you. I appreciate you telling me."

In the hallway, James strode toward the elevator. Odette ran after him, forced to take three steps for each of his in order to keep up. Inside the elevator, she reached out and grabbed his hand as they rode down to the lobby. Odette watched as his mouth twisted, his jaw jutted forward, and his eyes squinted. She had believed, after forty-two years of observing nearly every twitch of his lips and contortion of his brow, that experience had shown her how any emotion would present itself on James's face. The worries and joys of raising Jimmy, Eric, and Denise. The blinding grief of losing family and friends. The stress of keeping a roof over their heads in the hardscrabble years. Now she gazed up at him and was both amazed and frightened that this face she knew so well could still produce an expression she had never seen.

CHAPTER 16

A fat orange tabby leapt onto James's lap. The purring cat marched a slow circle in a futile attempt to find a comfortable resting place atop James's bony thighs. Then she gave up in frustration and stretched out beside him on the living room sofa.

James reached out and cradled the cat's chin in his palm, lifting her face. This one might be a new one. He would have to ask Odette the cat's name. Of course, there was no guarantee that she actually belonged to them. Unfamiliar felines appeared in the house frequently enough that James often couldn't distinguish the permanent residents from the visitors.

Word had spread among the animals of the area that a sweet deal was available at the Henry home: indiscriminately affectionate humans, a dog-proof fence, and an ample food supply. Cats flocked there to take advantage. The Plainview Humane Society regularly sent people to Odette and James to inquire after lost pets. Anxious strangers who came by in search of their wayward cats often found their animals fatter and better groomed than they'd last seen them and, more often than not, highly displeased to be dragged away from their vacations.

When Odette was a little girl, it seemed that cats always accompanied her. Throngs of them pranced along after her, darting between her feet as she walked and coiling themselves around her ankles when she stood still. They waited patiently outside the doors of the school for Odette to leave at the end of the day, so they could accompany her as she walked home.

The way the cats assembled to greet her every day seemed like a magic trick to James and the other children. It therefore struck her schoolmates as logical that Odette could attract and communicate with animals. She had that kind of reputation. By the time Odette was in the first grade, most of her classmates had heard some version of the story of her birth in a sycamore tree. Even if they hadn't been told the entire tale, the kids had heard the superstition related to it: that the novel circumstances of her entry into the world had cursed her with fearlessness. Also, several of the other children's fathers had been left physically and emotionally damaged by encounters with Odette's aunt Marjorie in her capacity as the Pink Slipper Club's volunteer bouncer. Odette's classmates had been instructed to give her a wide berth, and for the most part, they did.

There was, in fact, a far simpler explanation for the cats seeking her out. Dora Jackson was such an extraordinarily terrible cook that, from kindergarten on, Odette's grandmother would fill her granddaughter's pockets with supplementary food to substitute for the unappetizing or downright inedible lunches Dora prepared for her daughter. While the cats might well have connected with some unique and shining facet of Odette's soul, it was more likely that they gravitated to her because of what she carried. Any halfway sensible cat would cozy up to a chubby girl who often traveled with a couple fried-perch sandwiches in her sweater pockets.

During their elementary school days, Odette had been known as the girl from an oddball family who was born in a tree. Just as Clarice was thought of as the spectacularly gifted daughter of the religious zealot who handed out miniature Bibles on Halloween instead of candy, Barbara Jean was the child of a whore. The scar on James's face had set him apart from other children. Even before his first day of kindergarten, James had been pointed out to his schoolmates as the unfortunate boy whose junkie father had slashed his face. That shorthand had served the parents of the other kids well, and it was eagerly adopted by their offspring.

James's scar ran from the tip of his right earlobe, down along his jaw, and curved up slightly toward the center of his lower lip. When they were bored, or couldn't come up with a more exciting diversion, a group of boys entertained themselves by following James to or from school, teasing him about the scar.

At first it happened only once every few weeks. Then one of his tormentors hit upon the idea that the thick, raised line along James's jaw looked like something from a horror movie. Suddenly it became a daily game for some of the boys to swarm around James. Walking with a teetering, stiff-legged gait, they would extend their arms straight out in front of them as they yelled, "Frankenstein!"

Their taunts never advanced to physical violence. James was several inches taller than the majority of his classmates from his first day of school until the day he graduated. While he was never one to start a fight, his height and serious demeanor gave him the appearance of someone who could easily end one. But his unwillingness to use his fists to put a stop to the harassment made him a safe target.

The first time they called him a monster, James ran home and sobbed on his mother's shoulder, insisting that he would never return to school. Ruth Henry's response was to wipe his tears and say, "Baby, you and me are too poor to be this tenderhearted. You'd better learn to make fools invisible. These won't be the last ones you meet."

It hadn't been easy, but James had taken his mother's advice. The situation quickly improved. There was little sport for his tormentors in abusing someone who barely noticed. Only a few of the older bullies had been tenacious, a devoted contingent that performed the "Frankenstein" routine nearly every time they saw James. They kept it up until Odette and her cats brought it to an end.

Odette and James hadn't been close friends at the time. That would've been impossible for a boy and girl of their ages. But like all the other children, even those who professed to be afraid of Odette and what they saw as her supernatural powers, James had been a guest at Odette's birthday parties.

Dora and Wilbur Jackson threw extravagant parties for both of their children's birthdays. More than fifty years later, James still recalled the amazement he'd felt entering the Jackson home for the first time. It was a palace. Unlike the walls of his home, which were perpetually eggshell white, as dictated by their agreement with the landlord, it seemed that a twenty-four pack of crayons had been set free on the walls of Odette's house. The kaleidoscopic windows borrowed their shapes from geometry books or puzzle pieces. Stairways curved artfully from one floor to the next.

And the food. The spread on display at Odette's birthday party that first time, and each time thereafter, was just as impressive as the house. There were tables of cookies and cakes, baked hams adorned with pineapple rings, and piles of golden fried chicken. If something could be roasted, candied, pickled, jellied, or spiced, it was on display. Every bite of food was cooked to loving perfection by Odette's grandmother and an assortment of relatives who believed that no one should be condemned to eat food prepared by Dora Jackson.

Young James's words upon stepping inside Odette's childhood home for the first time would become a running joke throughout their marriage. He had looked around at bounty that was an absolute wonder to the eyes of a desperately poor child and asked, "Odette, what's it like to be rich?"

The last day the boys called James "Frankenstein"—at least the last time they dared say it to his face—was just a few days after Odette's ninth birthday party. James was walking home along a stretch of dirt road that was surrounded on both sides by the distinctive twisted trees that had given the neighborhood of Leaning Tree its name. He heard them coming up from behind him, all of them grunting and howling, doing their best imitations of the Frankenstein monster.

James walked faster, but the boys soon caught up with him. He didn't run. He was determined never to run from them. Chin high and set straight ahead, he thought of his mother's words and tried to make the lurching boys invisible.

They continued their monster imitations, breaking character only to laugh.

Then Odette appeared. More precisely, the cats appeared. First one, then another. Then a half dozen, and, ultimately, twenty more. Mewling and yowling, they zipped between and over the feet of James's persecutors.

Finally, Odette crashed her way out of the underbrush that lined the gully. She rushed onto the rutted road, shrieking, "Leave him alone!"

The brigade of cats parted to make a passageway for her as she threw her solid four-foot frame at Ramsey Abrams, the largest of the boys who had been harassing James.

As Odette pounced onto Ramsey's back, the pack of cats attempted to scale his legs to get at whatever delicious snacks lay hidden inside her pockets. The cats clawed at Ramsey's legs, and Odette wrapped an arm around his shoulders, pummeling his head with her free hand. Soon he was on the ground, held down by a round girl and a throng of cats while his friends looked on, their mouths open in astonishment.

In nearly every retelling of the story over the coming half century, James would joke that the finale of the scuffle had been the true definition of an ass kicking. Odette, having brought Ramsey to the ground, aimed her shoes at his rear end. She stomped on him until he cried and begged her to stop. All the while, she kept shouting, "Leave James alone!"

The other boys ran off, abandoning their ringleader to Odette's harsh punishment. James stayed and watched her short, thick legs churn, her scuffed saddle oxfords repeatedly finding their target. With each strike, she made an indelible impression on Ramsey and solidified what would become a lifelong reputation as a fierce, if somewhat unhinged, guardian of justice.

At ten years of age, James had been old enough to understand that having a girl fight for his honor and, even worse, win that fight was not something he wanted anyone at school to hear about. He imagined—correctly, as it turned out—arriving at school the next morning to hear the boys who had once called him Frankenstein instead chanting, "James loves the fat girl!"

As Odette continued to work Ramsey over, James scampered away. Running home, he grinned and thought, *I love that fat girl.*

DINNER WAS LATE. In the two days since Clarice's recital, Odette hadn't been able to do anything around the house with her usual efficiency. The roast chicken with herbs that normally took her an hour to cook had been a two-hour project tonight. James was even more preoccupied than she was. His mind had taken him off somewhere. Maybe his thoughts were in the tiny house in Leaning Tree where he had grown up, struggling so hard with his mother, or maybe in a hospital room across town with the man he had glared at with a searing hatred but claimed to have forgiven.

Since leaving El's hospital room, James hadn't uttered a word about his father. Odette had prodded and probed, wanting to know what he was feeling, but that had only made him become quieter. Throughout their years together, she had been grateful for James's hushed restraint and serenity. She couldn't imagine living with one of those boisterous men who spilled out every half-baked thought in their heads. But this was a deeper silence than ever before.

Like a song, a long marriage had its own rhythm. Neither of them had been hitting the beats they were supposed to. It had been only two days, but that was an eternity when you knew how your song was supposed to go and heard clanging and banging instead.

Odette had talked through her worries about James with her mother in the gazebo that morning. The conversation with Mama had gotten off to a rough start when Odette had asked why, in the nearly six years since she'd been visiting from beyond the grave, her mother had never mentioned that James's father was still alive. Mama had been insulted by the suggestion that she'd been holding back such important information. She'd also been highly offended by the insinuation that all dead people knew each other.

Odette had said she was sorry and pointed out that her mother's habit of regularly popping in with two such unlikely companions as Aunt Marjorie and former first lady Eleanor Roosevelt could lead a reasonable person to assume that the world of the dead was a small one. Mama had remained surly, but she'd eventually accepted Odette's apology.

Odette's mother had provided some information about El from the old days, including his real name, Marcus Henry. He and Miss Ruth had been several years younger than she was, so she hadn't known him well. Aunt Marjorie, who'd visited the Pink Slipper daily, would be the person to ask about El, Mama had said. But Aunt Marjorie and Eleanor Roosevelt had shared a bottle of corn liquor that morning, and the two of them had carried on a friendly slap-boxing match outside the gazebo the entire time Odette and her mother talked. Odette had hoped to chat with Aunt Marjorie about El, only as soon as the boxing match was over, her aunt had run off. Mama and Mrs. Roosevelt, fox stole waving in the breeze, had followed her.

James arrived in the kitchen just as she placed his dinner on the table. He sat down as she filled the cats' bowls in the corner of the room and then prepared her own plate. As Odette passed his chair on her way to her place at the kitchen table, James reached out and wrapped his arm around her waist.

He said, "Seeing you with all those cats reminded me of that time with Ramsey back when we were kids. Man, you tore his butt up. I bet he still remembers it."

Odette said, "I hope he does."

When James released her, she sat down across from him. Before taking the first bite, Odette said, "Things will get better soon."

"Everything is just fine," James said.

She sliced into her chicken and tried to recall the last time he had told her a lie.

CHAPTER 17

The door of room 426 was just slightly ajar when Barbara Jean approached. She tapped three times and received no answer. When a quiet "Hello" elicited no response, she entered. The room was dark, and El wasn't in his bed. She saw the open guitar case lying across one of the two visitors' chairs and then heard a sweet, meandering tune.

El sat in the far corner of the room with his chair angled toward a large window with its curtains drawn partially open. Taking no notice of Barbara Jean, he strummed. His gaze traveled back and forth from a pair of crutches leaning against the arm of his chair to the aluminum walker that stood directly in front of him, enclosing him like a cage. He wore a tattered red wool sweater with unraveling cuffs over his hospital gown. He also wore his newly fitted prosthesis. Continuing nearly to his knee, the high-tech appendage completed his foot and attached to his shin.

She said, "Hi, El. It's good to see you out of bed."

He stopped playing in mid-phrase, and his head jerked upward in surprise. "Hey, Barbara Jean," he said.

She set a vase of fresh flowers beside the wilting arrangement on his side table. "How's it going with the prosthesis?"

"I took a few steps this morning."

She waited for him to say more, but he went back to studying the crutches and the walker again as if they were new to him. She said, "Every step is a good one. Pretty soon you'll be walking just fine."

She sat on the corner of his bed and adjusted her tweed Chanel dress to cover her knees. She said, "I heard about what happened after Clarice's recital. Are you okay?"

"I guess I caused enough of a ruckus that everybody 'round here is talkin' about me."

"No, they're used to folks getting upset. Everybody who works here understands that people getting overwrought is part of the job. It's just that you've been such a mellow guy since you got here that you surprised them. Anyway, I didn't hear about it from anyone at the hospital. I heard about it from my friend Odette. She's married to James."

"I see," El said. "Now you know that I'm the worst father there ever was. My son hates me."

"Odette told me that James forgave you."

"Yeah, that's what he said. But I was lookin' in his eyes."

Odette had told Barbara Jean that James pretty much wanted El dead. But Barbara Jean had decided before she'd knocked on El's hospital room door that she wouldn't be sharing that.

She had thought a lot about El since discovering that he was James's father. She had lain awake for two nights wondering how she could go on being his friend. Finally, she'd decided she had to believe that, with time, faith, and patience, people changed. Otherwise, what had five years of AA meetings meant? This man had changed. No matter what he had once done, the El Walker she'd talked and laughed with over the past two and a half weeks wasn't a man who hurt people, not anymore.

She said, "James is a good man. He doesn't want you or anybody else dead. He's probably just in shock. I'm pretty sure he never thought he'd see you again."

El said, "I shouldn't be here. This town ain't never done me anything but bad."

She stood and walked to El. She came close enough to him that the tips of her sleek tan high-heeled pumps were nearly even with the neon-green tennis balls attached to the legs of his walker. "I told you that I used to drink, but I never told you how bad it got. I nearly ruined everything good in my life when I was drinking—my marriage, my friendships, everything. I piled up enough regrets to last three or four lifetimes. It's a miracle I didn't kill myself or accidentally kill somebody else.

"I go to AA meetings at least once a week to keep from sliding back into all that. Every time I'm there, I hear a story like mine, or worse. What I've learned is that anyone can change, no matter what they've done. And everybody deserves forgiveness."

"Pretty girl, you're wrong about that. There are some things you can't ask anybody to forgive."

"Then you ask God to forgive you and you forgive yourself." She placed one of her finely manicured hands just below the faded needle marks on his exposed arm. "Taking responsibility for the things you did when addiction had a hold on you doesn't mean you have to punish yourself forever."

"Did you ever get so messed up that you lifted a razor in the air and brought it down on your child's face?"

For just a second, Barbara Jean pictured her son, Adam, whose angelic face she'd last seen in a coffin when he was just eight years old. The vision of a glinting blade swinging toward his smooth cheek caused her to wince involuntarily.

"I didn't think so," El said. The furrows of his forehead compressed and his crow's-feet deepened as he shut his eyes tight. She could tell that an old movie he'd seen thousands of times was playing again behind his eyelids.

El said, "You know, it's not the memory of the blood or the scar on James's face that comes to me at night. It's the way he reached for me after I cut him.

"See, James was my baby more than Ruthie's, really. His mother worked all day, so I spent more time with him than she did. I went crazy that night 'cause Ruthie hid my stash. She'd done it before and gotten me to clean up for a few weeks. That night, I lost my mind, though. I just wanted to scare her. At least I think that's all I would have done. I don't know the truth anymore, if I ever did.

"What I know for sure is that I had to get my heroin, and I thought wavin' the razor at Ruthie would get it for me. All of a sudden, James was there between us and the razor was sliding across his face. As soon as he was cut, he put his arms out for me to hold him because that's what he always did when he was hurt."

El lifted his guitar and cradled it in his arms. One hand gently held the body of the instrument, and he tenderly cupped the other over the tuning pegs. "I snatched him up and put my hand over the cut to stop the blood. He wasn't even crying at first. But Ruthie screamed, and then we were all screaming. She grabbed James from me and ran out the door with him. The way I picture it, he was callin' out, 'Daddy, Daddy!' when she carried him away. But I can't tell the true memory from the nightmare anymore.

"You can say all you want about forgiveness and folks changin', but I know I'm no better now than I was back then. I'm just older and slower."

"I don't know what kind of man you used to be, but you've been good to me and you were a friend to Loretta."

"No, I wasn't. I'd like to lie to you and say I was always your mama's friend, but I got no lies left in me today. I didn't do right by Loretta."

"No man ever did," Barbara Jean said. She sat on the edge of the bed again. "I can guess what might have gone on between you and Loretta."

"You don't know the half."

"Maybe not, but I know you've done right by me." She looked out the window and watched cars climb the hill toward town. Ballard House stood at the crest of that hill. The weather vane of the mansion she owned but rarely stepped inside anymore was visible from where she sat. She said, "I've got all the things Loretta said would make me happy, but I've never really felt that way. I used to think it was because my mother was a drunk. Then I thought I was sad because I was a drunk, too. But when you started showing me those pictures and told me how Loretta was sad even before she started drinking, both of us made a little more sense to me. Now I know it was in my blood."

El said, "If there's one thing a blues man is good for, it's letting you know you're screwed from birth."

"That's not what I meant, and you know it. You did a good thing for me, and I'll always be grateful." Barbara Jean adjusted the hem of her dress again and then played with the clasp of her purse. "I've been thinking. You told me once that you could have steady work in Europe. I'm a wealthy woman. I'd be glad to help you get wherever you want to go, once you're out of here. We could call it payment for all the pictures you let me copy. They've been valuable to me."

El said, "You're a generous woman. Loretta would be proud of you."

Barbara Jean laughed. "Maybe, if she wasn't too busy stealing from me."

"Loretta would try to take her cut, all right. But she'd be proud, too," El said. "I appreciate the offer, but I don't need it. Forrest dropped by yesterday and paid me for a gig he knows I'll never perform. He even threw in a bonus, called it 'overtime from 1949.' I tell you, that man's conversion from sinner to saint must be for real. Only the Lord could loosen that cheap bastard's grip on his wallet."

Barbara Jean stood and returned to El's side. "If you change your mind and decide you want some help, my offer stands." She squeezed

El's shoulder. "I'll come by to see you tomorrow. Maybe you can play some music for me. I'd love to hear you sing again."

El gave out a grunt that Barbara Jean chose to hear as a yes. She waved good-bye to him from the door of his room, but his attention was focused on the guitar cradled in his lap.

CHAPTER 18

*I*n the fall of 1976, El sang at Forrest Payne's second wedding. Forrest's bride, just nineteen years old, had been a dancer at the club. She was pretty, but she was worldly beyond her years and had a hot temper. Everyone—except Forrest—saw the end coming long before the vows were spoken. A small fortune was wagered on the date by which the marriage would fall apart and whether or not there would be police intervention. (The union lasted five years, four of them mostly peaceful. Half a dozen policemen were on hand to witness the climactic scene. Marjorie won all the money.)

Just as he would decades later, Forrest set El up with free lodging for the three days he'd be in Plainview for the wedding. El figured that if he stepped outside only to perform at the ceremony, he could slip in and out of town quickly and anonymously. Most of the wedding guests were too young to remember him from his days as Marcus Henry. He would stay in Plainview long enough to play Forrest's good-luck song, and then he'd catch a ride south the next night with one of his bandmates for two weeks of gigs in Texas.

In the excitement of his nuptials, Forrest forgot to bring the envelope containing El's pay to the wedding service. So El settled into a shadowy corner at the Pink Slipper Gentlemen's Club the afternoon after the wedding and waited for Forrest to deliver what was due. By way of apology, Forrest had told the bartender to give El all the free drinks he wanted at the bar that day, and El intended to make ample use of Forrest's conciliatory gesture and be fully fortified for traveling by the time his drummer friend pulled into the parking lot outside.

Each time the door to the club opened, El glanced over to see if it was Forrest entering. Around three o'clock, a figure who was as broad across the shoulders as Forrest but a foot shorter swaggered in. Clad in overalls with a nameplate on the breast pocket that read simply, "M," Marjorie Davis tipped her cap at the doorman and strode for the bar. She walked behind the counter, squeezed past the bartender, and pulled an unlabeled glass jug from the liquor shelf. Marjorie tugged the cork from the jug and poured cloudy liquid the color of weak iced tea into a beer mug. After filling the mug, she corked the bottle and placed it back on the shelf. Then she slid past the bartender again, came around the other side of the bar, and sat down next to El.

His first instinct was to stand up and run. Marjorie had that effect on people. Just the sound of her coarse voice, which brought to mind the creaking of rusty nails being pried from boards and the bass rumble that came from the settling foundations of old houses, made him feel as if he had just been caught at something and was about to receive his punishment.

El had changed quite a bit since the last night Marjorie had seen him, one of the many Plainview nights he longed to erase from his memory. He was two decades older. He had a thick beard now and a new name to go with it. She didn't glance his way as she dropped her cap onto the bar top and then sipped a brew with a harsh, paint thinner odor that assaulted the air around her.

She doesn't recognize me. He relaxed as Marjorie looked straight ahead. Then Marjorie rumbled, "Good to see you. I like the beard."

He took a deep breath and released it slowly to calm his nerves. Hoping that his voice wouldn't squeak as if he were thirteen years old, he said, "Good to see you, too. I like your haircut. It suits you."

She ran her hand over her head, which was now shaved down to the scalp. "Thanks much, Marcus. No, that's not right, is it? You go by El Walker now."

"Yeah, most folks call me El these days. I guess I'll always be Marcus Henry here, though." He smirked. "That's why I haven't been back."

"Whatever you want to call yourself, I'm glad you're here. Maybe we'll start havin' some good music up in here for a change. It's truly sad what passes for blues singin' these days."

"I'm only here till tonight. I'm just waitin' for Forrest and havin' a few drinks." He drained his glass and signaled to the bartender to bring another. To himself mostly, he said, "Don't wanna stick around too long. This town has always been bad luck for me."

"I can see how you might look at it that way." She pulled a cigar from the breast pocket of her overalls. She struck a match against the rough wood along the edge of the bar and, with a series of loud sucking sounds, lit a stogie that smelled almost as bad as her liquor. "Listen, I feel bad about the stuff I said to you the last time I saw you. I should have minded my own business, but I was so mad I couldn't help myself. I was always fond of Ruth, and that boy of yours was such a sweet little thing. Still, it wasn't my place to tell you that you weren't welcome here. You built more of the Pink Slipper than anybody."

"Hell, you probably saved my life. I can think of half a dozen men and twice as many women who would gladly have stabbed me in the heart if I'd tried comin' back to the club after what I did to James. I would have deserved it."

"Maybe, maybe not. All I can say for sure is that nobody has made music like you and Lily and the band since y'all went away."

"I appreciate that." El lifted his refreshed glass of whiskey and the two of them clinked a toast.

Marjorie noticed the ring of El's possessions—his guitar, amplifier, and two suitcases—stacked against the wall behind him. "All that yours?" she asked.

"Yeah, I'm staying at one of the little houses down the road that Forrest rents out to the girls. I didn't want to leave my stuff there unguarded."

Marjorie said, "Wise move. I'm friends with most of the girls, but I wouldn't trust a single one of 'em near anything that can be pawned."

She waved her cigar toward the suitcase in which El kept his sheet music. It was covered with stickers and decals he had picked up at music festivals and assorted train and bus stations over the years. "You've been gettin' around, I see."

"Stay still too long and you starve."

Marjorie read locations from the stickers: "Los Angeles, New York City, Paris, London. Looks like you've done all right. Just don't forget about your home. A lot of folks around here would be happy to have you stay and make music for a while, especially me. After all, you and me are kin now."

"What?"

"Yeah, you know Odette's my niece, right?"

"Who's Odette?"

"She's my sister Dora's daughter."

"I remember Dora, but what's her daughter got to do with me?"

"Odette married James. Didn't you know that? They got a baby and another on the way."

"Well, I'm be damned," El said. "How long have they been married?"

"Oh, five, six years now."

"Happy?"

"I think so," Marjorie said. She snickered and added, "It wouldn't be like Odette to keep it to herself if she wasn't."

A memory tickled the back of El's mind. "Wasn't there some kind of weird story about Dora and her daughter?"

Marjorie twisted her mouth and scratched her head. "Nothing weird that I can think of."

Hours later, half asleep in the passenger seat of his bandmate's car, El would startle the driver by bursting forth with laughter as he remembered the tale of how Marjorie's sister, Dora, had climbed into a sycamore tree and given birth to Odette up there after getting stuck. Only Marjorie Davis could have thought there was "nothing weird" about that story.

"Did you know that James is a cop?" Marjorie asked.

"You're kiddin' me. *My* son is a cop?"

"I'm serious as a heart attack. He's a state trooper. James is cool, though. He's not out there tryin' to mess with folks for the fun of it. Everybody likes James."

El took another sip from his glass. He looked past Marjorie as if he were gazing through the wall at something disappearing over the horizon. "What's she like, this girl who married my son?"

"I guess the best way to describe Odette would be to say that she could be my twin, except she's tougher and more manly than me."

The shocking implications of such a thing—a woman tougher and manlier than Marjorie—caused El to choke on his whiskey. He coughed and gagged as liquor traveled upward and sprayed out of his nose and onto the front of his shirt.

Marjorie let loose a loud bark of a laugh and said, "Calm yourself, El. I'm just messin' with you. Odette's not much like me, really. Come to think of it, Odette's not much like anybody, exactly. She's strong, like Dora, but she's got her daddy's sweetness. And she's got more brains than anybody in the family. Nobody puts nothin' over on that girl.

"She looks a lot like Dora. She's big like Dora, too. Odette's pregnant now, like I said. But she's always been big." Marjorie elbowed El in his side and said, "That's right, your son went and got himself a big woman. We both know there ain't nothin' like the love of a big woman." She winked at him and took another swig from her mug.

El thought of his own wife and how she had once been as round as a plum. Then he thought of how poverty and worry had worn Ruthie down to a stick. That had been his fault. He pictured James and Ruthie the last time he had seen them, and his spirits began to crumble. El was just a month off of heroin, and that image—his wife, his son, and the life he had burned to the ground—made him crave something stronger than whiskey to drive the memory away. He waved a hand quickly back and forth in front of his eyes to erase that troublesome picture, as if he were sweeping away writing in the sand.

"I wonder what's keeping Forrest," he said.

Marjorie issued a loud cackle. "Forrest married a girl less than half his age last night. It'll probably take him a while to gather the strength to walk today."

El laughed along with her. The two of them sat listening to R&B on the jukebox and sipped their drinks.

After a couple of songs, Marjorie asked, "You been to see Ruth?"

"The last time I saw Ruthie and James, it didn't go too good. I figured it was better to stay away."

"You know she's sick, don't you?"

El's glass of whiskey slipped from his hand and landed on the bar top with a clack. He used a paper napkin with the silhouette of a naked woman on it to wipe up the drops that had escaped onto the scratched and grooved surface of the bar. "I didn't know."

"She's in the hospital. Bad lungs and worse heart is what I was told."

"Shit."

Marjorie said, "You can say that again. She's still a young woman."

"Is she in Evansville?" When he had lived in Plainview, all the black residents in town had gone to the hospital in Evansville for medical care.

"No. Times have changed. She's over at University Hospital. Everybody goes there now."

El picked up his whiskey again. He swirled the liquor around in the glass, first in one direction, then the other. Then he drained it in one long draw.

"Goin' to see her?" Marjorie asked.

"If I don't lose my nerve."

Marjorie poured two fingers of noxious-smelling liquor from her mug into his glass. "Drink this. I made it myself. I call it my 'doubt remover.' Swallow this down, and I guarantee you'll follow through on any plan you set your mind to."

El chugged the corn liquor. He shivered as it clawed its way from his tongue to his stomach. When he recovered, he reached for Marjorie's mug, thinking that he might pour himself another.

She snatched it away from him. "No, baby. One takes away all your doubts. Two will take away your liver, your eyesight, and your common sense, if you're not used to it."

Marjorie watched El begin to strap his suitcases to his back. When he reached for his guitar and amplifier, she said, "I can keep an eye on those, if you want."

El was so used to carrying his life on his back that, for a moment, he didn't know what she meant. When he understood, he said, "No, I'm good." Fully loaded up, he did a quick soft-shoe to demonstrate just how comfortable he was. "Light as a feather." Then he said, "If Forrest comes in while I'm gone, do me a solid and ask him to leave the envelope with the bartender. I'll be back before long."

"No problem," Marjorie said. She lifted her glass in salute.

THE WOMAN ASLEEP in the hospital bed bore such scant resemblance to the Ruth he remembered that he wouldn't have recognized her. She looked far older than her forty-three years, and there was so little flesh on her that he could see the slow pulsing of her veins beneath her skin. He checked the green paper visitor's pass upon which the man at the reception desk had written Ruthie's room number to make sure he was in the right place. After reading the number once more, he set his guitar, amplifier, and suitcases against the wall and approached the bed.

It took him a moment to coax his lips into forming words. "Hey, Ruthie, I came to see how you were doin'. I was real sorry to hear that you were feelin' poorly."

He stepped forward and placed his hand over hers. Her bones felt as fine as guitar strings beneath his callused fingertips. "Seems like there should be so much more to say, but I can't think of anything. Maybe it doesn't matter now, anyway."

The curtain that divided the two sides of the room rustled. Just behind him, El heard the clacking of metal fasteners sliding along the track that connected the curtain to the ceiling as the fabric was pushed aside.

"Marcus Henry, leave that woman alone," a voice demanded from the bed on the other side.

He turned and saw Ruthie lying in her bed. With visible effort, she supported herself on one elbow while holding open the dividing curtain. She was thinner than she had been when he'd last seen her. Her skin had a grayish tint, and her short hair was held tight against her scalp with bobby pins. A piece of translucent tape on her cheek held the oxygen tube under her nose in place. But Ruthie was still very much herself.

If the other patient had been awake, there would have been no confusion. No one had eyes like Ruthie. They were amber with silver streaks. He had seen those extraordinary eyes from the stage of the Pink Slipper the first time she'd come in to hear the band. He had noticed her irises glittering as they reflected the spotlights, and he had spent the entire night singing directly to her. El backed away from the sleeping stranger in the other bed until he was beside Ruthie.

He stood, embarrassed, in the dull fluorescent light of the hospital room, trying to think of something to say that might lessen the awkwardness of the moment. He thrust his visitor's pass toward her and said, "It says here that you're supposed to be in bed A, not B. 'Course I was pretty sure she wasn't you. I was just tryin' to be friendly."

Ruthie said, "It's sweet of you to honor tradition by getting straight to lying to me. Feels like old times."

He stood there, shifting his weight from foot to foot, until she said, "Don't worry. The last thing I wanna do is waste time getting worked up over stuff that happened when we were dumb-ass kids." She pointed to a chair near the window and said, "Sit."

As El pulled the chair closer to her bed, Ruthie said, "I like your beard. I always wanted you to grow one."

El stroked the dark bush on his face. "I wanted one, too, but it wouldn't grow in till I was almost forty."

Ruthie studied his face for a while. "So you've got a new beard. And I heard you have a new name. You must have warrants out on you."

"No warrants," he said. Ruthie looked at him with a raised eyebrow. In response to her skepticism, El added, "Well, no warrants in Indiana."

Ruthie wheezed and gasped as laughing made her already troubled breathing even more difficult. After she recovered, she inclined her head toward the stack of possessions El had brought into the room. "Still loading yourself down like a pack mule."

"Old habits are hard to break."

"Looks like the same case, too. You still got that old guitar?"

"Oh, yeah. I'll never say good-bye to Ruthie."

"And you're still a traveling man?"

"Mmm-hmm. I've been gettin' around. I went to Europe last year, and I'm goin' back next summer. They know their blues over there, a lot better than here. Not too many folks in the States wanna listen to the old stuff anymore. But in Berlin and Paris, man, they treated me like I really was somebody."

"I'm glad for you. I really am," Ruthie said. She turned her head slowly away from him to look at the clock on the wall. El saw just how weak she was from the deliberateness of her movements and the way she fell back onto her pillows when she turned toward him again.

He said, "I hear we're grandparents now."

A grimace came over her face, as if she'd been seized with a sudden pain. After a moment, the discomfort seemed to pass. She said, "Sing me a song, why don't you?"

He glanced in the direction of her dozing roommate.

Ruthie said, "She won't mind. The poor thing hasn't spoken a word since they brought her in yesterday night. I don't expect she ever will. Between her condition and mine, I think they're likely to turn this room over pretty quick."

"Don't say that."

"Just speaking the truth. Now, how about that song?"

El rose from his chair and retrieved his guitar case. He was glad to see that the sight of his spotted guitar with her name splashed across its body seemed to please her. He sat on the edge of his chair and strummed the strings, performing a fast tuning. Unplugged from the amplifier, his guitar made a hushed, almost plaintive sound, and he matched that timbre with his voice as he sang.

"Baby, dry your eyes. I'm here. I'm here to stay—"

Ruthie interrupted, "What's that?"

"It's 'Love Returns.' Don't you remember? It was one of the first songs I wrote. I wrote it so you wouldn't be mad at me when I got back after that first tour."

"What made me mad was that you got back from that tour, but didn't come home for another two days."

El said, "I can't say that I recall."

"You wouldn't. That's not the one I want to hear, though. Sing 'Happy Heartache.' That's my song."

"It's kind of a sad one. Sure you don't want to hear something cheerier?"

Ruthie lifted her hand and gestured at their surroundings. "After all these years, we're saying our last good-bye in a hospital room. I can't think of a better time for a sad song."

El said, "Guess you're right, like always." He cleared his throat and sang: *"Love, love, oh love, if you stay away I don't know what I'll do . . ."*

Ruthie closed her eyes as he crooned. She rocked her head from side to side and occasionally hummed along. As he sang, she became more and more still. By the end, her only movement was the smile that widened as he intoned the final words.

She opened her eyes and watched him as he continued to strum chords. For a while, both of them enjoyed being lost in another time, picturing bright, optimistic days that had faded into passionate, foolish nights.

Finally Ruthie spoke. "All these years, I believed you wrote that song for me. I figured, *Who else would he be writing a love song about? I'm the love of his life.* I was proud of that. But now, *just* now, I realized that it isn't about me. It's about you and that *other* Ruthie. *My song* is about you and music."

El played a few more chords, and then he looked into the eyes that he had fallen in love with decades earlier and said, "I'm sorry."

"Don't be sorry. I was always going to be second. I just wish I'd figured it out sooner."

She turned her head toward the wall clock even more slowly this time than before. "Thank you for coming by. It was good to see you."

Accepting that he was being dismissed, El stood and returned his guitar to the case. When he came back to her bedside again, he said, "I want you to know that I'm sorry for everything that happened. And I've changed. I've cleaned up. . . . Well, mostly. I'm tryin' to be a better man. I'm gonna do better by James."

The warm expression she had worn since he had pulled his guitar from the case left her face. Ruthie struggled to sit up in the bed, her eyes bulging and wet as she shook with anger. "No! Don't say that to me. Don't talk about changing. I heard it too many times. And don't you talk to me about James. You don't have the right."

El raised his hands in surrender. "I'm sorry. I didn't mean to upset you. I was tryin' to say that I'm gonna make up for the things I did wrong. I don't want you to worry that James'll be alone."

"James won't be alone. He's got a good wife. If you knew anything about your son, you'd know that he has wanted Odette and nobody else since he was ten years old. Now he's got her and a child and another one coming. Even if he was gonna be alone, you are the last thing he'd need."

She grabbed El's wrist with her small hand. "I'm not trying to hurt your feelings. I know you never meant to cut James. I've made sure he knows it, too. But you'll scar him again if you ever get close enough. You won't mean to, but you will. It's who you are. You can't help it."

Ruthie's voice grew weaker, but her hold on his wrist became tighter, and his hand began to throb. "I need you to promise me something. Promise you'll never come back to Plainview again. Promise you'll never see James."

"I can't—" El began. But she cut him off.

"Promise. I have to know that James is safe." Her tone softened as she said, "I'm not asking you to do anything new. Just stay away, like you've done most of his life."

His voice, which had been smooth and confident since the first notes he had sung to her, began to break. "Okay, Ruthie. Okay."

"Swear," she said. "I need to hear it."

"I swear on my mother's grave—"

"No. Swear on *my* grave."

"Jesus, Ruthie."

"Please."

El took a shaky breath and said, "I swear on your grave that I will never come back to Plainview and I will never see James again."

Ruthie released her grip on his wrist and collapsed onto her pillows. "Thank you."

Unable to summon the strength to turn her head, Ruth angled just her eyes toward the clock on the wall. "You should go. James is off work. He'll be here soon."

On unsteady legs, El walked over to the possessions he had unloaded earlier. He strapped his suitcases to his back and lifted the amplifier and the guitar case. He returned to Ruthie's bedside one last time and said, "Good-bye."

Between panting breaths, she said, "Giddyup, old boy."

MINUTES LATER IN the hospital parking lot, El saw James and Odette walking toward him. It was almost funny that a chance meeting would cause him to break even his last promise to Ruthie so soon after making it.

He recognized Odette first. Anyone who had ever seen Dora Jackson would know immediately that this was her daughter. As Marjorie had related, her niece's round face and wide mouth were identical to Dora's.

And James. He was noble and proud as he strode toward the hospital in his Indiana State Police uniform. El was thankful that James was just far enough to his left side that he couldn't see the scar he knew was on James's cheek.

James amused the toddler on his hip by making funny faces and imitating animal noises. As he approached El, he altered course to give ample room to the heavily burdened stranger. James walked past his father, bouncing his giggling child and clasping the hand of his big woman.

CHAPTER 19

*I*t was an unusually quiet Sunday supper at Earl's that week. Richmond, the real talker among the men of our group, had yet to arrive. James and Ray sat, with Richmond's empty chair between them, acknowledging each other with an occasional brief sentence. My husband and Barbara Jean's had been close friends for nearly as long as Clarice, Barbara Jean, and I had been a trio. Unless the river was frozen over or summer storms had washed out the back roads, they met nearly every weekend to go fishing together. Still, whenever I asked James what they talked about while standing on the shore or floating in James's boat, the answer was always "Nothing." Given their tight-lipped natures, I believed him.

Clarice, Barbara Jean, Ray, James, and I hadn't waited for Richmond to arrive before filling our plates and beginning to eat. It was Revival Week at Calvary Baptist, so there was no way of knowing when their service might end. When Reverend Peterson dug his teeth deep into a juicy vein of sin, he'd been known to gnaw at it until sunset.

I was glad that we had food to distract us. With the array of frayed nerves, dark moods, and awkwardness at the window table, it would have been a shame to add hunger to the mix.

Clarice was nearly as quiet as James and Ray that afternoon. As the date of her Chicago concert grew closer, she had become more withdrawn. So Barbara Jean and I did most of the talking. Since I was preoccupied with fretting about James's refusal to admit that he was fretting, Barbara Jean was stuck with most of the work of keeping our conversation going. That was a tough job, because we were both avoiding saying too much about El Walker, the topic that was on both of our minds.

Barbara Jean had become El's friend. She felt sorry for him, and she visited him almost every day. I knew that hearing his stories and looking at his pictures helped her imagine who her mother might have been if she'd survived all her trials and lived long enough to make amends for the misery she'd caused. Loretta had beaten Barbara Jean, humiliated her, and left her vulnerable to dangerous men. It was part of the wonder of Barbara Jean that, all these years after her mother's death, she still wanted to find evidence that Loretta was deserving of the forgiveness Barbara Jean had already granted her.

El Walker wasn't showing me any pictures or lightening my load with blues songs and stories of the past. I couldn't see him as anything but a lowlife who'd cut James and then come back fifty-seven years later to injure him again. So Barbara Jean said little about her new friend, and I tried not to speak ill of him.

In the week since the shit had hit the fan, I'd tried to get James to talk to El. More than once, I'd said, "Don't you want some answers? Don't you want to know where he's been and why he never came back?" I told him, "You should march over to that hospital and demand an apology. That's the least you're owed."

Last night, calm, sweet James, who rarely raised his voice in anger, had actually shouted at me. He'd yelled, "Dammit, Odette, leave it alone!" Because he is James and had shocked himself as much as me with his outburst, or maybe because he'd recognized he was proving my point that he wasn't done with his father like he claimed to be, he had apologized right away and then acted as if none of it—the yelling or meeting his father—had ever happened.

The only person who wanted to talk about El was Mama, and I didn't want to hear what she had to say, because she didn't agree with me. My mother, who had advocated the hard line since she and Aunt Marjorie had taught me the techniques I'd used to kick Ramsey Abrams's ass back in grade school, was suddenly a fan of moderation. When I'd confessed my fantasies of marching over to the hospital and pistol-whipping James's father, she'd sided with James, telling me to back off. "You're a hard woman," Mama had said. "Hardness ain't likely to bring you peace."

Barbara Jean said, "Did you know that Wayne Robinson was sick?" She leaned forward and whispered so that only Clarice and I could hear her. "Darlene Lloyd told me it'll be a miracle if he lives through the week."

"Yes, I heard about that," I said. I didn't bother to mention that I'd heard about it directly from the comatose patient himself.

True to her sweet nature, Barbara Jean tried to come up with something nice to say about Wayne Robinson. She had heard me say plenty about him back when Terry, afraid at school and unwelcome at home, was spending a lot of time with James and me. She'd encountered Mr. Robinson often enough when his wife was receiving treatment at the hospital to get a sense of his character. Barbara Jean moved food around on her plate as she struggled to conjure up a kind word about the man. She opened her mouth a few times as if something had come to her, then gave up. She sat back in her chair and sipped her tea.

Finally, she asked, "Have you talked to Terry?" Like nearly everyone else in Plainview, Barbara Jean had heard the story of Terry's vow to take revenge at his father's burial. She also knew that I had promised Terry I would notify him when the end came for his father.

"I spoke to him," I said. "He hasn't changed his mind."

"Did you try to talk him out of it?" Barbara Jean asked.

"It's not my place," I said.

She cast me a disapproving look. She was too much of a lady to ever applaud Terry's plan to drop his drawers at his father's graveside, and I knew she thought I should encourage my young pal to take the high road. She didn't argue with me, though. We were already seeing enough of life differently.

Since she'd sat down at the table, Clarice had been smiling and nodding her head as if she was listening, but I was willing to bet she hadn't heard most of what had been said that day. She proved me right then. When Barbara Jean and I took a break from making conversation and turned our attention back to our food, Clarice figured we were waiting on her to say something. With no idea what we'd been talking about, she jumped directly to the topic we'd been avoiding. She looked at me and asked, "What do your kids say about their grandfather showing up in town?"

She took me by surprise, but her question was easy to answer. My children and I had talked on the phone about James and El Walker every night that week. They had reacted pretty much like I'd expected. Our eldest, James Jr., thought that we should pretend we'd never met the old man and forget the whole thing had ever happened. Our "let bygones be bygones" middle child, Eric, thought it was wonderful that his father wanted to forgive. Our daughter, Denise, asked me if El had ever apologized for all he'd done to James and Miss Ruth. When I told her that he hadn't, she asked me how many times I'd hit the old man. Not *if* I'd hit him, but *how many times.*

I told Clarice, "James is acting like our peacekeeping son, but if you catch him when he thinks you're not looking, you can tell he feels like our hell-raising daughter."

Then Clarice rescued us from the topic of El Walker. She put her hand to her forehead and exhaled loudly. She whispered, "I'm having trouble with Richmond."

Barbara Jean and I exchanged glances. We knew all about the struggles Clarice had had with Richmond's cheating throughout their marriage. We'd thought, though, that they'd come to an agreement now and those particular difficulties were in the past.

Clarice picked up on what we were thinking. "Not the old kind of trouble. He's keeping it in his pants, as far as I know. That's part of the problem. He's acting strange. He wants to cuddle, even when there's no sex in it for him. He notices what I'm wearing. He's caring and considerate. It's horrible. His sensitivity isn't what kept me with him all those years, and it's certainly not what I need from him right now.

"Forty years ago, I'd have loved the husband he's decided to turn into. But today, I just want him to shut up, strip off his clothes, and make himself useful." She crossed her arms over her chest and leaned back in her chair, pouting.

Barbara Jean twirled her fork in her spaghetti. With a sheepish expression on her face, she said, "I might know a little bit about what's happening." Then she uttered what is maybe the least useful sentence in the English language: "I was just trying to help."

Sounding remarkably like my aunt Marjorie, Clarice growled, "What did you do?"

"It really wasn't much. Richmond came by the house a few weeks ago wanting some advice. He said that things were going well between you and him, but he wanted to move your relationship further along. He asked what Ray and I thought he should do to convince you that he was different now."

Clarice glared at Barbara Jean. "What did you tell him to do?"

"We just told him you'd probably like him to be more attentive and show you that he appreciates you as more than a bed partner. We also suggested that he might want to ask you how you were feeling and what you were thinking. You know, small things like that."

As Clarice groaned, Barbara Jean said again, "I was just trying to help."

"Barbara Jean," Clarice said, sounding more like herself, "you know I love you and Ray. But if either of you give Richmond one more word of advice, I can't be held accountable for my actions. Since the day we got married, my husband has consistently done one thing extraordinarily well. You and Ray are screwing up that one thing."

Clarice cast her withering stare my way. "Did Richmond talk to you and James, too?"

"I'm happy to report that we haven't given him one single word of advice," I said. I didn't mention that Richmond had called a week or so earlier and suggested getting together for dinner—just him, James, and me. One good thing about the revelations of the previous week was that we'd been too off-kilter to have much of a social life, so we'd avoided an advice session that might have put us in Clarice's doghouse along with Barbara Jean and Ray. At long last, El Walker was good for something.

The bell above the door of the diner rang and, led by Miss Beatrice and Clarice's new stepfather, Richmond walked in. Their appearance allowed us to escape from the uncomfortable topic of the latest twist in Clarice and Richmond's love story.

The two men went to the buffet line. Miss Beatrice headed straight toward our table. I had hoped it might take a while for her to work her way over to us. The Sabbath tended to get Clarice's mother so hopped up on Jesus that she was hard to stomach. When she took her time winding her way through the after-church crowd, she got a chance to burn off some holy energy by politely judging and criticizing people as she greeted them along her way. But that Sunday, we were out of luck.

Miss Beatrice stepped up to the window table and, without saying hello, began needling Clarice. She started by telling us what an inspirational service everyone in the family, except Clarice, had enjoyed at Calvary Baptist Church. "It was so moving. You could feel the Spirit." Miss Beatrice brought her fingertips together in a prayerful pose and said, "You remember what that was like, don't you?"

Clarice said, "I remember *everything* about that church, Mother."

Not hearing, or choosing to ignore, the sarcastic tone in her daughter's voice, Miss Beatrice said, "And still you refuse to go back. I'll never understand it." She looked down at Clarice's half-eaten plate and said, "Have you been here long?"

"Not too long. Maybe twenty minutes."

To Barbara Jean and me, Miss Beatrice said, "Those Unitarians sure do zip those services right along, don't they? I suppose you save a lot of time if you aren't concerned with saving souls, like us."

It made my head spin to have Miss Beatrice turning to Barbara Jean and me for support on religious matters. Clarice's mother had never thought much of my church, Holy Family Baptist, or of Barbara Jean's, First Baptist. She'd told me many times that my church's sinner-coddling ways guaranteed that none of our members would make it into the King-dom of Heaven. The large number of wealthy members of Barbara Jean's church meant they were cursed, too. " 'Easier for a camel to go through the eye of a needle,' " she liked to quote when she spoke of First Baptist. But Miss Beatrice wanted us on her side in her ongoing holy war with Clarice. That Sunday, she was willing to pretend that, being Baptists, Barbara Jean and I had some hope for redemption, even though we'd chosen the wrong churches. She had no such hope for her Unitar-ian daughter.

Clarice had once told me that when her mother was driving her crazy, she thought of the fact that Barbara Jean and I no longer had mothers at all. The idea of losing Miss Beatrice helped her endure her mother's lectures. At the time, I had thought it was a touching thing to say. But as Miss Beatrice stood there hammering away at the topic of her daughter's religious choices, the cold-eyed, crocodile smile on Clarice's face caused me to wonder if I'd misinterpreted her meaning. If she was imagining Miss Beatrice dead at that moment, she was taking at least some small amount of pleasure in the fantasy.

Miss Beatrice turned to Barbara Jean and me. She said, "Wouldn't you think the Unitarian services would go slower, since they probably have to stop the sermon every few minutes in order to keep those heathens from indulging in sins of the flesh right there on the spot?" She arched an eyebrow, proud of herself for the insult.

Clarice said, "Don't be silly, Mother. Everybody knows the orgy is *before* the service. We wouldn't want those friendly, nondenominational homilies to distract us from our fornicating."

"That's not funny," Miss Beatrice snapped. But Forrest Payne appeared then and, having heard the tail end of their conversation, let out a high-pitched, howling laugh. To my surprise, Miss Beatrice stopped twisting her mouth in disapproval and began to laugh along with her new husband. Loosening up that woman on a Sunday was no small achievement. As they headed to their table, I thought for the first time that maybe Forrest Payne was the perfect man for Miss Beatrice after all.

Clarice's family reunion expanded when Veronica strode in with her husband, Clement, trailing along behind her. Veronica had taken her habit of overdressing for every occasion to new heights since her promotion from annoying church member to bothersome associate pastor. That day she was encased in layers of puce-colored taffeta from her neck to her ankles. She was perspiring heavily from wearing such a heavy outfit on a warm June day. The length of the gown made it difficult for her to maintain her usual jerking, goose-step style of walking.

I hadn't seen Veronica since the news of El Walker's connection to James became public knowledge, and I wasn't looking forward to hearing her offer her opinions about matters that were none of her business. Veronica and I had butted heads since we were schoolgirls. Though I saw the foolishness of it, I still let her get under my skin. The moment I laid eyes on her, I felt myself becoming angry, and I began to ready myself for a fight.

Rather than preparing to pounce at the first provocation, though, I decided to try Clarice's approach. I imagined how sad I'd feel if Veronica suddenly dropped dead. But I quickly gave that up. Given the years of hostility I had harbored toward Veronica, it wasn't safe for me to indulge in that fantasy with so much cutlery lying around. I stuffed a forkful of salmon into my mouth and attempted to think kind thoughts, like genteel Barbara Jean.

Panting in her unwieldy dress, Veronica marched up to our table and said, "I can guess from your smiles that you've all been celebrating the good news."

That wasn't exactly the way I, or anyone else at our table, had been looking at the return of James's father. I was surprised to hear Veronica describing it as cause for celebration. But as Veronica continued, it became clear that she had other news on her mind. She said, "Clarice, I've been thinking maybe the two of us could put something together for the occasion. A little music is always nice and folks will think it's cute, us being cousins and all. I could also use your help picking my outfit. You used to have such good taste."

When Veronica saw the mystified expressions on the faces at the table, she said, "You have heard about Reverend Biggs's accident, haven't you?"

Barbara Jean said, "What are you talking about? I just saw Reverend Biggs at church an hour ago."

Clement said, "The accident must have happened right after that. He fell down the stairs after the service. He tripped on the top step and fell all the way down to the bottom."

"Good Lord," Barbara Jean said. "There must be twenty steps in front of First Baptist."

"He didn't fall down *those* stairs. He fell on the steps in the back. There are only four or five stairs there," Veronica said.

Barbara Jean asked, "How is he?"

"He's doing okay, considering. But he'll be out of commission for about a month, they say. He's got a broken leg, and he hurt his back." Pointing a thumb at her puffed-out chest, Veronica said, "I'm the one who found him. And he's lucky I did. Most of the members had gone home by then. He could have ended up lying there for who knows how long.

"I have no idea why he was going out the back door of the church. He knows I always wait for him in front with my suggestions for the next week's sermon."

I pictured Reverend Biggs's accident like an episode of a nature program on TV. I saw Veronica stalking the poor man through his church like a lion after a gazelle until she brought him down, wounded, in the rear parking lot.

Barbara Jean said, "Wait a minute. You said something about us celebrating good news. What's good about this news?"

Veronica said, "I'm going to preach. With Reverend Biggs out, we associate pastors got together and decided that we would split the sermon duties between us until he gets better. My turn comes in three weeks."

Veronica leaned toward us as if she were sharing a secret. But in typical Veronica fashion, she spoke loudly enough for anyone within ten yards to hear. "Madame Minnie was right on target about this whole thing. Charlemagne told her ages ago that I would have my own church."

Clarice said, "It's a little soon to claim First Baptist as *your* church, don't you think? Reverend Biggs isn't dead. He'll be back as soon as he's healed."

Veronica said, "I didn't mean it that way, of course. I'm praying nonstop that he'll have a speedy recovery."

That last part would have been more believable if she'd been able to stop grinning for just a few seconds. Family loyalty wouldn't allow Clarice to say it out loud, but I'd have bet anything she was thinking that her cousin had shoved Reverend Biggs down those stairs.

Veronica glanced across the room toward the fortune-telling table in the corner, where Minnie, in one of her showy trances, sat rocking from side to side with her palms on her crystal ball. Above the noise of the diner, we heard the occasional tinkling of the silver bell that stuck out of the top of Minnie's turban.

Veronica said, "I'm going to consult with Madame Minnie about the topic for my sermon. I've been thinking either the Good Samaritan or Daniel in the lions' den. But there's no reason to leave it to chance."

Clement fetched a chair for his wife, and she sat down between Clarice and me. "I wish Madame Minnie would hurry up. I've got a lot to do today. It's not easy running a church."

"In the meantime," Veronica said, "let me show you the video of Apollo that Sharon sent this morning."

Clement retrieved Veronica's phone from her purse so she could treat us to the video of their grandson.

Apollo sat in his father's lap. The camera angle exaggerated the strange shape of the baby's nose, which looked even more like a snout than it had in his earlier pictures. He seemed to have become hairier, and his plump cheeks squeezed his small eyes into tiny black dots. The baby opened his mouth so that it formed a frighteningly large, gaping pink cavern. Then Apollo let forth a shriek: "Gaah!"

The young father's reaction to the racket his son made was to grin with pride as if his infant had recited a Shakespeare soliloquy.

Veronica and Clement waited for us to express our admiration. Barbara Jean and I chose that moment to fill our mouths with food. The proud grandparents turned to Clarice. "He really is sweet," she said.

Clarice didn't have to elaborate because Veronica's attention was suddenly drawn elsewhere. "Madame Minnie's free," she squealed. She rose, shook out the ruffles of her dress, and stomped over to Minnie's table.

With Veronica gone, we resumed our conversation. We talked grandchildren, clothes, and recipes, each of us carefully avoiding the subjects that were eating away at us.

Clarice might have been annoyed with her husband, but I was thankful he was there. For most of the time I had known Richmond, his infidelity and vanity had irritated me so much that I'd had to devote a considerable amount of energy to restraining myself from throwing whatever I might have been holding at his head. That afternoon, I was glad to see him being his usual big, blustery self, talking louder than anyone else in the room and enjoying his own jokes enough to make up for James's gloominess. Richmond couldn't quite coax a chuckle from James, but his brazen good humor temporarily took away the sour, angry look that had lingered on my husband's face for the past week.

Clement, who had joined the men at the other end of the table after Veronica marched over to Minnie, was showing them the video of his grandson and son-in-law. I heard Richmond, the most accomplished liar I've ever known, begin to gush over the handsomeness of little Apollo. The video was passed to James. He held the phone in his hand and examined the image as if he were trying to memorize it. Eight days ago, I wouldn't have tried to read anything into James's behavior or his facial expression. Today, I wondered if this intimate moment on the screen, as well as the thousands of others like it that James had witnessed or been a part of as a father himself, had prodded at a spot of pain inside him. Being the hard woman I was, that thought made me furious at El all over again.

CHAPTER 20

I knew something was wrong when I arrived home from work and found James standing beside his car in the garage. Even when I worked full-time, instead of the limited summer schedule I was on, James never beat me home on a weekday. He was always out the door before I was in the mornings and came back an hour or so later than I did in the evenings. If something major was going on at the station, he dragged himself in late at night and slid into bed next to me as I pretended to sleep. But there he stood, home two hours early, hands on his hips, looking around the garage as if it were an uncharted planet he'd just landed on.

I pulled my car in alongside his. When I stepped out, I asked, "What are you doing home?"

He tried to make a joke out of my question. "You sound like you're disappointed to see me," he said.

I asked again, "What are you doing home?"

James's eyes wandered to the floor, then to the ceiling. His gaze fixed at a point high on the wall behind me. Then he said, "I'm taking the week off. I've got some sick days coming, and there's a lot of stuff I've been meaning to do around the house. I'd like to organize the basement so the grandkids'll have someplace inside to play when they come. Maybe I'll get the Ping-Pong table set up and hang the dartboard. And that retaining wall in the backyard could use some patching. This would be a good time to start."

He rattled off a long list of the household tasks he had in mind to accomplish over the coming days. All the while, I thought, *This man is talking horseshit.*

James loved being a state trooper. He never wanted to miss a day of work. In a week and a half, he and I were planning to meet our children and their families in Chicago for Clarice's concert. Then we would all come back to Plainview to spend a few noisy, hectic days together here at the house. It had taken countless hours of manipulating, cajoling, and threatening just to persuade James to take time off for a few days of sightseeing in Chicago and for the family visit afterward.

Dozens of his half-done projects, some dating back to the early days of our marriage, leaned against our garage walls or were lashed to the dusty brown pegboard that hung above the work table. His inability to finish them was a running joke between us. There were bookshelves he'd never gotten beyond sawing the wood for, a bunk-bed frame he'd started building for our sons when the boys were twenty-five years younger and two feet shorter. We were inches away from a rocking chair he'd begun making for me so that I could soothe grandbabies who were now far too big to fit on my lap. Today, this man who never wanted to miss a day of work and happily left his household masterpieces incomplete claimed to have taken a week off for chores he had avoided for years.

James rocked back and forth on his heels. He mumbled something about drill bits and waved his open palm at a flying insect I didn't see or hear. Then he said, "I'm going to change the oil in the Honda." He moved to the front of his car and began to feel around for the hood latch.

My husband is no one's idea of a mechanic. Still, if he'd been thinking clearly, he would have remembered that it had been ages since we'd owned a car with a hood that could be opened that way. I let him keep at it. I hoped he would soon get uncomfortable enough that he would tell me what was going on.

The phone rang then and he said, "Would you mind getting that while I get started here?"

I left my relieved husband groping at the front end of his car and hurried into the kitchen to answer the phone.

The call was from Calvin Bayless, who had shared a highway cruiser with James in their younger days. The two of them had maintained a good relationship over the decades, in spite of being drastically different. Calvin was heavyset and several inches shorter than James. Blond and fair-skinned, he was so pale that three minutes in the summer sun turned him the color of a pickled beet. As long-winded and gossipy as James was quiet, Calvin was a man who couldn't keep a secret. In my information-starved state, there were few voices I would rather have heard on the other end of the line than Calvin's.

He said, "Hey, Odette. I was just calling to check on James. Is he okay?"

"No," I said. "What happened?"

The way Calvin told the story, the trouble began when a man was brought in for domestic abuse—fourth time. The man had roughed up his wife and tossed his ten-year-old daughter against a wall when she'd tried to stop him. The woman and the girl were bruised, but not badly hurt. The wife had refused to cooperate with the police, and they'd had to release the man after a night in lockup. It was after the release that the incident occurred.

Calvin said, "James and I were coming back to the station after lunch, and the man and his wife were on their way out. Apparently his wife said something that the fellow didn't take kindly to. They started shouting at each other, and the guy hauled off and slapped his wife so hard she ended up on her backside on the sidewalk. Then the little girl ran at the guy, throwing punches. Before I could take two steps, James was on him, fists swinging."

I tried, but I couldn't imagine it. James wasn't the type to punch someone, no matter what they'd done. I came close to telling Calvin the story of ten-year-old James and the bullies who had called him "Frankenstein" to illustrate that he had to be wrong about the fight.

Calvin said, "It took me and another trooper to pull James off that asshole. Excuse my language."

So that was why James was at home. My quiet, peace-loving husband had beaten a man. "How bad was the guy hurt?" I asked.

"Not bad. He had a swollen lip. His eye'll be black tomorrow, and he'll ache for a while. But he'll be all right. Everybody at the station was more worried about James than that loser. That wasn't the sort of thing you expect from James, you know? Some of the other guys around here are hotheads and get in tussles pretty regularly. But I've worked with James for forty years, and the man I saw today was a total stranger to me."

"I know what you mean," I said. "Is James going to be in trouble?"

"I don't think so. The guy James knocked around isn't going to be making a fuss about it. He's dumb, but he's not that dumb. He knows we'll be picking him up again the next time he gets drunk and starts in hitting somebody. He won't want us to be pissed off at him from the get-go. I'd say James doesn't need to worry."

Calvin told me that James had walked into the station after the fight and taken a week of sick days. Then he talked for a while longer about how everyone at the job was worried about James and wished me good luck.

I thanked him for calling and headed out to see my husband.

When I stepped into the garage from the kitchen, James was staring into the engine of his car. He had opened the hood, but he seemed totally confused by what he saw in front of him. The perplexed expression on his face suggested that he had just discovered that his car was powered by a horde of hamsters on a treadmill. He said, "These modern motors don't even look like car engines anymore. This might as well be a rocket ship."

I said, "Calvin just called and told me what happened."

James shut the hood of the car. He turned around and sat on the front corner of the passenger side with his heel propped up on the car's bumper. Looking exhausted, he slumped forward and dropped his chin to his chest.

"I didn't intend to hit him. I saw him hit her, and I thought I'd try to get him to simmer down. But the little girl was on him and the woman was on the ground, and the guy was telling them both to shut up. I remember hitting him the first time and then I remember Calvin pulling me off him. The in-between part, it's like that was somebody else."

James brought his hand to his face and rubbed his scar. "I beat that man in front of his wife and his daughter. When Calvin stopped me, the guy's wife was screaming and the man I hit was crying. Their daughter had her hands pressed over her ears so she wouldn't hear it. Odette, I gave that little girl a terrible memory to take with her for the rest of her life. And believe me, that child already had enough ugly memories without my help."

He used his left hand to massage the knuckles of his right. "Why did that old man have to come back?" he said. "I was doing fine thinking he was dead. Now I'm a sixty-one-year-old man getting into fistfights like a hotheaded boy.

"After all these years, you'd think it wouldn't matter anymore. But you pick at that old scab and it still bleeds."

He saw me looking at the rough line along his jaw and said, "I'm not talking about this old scar. I mean all of it, that whole father thing. It's hard to explain, but when your father takes off, it's like you get to be a member of a club that you don't wanna be in. At first, you and everybody else in the club talk about how your old man's gonna come back and make everything good. When you figure out that he won't be coming back, you get mad. You get mad because you know you got cheated. You wonder if maybe everybody else is better than you because their fathers stuck around.

"I know that's stupid. I know it's something I have to let go of. I thought for sure I *had* let it go. I had Big Earl, and he was like a father to me. But Big Earl had his own kids. *Like a father* and a *real father* are two different things.

"So here I am, almost an old man myself, and I can't sleep at night, and I'm as pissed off as if that son of a bitch walked out on Mama and me yesterday. I can't stop feeling that way, no matter how hard I work at it.

"I think about what Big Earl would have wanted me to do. He used to tell me, 'The way to be a good man is by always being the bigger man.' And I'm trying. I really am."

"Maybe you should stop trying," I said. "Aunt Marjorie used to say that you can't be good all the time. She said sometimes you have to do what's right for right now, and clean up the mess later."

"Your aunt Marjorie was a crazy woman."

"True enough, but she never fretted over the past, not that I ever saw. And she slept like a rock every night till she died."

"That was the moonshine," James said.

I couldn't argue with that.

"The worst part is that I see you looking at me like you don't know me anymore. I want to turn back and be myself again before I scare you off, but I can't. Not yet, at least."

I moved forward until I was standing between James's knees. I reached up and grabbed the hand that was still rubbing against his scar. I pulled that hand away, then kissed his face again and again from his earlobe down to the corner of his mouth. I wrapped my arms around his skinny waist and squeezed him.

"James Henry, did you forget I was born in a sycamore tree? There isn't a power on this earth that can scare me away from you."

James rested his chin on my forehead. He said, "I don't deserve you."

"I know you don't," I said. "But I didn't think I should be the one to say so." I held him tighter and pressed my cheek to his sharp collarbone. Then I stepped into the topic he had warned me a couple of days earlier to stay away from.

"I've been thinking. Maybe we can go face El Walker together. I really believe it will make things better for you if you have it out with him."

James said, "No." I felt his body stiffen. His arms loosened around my shoulders, and he went back to squinting at the garage walls.

I patted him on his back and said, "Wanna come inside and help me start dinner?"

He followed me toward the door to the kitchen. As we stepped into the house, he said, "I was thinking maybe I'd build window boxes for the living room windows while I have time. Would you like that?"

I tried to recall the name of that nice handyman who had come by last summer to finish the Adirondack chairs James had started and then wandered away from. That same man had also pieced together our spice rack a few years back, after James had given up on that project in frustration. He would probably do a good job on the window boxes, too, once James lost interest in them.

"Window boxes sound wonderful," I said.

CHAPTER 21

When the ringing of the telephone woke me, the first thing I did was look at the clock on the dresser across the room. I wanted to know just how deep a breath I needed to take to be prepared for the shock that was surely about to come. I saw that it was nearly three in the morning, so I inhaled big.

Clarice was crying when I picked up. "It's Richmond," she said between sobs. "He's had a heart attack. I'm in the emergency room at University."

I didn't want to ask if he was alive, so it was a relief when Clarice said, "They just took him into an exam room."

"I'll be right there," I said. And after waking and frightening Barbara Jean and Ray, James and I were on our way to University Hospital.

We found Clarice in the emergency room. She was alone, except for a few very drunk college students who seemed to be suffering from fight- and fall-related injuries. After an exchange of embraces, Clarice said that she had no new information. No one had been able, or perhaps willing, to tell her anything so far. She had to repeat herself just a few minutes later when Barbara Jean and Ray arrived. Then she began to tell us the details of what had led to her 911 call and the arrival of the paramedics.

It had begun when Richmond stopped by to see Clarice at her place in Leaning Tree.

"He came over to visit me after dinner," Clarice said. "We were talking, and he started to sweat a lot. Then he couldn't catch his breath. He said his chest hurt." She squirmed uncomfortably in her chair. She was wearing a terry-cloth robe, and the fluffy fringe of a black negligee was peeking out beneath the robe's hem. I began to get a clearer picture of what kind of activity had led up to Richmond's heart attack. Ray and James noticed the negligee, too. Ever the gentlemen, they excused themselves, saying they were going to find coffee for us.

After the men left, Clarice reached out and grabbed my hand and Barbara Jean's. "It's my fault," she said. "You know that problem I've been having with Richmond? Well, tonight he showed up at the house carrying a stack of old pictures of the kids and a bunch of scrapbook supplies, talking about all the wonderful memories we had and how we should paste the pictures into books to give to the kids when we see them in Chicago. I called the man to come see me at eleven at night, and he showed up prepared to do handicrafts. I almost shoved those crinkle-cut craft scissors he was holding right into his forehead.

"Then I noticed that he had a little jewelry box in his pocket, and I panicked. Before he could say another word, I ran upstairs and changed into this." She lifted the hem of the robe and showed more of the black negligee to Barbara Jean and me. "Then I jumped him. An hour later, he was on the bedroom floor, clutching his chest." She readjusted her robe to hide the negligee. "I'll never forgive myself if he dies."

Local skirt-chasing legend Richmond Baker might finally have been screwed to death. It was just the way anyone who'd known him since he was thirteen would have assumed he'd go. Not one of us would have thought his own wife would be the woman responsible, though.

I wanted to tell Clarice that my ghost-seeing ability was hinting that there was cause for hope. I often observed Mrs. Roosevelt hovering in the vicinity when someone was about to cross over. It was a positive sign for Richmond that she hadn't seen fit to show up that morning. But I hadn't talked with the Supremes about my communications with the spirit world since my near-death experience five years earlier, and this didn't seem like the right moment to start.

Barbara Jean, who had always found comfort in well-made articles of clothing, said, "That really is a beautiful negligee."

Clarice wasn't ready to take consolation in admiration for her outfit, especially not when she saw it as a potential murder weapon. She began to cry again as we muttered well-intended, useless phrases. "No news is good news." "It's all in the Lord's hands."

Clarice leaned back into the worn vinyl chair. She said, "I've loved Richmond since I was a little girl. Even when I hated him, I loved him. I don't want him to die thinking that I don't still love him just because I don't want to live with him."

Ray and James returned with cups of thick, bitter coffee for all of us. They saw Clarice crying and sprang into action, offering their own words of comfort.

We didn't stay in the emergency room area for long. Even at zero dark thirty, the presence of Barbara Jean, whose charitable giving had rebuilt so much of the hospital, prompted special treatment. A heavyset man wearing a well-made black suit hurried up to us. His sleepy eyes oozed sympathy as he ushered us into a lushly upholstered room, away from the harsh fluorescent light and drunken university students.

We had just settled into the brocade furniture in the warmly lit private waiting area when a doctor in green surgical scrubs stepped through the door. I tried to gauge the severity of the news he was about to deliver by his expression, but his face was unreadable.

He approached Clarice and said, "Mrs. Baker, could we have a moment in private?"

Clarice reacted as if she had just been slapped. She shivered and grasped Barbara Jean's hand and mine again. She said, "No, I think I'd like to have my friends with me."

The doctor said, "Really, I think it would be better if we spoke in private."

At not quite a shout, Clarice said, "Doctor, I don't have any secrets from my friends. Please just tell me how Richmond is."

The doctor was clearly reluctant to give Clarice an update with the rest of us around. But Clarice's insistence and the fact that she was there with Barbara Jean won out.

He said, "Mr. Baker did not have a heart attack. Our concern is that he needs to be persuaded to avoid continued self-medicating. The pills he has been taking can be quite dangerous."

In a tone of voice borrowed from her imperious mother, Clarice proclaimed, "You are mistaken. Richmond has never taken drugs in his life."

"I'm not talking about anything illegal," the doctor said. "What he's been using can still have dangerous side effects, though, especially when taken along with Mr. Baker's diabetes medication." He reached into the pocket of his pants, produced a small amber-colored glass bottle, and handed it to Clarice. "This belongs to Mr. Baker. He told me that he has been taking twice the recommended dosage for several weeks."

Clarice held the bottle out at full arm's length and still couldn't read the lettering on it.

Barbara Jean retrieved a pair of reading glasses from her purse and passed them to Clarice, who began to read aloud.

"Nu-Man. Extra-strength potency-enhancement supplements. The natural remedy for male erectile . . ." Her voice faded as understanding sank in.

The doctor suddenly became downright chatty. In a clinical tone, he said, "From the frequency and intensity of the activities he described to me, it isn't surprising that a man of Mr. Baker's age might have some difficulty matching his youthful level of performance. But these supplements aren't the way to go. As you saw earlier this evening, they can have side effects that mimic a heart attack.

"We have counselors here who specialize in mediating intimacy disputes between couples. Perhaps we could put you and Mr. Baker in contact with one of them."

Poor Clarice. She had changed a lot over the past five or six years. But underneath, she was still the same good Baptist girl I'd become friends with in kindergarten. Hearing a stranger explain, in front of all of us, how her insatiable sex drive had put her husband in the back of an ambulance was too much for her. While the rest of us struggled not to laugh and make her embarrassment even worse, she slumped down in her bathrobe and sexy negligee, looking like she wanted to crawl under the sofa.

The doctor said, "Mr. Baker is already feeling much better, and he'll be fine when he stops taking those pills. He should probably avoid any strenuous activity for a couple of days."

Clarice cut the doctor off before he could start listing the specific activities Richmond should avoid. "Can I see him?" she asked.

"Of course. He'll be out in a few minutes, but you're welcome to go back and be with him."

Clarice thanked the doctor and then followed him out of the private waiting area and down the hallway that led to the examination rooms.

Barbara Jean, Ray, James, and I were so relieved that Richmond was all right that we didn't laugh or make any of the nasty jokes that the occasion cried out for. It wasn't easy. As Mama used to say, "When shit is funny, it's just funny." And this was the funniest shit I'd heard in a long time. But we came to an unspoken agreement to celebrate Richmond's recovery by holding off on our mockery until we could tease him directly to his face.

CLARICE TOLD ME later that Richmond's proposal came when she entered the examination room. He had just finished dressing and was kneeling to tie his shoe. When he didn't rise, she thought that maybe he was having another sick spell. After she rushed to his side, though, she saw that he had a small, dark purple velvet box in his hand. The jewelry box contained a ring with a diamond that was the same cut as the engagement ring he'd given her in 1970 but was four times the size of that stone. When he asked her to marry him again and come back home, all she could think about was the way she had felt when she thought he was dying. She couldn't bring herself to say no.

CHAPTER 22

Since the Simon Theater's reopening, Audrey's following had grown steadily. She made enough in tips that she was only half a month behind on her rent. As she had walked to work earlier that day, it had struck her that in a few weeks she would likely graduate from dirt-poor to flat broke. That realization brought her out of the funk she had been in since Odette had called with the news that Audrey would soon become an orphan. Audrey's thoughts had gone back to Plainview, but the memories that came to mind onstage that evening were mostly happy.

She leaned into her microphone and said, "After my mother, the first person I told about how I liked to dress in women's clothes was my friend Odette. It took me a while to work up the nerve to say it. We were good friends by then and I knew she had a gay son, but people can surprise you when it comes to what they're a hundred percent cool with and what makes them freak out."

To the amusement of her audience, she began to play the disco classic "Le Freak."

"We were in Odette's kitchen when I told her, and I was shaking so bad I could barely get my words out. She led me to the mantel over the fireplace in her family room and showed me a framed picture of a muscular man with a shaved head holding a trophy. Odette said, 'That's my aunt Marjorie after she won the arm-wrestling contest at the county fair thirty-five years ago. If you think being somewhere between a boy and a girl is gonna shock me, you're mistaken.'

"I never met Odette's aunt, so the one person in Plainview who I knew was like me was my grandparents' bloodhound."

She played two phrases of "Hound Dog" while her audience laughed. A few of the more inebriated patrons howled.

"People never believe me when I tell them that, but it's the truth. That bloodhound was my inspiration. I was a sissified child, but I didn't get the idea to dress in drag until that dog did it.

"Daddy decided Grandma and Grandpa needed company and protection after the pointer they had died from old age. He bought a bloodhound for them, and my grandparents named him Pal.

"Pal was a natural guard dog, but he couldn't have been worse company. He wasn't even a year old when Daddy bought him and he was already mean as hell. Even Grandma and Grandpa took care not to aggravate him for fear they'd lose some fingers.

"Pal was a foul-tempered son of a bitch. But once he was finished barking and snarling at everyone and everything in his path, he was the best hunting animal in the state. Grandpa and Daddy went hunting every weekend, and they always took Pal."

She plinked out "A-Hunting We Will Go."

"Pal got meaner after Grandma died. It got so bad that Grandpa had to slide Pal's food dish across the floor to him and jump back so he wouldn't have to go near Pal's teeth.

"Then Grandpa had a brainstorm. He remembered how Grandma's mood always improved when she put on an accessory that made her feel pretty. So he went up to Grandma's closet and found her best hat, a red satin pillbox that I would kill to have now. He put that hat on Pal's head, and it was like night and day. The snarling stopped, and Pal just wanted to snuggle and have his tummy rubbed.

"At first, Grandpa figured it was hats, in general, that Pal liked. He put one of his baseball caps on Pal, but the dog bared his teeth and growled at Grandpa till he brought back the pillbox. From that day forward, Grandpa dressed up that nellie dog in the nicest hats in Grandma's closet. After a while, he added scarves and ribbons for extra splashes of color. Grandpa turned out to have quite an eye for fashion."

The audience chuckled. Audrey played "Who Let the Dogs Out?"

"The trouble started when hunting season rolled around again. Daddy and I went to Grandpa's house early one Saturday morning, like usual. Daddy just about lost his mind when he saw that formerly vicious dog curled up on the couch next to Grandpa with lavender painted nails and a pink Little Mermaid tiara that Grandpa'd bought for Pal's birthday sitting on top of his head.

"Grandpa warned him not to, but Daddy snatched the tiara off the dog's head. Next thing we knew, Daddy was on the floor and his hand was inside Pal's mouth. Daddy punched the dog in the head once or twice. But each time Daddy hit him, Pal bit down a little harder.

"Daddy started screaming for me to go to the truck and get his shotgun, but Grandpa told me not to move. He said to Daddy, 'Son, he'll give you your hand back once you let go of his tiara and tell him you're sorry.'

"Daddy dropped the costume jewelry onto Pal's head and tried to pull his hand away, but the dog still wouldn't let go. Grandpa said, 'Apologize, Wayne.'

"Sure enough, as soon as Daddy said he was sorry, the dog let him go and settled in on the couch like nothing had happened.

"Daddy's hand was scratched up some, but not actually bleeding. He went to the bathroom to put some antiseptic on it. By the time he came back to the living room, looking like he still wanted to go after Pal with his shotgun, Grandpa had adjusted that pink tiara the way Pal liked it and the two of them were as happy as could be.

"Great hunting dog or not, Daddy wasn't about to be seen with a bloodhound in drag. I've told you about my father before, so you know that he wasn't much for letting folks be who they wanted to be if it wasn't who Daddy wanted them to be. Grandpa didn't give a damn what my father thought, though. He took Pal hunting on his own, and Pal kept on being the sweetest dog in the world, as long as he had his ensemble the way he liked it.

"I was about ten when Pal started doing drag, and it made perfect sense to me. I couldn't imagine anything that could make me feel happier than polishing my nails and throwing on a cute hat before heading off to school. So that's what I did. The school and Daddy put a quick stop to my early experiments, though. I had to start doing my dressing up in secret. But you know what? Pal was right. Every day is a little better if you feel prettier by lunchtime than you felt at breakfast."

Audrey had just begun to sing "How Much Is That Doggie in the Window?" when someone shouted out from a table in the rear, "What happened to Pal?"

Because it was Audrey's nature to tell the truth, she almost told the story of how Terry had shared his bedroom with Pal for the six months between his grandfather's and his mother's deaths. She nearly related how Pal, like Terry, hadn't lasted long under the Robinson roof without the protection of Terry's mother. Terry had come home one afternoon exactly one week after his mother's funeral and found that Pal was gone. The look on his father's face told Terry that he'd better not ask for an explanation.

That story was too heavy for tonight, though. Audrey wanted to begin her set with everyone smiling. She said, "Pal was my dress-up partner until he was called home to doggy heaven." She reached up and tapped the black sequined beret that sat atop her head at a coquettish tilt. She said, "This was one of his."

In honor of Pal, Audrey sang, "I Feel Pretty."

CHAPTER 23

*T*hroughout the ride from the hospital to his temporary digs in a pale green clapboard house down the street from the Pink Slipper, El caressed the butter-soft leather upholstery of Barbara Jean's Mercedes. It was the most luxurious car he'd ever been in that wasn't following a hearse. Forrest had provided the house for El's use during his recuperation, more evidence of his post-salvation generosity. He had also, El found once he got inside, stocked the kitchen cupboard with a bottle of excellent whiskey.

Because Barbara Jean and Forrest had been so good to him, El felt guilty about what he was planning to do. Not so guilty that he changed his mind, but guilty enough to hope that it would be neither of them who found him.

When he'd awoken in University Hospital after his first surgery, he'd made the decision to shoot himself. Then he'd remembered that, like nearly everything he had once owned, the gun he'd kept for protection for fifty years had been swept away by Hurricane Katrina. Later, he had given some thought to gas. But he didn't own a car that he could leave idling inside a closed garage. He also had no garage. He had learned from a conversation with a talkative and equally depressed fellow hospital patient that modern stoves weren't efficient for gassing yourself. They were likely to blow up before they killed you. Even if some fool could have been persuaded to sell or lend a pistol to a downhearted old man freshly out of the hospital, or if he could somehow manage to fill the kitchen with cooking gas, he wasn't low enough to repay Forrest's generosity by leaving him a bloody mess to clean up or by blowing the roof off his house.

Drugs it was. El had gritted his teeth through his post-surgical discomfort and squirreled away half of the pain pills Darlene Lloyd had brought him each afternoon. Stockpiling the drugs had been easy, and doing it had filled him with excitement and nostalgia. It had been years since he'd last been high, but hoarding those pills was just what a junkie with access to opiates was meant to do.

El was relatively sure that he had enough of the precious white tablets to accomplish the job, especially if he washed them down with the whiskey Forrest had left for him. If the pills and booze weren't sufficient, he had a plastic bag to pull over his head to guarantee the proper result—another tip from that sad patient he'd met at University Hospital.

He sat at the chipped Formica kitchen table and took inventory of the items in front of him. The whiskey bottle—opened, but still full. Pills piled to the right of the bottle, alongside a plastic garbage bag. Spotted guitar in his lap. It would feel good to play for as long as he could. He attached a strap to the guitar and looped it over his shoulder to keep Ruthie from falling to the floor at the end.

El grabbed the whiskey bottle, tipped his head back, and took a swig. No reason to dirty a glass. His mouth filled with whiskey until his cheeks bulged. Then he reached for a handful of tablets.

It was then that he saw it. He caught just a glimpse of it in the corner of one of the kitchen windows. He thought his mind was playing with him at first. But after it disappeared from one window, it reappeared briefly in another. His eyes darted back and forth between the windows, waiting to see if he might spy it once more. His heart beat a tight, staccato drum roll. He saw it again. It was at the door that led from the kitchen to the backyard. El swallowed the mouthful of liquor. He inhaled with a whooping gasp and sat still, shocked into immobility.

Raja, his father's leopard, was prowling the back porch, searching for a way in.

El watched as Raja came closer to the glass panes of the kitchen door. The knob turned, and the door creaked. El's throat clogged with silty river mud, and he found himself unable to breathe as the door swung open and the leopard entered the house.

Raja crept across the kitchen floor toward him. The animal stopped just a few feet away from its prey. El watched as Raja transformed from a leopard into his spotted guitar, and then into a woman in a leopard-skin coat.

The leopard woman spoke to him. "I'm Odette. I'm married to James. We need to talk."

ODETTE SAT DOWN across the table from El. She had planned to begin by telling him what she thought of him, a listing of his offenses. But now that they were face-to-face, she hesitated. This was the first time she had seen him up close, and she couldn't help noticing traces of James. El was certainly the source of James's height. Miss Ruth had been five foot three, the same height as Odette. Like James, El's long appendages made it look as if he were sprawled out wherever he sat. Though James had inherited his mother's amber-and-silver eye color, the shape of his eyes and brow came directly from El.

She stopped herself before she saw too much of James in El. She had arrived at the house propelled by anger and a duty to fix what was wrong with James. Sympathy could interfere with her mission.

When Odette had talked with Barbara Jean that morning and discovered that El had been released from the hospital, the path forward
for James, and for herself, had become clear. She'd learned where El was
staying from Barbara Jean and then hopped into her car. First, she
intended to tell El that it was time he apologized to James. Then she
would explain to him that he owed James some hard truths. If El could
show pictures to Barbara Jean and bring her mother back to life with
stories about long-dead folks, El could tell James exactly what had caused
him to twist the course of James's life with the slash of a blade. She would
see to it that El explained to James just how he could have left him
and Miss Ruth to suffer through hunger and poverty while El was off
doing whatever the hell he was doing.

She'd even worked out a schedule. El would come see James at their
house on Sunday night. After a good sermon and a long, relaxing meal
with their friends at Earl's, James would be more likely to forgive her
for interfering even though he'd told her not to. At least she hoped so.

Part of her had argued that she should stay out of this and let James
sort out his feelings on his own. But now James hardly slept, and when
he did, he talked out loud to his long-dead mother. During the day, her
normally quiet James had gone nearly silent. And he had beaten a man.
The voice in her head that advised backing off had been drowned out
by the sound of Aunt Marjorie bellowing, "Do what's right for right now,
and clean up the mess later."

When Odette had arrived at the green house, she'd tapped her
knuckles against the front door. No one had answered. Knowing that
El was getting around with the help of a prosthetic foot and a walker,
she waited for a while before rapping on the door again. When she didn't
receive an answer to her third barrage of knocks, she left the front stoop
to investigate.

She peeked into the living room window first. Through the glass,
she saw a large, cheerful bouquet of pink and yellow roses that seemed
out of place on the battered coffee table in the center of the room. She

guessed that the flowers had come courtesy of Barbara Jean. When she didn't spot El, she went to the next window. On tiptoe, she peered into an empty dining room. Then she walked around the house toward the backyard.

Odette saw El through the first of the two kitchen windows on the west side of the house. He sat, unnaturally still, at a small table across the room. His walker stood just behind his chair, and his guitar lay across his lap. *Dead?*

She moved to the next window for a better look and saw that El's eyes were open. His face was turned toward the window through which she'd first seen him. Perhaps his eyes were following her. She wasn't sure. She walked to the rear of the house and climbed two weathered wooden steps leading to the back door.

Through the glass of the door, she saw El, just a few feet away. She knocked, but it was only after she turned the knob and pushed the door open that he looked her way. She slowly walked toward him across the creaking floor while he gawked at her as if she were something other than human.

She pulled back an empty chair at the table, sat down, and introduced herself. "I'm Odette. I'm married to James. We need to talk."

El adjusted his guitar in his lap, then lifted the whiskey bottle to his lips and took a swallow. "You were a leopard. Then you were my guitar."

For the first time that day, but not the last, Odette wondered if she should call for paramedics. With all the time she'd spent at University Hospital dealing with her own health problems, she'd had her fill of the place. And just one day had passed since Clarice had summoned her to the emergency room after what had turned out to be just the latest chapter in the long history of trouble caused by Richmond's genitalia. She was relieved when, focusing more clearly, El said, "Your coat. My guitar looks like your coat."

Odette was wearing the leopard-print jacket Clarice had given her years earlier. She looked from her sleeve to the guitar propped against El's belly. "I guess they do look alike."

It was then that Odette took in the items arrayed on the table—the pills, the whiskey, the plastic bag. This selfish man was ready to check out and leave James with the same old questions and anger. The shred of sympathy she had felt toward El upon recognizing the physical similarities between him and James disappeared.

She said, "Your plans for this afternoon have just changed. You won't be killing yourself today."

El sputtered, "I wasn't gonna do no such thing."

Odette held up a hand to stop him. "I'm not gonna waste my time arguing with you about this. You don't get to die yet. You've got unfinished business."

El opened his clenched fist and let a handful of white pills fall onto the table. He stared down at them and said, "I got no business with you or anybody else anymore. If you could leave me alone, I'd appreciate it."

"I know this is gonna sound cold, considering that you're clearly in a bad way. My own mother says I'm a hard woman, and maybe she's right. But the truth is, the only man I'm feeling sorry for right now is my husband. James is the one trying to make sense of everything you did to him and his mother. He's the one who'd end up paying for you to get a decent burial. He'd do that, you know. James would suck down all his anger to see to it that you got a respectful send-off. He would do it because, no matter how good a husband and father and man James is, he never believes that he's good enough. He's got to prove it, over and over again. So, you see, I couldn't feel sorry for you even if I wanted to. I'm too busy being pissed off about what you've taken from my husband and how you were prepared to leave this earth and take a little more."

She placed her elbows on the table and scooted forward in her chair until she was close enough to smell the alcohol on his breath. "Nobody takes nothin' from my James."

El inched away from her.

"I was going to try to set up a meeting between you and James, but I'm thinking now that I'll have to do something else," Odette said.

The further she stepped into El and James's conflict, the more she knew she shouldn't. But it was too late now. The mess she'd have to clean up was growing, and she couldn't stop adding to the pile.

She pushed one of the pills around on the tabletop with her index finger. Then she sat back in her chair. "You're gonna have to come with me."

"Look," El said, "you're wrong about me killing myself. I was just gettin' some stuff organized here. If James wants to talk to me, that'll be okay. We should just do it on another day."

Odette's hand sprang up again. "Two things. First, everything I know about you leads me to think that trusting your word isn't the smartest move a person can make. Second, this isn't about what James wants. It's about what he needs, and I'm in charge of that right now. Let's get your stuff together. You'll stay with James and me, so I can keep an eye on you till you two come to some kind of reckoning."

She grabbed the plastic bag on the table and shoveled the pain pills into it with a swipe of her hand. "I promise you can still kill yourself later, if you've got to. I won't stop you."

El said, "You're Marjorie's kin. That's for damn sure."

Odette said, "I'll take that as a compliment."

Thinking out loud, she said, "James is out fishing. I can get you settled in while he's gone. We'll figure out later what to do with you when we go to Chicago."

"Chicago?"

"Clarice is playing a concert there, and James and I are going. That's still a week and change away. We'll figure that out when the time comes. For now, let's get you packed up."

She prepared herself for more arguing. Then, just as she was wondering if she had enough of Aunt Marjorie in her to drag an eighty-year-old man out to her car against his will, El became cooperative. He began the lengthy, awkward process of rising from his chair. After carefully placing his guitar in the case that leaned against his walker, he said, "I'm about ready. All I've got is what's here and a couple things in the bedroom up front."

AS ODETTE AND El drove across town, he pressed his nose against the passenger-side window and watched the early summer greenery of Plainview pass by. For the first time since coming back to Indiana, he felt that there was a reason for his return. From the moment he had seen Raja bounding onto the back steps and then bursting into the room, things had changed. Sixty years ago, El had walked into a pawnshop on his way to quitting music forever. Instead, he'd found his leopard-spotted guitar. Now his father had sent Raja to him in the guise of James's big woman, and the leopard herself had said that El had unfinished business.

Thank you, Daddy.

He would follow this new incarnation of Raja. He would make things as right as he could with James. He would accompany the leopard to Chicago and rescue Lily, as he should have done all those years ago.

CHAPTER 24

*E*l went to jail for the first time in 1953, after he'd been an addict for nearly a year. His band had just left the stage after their first set at a tavern in Louisville when the police raided the place for liquor law violations. In the process, the cops happened upon a thriving heroin sales operation. Back then, customers purchased the drug in capsules that were wrapped in aluminum foil. When the police burst in, squares of foil were tossed from pockets and purses throughout the tavern until the floor was covered with what looked like a shimmering silver carpet. When El was searched, it was discovered that he had neglected to get rid of an empty capsule he had tucked into his shirt pocket. The other band members had been more thorough than El, so he was arrested while they were all released.

There hadn't been enough heroin on him to make a possession charge stick. But the district attorney's office kept him locked up as long as they could, hoping to sweat him until he gave up his dealer. His one-night Kentucky gig turned into three months away from home.

The police had been sure that Bubba, the band's sax player, was the dealer. Bubba fit the cops' image of a pusher. He was black. He wore flashy clothes and carried himself with the smoothness of an outlaw. Between his attitude and his size, he was the kind of man who could stroll through a crowd of tough characters with cash bursting from his pockets without the slightest fear that anyone would dare to touch him. But Bubba was far too busy juggling his dangerous women to handle the demands of a drug business.

El's foster brother Harold had been dealing to the band and all of the other users at the Pink Slipper since he was a high school junior. Unlike Bubba, Harold didn't look the part. Long-limbed and hulking, Harold was already losing his hair at twenty. His round, pink face always shone with perspiration, and he had a country way about him that he could crank up to a higher volume when it suited him. Good ol' boy Harold could run right past a phalanx of police with a pile of white powder in his cupped palms and the cops would suspect only that he was a harried farmer rushing home to bake bread. The police interviewed everyone in the band after raiding the Louisville joint, but they never once asked about Harold during those interrogations or during El's weeks behind bars. They were interested in Bubba and didn't want to hear about anyone else.

Even if the cops had been willing to suspect someone other than Bubba, El wouldn't have given up Harold. They weren't as close friends as they'd been when they were kids. But they were brothers. El couldn't snitch.

Also, Harold had become the band's manager in early '52. Drug dealer and band manager were one combined position in lots of bands back then. It made things easier. Only Lily and Bubba abstained, so most of the band's money was going to drugs anyway. This way, they skipped the middleman. Harold had turned out to be a pretty good manager. He had a head for numbers, and he was more ambitious than any of the musicians in the group. After taking the reins, he booked the band in blues clubs throughout the middle third of the country.

It was Harold who set up the gig that turned Marcus Henry into El Walker. They had gone to Chicago to play at a little South Side place called the Blues Pot. The club paid their performers next to nothing, but the word on the street was that record company executives regularly showed up there. The rumor about the record execs turned out to be entirely untrue, though El and the other band members didn't know that at the time. For three nights, El, Lily, and the rest of the musicians gave the club's audience their very best.

The Blues Pot was one of the nicer places on the circuit. The outside walls were sky blue. A huge guitar-shaped white sign with a robust 1930s-style, blues-shouting woman painted on it hung above the front door. Inside, there was a beautiful oak bar and a minuscule but well-lit stage. The seating area was small but comfortable. Unfortunately, the Blues Pot sat just yards away from Chicago's famed elevated train tracks. Every time the "L" passed, it created such a racket that nothing else could be heard until the train was gone.

The band was performing the first song of the set when the "L" came by. Lily surrendered and stopped singing as the metallic roar grew. But because they had been near the climax of the song, El refused to be outdone by the clatter of the train. He battled on, increasing the volume of his voice until the thundering train was only the second-loudest sound in the room.

At the end of the set, the club owner came to the stage and slapped El on the back. "You outsang the 'L,' son. That's a first here."

Calling Marcus Henry " 'L' Train" became an inside joke among the band members. It was eventually shortened to "El." The surname Walker came a few years later, courtesy of another band manager who thought El's guitar-playing style was similar to T-Bone Walker's. T-Bone was still riding high with "Call It Stormy Monday," and El's manager thought they could create some confusion and make a few bucks off it. No one mistook El for the more famous Walker, but—unlike Marcus Henry—no arrest warrants had been issued for El Walker. So he hung on to the name.

When El was finally set free from the Louisville jail, his first stop back in Indiana was the Pink Slipper. He walked into the club in the late afternoon and found the place occupied by a few of the usual early drinkers and daytime hustlers. As El had expected, Harold was there, doing business at a booth in a back corner. El stopped at the bar and put a shot of whiskey on his tab. Then he headed over to see his foster brother.

El sat down across from Harold in the booth and said, "Hey."

"Hey," Harold replied, not looking up as he scribbled into a black book. "I didn't know you were out."

"Just got back in town. I haven't even been home yet."

Harold continued writing. "We'll see you onstage later, right? It hasn't been easy on the band since you got locked up. Forrest'll want to let his regulars know you're back."

"I'll be here. I'm just gonna go home and clean up first."

Harold muttered, "Good. See you tonight."

El was hot-tempered in those days, and few people infuriated him more than his foster brother. He slapped his palm down on the table-top and shouted, "Three months, you asshole! I could've walked out of there on day one if I had given 'em your name, but I sat in that damn jail and kept my mouth shut. I expected to see some kind of gratitude!"

El waited for Harold to yell back at him. The two of them had hollered at each other for years at the foster home and battled over assorted business matters at countless band rehearsals. Harold lifted his gaze from his black book for the first time since El had sat down with him. He carefully rested his gold fountain pen on the table between them and reached into the breast pocket of his jacket. "Here's some gratitude," he said, tossing two small foil packets across the table toward El. "Thanks for your help." He turned his attention to his ledger.

El thought of a thousand things to say. He could remind his brother that he had been the one who'd founded the band, and that his music was what kept it going. He could say that people were whispering behind Harold's back that too many years living with his crazy mother had messed up his brain and that Harold was getting more like her every day. But somehow the act of tucking the heroin into his pants pocket drained the fight out of him. El stood and left the club.

The two heroin packets whispered to him all the way from the Pink Slipper to the front door of his home. The drug's call grew in volume like an oncoming train. But when El stepped inside the house, the demanding voice of heroin was temporarily blocked out by the sound of his son's voice shouting out, "Daddy!"

Little James launched himself at his father, and El lifted his child into an embrace. El buried his face in the four-year-old's hair and inhaled as his son squeezed him with all of the strength in his small body.

Ruthie was less welcoming. She stopped several feet away from El and stood watching as he continued hugging James. El stepped forward and attempted to kiss her, but Ruthie turned her lips from him, offering only her cheek. "Your son missed you," she said.

Immediately angry and defensive, El said, "It wasn't easy on me either, you know. I wasn't in Louisville on some kinda vacation. James'll forget all about this. I'm the one who'll remember sittin' in that jail and missin' my boy and thinkin' my wife was missin' me."

A junkie will always offer an excuse or an accusation instead of an apology, El would later understand. And true to form, that night he gave Ruthie an addict's response. Fully committed to his vision of himself as the victim, he used her failure to offer him sympathy to reinforce his belief that he had been wronged. El's righteous anger was made even worse because, with James against his chest, he couldn't say what he wanted to say. Or at least he couldn't say it as loudly as he wanted to.

He cupped a palm over James's ear and pressed his son to his heart, so James couldn't hear his words. He hissed, "This is no kinda way for a loving wife to welcome her husband home, not after what I been through."

"Nothing has changed since the last time I saw you. Nothing *will* change until you're done with that stuff for good."

There it was. They had spent the week before his ill-fated trip to Louisville arguing about the addiction that she felt was ruining their lives, an addiction that he insisted did not exist. Now they were at it again.

"Well, you'll be happy to know I'm clean. Three long months in a jail cell will do that for you."

Ruthie eyed her husband with a twisted mouth and a raised eyebrow. "You've been *clean* before."

"It's true this time. Maybe it would've been true before if you hadn't been on my back about it every damn day."

Ruthie reached out and took James from El. She set her son on his feet beside her and said, "It's time for his dinner." As she left the room with James at her side, she called over her shoulder, "Welcome home."

The reunion with Ruthie that El had imagined repeatedly during his weeks in Louisville had been romantic and pornographic. It had definitely not included Ruthie nagging him with her accusations of drug addiction. In his bedroom, undressing for his bath, he thought of the heroin in his pants pocket. He pulled out the foil squares and opened one, just to reassure himself that it wasn't empty. He touched the four powder-filled capsules with the tip of his finger, rolling them back and forth in his hand. It would serve Ruthie right if he shot up right then. No, she'd know he was high and would throw it in his face. It was better if he waited.

He went to the bedroom dresser and hid his stash at the back of his underwear drawer inside a tin with his needle, his spoon, and a tiny quantity of heroin he'd bought just before his jail stint. He smiled as he thought about how much he would enjoy the look on Ruthie's face when he showed her the little foil squares a month, maybe two, from now. He would wave them in front of her nose and say, "Who's hooked, Ruthie? Who's a junkie?"

He talked a lot through dinner to show Ruthie how sober and alert he was. He discussed some new songs he had written while he was away. He described some ideas he'd had for the band that he'd be presenting to everyone later that evening. By the time he left for the club with his guitar strapped to his back, dressed in his best high-draped, pin-striped pants and a crisply ironed white dress shirt, he felt that he'd made his point to Ruthie.

All of the band members, except for Lily, were at the Pink Slipper when El arrived that night. They began the first set without her. It would have been better with Lily, but the other band members were so happy to have El back that they all played their best. Bubba was on fire. He danced across the stage with his saxophone as if he were gliding over the floor with one of his many ladies. Leroy's fingers were a blur as he attacked his bass. The drummer had the audience rocking in rhythm.

El was glad to be back at work, but he kept looking for Lily to show up. El and Lily were each good on their own, but together, they were special. While he'd been locked up, El had gone to sleep each night thinking about the music he and Lily would make with the band. It was the only thing that quieted his mind long enough to allow him to rest.

Lily and Harold walked into the Pink Slipper just as the first set ended. They made their way through the crowd and headed for the small greenroom behind the stage. At the sight of Lily, El began planning the playlist for the second set. The other band members hurried to the bar as soon as the applause died down, but with the late-set songs in his thoughts, El parked his guitar in its stand and rushed to the greenroom.

Harold was dressed up that night. Once he'd started dealing, he'd bought a suit every month. He wore each ensemble for four straight days. One day to show off, the other three to prove to everyone that Mrs. Taylor no longer forced him to return his new clothes to Clancy's Department Store.

He was decked out in a violet-and-gold plaid suit that was as much a country boy's fantasy of how a wealthy man dressed as Forrest Payne's yellow tuxedos were. His purple shirt and shiny gold tie squeezed his thick neck, and his hair was slicked with pomade in the fashion of the mobsters he'd seen in Louisville and Chicago. Somehow it all came together in a way that made Harold look even more like a shitkicker than he had before his style transformation.

Lily didn't look up at El when he came into the greenroom. She sat slumped in her chair with her chin resting on her chest, playing idly with the leopard-patterned scarf draped across her shoulders. The scarf had been a birthday gift from El and Ruthie, a little something special so she would match his spotted guitar.

When Lily finally raised her head, El knew. He didn't have to roll up her sleeves and look for tracks. He could see it from across the room.

On shaking legs, El walked to Lily and knelt beside her. He asked, "Lily, honey, what did you do?"

She squinted at him, trying to bring him into focus, though he was just a few inches away. Lily smiled as if she were surprised by his presence. She said, "Is it time to sing?"

El stood and glared at Harold, who was admiring his reflection in a full-length mirror on the other side of Lily's chair. El tucked his hand into his pants pocket and touched the straight razor he kept for protection when he was going to be paid in cash. "I should kill you," he said.

Harold flicked his fingers at his ear as if he were chasing away a gnat. "You ain't got it in you to kill anybody, and we both know it."

El rolled the folded blade in his palm and tried to imagine that he was another kind of man, a tougher man who could lash out in defense of his precious sister. El squeezed the razor for several seconds, before releasing it and admitting to himself that Harold was right. He didn't have it in him.

Harold said, "You should watch how you talk to me. I'm gonna open up a club in Chicago, and if you behave yourself, I might let you play there sometime. It's gonna be a real nice place."

"What the hell are you talkin' about?"

"The Blues Pot. I bought it. I'm gonna fix it up and make it better than this dump ever thought about bein'." He stroked Lily's hair. "I'm movin' to Chicago, and Lily's comin' with me."

"Lily can't go to Chicago. We've got a whole bunch of gigs comin' up. We're gonna make a record this summer. If you want to move to Chicago, fine. But Lily is staying here."

Harold said, "What kind of man would I be if I left my wife behind?"

"Your wife?"

Harold grinned like a gambler laying out a royal flush. "We got married last week."

"You're lyin'."

Harold turned to Lily. "Sweetheart, show him the ring I bought you." Lily slowly lifted her left hand and showed El a wedding band. Harold said, "We accept your congratulations."

"You could never get her to look at you twice, so you got her hooked. That's as low as a man can go," El said.

Harold's jaw flexed, and he balled his hands into fists. He stomped over toward El until they were nearly chest to chest. "Since you and my wife are friends, I'm not gonna kill you for sayin' that. I want you to remember this day, though. I want you to think about how I came out on top for once. Me, the man whose own mother you turned against him."

"What the hell are you talkin' about?" El said.

"Like you don't know, you damn snake. From the second you walked into my house, you made my life harder, always grinnin' and suckin' up to Ma the way you did. She threw you and your songs in my face every day."

"That's bullshit and you know it, Harold. Your mother beat the hell out of all of us. Nobody came out of that place on top. That bitch was insane."

Bits of spittle hit El's face as Harold shouted, "Shut the hell up! You don't get to say that about her. She's *my* mother. Only I get to say that."

El watched as Harold began to pace behind Lily's chair, speaking louder and faster with each step. He waved his hands in the air as he became more agitated. El thought, *Shit, if he had a Bible in his hand, I'd hardly be able to tell him apart from his mama.*

"From the day you showed up with that guitar, I got the worst of it. I'm not forgettin' how you tried to steal Lily from me from the moment she got there, neither. But she's mine now. I'm the one she married. Remember that. I won."

Harold stopped in front of the mirror and adjusted the lapels of his jacket. He loosened his gold tie and unfastened the top button of his too-tight shirt. Some of the red left his face now that his neck was less constricted. Echoing El's words from that afternoon, Harold said, "I expected to see some gratitude. We didn't have to come by to see you. I'm bein' nice, lettin' her sing with you one last time."

Lily asked again, "Time to sing?" She looked at El through droopy-lidded eyes and smiled as if she'd heard a joke that no one else was in on.

Exhausted, El took a seat in an empty chair next to her. The chair's worn-out springs wheezed as he fell onto it.

Harold placed a hand on Lily's shoulder. He said, "Baby I'm gonna go out and get a seat up front, so I can cheer for you." He bent down and kissed her on the lips. Then he left the room.

El and Lily sat listening to the jukebox music that filtered into the room from the tavern. Soon the sound of the crowd grew louder and they could hear Bubba honking out a few notes on his sax. El extracted himself from the chair and walked to the sink in the corner of the green-room. He poured a glass of water and brought it to Lily. He knelt beside her as she drank slowly, taking tiny sips. By the time she'd finished the glass, she was more awake.

El said, "Why would you marry him? You don't love him."

"Harold loves me. He always has. And I don't want to be on my own. I can't be."

"Don't go, Lily. Stay here and sing with me and the band."

She shook her head. "I'm tired of being alone. I want a husband. Maybe some kids. I want what you've got with Ruthie."

"Please, just stay here and sing with me."

Lily rose unsteadily to her feet. She patted El on the top of his head. "I hear Bubba warming up. It's time to sing."

They sang, and it was as good as it had ever been. They performed every tune in their repertoire. When they finally ran out of songs, Lily hugged El and said, "Good-bye, brother." She stepped off the stage and left with Harold.

Three hours later, after shooting up with Leroy in the parking lot and downing half a bottle of Old Crow, El confronted Ruthie in the living room of their little house in Leaning Tree. He had returned home with his mind thoroughly scrambled, wanting nothing more than to drift further away from reality. But the compact tin box he had hidden away at the back of the top right dresser drawer was missing. Ten minutes after the ensuing argument with Ruthie began, El was waving his razor in the air, unaware that little James was running toward him.

CHAPTER 25

*E*l was exhausted by the time I got him into the guest room. He climbed into bed and was snoring within seconds. I went straight to the kitchen to begin dinner and to figure out what I would say to James.

I had a special meal in mind for James to take the edge off the news that I'd dragged El home with me. Short ribs braised in red wine, green beans with bacon, and twice-baked potatoes, followed up by lemon cake. Was it too much to hope that I could delay James's finding out that his father was there until dessert? Maybe El would sleep until late. James and I could eat most of our meal alone. Then, as the first bite of cake hit James's lips, I would whisper, "By the way, darling, your father's going to be staying with us until you start acting more like yourself."

"This is a mistake," someone said. I looked up from the open cookbook on the counter and saw Mama standing next to the stove with her hands on her hips and an expression on her face that I remembered from my childhood as her lecturing face. Mama said, "You can't just bring some-body into the house without telling James and hope it's gonna go fine."

"It's not just somebody, it's his father."

"That's even worse. It's like you're goin' out of your way to push James's buttons."

"I'm trying to help him, not push his buttons."

"It doesn't look that way to me. And it won't feel like that to James."

It was like I was in high school again, Mama giving me a talking to that I didn't want to hear. She was even dressed in an outfit I recalled from my teen years—a faded blue cotton housedress with red terry-cloth pockets, black-and-gray plaid sleeves, and an orange wool collar. It was one of the dozens of dresses my grandmother had sewn for Mama and me from the same not particularly flattering pattern. Grandmama loved to sew, and she cranked out clothes for the family like a one-woman factory. She was also blind, which freed her to enthusiastically mix and match colors and fabrics with no regard for how they would look when thrown together. I stopped wearing my Grandmama originals after she passed, but Mama hung on to those monstrosities until the end of her life. Mama had been in one of the worst of my grandmother's crazy-quilt creations when I'd found her lying lifeless in her garden back in 1999.

Mama said, "You always were too bossy for your own good. Even when you were a child, you were forever tellin' other people what to do. That's something you should work on before it gets you in trouble."

"That's quite a statement, coming from the woman who jumped across the divide between life and death to stand in my kitchen and deliver unsolicited advice," I said.

Mama made a harrumphing noise and walked around me to inspect the ingredients spread out on the counter. I felt a childish thrill from having rendered my mother speechless for once. I knew her silence wouldn't last long, though, so I continued. "James has got to sit down with his father and get some things off his chest. Pretending to forgive and forget isn't working. James will understand once I've had a chance to talk to him. He'll see that I'm right."

Mama said, "What if he doesn't?"

"He will."

Mama moved over till she stood next to me. In the deep voice that I knew from long experience meant that she should be heeded, Mama said, "Odette, pay attention."

I stopped chopping herbs and listened.

"It doesn't matter if you're right. You think you and James have been together so long that you can treat him however you want and have him accept that it's for his own good. You watched how I was with your daddy and picked that up from me, I guess." Though I couldn't feel it, she laid her hand on mine. "Even after a lifetime together, it's still possible to put a distance between you and him that won't ever go away. I know that for a fact. Ask your daddy if I was always thinkin' of his best interests every time I stepped on his pride, and I'll bet he'll say yes. Then think about how often you see him with me now that he can be wherever he wants to be."

"I understand what you're saying, but it's too late to change course now. Besides, I know James better than he knows himself. He might be a little mad at first, but he'll come around to my way of thinking."

Proving, once again, that there are no etiquette schools in the next life, Mama said, "I have to hand it to you. You got some big-ass balls."

"Thanks," I said, pulling eggs and butter from the refrigerator. I would never admit it to Mama, but I agreed that I had overstepped by bringing El home with me. Until I'd parked the car in the garage, I'd debated taking him to Barbara Jean's house. She could even have let him choose between staying in the new house in Leaning Tree Estates that she shared with Ray and playing lord of the manor in her Victorian mansion downtown. But if I had taken El to Barbara Jean's, I'd still be stuck trying to get two unwilling men together. So El was in my guest room.

Mama said, "I don't wanna nag you about this."

"Too late," I interrupted.

Sounding as annoyed with my sassiness as she used to fifty years earlier, Mama snapped, "There is no way James is gonna be happy with you forcing all this high-drama mess on him."

"He's not happy now. This can't make it any worse."

Mama's expression softened from irritation to pity. She said, "Oh, baby, things can always get worse. I thought you knew that."

Like I used to when I was a teenager, I blocked Mama out. I cooked while she offered more of her opinions.

Dessert was in the oven by the time James came in. He was holding a cooler and smelled of the river. As he walked into the kitchen, I plastered on a big smile and asked him how the fish were biting. He put out his hand, palm down, and waggled it to indicate that it had been just so-so.

I announced the dinner menu, emphasizing the lemon cake. Then I waited for him to smack his lips and gush with enthusiasm. That's not what happened, though.

As had often occurred during the years of our marriage, right about the time that I'd be congratulating myself for knowing every aspect of James, he'd turn it around and show that he knew me just as well. After hearing what I'd cooked that evening, James placed the cooler on the table and crossed his long arms over his chest. Leaning back against the kitchen counter, he said, "What's going on, Odette?"

"Nothing's going on. Not much, at least," I said. "Why don't you get cleaned up, and then we can talk about it over dinner?" I repeated that we'd be having twice-baked potatoes, in case he'd missed it the first time.

James stayed put. "Short ribs *and* lemon cake mean this is a punch-softening meal. Let's have the punch."

Right on cue, the blow I'd hoped to cushion with cake pushed his walker into the room and said, "Hello, James."

"Here we go," Mama declared.

James gawked at El. He looked as shocked as I imagine I did the first time Mama appeared to me, in this very kitchen, six years after she died. El scraped his walker a few inches closer, and James said, "Excuse us for a minute."

James stalked out. I excused myself and followed him upstairs to our bedroom.

The moment I shut the door behind myself, James growled, "Why is that man here?" He was as angry as I had ever seen him. His entire body vibrated with barely contained rage, and his eyes bulged as he glared at me.

I led with what I believed to be my most effective pitch. I said, "I had to bring him here, James. When I went to see him, he was about to kill himself. He had pills laid out and everything. I couldn't just leave him."

I had hoped that the dutiful-policeman part of James would overcome the pissed-off husband part of him and he would understand that I'd witnessed an emergency situation and been forced into life-saving action. But he stood there clenching and unclenching his fists. He asked, "Why did you go to see him in the first place? Didn't I tell you to stay out of this?"

I placed my hand on his shoulder and was relieved when he didn't jerk away from my touch. I said, "James, are you listening to yourself? You just heard that a man was about to kill himself and all you want to know is why I was there. That's not you, James. I went to see El because you wouldn't go. I went to see him because you've been acting a little less like yourself every day since we saw him at the hospital. And I'm scared."

James snorted and said, "Since when have you been scared of anything?"

"Since you stopped sleeping at night and started snapping at me and getting into fights."

James seemed to relax a bit then, and I thought maybe the worst had passed. He turned away from me and clutched the edge of the mahogany wardrobe against the far wall. "Odette, you shouldn't have brought him here," he said to the perfume bottles and cream jars on top of the wardrobe.

"If you saw me drowning, wouldn't you save me whether I wanted saving or not?" I asked.

James said, "My situation with him is nothing like that."

"Yes, it is. You're drowning, and you won't admit it. The question is whether you're going to trust me not to let you drown."

"No," James said. "The question is whether you respect me enough to treat me like a man in my own home."

That stung me so bad that my throat went dry and my lungs felt emptied of air. I said, "You know I respect you. I'm trying to help you."

The buzzer on the oven timer sounded in the kitchen, calling what I hoped was an end to this round of our argument. "That's the cake," I said. "We could both use a good meal, and El's a diabetic. He should get some food in him."

Buzzer or not, we weren't done. James spun around toward me. For the second time in two weeks, I saw an expression on his face I didn't recognize. This time, I had put it there. I'd hurt him. Insulted him. Cut him.

He said, "This isn't okay. I would never do something like this to you."

Before I could say more, James snapped, "I'll be back later." He stormed past me. I was still standing in our bedroom when I heard the sound of the garage door opening and the roar of the car engine.

Mama was sitting next to El at the kitchen table when I got back downstairs. One of the many lovely things about my mother is that she rarely gloats. She watched me prepare plates for myself and my houseguest without offering a single "I told you so." What she did say, midway through my meal with silent El, was "It'll be all right with James. Just don't wait for it to get right on its own."

She kept me company through the rest of the meal and as I saw El off to bed. My good mother left my side only to give me privacy as I sought solace in eating half of the cake.

I WAS IN bed when James returned. I'd lain awake watching the glowing red numbers of the digital clock, the way I did when he was late getting home from work. Sleep never came if he wasn't beside me. From the day he had joined the state police, I'd been convinced that my staying awake kept him from all harm.

As he'd done hundreds of times, James undressed in the dark. Pretending to believe I was sleeping, he climbed in next to me.

I said, "Did you eat?"

"Went to Earl's."

We both flopped around in the sheets, trying to get comfortable. We pounded our pillows and wrestled with the blanket. James wound up with his back to me, as far away as he could be in our king-sized bed.

I said, "I'm sorry. I know I did the wrong thing. I just couldn't sit back and watch you be unhappy. I'll never be able to."

James snorted. "So you're saying you're sorry but you still might do it again. That's just about the shittiest apology I've ever heard."

"It's an apology, though." I slid over toward him and laid my fingertips on his back. "I'd sooner die than hurt you."

"I know." He rolled over till we were facing each other. He gave me a peck on the lips, and then he escaped back to the other side of the bed. "What's done is done. He can stay till next week."

CHAPTER 26

The days El spent in our house zipped by quickly. That was partly because I'd thrown James, El, and myself into a situation that required us to be on the alert each second so we wouldn't say the wrong thing and upset the delicate diplomatic balance in our home. Living on the edge has a way of making time go faster. Also, we had a stream of people in and out of the house, creating a constant buzz of activity.

Barbara Jean dropped by daily, sometimes alone and sometimes with Ray. A physical therapist from the hospital came over to work with El every afternoon. Clarice was too busy practicing for her big show to come much, but she called each evening. We talked about El, her ongoing spiritual battle with Miss Beatrice, and the joys of grandmothering. We never once discussed her upcoming move back into the house with Richmond, and she didn't have a word to say about what I could tell was near panic over the Chicago concert. I was already doing more than my share of pushing other folks to open up. I didn't pester Clarice. Besides, I had a strong feeling that that dam would burst soon enough.

Forrest Payne came by the second day El was with us and almost every day after that. He arrived laden with stories of the old days at the Pink Slipper to relive with El, most of them at least a little bit dirty. I'd thought I knew all the stories about Aunt Marjorie, but it turned out there were still one or two more. And they were doozies.

The first night Forrest came by, we sat in the family room—Forrest, Miss Beatrice, El, and me. I'd served everyone lemonade, except Miss Beatrice. Though it was less than a week from the Fourth of July and sweltering outside, she drank her customary hot tea. She was visibly saddened by both the brand of Earl Grey in her mug and the low quality of the mug itself. Her frown deepened when Forrest mentioned my aunt.

"Did you hear about Marjorie and the fire?" Forrest asked me.

When I said that I hadn't heard that story, he said, "The dancers were doin' a patriot show with sparklers, and one of them accidently tossed her sparkler off behind the band. Next thing we knew, the curtains were on fire and the place was filling with smoke. You remember, El?"

El said, "Yeah, I remember." I saw him smile for the first time then, and I was looking at James with a couple of added decades.

"Smoke was everywhere, and the customers started runnin' for the front door. So many folks tried to squeeze out at once that they made a logjam and nobody could move. I started to think I was gonna die. But Marjorie barreled through the crowd, pickin' people up and tossin' them out of the way till she got to the head of the line and cleared the jam. She was a sight to see."

I asked, "Did anybody get hurt in the fire?"

Forrest peeped out his high-pitched giggle and said, "That's the best part. Turned out the fire was mostly smoke. Bubba, the sax player, opened his pants, peed on the curtains, and doused the flames. But since Marjorie was the real hero that night, we told everybody it was her that pissed the fire out. Marjorie bein' Marjorie, she went along with the lie. Not a single person we told doubted it was true."

Poor Miss Beatrice was thoroughly scandalized. She'd only come with

Forrest so she could lead a prayer at the end of their visit, but she had ended up being subjected to my cheap tea, a dollar-store mug, and a tale about dancing girls, urine, and Aunt Marjorie.

The reminiscing tickled Forrest. His voice going even higher, he squealed, "Were you there when Marjorie chucked off her overalls and spun around the stripper pole?"

He turned to me and said, "Big Marjorie yanked that pole clean out of the floor. I'm tellin' you, the audience saw more ass in that five minutes than they'd seen all month."

Miss Beatrice launched into some heavy-duty entreaties to Jesus then. She prayed for a solid half hour. Forrest never did get to the end of his tale about Aunt Marjorie. On his way out the door, though, Forrest whispered in my ear that he'd finish the story the next time he saw me.

With all the talking going on at the house, precious little of it was between James and his father. El was more of a talker than James, but that's not saying much. James can make just about anyone seem like a chatterbox. El was downright animated when the conversation touched on music. He was proud of the places he'd played and the songs he'd written—150 of them, he claimed. The darkness that nearly always emanated from him lifted whenever he spoke of his songs, his bands, or his guitar.

James was the true music lover in our house, though he practically bit my head off when I suggested that he might have inherited his affinity for music from El. James had bought most of the recordings we owned. It was James, not me, who had decreed that our daughter, Denise, would become a pianist. He dragged her to lessons with Clarice every week for five years, until Clarice called a halt to the torture—Denise's and her own. It was due to James's desire to have musicians in the family that Jimmy and Eric tormented our neighbors with, respectively, the drums and the trumpet. James wasn't interested in sharing much of anything about himself with his father. He made no mention of our amateur-musician children.

We were having dinner on Friday night when I told El that it had been a surprise for us to learn that he was a musician. I thought that was a safe way into a topic they'd both enjoy. But there was danger in every subject where El and James were concerned.

El froze with his fork at his lips. After he set his fork back on his plate, he stared at me as if he were in shock. "Ruth never told you I was a blues man?"

James said, "Mama told me you played the guitar, but she never made it sound like it was a big deal. She didn't tell me it was your job."

With no bitterness, as far as I ever saw, Miss Ruth had explained to James that El was a man who carried misery with him wherever he went. She'd told James that his father was a junkie. She'd been direct with him about how El had disappeared from their lives and left them without a penny. El knew all of that. I'd told him myself in the car ride to our house. But, amazingly, what El couldn't bear to hear was that Miss Ruth had left out that he was a blues man.

El said, "I suppose Ruth did what she thought was best. I just figured my music would be the one thing she would tell you about me for sure." Then he said to James, "When I'm gone, I'd like for you to have my guitar. It has your mother's name engraved on it."

James surprised me by angrily spitting out, "I don't play the guitar."

Here it comes, I thought. He's finally going to let loose the explosion that I had hoped to engineer. The truth would be spoken, or yelled, at last. The right questions would get asked, and some real answers might be offered. But James caught himself and added, in a calmer, more even tone, "I'm sure one of the grandkids would be happy to have it." The subject was abandoned for a chat about the weather.

After dinner the next night, El went to his room and brought out a picture of James as a toddler; he was sitting in his father's lap, next to El's leopard-spotted guitar. In the picture, smooth-faced young El was dressed in a tight-fitting shirt that showed off his muscular arms. His teeth, now deeply stained, gleamed white as he grinned at the camera.

It wasn't just that he had aged. In 1952, El'd had a wild energy about him that made you think the picture might burst into flame at any second. He was all vitality and light.

The most remarkable aspect of the photo was that young El's affectionate gaze was clearly fixed on his guitar, not on the child squeezed next to it on his lap. He looked at the instrument so intently that I wondered if the baby hadn't been tossed aside the moment the camera's flash died out.

In a dreamy voice, El said, "I still remember when your mother took that picture. I had just got the camera, and I said, 'Ruthie, I want a picture of me and my baby.' It was a real nice day."

I am not, by nature, a forgiving woman. I hold grudges, and to be honest about it, I often enjoy holding them. But right then, as I listened to El talk about that day, decades ago, when his wife snapped a picture of him and his son, I knew I couldn't maintain my hatred of him.

El was a frail old man who wore his regrets like a weight around his neck. He deserved to wear that yoke, and I wasn't making excuses for him or even thinking about granting him the forgiveness he hadn't been man enough to seek from James. I just couldn't stoke that furnace of anger like I had been doing. Here he was, smiling with nostalgia about his sweet memory of taking a picture with "his baby," and nearly sixty years later, this pitiful man still couldn't see how plainly the photo advertised to the world that his real "baby" wasn't his son.

CHAPTER 27

Veronica stood in the lobby of First Baptist Church greeting congregants in advance of her pulpit debut. She was flanked by her husband, Clement, her daughter Sharon, and her grandson, Apollo. Her son-in-law had arrived at the church with his wife and child, but not long after he'd entered, Veronica had ordered him to go into the chapel and reserve seats for the family. He'd been given specific instructions as to which locations were, and were not, acceptable. No farther than eight rows away from the front. No closer than three. The family should be seen, but Apollo shouldn't be so near the pulpit that his cuteness might detract from the solemnity of the occasion.

They stood in a spot that Veronica had chosen after scouting the lobby for weeks. Their location, in front of the wooden kiosk where visitors signed the welcome book, provided excellent sight lines and was bathed in morning light from a window high on the east wall. Whoever was parked in the center of the shaft of light created by the window was imbued with an angelic glow. The sunbeam that suggested God's favor produced a blinding glare that caused Clement and Sharon to squint. But Veronica, who had come fully armed for the weekly fashion battle her church was known for, sported a three-foot-diameter hat that successfully blocked the sun. The hat—like her dress, scarf, gloves, and shoes—was Barbie-accessory pink and featured a cascade of bubble gum–hued ostrich feathers that flowed down from its crown, creating a fluffy, domed effect. Summer fruit—peaches, strawberries, and pears— rendered in glass were artfully interspersed among the plumage. Perched atop it all were two small silver-and-white sequined doves. There had originally been three birds, but Veronica had removed one of them, fearing that the third dove pushed her headdress across the thin line that separated festive from ostentatious.

Nadine Biggs, the wife of the injured pastor of the church, was among the early arrivers. When they made eye contact across the lobby, Veronica lifted a pink-gloved hand and waggled her fingers at Nadine.

Sharon said, "Mrs. Biggs looks like she was up all night. The reverend must not be doing too well."

"That's just her face, honey." Veronica lowered her voice and added, "I wouldn't be surprised if she was up late, though. I have it on good authority that she's been sleeping with the choir director for close to a year. They say she's more brazen than ever since Reverend Biggs has been laid up."

"No!" Sharon cried out.

"Yes, indeed. But you didn't hear it from me."

Nadine began walking toward Veronica, weaving her way through friends who all wanted updates on the pastor's condition. As she approached, Veronica whispered to Sharon, "I heard her daughter steals from the collection plate."

She reached out and grabbed Nadine's hand. "How is Reverend Biggs? I hope he's making a speedy recovery."

Nadine said, "His progress is a little slower than we expected, but we're hoping it'll pick up soon."

Veronica took no pleasure in the prospect of Reverend Biggs being laid up longer than his doctors had estimated. She wasn't that type of person. But Madame Minnie had predicted that Veronica would soon have her own church, and it wasn't like the church could have two pastors.

She laid a sympathetic hand on Nadine's shoulder. "I'm sure he'll be better in no time with an angel of mercy like you tending to him." Then she said, "Have you met my grandson, Apollo?"

Nadine leaned forward to get a good look at the baby. She gasped and said, "He is as precious as he can be. I love how his little bow tie matches your dress." She congratulated Sharon and backed away to say hello to Clement. After telling Veronica how much she was looking forward to her sermon, Nadine excused herself and went to fill in other church members on the health of the pastor.

Odette and James, Barbara Jean and Ray, and Clarice and Richmond entered the church. Several people surrounded Clarice. Even from yards away, Veronica could hear them carrying on about the upcoming Chicago concert. Others shook Richmond's hand as if he were still a football star. Women ran up to Barbara Jean and gushed over the simple blue sundress she was wearing. The same women turned to bat their eyes at Ray.

What was wrong with these fools? They saw Barbara Jean and Ray every Sunday. Was it surprising that a rich woman owned a decent dress or that a handsome man looked as good today as he had seven days earlier?

"That Clarice just can't stand to have the spotlight off of her for one second," Veronica said. "Insecurity is what it is. It's sad. If you ask me, Barbara Jean looks cheap. That's a very short dress for a woman her age."

"It's like Grandma Glory used to say: all the money in the world can't buy class," Sharon remarked.

When Clarice and the other Supremes stepped into Veronica's sunbeam, they showered her with hugs and wishes for good luck. The men said their hellos and left to reserve seats in the rapidly filling sanctuary, leaving Clarice, Barbara Jean, and Odette behind.

This was the first time Barbara Jean and Odette had seen Sharon since the birth of her son. She was fussed over and heartily congratulated. Odette tickled Apollo above the pink bow tie, which was partially buried in the folds of skin around his neck. He opened his mouth and bellowed, "Gaah!"

Odette apologized for upsetting him, but Sharon assured her that Apollo's unearthly howl was, in fact, a laugh.

"He's extraordinary," Odette said.

Barbara Jean added, "He's all boy."

"He's so sweet," Clarice said.

Veronica's aunt Beatrice appeared on the arm of Forrest Payne. Beatrice wasn't happy to be in a house of worship that went easy on sin and was largely Holy Ghost–free, but she was pleased enough to finally have a preacher in the family that she was willing to tolerate a few hours at a substandard church. She accepted kisses from Veronica and Sharon and was introduced to Apollo.

At the sight of her great-grandnephew, Beatrice let out a squeak of astonishment. She'd seen countless pictures, but she had never had the opportunity to experience him in the flesh. "He is truly something," she said.

Forrest patted Apollo's head and drew Veronica's ire by coming too near her in his yellow tuxedo, the brightness of which caused Veronica to recede into the shadows, even as she stood, in all her pinkness, in a circle of sunlight. To Veronica's relief, the Supremes, Forrest, and Beatrice soon headed into the sanctuary. They were replaced by other members of the congregation, who stepped into Veronica's patch of sun to wish her luck.

When the crowd thinned to just a few stragglers, Sharon turned to her mother and said, "That was the rudest thing I have ever seen."

"I know," Veronica said. "It makes you wonder why you even bother to get dressed up. All the money I put into looking like this, and nobody said a thing."

"I'm talking about Apollo. Did you hear what they called him?"

"They all said he was cute," Veronica replied.

"No, they most certainly did not. Aunt Beatrice said my son was 'something.' Odette called him 'extraordinary.' Barbara Jean said he was 'all boy.' Nadine Biggs called him 'precious.'" Saving the worst for last, Sharon added, "Clarice said that he was 'sweet.'"

Veronica and her daughter both understood that *sweet* was merely a code word well-raised people used to describe ugly babies. "Why use an unkind word like *ugly* when *sweet* says the same thing so nicely?" her late mother had always maintained. Like saying "bless your heart" when you meant "kiss my ass," it was basic good manners.

Clement, sensing an oncoming tempest, offered, "I'm sure they didn't mean anything by it. People get careless with their words sometimes."

"They meant it, all right," Veronica said. "Monsters, each and every one of them."

She was about to elaborate when the church secretary appeared. Gently touching Veronica's arm, she said, "Sister Swanson, you should make your way to the pulpit. It's baptism week. You know how that can drag on if you get behind."

As Veronica walked down the side hallway that led to the sacristy behind the altar, she was unable to think of anything but the unjustified attack she had just endured. The church secretary rattled off some last-minute details about the order of the day's events and the baptismal procedure. Veronica barely heard her. She was busy reliving the episode in the lobby.

Veronica was so angry that her body shook as she tried to contain her fury. The church secretary noticed her shuddering as she fastened the pastor's microphone to Veronica's collar. Mistaking the trembling for nervousness, she said, "Don't be scared. I'm sure you'll do fine. Just remember to tap the button on the microphone to turn it on."

As Veronica stepped through the side door that opened onto the dais and made her way to the red velvet pastoral throne at its center, she went over all the things she could remember having heard about Apollo over the past months. She couldn't recall a single "cute," "handsome," or "gorgeous" among the reactions to his photographs.

Her mood deteriorated further when she looked out into the crowd and saw that, contrary to her instructions, her son-in-law had found seats in the sixteenth row of pews, fourth from the back. Veronica took a moment to count and recount each row, because she wanted to have her facts in order when she confronted him about his ineptitude at supper later that afternoon.

So great was her irritation with her son-in-law's inability to follow simple instructions that Veronica threw up her hands in a gesture of frustration. In the process, she whacked her grand hat, pushing it back on her head and dislodging one of the hat's fruits. The crystal peach rolled across the floor and was crushed—intentionally, Veronica suspected—beneath the heel of a fellow associate pastor's shoe. The hat's two sequined doves slipped down onto the ostrich feathers and fell upon each other in an arrangement that looked as if they were in the process of mating. This was immediately noticed by a pair of adolescent boys, members of the children's chorus seated directly behind her. The boys giggled and elbowed each other until their choir director noticed what was going on. He tapped Veronica on the shoulder and said, "Excuse me, Sister Swanson. I hate to tell you, but your hat has gone pornographic."

Veronica turned to the choir director and thanked him, even though she felt that the smirking expression on his face conveyed an unseemly amount of prurient pleasure. Adjusting her hat, she added, "Bless your heart." As she said it, she glared at him in a way that let him know which interpretation of "bless your heart" she meant.

On the monthly baptism day at the church, new members were presented to the congregation at the beginning of the morning service.

Before proceeding to the dressing rooms, where they could change into robes for their submersion in the baptismal pool behind the choir stand, they were invited to testify about their salvation. This Sunday, there were two candidates for baptism, and both of them chose to address the assemblage.

The first new member was a very old man who spoke of how he had been attending services at First Baptist for years and was just now getting around to being baptized because the Angel of Death had spoken to him in a dream and told him to get his house in order. The man's story of late-life salvation was the kind the congregation usually enjoyed, but he soon revealed himself to be a touch senile. He described, at great length, how the Angel of Death had resembled Sammy Davis Jr., illustrating his point with an energetic rendition of "Mr. Bojangles." The elderly man would have gone on for hours if Veronica hadn't cued the organist to begin playing so the secretary could discreetly guide him away from the lectern.

Next, a girl of fifteen stood before the church and thanked her parents for providing her with strong moral leadership. She smiled innocently and swore that she would try to be more Christlike every day. It was a lovely sentiment, but everyone in the church, except the girl's parents, knew that she had a reputation for being a pill popper and the most promiscuous student in her high school. Veronica had heard from multiple sources that the teenager had bragged for months that her Christian rebirth was merely a ploy to get a new car for her upcoming sixteenth birthday. The girl's gullible parents sat smiling like idiots as they ate up every word their daughter said.

The church secretary made the weekly business announcements and read the names on the sick list. When she finished, Veronica took her place at the lectern.

Serenely smiling down at the congregation, Veronica said, "I'd like us to reflect upon the parable of the Good Samaritan. Please open your Bibles to Luke 10:25."

She stopped. Struck by a moment of divine enlightenment, she understood the cause of all her troubles. It was pride, the bitter fruit of the thorny vines of vanity, lust, and envy that had taken root in the church. Clearly, all of the people who had insulted her and her innocent grandson had been corrupted by the sin of pride. Why had it taken her so long to see it?

Having solved this mystery, Veronica felt her spirit lightening. Her anger mixed with something close to elation. Abandoning her planned remarks, she said, "No. Let's turn to Proverbs." She opened the Bible on the lectern and read, " 'Where pride comes, then comes dishonor. Pride goes before destruction, and a haughty spirit before stumbling.' " Then she quoted from the Book of James. " 'God is opposed to the proud, but gives grace to the humble.' "

She fixed her eyes on Nadine Biggs in the first row of pews, and said, "The prideful drip with hypocrisy and will not be corrected, even as they wallow in depravity." She glanced over her shoulder at the choir director to make sure he knew she hadn't been deceived by his pious act. She glared at Odette and pronounced, "Pride can cause people to stew in jealousy for years and then act out in vile ways." With her focus on Barbara Jean, she said, "It is pride that makes people forget their humble origins and pretend to be someone they are not."

Several church members saw her staring into the pews and understood that her comments were targeted at specific individuals. Though no one was completely certain at whom the accusations were directed, the crowd gave in to human nature and took pleasure in hearing their neighbors being chastised. Loaded with passion and thinly veiled malice, this wasn't the type of sermon often heard at First Baptist Church. But the congregation enjoyed the change of pace, rewarding Veronica with shouts of "Preach!" and applauding her rapid-fire invective.

Buoyed by the positive response of the audience, Veronica gave them more of the same. She left the dais and strutted through the aisles.

She stopped at the end of the row where Clarice sat. Frowning toward her cousin, she declared, "The bottomless insecurity of the prideful results in their desperate need for attention. They demand to be seen, but are determined not to see themselves. They are driven to acts of unkindness because pride has destroyed their ability to feel for anyone but themselves."

She continued to march through the aisles of the church. She warned, admonished, and threatened her way from the first row to the last. When she reached the pew were her family sat, she took Apollo from his mother's arms. "I dream of a world where my beautiful grandson can be free of the despicable consequences of pride. I pray for a world where the righteous will not be attacked by weak-minded and prideful sinners."

Apollo screamed, causing everyone to jump or cover their ears. Several of Veronica's next sentences were lost before she realized that Apollo had fastened his mouth to her microphone and shut it off. When she could be heard again, she worked her way back to the front of the church, picking out of the crowd people who had slighted her in some way, real or imagined, over the past half century, calling the miscreants to task for their pride.

As Veronica ended her sermon, a chorus of amens rose from the parishioners. With Apollo in her arms, she left the podium to change into her robe for the baptisms, tingling with pleasure from having successfully and forcefully made her point.

Clement left his seat in the sixteenth row and exited the sanctuary through a side door. He followed his wife down the hallway, catching up with her just in time to open the door to the pastor's office for her and Apollo. "That was great," he said as they walked inside.

She passed the baby to him. Then she removed her pink dress and tossed it over Clement's shoulder, where it was promptly seized by Apollo. He pawed at it and screamed, "Gaah!"

"You should be proud of yourself. It wasn't what you practiced at home, but it was a good talk."

"Oh, my sermon was a damn sight better than they deserved. Especially after those lame-ass testimonies almost ruined the whole thing. Those two new Christians just about bored the old Christians to death.

"Neither of the other associate pastors had to deal with that. The new member that the first one got was a good-looking recovering crackhead with a voice like James Earl Jones who talked about how he found the Lord just as he was about to jump off a bridge. The second associate pastor got to baptize an identical-twins singing duo with voices like angels. They performed a hymn they'd written about finding the Lord beside their grandmother's deathbed. It's not fair. I get stuck with a crazy old man and a teenage slut who'll forget all about Jesus as soon as her parents give her a new car. Well, at least she can drive herself to the VD clinic. Let me tell you, when this church is mine, there's going to be a whole new quality-control system put in place."

Clement said, "Calm down, honey. You're still a little worked up over what Sharon thought those women said about the baby."

"Believe me, I'm not done with them, either," Veronica said. "Mean-spirited vipers is what they are. Those heifers had better be glad we're in church. I only wish I'd called them out by name. It would've served them right.

"The nerve of them. Clarice, with that out-of-control ego of hers. I've got half a mind to skip that stupid concert. It's not like she needs any more of a fuss made over her. And Odette. Have you ever seen a fat woman who thinks so much of herself? Barbara Jean is a whore's daughter, for Christ's sake, and the fools at this church are lining up to kiss her ass. And don't get me started on Nadine Biggs. If I was screwing a man as trifling as that choir director, I'd be ashamed to show my face."

She was interrupted then by a loud knock on the office door. Clement cracked open the door, and a distraught Sharon rushed into the room. Her husband followed her in.

Sharon spoke in a hushed tone: "Mama, your microphone is on."

"What?"

"Your microphone is on, and they can hear every word you say in the sanctuary."

Veronica turned toward Clement, who stood with her pink dress over his shoulder. Then she saw the offending microphone on her dress's collar, twisting and turning in Apollo's tiny hands. Before the mic went quiet, the rapt crowd in the pews heard Veronica bid good-bye to her days as a member of First Baptist Church with the words "Holy shit."

The congregation sat hypnotized, hoping there would be more to come. They wouldn't learn until a bit later that Veronica and her family had escaped through the back door, running to the parking lot down the same steps where Reverend Biggs had suffered his fall. As the audience waited, Odette turned to James and saw that he was biting his lower lip to keep from laughing. That one moment of eye contact between them was all it took. James let out a rumbling hoot that echoed around the quiet room. Odette followed with a squawk. Soon the entire church was filled with sounds of unrestrained hilarity.

Odette relished the sight of the first genuine grin to grace James's face since the day he'd encountered El. And, after half a century of both overt and concealed hostility, she experienced unqualified feelings of affection toward Veronica.

CHAPTER 28

*T*he glow James and I picked up from Veronica's sermon stayed with us through our traditional post-church meal at Earl's. We were still feeling good when we returned home and said good-bye to the health-care aide who'd kept an eye on El while we'd been out. El, James, and I were at the kitchen table eating what was left of the chess pie I'd made the night before when James surprised me by asking El about his—their— family. His questions had the air of an interrogation, but that was better than nothing.

El seemed eager to talk that evening, too. He told us about his life in a foster home with a crazy woman who was obsessed with snakes. He revealed that he'd never married again after Miss Ruth. He said he'd never had more children, though from his tone of voice, I suspected he wasn't quite sure about that.

El said, "My mama and daddy both passed when I was a kid. Neither of them had any folks that I ever met. All that's left now is my brother and sister."

James and I both did a double take when we heard him mention siblings. El saw our shocked expressions and explained, "They ain't blood relations. They're my foster sister and brother, Lily and Harold. They run a little blues bar in Chicago."

He entertained us with a cute story about singing louder than the elevated train. Then he took a bite of the chess pie and carried on for some time about how it was the best he'd had since leaving New Orleans. Looking back on it, I have a vague memory of feeling that he was buttering me up. But it's easy to see it that way now. I was, and am, vain enough about my baking that I didn't suspect his motives at the time.

He said, "Speaking of Chicago, I was hoping maybe I could ride along with you when you go. I'd like to spend a few days with Harold and Lily. I wouldn't ask, except it's hard for me to get around on my own right now." He reached down and rapped his knuckles against the plastic prosthesis beneath his pant leg.

Trapping James and El in a car together for the eleven hours it would take to get to Chicago and back struck me as a wonderful idea. I wasn't going to express an opinion about it, though. I couldn't claim to be a changed woman, but the lessons from the fight James and I were just beginning to get past hadn't been totally lost on me.

My interference wasn't necessary. James said, "Sure. We'll give you a ride."

Excitement made me get ahead of myself. I said, "We're all going to our friend Lydia's restaurant for dinner in Chicago on Thursday night. Maybe you can join us. Your grandchildren will be there. Their families, too." I glanced over at James to gauge whether I had gone too far, inviting El to come with us to the Thursday night dinner. But he didn't seem bothered by the idea.

I should have shut my mouth then and celebrated, in silence, how well the day had gone. Instead, I said, "Lydia is Big Earl and Thelma McIntyre's daughter. Did you know Big Earl?"

In my defense, it's almost impossible to avoid a misstep when every inch of the terrain is littered with hidden dangers. Mentioning Big Earl was like heaving over a boulder. One name was spoken, and nasty bugs that weren't used to the light of day scampered off in all directions.

El said, "Of course I knew Earl. He was a good guy."

James jumped in with "Damn right, he was a good guy. He gave Mama a job at the All-You-Can-Eat before the place was breaking even. He kept us from starving. Big Earl took me fishing when I was a kid. Big Earl taught me how to shave. Big Earl showed me what it meant to be a man. Anything I've got, I owe to him. Big Earl McIntyre was like a father to me." He said this last part slowly, making it sound exactly like the accusation it was.

I thought he would say more, but the storm soon passed. James and El ate the rest of their chess pie hunkered over their plates like convicts. There was no more talk of family. Neither of them said another word to the other that night.

EL WAS SITTING at the kitchen table when I walked in to start the coffee on Monday morning. He was dressed up. He wore a pair of black trousers and a white dress shirt that was creased from being stored in a suitcase but was otherwise neatly pressed. I guessed, and El confirmed, that Barbara Jean was coming over to take him out for breakfast. El, like most men, cleaned himself up as much as possible in anticipation of spending time with Barbara Jean.

Dozens of El's photographs were spread across the tabletop. Even though I told him that it wasn't necessary, he began to gather them up to clear a place at the table for me. He said, "I was lookin' for more pictures to give to Barbara Jean."

He sifted through the photos, squinting as he inspected each one. He waved a photograph at me and said, "I've got a picture of James's grandfather that I can show you."

I told him I thought James would be thrilled. As it turned out, the morning soon took an odd twist. James and I wouldn't see the photo of his grandfather Joe until several days later.

James entered the kitchen, stretching out his long legs with each step and yawning as he walked. Every few paces, he paused to puff out his chest and push the knuckles of his fists into his lower back. This was his routine. Seven mornings a week, James slowly made his way through our house, moving as if he had to wake up each part of his six-foot-four-inch frame separately.

El lifted a picture and announced, "There it is." It was a snapshot of Loretta Perdue, looking remarkably like Barbara Jean, perched on the edge of a stage as a round-faced blond singer behind her leaned into a microphone.

James looked at the picture and suddenly ended his morning stretch. He and El exchanged a glance and quickly turned away from each other. It was evident that, like the previous night when I'd mentioned Big Earl McIntyre, another rock had just been rolled over. Again, something unpleasant had been uncovered.

El shoved the picture into his shirt pocket. James poured a cup of coffee and then excused himself, saying that he had to do something to the car to prepare for the trip. I weighed whether or not to ask what had just happened. But El announced that he was going to lie down for a little while before Barbara Jean arrived to fetch him. He was up and shuffling out of the room with his walker a few seconds later. It was the fastest I'd seen him move all week.

Just after James and his father vacated the kitchen, my phone rang. I didn't recognize the voice at first. The woman calling didn't introduce herself; she just started talking the moment I answered. A few sentences in, though, I realized it was Darlene Lloyd. She was calling to tell me that Wayne Robinson was dead.

Darlene said that although it was a minor breach of hospital protocol to pass this news along to me, she felt it was her Christian duty to try to get word to Terry. Like any good gossip, she was happy to employ the Lord if she needed an excuse for getting into somebody else's business. I thanked her for calling and said good-bye.

Her call had been unnecessary. By the time I'd lifted the ringing phone from the countertop, I'd known that Wayne Robinson was gone. Out my kitchen window, I saw him in the garden talking to my mother and Eleanor Roosevelt. He was waving his hands as he spoke, pleading his case, no doubt—claiming that he'd been a good husband, a well-intentioned father. Mrs. Roosevelt might have been inclined to give him a sympathetic ear. She was sweet that way. He was barking up the wrong tree with Mama. And he had better beat a hasty retreat before Aunt Marjorie showed up. If Mama had shared with her manly sister that Wayne Robinson had thrown out his teenage son for being too girly, Aunt Marjorie would be likely to exact vengeance. If anyone could whoop a dead man's ass, it was Aunt Marjorie.

But none of that was my concern. I called Terry.

CHAPTER 29

*T*he Simon Theater was decorated for Independence Day. Red, white, and blue metallic streamers hung from the wall sconces. Each table in the main room was adorned with a patriotic centerpiece that contained miniature American flags and small cut-out caricatures of the founding fathers. Audrey was also decked out. She saluted America in a vintage World War II WAC uniform. She had planned an evening of songs that coordinated with her outfit—"I'll Be Seeing You," "A-Tisket, A-Tasket," "Don't Sit Under the Apple Tree."

Once the stage lights hit her, though, she veered away from her script.

As the applause died down, she said, "I'm going back to southern Indiana Sunday morning."

A few boos and shouts of "No!" came from the regulars. Audrey smiled and said, "You're sweet. But don't you worry; I'm not going there to stay. I'll just be gone for a couple of days." The booing transformed into whistles and more applause.

"Some of you might have been here when I talked about the little chore I promised to take care of down there. Well, the time has come. As usual, the great challenge is picking just the right outfit for the occasion. I've been calling old friends and soliciting advice, but I'm still trying to make up my mind."

Audrey sang the Ella Fitzgerald standard "Undecided."

Earlier that day, Terry had called his former home in Plainview for the first time in five years, hoping that whoever answered would be able to supply him with a phone number for his sister.

It had been James Henry's idea for Terry to call Cherokee. Terry had been having doubts about whether to follow through on the promise that had been so easy to make in Bailey's Laundry and Dry Cleaning. His fury had been raw then, propelled by years of pain. Later, when the tiny nest egg he'd brought with him from Plainview had been exhausted, he had swallowed that anger and resentment until it filled his empty belly. Even after Odette and James had hooked him up with free meals and a job at their friend Lydia's South Side diner, he'd thought of his father every day and tasted his revenge with every bite of food he ate.

But now that Wayne Robinson was dead and retribution hung within reach, Terry was amazed to find himself wondering what to do. Long-buried memories had crept forward to complicate his feelings. Camping trips with Mom, Daddy, Cherokee, and Seville. Daddy teaching him to ride his bike. Playing in the cars at Daddy's repair shop. Recollections of better days in the distant past competed for his attention with the ugliness that came later, threatening to reduce his ogre to a troll.

He'd called Odette for advice. She hadn't been at home, so he'd spoken with James. As Terry had expected from speaking with James many times throughout his tough high school years, James had counseled that Terry should be the bigger man—or woman, depending on whether Terry or Audrey showed up in Plainview. "You've got to forgive. Forgive your father, and forgive your sister, too. That's what your mother would want you to do."

James had made it sound easy. He'd told Terry about the return of his own father and how therapeutic forgiving El Walker had been for him. Not having spoken to Odette about El and James's relationship, Terry didn't understand that there was a far more complex scenario playing out in the Henry home than James was letting on. It was with James's urging toward forgiveness on his mind that Terry called Plainview.

To his surprise, when he dialed the number that had been his throughout his boyhood, Cherokee answered. "Hi, it's Terry," he said when he heard her voice. He listened to the sound of his sister breathing as a television commercial blared in the background. He asked, "How are you?"

When she still didn't answer, he continued: "I heard about Daddy. I'm going to come to Plainview for the funeral and—"

"I can't believe you have the nerve to call here," Cherokee said. "Haven't you caused enough trouble? All I've heard about since Daddy got sick has been that nasty thing you said you were going to do." Her voice quavered, and Terry heard her sniffling. She said, "I hope you know you won't get away with that filth. Seville's coming, and he's bringing friends with him to keep the peace. You'd better not try to come anywhere near Daddy's funeral."

Cherokee wailed about the humiliation Terry had brought to the family and the years of suffering she and Wayne Robinson had endured because of him. As she continued to toss accusations at him, Terry felt his hunger pangs of the past return. The anger he'd feasted on to soothe those pangs came back, too. When Cherokee paused in her recitation, he said, "So our brother, who I'm guessing is fresh from his latest prison stay, is going to stand guard at the cemetery to stop *me* from bringing shame on the family?"

Cherokee stopped crying. Terry heard another, cheerier television commercial through the phone. He inquired then about his sister's husband. A year after Terry had left Plainview, Cherokee had married the handsome dry-cleaning heir for whom her younger brother had once danced in his homemade Dior. "How's Andre doing, Mrs. Bailey?"

The phone had gone dead then.

To her Simon Theater audience, Audrey said, "There's nothing quite like family. Just when you start to forget the past, they remind you where you came from."

She played a jazzed-up version of a bugle call on the piano that would serve as a lead-in to "Boogie Woogie Bugle Boy." The bugle call turned into a series of arpeggios up and down the keyboard. Out of that rush of sound emerged the opening of a Brahms intermezzo.

"Before I go to Indiana, I'm going to go to a concert in Millennium Park. Have you seen those ads for the recital by Clarice Baker?" A few handclaps sounded from the audience. "Mrs. Baker was my piano teacher when I was a kid."

Chopin. Louder and faster. Several patrons whistled and shouted, "Bravo!"

"That's right. Your little Audrey studied the piano with a genuine virtuoso. I was going to be a great piano soloist, like Rubinstein. Well, maybe like Van Cliburn." Then she lifted her hands to show the crowd the chunky, glittering rings on each of her fingers and raced through a chromatic run from the lowest key of the piano to the highest. "Okay, more like Liberace.

"After Mrs. Baker's concert, I'm going to catch a ride to Plainview with my friend Odette. The question is, do I head for a thrift shop and find a dark men's suit to wear? Or do I paint my fingernails fire-engine red and break out the imitation Chanel? I'll tell you what, I never imagined when I was a youngster that so much of my life would boil down to that one quandary."

Audrey sang the first few bars of that 1940s favorite "Sentimental Journey." Then she modulated to a new key. She winked a heavily mascaraed eye at the crowd and belted out, "Walk Like a Man."

CHAPTER 30

The night before their departure for Chicago, Barbara Jean and Ray went to bed early, each claiming that the day had left them exhausted. An hour after they had kissed good night and clicked off the lamps on the nightstands beside the bed, Barbara Jean lay awake. She looked at the shadows on the ceiling cast by moonlight peeking through the gangly trees outside the house. She listened to the hissing of the wind through the leaves of those trees, hoping it might lull her to sleep. She turned her head and saw that Ray, too, was watching and listening instead of sleeping.

She asked him the question that had been on her mind all day. "Are you happy?"

The question shocked him, but his answer came without hesitation: "Of course I'm happy. I have everything I've ever wanted." Ray scooted closer to her. He slid one arm beneath her neck and brought the other across her body so that his arms encircled her. He took a fortifying breath and said, "You're scaring me."

Barbara Jean shifted in the bed until she was facing Ray, their lips just inches apart. She said, "I'm sorry. I didn't mean to scare you." She kissed him. "What I meant to ask was, do you think of yourself as a happy person?

"El and I talk about happiness and sadness a lot when we're together. I suppose that goes along with the territory when you're hanging out with a blues man. El says Loretta was sad from the day he met her. She was only happy when she was dancing. There's no real joy in El until he pulls Ruthie out of her case. Sometimes I think maybe I'm like the two of them. I'm happy when I'm with you. I was happy when I was with Adam. I'm happy when I'm acting a fool with Odette and Clarice. That's the only way I know happiness; somebody or something comes along and makes me light up. It never comes from inside. It's not like I'm *un*happy. Happiness just doesn't make a lot of sense to me. Know what I mean?"

Barbara Jean felt the tense muscles of Ray's arms relax around her. He said, "I don't think about it a lot, but it's like that for me, more or less. When I'm with you and sometimes when I'm in the middle of a really good day at work, I feel great. Otherwise, it's like I'm faking it. Well, not *faking* it exactly. More like I'm standing outside of it. James feels the same way. We've talked about it a few times while we're fishing."

Because both Ray and James were exceptionally quiet men, Barbara Jean had always imagined that they fished in silence. She'd often pictured them as two mute statues, floating along the river together until they agreed, through telepathic communication, that it was time to row back to shore.

"James believes it's the fatherless thing. He thinks maybe growing up without dads screwed us up some."

"He might be on to something," Barbara Jean said. "I didn't know anybody who had a father until I started hanging around with Odette and Clarice. I remember thinking it was like they lived on a different planet. Once, back when we were teenagers, the three of us were over at

Odette's house. All casual, like it was nothing, Clarice said that she'd never had a moment in her life when she didn't feel like everything was going to be all right. No matter how bad things were, she *knew* there'd be happier times ahead.

"At first I thought she was talking about something she'd heard in church; Miss Beatrice dragged Clarice off to Calvary Baptist almost every day back then. But Clarice said she knew things would be okay because her daddy said they would be. I actually laughed when I heard that. When I looked at Odette, she wasn't laughing with me, though. You know what Odette said?"

"What?"

"She said, 'Of course.' Can you imagine that? 'Of course.' That's the way they grew up, believing they were going to be happy and that things would work out all right because their daddies told them so."

They lay, forehead to forehead, listening to the wind sing. Then Ray said, "I think I know what our solution is. We've got to spend more and more time together until we get so damn happy that it starts to come naturally."

Barbara Jean said, "I like that plan. Who wouldn't be happy to spend time with the King of the Pretty White Boys?"

"Oh, stop it," he said.

She wrapped one arm around his waist and placed her palm against the small of his back. She brought her mouth to rest at the hollow at the base of his neck just above his collarbone, that place she'd been convinced had been made just for her when she was a teenager and first in love with him. "Between the two of us, we're gonna kick happiness's ass."

EL SAT WITH his back supported by two pillows propped against the brass headboard of his bed. He held a black felt-tip marker that he'd found among several other writing utensils in a misshapen mug that had a childishly scrawled "Grandma" baked into its glaze. He wrote, "My friend Bubba and my brother Bert" on the back of the photograph on his lap and placed that photo on top of a stack to his right. He reached for another.

Some of the pictures would go to Barbara Jean. He'd discovered several more with Loretta in the background. Not all of them were the kind of images she would want to see. A few, though, captured Loretta at her best, when her beauty was so spectacular that just looking at her was like stepping out of this world and into paradise.

The rest of the pictures would go to James. The same with Ruthie. James had said he didn't want her, but he might change his mind once El was gone.

El had worked out the end. It had come to him when Odette, as the leopard woman, had stopped him from swallowing the pills. Several days and a few lies later, the time had come.

He had lied when he'd told Odette and James that his brother and sister were expecting him. The last time he had spoken to Lily had been ten or eleven years back. She'd shown up at a club he was playing in Gary, Indiana, and, as she'd done dozens of times over the years, had announced that she was done with drugs and with Harold. She wanted to get clean and sing again before it was too late. Close to seventy, she'd been stuck in an addict's cycle of dreaming and never acting. She had disappeared by the end of the evening, and El hadn't seen her since.

That was just as well. Lily would likely be dead by now if she had come with him. He had been flat broke and in the midst of his final relapse that night in Gary. The best he could have offered her was a room in his run-down house in New Orleans, where they would both have fallen deeper into addiction. Now, though, he was clean and had enough money to get Lily to New Orleans. He had lined up some friends to help her get settled there, mostly old guys who remembered the tiny white girl with the Bessie Smith voice. They would take care of her.

His reunion with Lily wouldn't be all he had once hoped for. Too much time had passed for the fantasy of the two of them singing and traveling together again to come true. But he had dreamed of fulfilling a promise to protect his little sister that he'd made on a log in the woods as a boy. Giving Lily this last chance, financed by Forrest, would have to be enough.

El had also lied when he'd told Odette and James that he would be coming back to Plainview with them. Once Lily was on her way with Forrest's money in her pocket, El would get a cheap room in Chicago and make use of that bottle of good whiskey from Forrest and the painkillers he'd saved from the hospital. True to her word, Odette hadn't tossed the pills away. He'd seen her tuck them into a cabinet the night he'd arrived at her house, and he had filled his pocket with them the previous night.

For forty years, he had begun every song in every club he'd played by looking out into the audience. He'd been certain that James would walk in one night. Sometimes he imagined James running up to him with open arms and a forgiving heart. Other times he imagined James striding in, a rightfully angry man determined to balance the scales. Either way, he saw himself impressing his son with one of his best numbers and showing James who he was, even if he couldn't manage the words to tell him.

Now he realized that all those years of squinting into the lights had been a foolish waste of time. James hadn't known that El was a blues man until El had come, as a broken-down charity case, to stay under his son's roof.

But James had heard him sing his best song, the one that said everything about him, in a beautiful church, on the last day El had been able to walk on his own two feet. Like getting the money to Lily so she could be safe at last, that would have to be enough.

He flipped another photo over and wrote, "My family. Me, Lily, Bubba, Leroy, Bert."

HE'S NEVER GOING to shut up, Clarice thought as Richmond, beside her in her bed, asked another question about the venue for their renewal of vows. They had agreed not to discuss the ceremony or, as Richmond referred to it, "the wedding." Somehow the conversation kept ending up there anyway. At first, the chatter had seemed like an improvement over long discussions about her feelings or the minutiae of her day. Then he'd become relentless, circling back to the same topic repeatedly. Now the sound of his voice made her want to scream.

She stared at the moon through the triangular window high on the opposite wall of the bedroom. She listened to the tinkling of the wind chimes outside as they spun in the steady breeze. She imagined that she was ripping into the first movement of Beethoven's *Pathétique* Sonata. Nothing made his voice fade away.

"What would you think of a 1970s theme? You know, since that's when we got married," he said. "The whole wedding party could have fun with the clothes. We could have the same music at the reception that we had at our first wedding."

"Sweetheart, I'm a little tired right now," Clarice said. "I did a lot of practicing today. Let's talk about it in the car tomorrow." She intended to take a sleeping pill before she sat down in the passenger seat of the car so she could doze the entire way to Chicago. But there was no reason to reveal that.

"No problem," he said.

A few minutes later, he was rattling off ideas that had obviously come from her mother. "It wouldn't be such a bad thing to have the service at Calvary Baptist, would it? It's where the first one was, and Calvary's still the most beautiful church in town. It sure would make Miss Beatrice happy."

"I don't know if I want to give Mother that kind of false hope," Clarice said. "If she sees me walk into Calvary, she might slam the door behind me and never let me out."

He spoke over her, shifting now from discussing the renewal of their vows to talking about Clarice's move back to his house. "I've got somebody coming over to paint your closets while we're in Chicago. It should be done before we get back."

Clarice began to grind her teeth.

It wasn't entirely Richmond's fault that she was feeling so irritable. She was nervous about the recital. No amount of hand holding or back patting was going to change that. And the one thing that might help her wasn't being offered, at least not recently.

Though Richmond was now a nightly guest at Clarice's house in Leaning Tree, they hadn't made love since that time he had ended up in the emergency room. He'd been given the medical okay to proceed, as long as they used reasonable restraint. But the scare had left them both too nervous to initiate sexual intimacy.

"Carnations," Richmond said. "Did you know they can dye them any color you want?"

She would have sworn that Richmond didn't know a daisy from a rose, and yet he wanted to discuss floral arrangements.

This was just too much. She rolled over in his direction and wiggled across the sheets toward him. She threw a leg over his hips and sat up astride his waist. Then she leaned down and kissed him on the mouth.

When their lips separated, he said, "I don't know if we should."

She kissed him again and pulled off the T-shirt she'd worn to bed. "Honey, tonight we're going to gamble with your life," she said.

Moments later, Richmond's true nature staged a revival. Soon his arms were around her and they were rolling across the bed together. For an hour, she forgot about Beethoven.

ODETTE GAVE UP on sleep and rose from the bed. At the sound of the creaking of their worn bedsprings, James snorted and rolled over. He was sleeping well, a rarity. She shut the door behind herself as quietly as possible.

She walked down a hallway lit by the glow of yellow-green night-lights. Purchased by James to comfort the grandkids when they woke during the night, the lights were in the shapes of cartoon characters.

Lately, that cheerful illumination had helped their elderly houseguest find his way to the bathroom after dark.

Odette heard the sound of El snoring through the closed door of his room. If she hadn't just left James, she would have sworn it was him making that racket. The only difference between their snoring was one of volume. It sounded to Odette as if El had connected himself to that old amplifier he'd brought to the house with him.

The cats—there were five living with her and James that week— followed her through the house, thinking that perhaps they would be getting a midnight snack. When Odette didn't go to the kitchen, where their bowls lay, the cats put aside their disappointment and accompanied her as she proceeded to the family room.

From the table beside the couch, Odette picked up the book she had been reading, the latest in a series of slightly dirty mystery novels about a handsome detective. She didn't open the book or even turn on the lamp. Instead, she stretched out on the sofa with the paperback resting on her stomach as the cats settled in at her shoulder, hip, knees, and ankles.

Since El had come into their lives, Odette had found herself thinking about her own father more than she had in years. Maybe more than ever. Wilbur Jackson had built the house she'd grown up in. It might be more accurate to say that he'd built and rebuilt it. The place in Leaning Tree had begun its life as a one-bedroom farmhouse that had been just big enough for her mother and father when they'd married. As Wilbur and Dora's family had grown, the house had expanded accordingly. One of Odette's earliest memories was hearing the sounds of construction—sawing, hammering, cussing—as her father added rooms.

The day Odette's father finished his biggest renovation, two additional bedrooms, a bathroom, and a new kitchen, Odette and her brother, Rudy, had run through the house, hopping into each room and declaring, "Mine!" It didn't matter whether they stood in a bedroom or a closet. Every inch of the house was so special that each of them wanted to lay claim to it. Odette still marveled at the castle her father had fashioned for them with his skilled hands, his strong back, and the fertile soil of his imagination. A part of her was always surprised and disappointed each time she drove up to visit Clarice at the old house and saw that a new room had not been framed out on one side of the place or the other.

Odette's father had kept on building until a few weeks before he passed. At the end, though his arms were too weak to drive a nail, he'd proclaimed his plans for the next round of renovations from his sickbed. Odette remembered her father, slipping in and out of time and unable to distinguish her from her mother, declaring, "I gotta get over to Odette's place, Dora. I wanna give her a skylight." His passion for that project had remained undimmed even after she'd reminded him that he had installed a skylight in her and James's house the week they'd moved in.

It was only after Odette herself had lain in a hospital bed believing that she was about to breathe her last breath that she'd truly understood her father's final days. With her adult offspring gathered around her, saying good-bye, fear that she hadn't managed to construct enough good memories to sustain them had taunted her. Like her father, Odette had wished more than anything that she could rise from her hospital bed and cut a hole through the ceiling, so Jimmy, Eric, and Denise could see the sky.

Whether our daddies do us right or wrong, she thought now, they never really turn us loose. Abraham Jordan, despite his endless string of women and his countless bastard children, had been convinced that his Clarice was the sun and the moon. Somewhere, deep down, Odette was sure that Clarice believed it, too. They still laughed when they recalled the way Mr. Jordan used to stand, rather than sit, at the back of concert halls while Clarice performed, because he couldn't contain his excitement for long enough to stay in his seat. When the rest of the audience applauded, Abraham Jordan jumped, whistled, and yelled as if he were in the stands at a football game.

Richmond's preacher father never saw his son's flaws, so, for most of his life, Richmond was blissfully unaware that he had any. With all that love and approval behind him, Richmond grew up to be so charming that other men didn't know he was a scoundrel until they caught sight of him walking off with their girlfriends, and women didn't realize he was insincere until he was hustling them out of his hotel room door.

Then there were Barbara Jean, Ray, and James. Knowing them had shown Odette what she had taken for granted. It had been left to Big Earl McIntyre to fill in for each of their fathers—a deadbeat deserter, a petty criminal who'd died in prison, and a selfish drug addict.

All of them were sixty years old or older now, but each of them still struggled to either stay true to or avoid the roads their fathers had paved for them long ago. Uphill or down, smooth or treacherous, straight or crooked, those paths kept drawing each of them back.

She stretched and yawned, but she didn't feel any sleepier. Lying on the sofa was beginning to make her lower back talk to her. She twisted herself into a slightly more comfortable position. Odette and the cats lay together, staring up at the stars through the skylight her father had created for her.

CHAPTER 31

On the Wednesday morning before Clarice's Chicago recital, the Supremes left Indiana as a three-car caravan. Barbara Jean and Ray led the way in their Mercedes. Richmond and Clarice followed in Richmond's oversized Chrysler, while Odette, James, and El took up the rear position.

The three drivers stayed within sight of one another at the start of the journey, but they soon separated, and they finished the trip hours apart. Ray and Barbara Jean branched off before Indianapolis to visit a bird sanctuary in Connersville. Richmond woke Clarice from her sleeping pill–induced rest for a lengthy lunch stop near Lafayette. Being a policeman and unaccustomed to strictly obeying speed limits, James put his foot to the floor and made excellent time, arriving in Chicago a half hour before a more law-conscious driver would have.

It was two o'clock when Odette, James, and El parked in front of the Blues Pot. The neighborhood had changed in the decades since El had last seen it, and the Blues Pot had changed with it. Most of the mom-

and-pop businesses he remembered were gone. The sharply dressed young men and women who used to parade up and down the block all day had also vanished. The outside of the tavern was, like the by-the-slice pizza joint east of it and the vacant storefront to the west, badly in need of a paint job. The guitar-shaped white sign El recalled from the past still hung above the doorway, but the colorful rendering of the round-bodied woman that had once graced the sign had faded away completely. The faintly legible words "Blues Pot" and a more visible but crudely lettered "Harold's" occupied the space where the singer's image had been. Only the "L" tracks that stood just a few yards away from the place remained unchanged.

Odette opened the tavern door for El and James, who was carrying his father's guitar and suitcase. The three of them walked inside. After their eyes adjusted to the shift from afternoon sunshine to the dimness of the tavern, they looked around at a room that was in the same state of shabbiness as the outside. An ancient television with snowy reception hissed from its perch on the wall. Two men sat at the bar, hunched over their beer bottles, each seemingly unaware of the other's existence.

A stage on the opposite side from the bar appeared not to have been used in ages. Cardboard boxes marked with the names of low-end liquor brands surrounded a tarp-covered piano. Four rusty microphone stands, strung together by worn black cords, stood sentry at the stage's edge. Dust motes swirling through the air created the most movement in the room.

A toilet flushed, and then a door beneath the television opened. A man with a deeply lined red face stepped out of the men's room, wiping his hands on a stained bar towel. He had a gleaming, bald head with a sparse fringe of white hair near his ears. He was big—both tall and wide. His belly extended well beyond and below the waistband of his pants. He moved like a younger, fitter man, though. He strutted toward the oak bar, every movement warning observers that this old man was not to be messed with. As he opened the half-door that led to the area behind the bar, he flashed a mouthful of yellowed teeth at the newcomers and asked, "What can I get for you?"

He stopped and fixed his eyes on El. He backed up, then took a few steps in El's direction. "I'll be damned."

"Hi, Harold," El said. He turned to Odette and James. "This is my brother Harold." To Harold, El said, "This is my son, James, and his wife, Odette."

Both Odette and James said, "Pleased to meet you."

Harold passed the bar towel back and forth between his hands, all the while watching El as if he believed his former nemesis might disappear if he looked away. He said, "You are the last person I ever thought I'd see again; that's for damn sure. I figured you were dead by now."

Odette and James exchanged glances as they realized that Harold hadn't known they'd be coming. El hadn't exactly said that they were expected, but he'd implied it heavily enough that it was clear he had misled them.

A slice of sunlight cut through the room, and an elderly woman shuffled in from the front door. She was small and thin and so extraordinarily pale that she was almost blue. Her cheeks were dotted with perfectly round circles of rouge that accentuated the gray of her eyes. Her hair had been dyed the orange-yellow color of a manila envelope. She moved very slowly, like someone afraid of tripping and falling. The woman held a plate that contained a sandwich on white bread, a stack of potato chips, and a chocolate cupcake. She mumbled greetings to the two men on the barstools as she walked behind the bar and set the plate down next to the cash register.

As she headed back toward the front door to leave, El called out, "Hey, Lily."

She turned around and squinted at El. Then she cried out, "Brother?" She moved to the center of the room where he stood. Lily fell against El in a combination embrace and swoon, forcing him to rock awkwardly on his walker. "My brother," she said, tears rolling down her cheeks and carrying her rouge away.

Lily cupped El's face in her blue-veined hands. She said, "I can hardly believe it." Her voice was low-pitched and slightly scratchy.

Lily looked over her shoulder at her husband and said, "See, I told you he'd be back." She stroked El's face.

Her speech came in bursts that were separated by sudden pauses, as if she occasionally forgot she was having a conversation. *She's almost here, but not quite,* Odette thought.

Lily pulled a handkerchief from the pocket of her faded green house-dress and wiped her eyes. She said, "What has it been? Two, three years?"

El looked down at his hands and moved his bony fingers one at a time, counting. "More like ten or eleven, I'm afraid."

"No, that can't be right," she said. She stared up at the television as if she might find verification of the date there. She stuffed her hand-kerchief back into her pocket and then grasped El's shoulders. "It doesn't matter how long it's been. I'm just glad you're here, Marcus."

"That's Mr. El Walker now, Lily. Remember?" Harold said.

"Of course, I do." Lily pointed at the cluttered stage across the room. "We named you that right over there."

"That's right," El said. Then he introduced her to James and Odette.

Lily shook Odette's hand and looked James up and down. "Little James, all grown up," she said. "Come sit down, y'all. Can I get you something to drink?"

They declined refreshments but allowed Lily to guide them to one of several tables that surrounded the stage. Its imitation-wood top was coated with grime, and the rickety chairs complained as they sat. The votive candle in the center of the table was the home of a large black spider and its ornate web.

Lily said, "I wish I had known you were coming. I'd have made myself look like something."

"You look fine," El said, his voice cracking. He cleared his throat. "I was hopin' I could take you out for a little something to eat, so you and me could catch up." He angled his head toward Harold. "You wouldn't mind that, would you?"

Harold scowled in a way that made it plain that he would, indeed, mind. But he said, "Wouldn't bother me at all. I just think it would be nicer if we all had supper together, don't you, Lily? I can close the place early for the occasion."

Lily said, "Yes, we should all have dinner here. That'll be nice." She turned to James and Odette and paused, trying to remember their names. After several seconds, she asked, "Can you two join us?"

James said, "Thank you, but we're having dinner with friends." Odette was about to correct James and say that their dinner plans were for the following evening, but he looked at her with an expression that indicated that he wouldn't appreciate being contradicted.

An air-conditioning unit above the front door made a loud thud. Lily could barely be heard above the whirring noise that followed. "Maybe some other time." She rested one hand on El's arm and the other on Harold's. "Tonight we'll have a celebration for the three of us."

One of the men at the bar called out for a fresh beer, and Harold excused himself. After he rose from his squeaking chair to serve his customers, El said to Lily, "I really want to talk to you, just the two of us. Maybe we could take a walk around the block while Harold's tending bar."

Lily twisted around in her chair and shouted out to the two men at the bar. "Hey, Perry. Hey, Jerome. This man here is a star. He's the best blues man in the country, maybe the whole world." They looked up and aimed their eyes in El's direction. They lifted their empty bottles in a toasting gesture, then turned away again, waiting for Harold to supply replacements.

Lily reached out and put a palm to El's cheek again. "You know what we should do? We should sing. You and me could show the young ones how it's done."

She took her hand away from El's face and brought her palms together with a smack. "It'll be so much fun. I've got my old costumes upstairs, and I still fit into them. Maybe we could get Bubba and Leroy to come play with us, just like the old days. Wouldn't that be something?"

Harold reappeared, chuckling, "It would be somethin', all right. Bubba and Leroy have both been dead more than thirty years."

For a moment, Lily looked shocked by the deaths of her old friends. Then she said, "I know they're dead. I was thinkin' out loud." She toyed with a tendril of her orange-yellow hair. "If we put the word out that El's here, all kinds of folks would come see us. Won't they, Harold?"

Harold said, "They sure will, hon."

Odette watched El as he gazed at Lily through reddening eyes. Lily continued to talk, in her stumbling way, about the show she and El could perform. She named songs and described her costumes. She spoke with the innocent excitement of a child describing her class Christmas pageant. El looked nearly as miserable as he had the day Odette and James had first gone to his hospital room. *This,* Odette thought, *is truly a defeated man.*

Harold said, "I think Friday night would be perfect. I'll get the kid who cleans up the place to come in early and move the cases off the stage and set things up. This is gonna be something special. I'll put together some flyers tellin' folks El Walker's gonna grace us with his presence and have the kid nail 'em up outside every blues and jazz club in the city. I'll fill every seat in the house, if it's the last thing I do."

"I don't know if that's such a good idea," El mumbled.

"Of course it's a good idea. You don't want to disappoint your little sister, do you?"

Lily said, "You have to stay with us. We've got plenty of room. You can stay in the apartment in back. It's empty, except for a bunch of my clothes." She looked toward her husband. "He can stay. Can't he?"

Harold said, "Wouldn't have it any other way."

"That'll help us prepare for the show, too. We can rehearse all day tomorrow and Friday afternoon."

Lily asked James, "Will you come? It'd be real nice. Almost like having Ruth here."

James fidgeted in his chair and looked toward the exit. Odette jumped in. "We'll be here," she said.

"We'll do an eight o'clock and a ten o'clock. No, a nine and an eleven. That'll be good."

Lily stood up from the table and said, "I'll go fix the room right now." Both Odette and James offered to help, but Lily insisted that they sit and relax. She disappeared through a door beside the stage.

In her absence, conversation ceased. Harold kept watch over El. James listened to the sounds of the thrumming air conditioner and the traffic passing by outside. Odette studied the spider in the candleholder. Finally El said, "Thank you, kids. I can take it from here."

Odette saw the two old men eyeing each other like pumped-up boxers in a ring. She was just formulating words to suggest that El might want to come to the hotel with them instead of staying here, but James stood to leave. He said "Good-bye" to his father and "Pleased to meet you" to Harold before she could speak. James helped Odette from her chair and, with a hand at her elbow, tugged her toward the door. She had just enough time to call back, "See you Friday night," before she and James were outside, squinting in the sunlight.

THE DOOR SHUT behind Odette and James, and El asked Harold, "What's Lily on?"

"Nothin', far as I know."

"I know high when I see it."

"Anything she's takin' now, she got from one of her doctors." Harold crossed his arms across his belly. "You've got a lot of nerve showin' up here and actin' like you know anything about Lily. I'm the one who's been takin' care of her since she fried her brain."

"You mean since *you* fried her brain."

"I never forced a damn thing on her. She only wanted to do that shit in the first place because you did it. She's lucky I was there to supply it, too. Anybody else and she'd be dead." He held up one hand, fingers extended. "Five times I found her OD'd on the floor, and the great El Walker sure as hell wasn't there to save her."

El said, "You can't talk about how you've been takin' care of Lily and then let her get up in front of people and sing, not the way she is. You can't let her embarrass herself like that."

"Saturday morning, Lily will take her medication and won't remember the show ever happened. You're the one who'll be embarrassed. You'll finally look like what you've always been, just a little piece of a man. Even Lily's gonna be able to see it." Harold snorted. "I only wish Ma was here to get a load of how you turned out. My mother died callin' out for you." Harold pinched his mouth into a tight circle and in a screeching falsetto said, " 'Where's Marcus? Go get Marcus. I wanna hear some music.' "

El said, "Come on, man. That was a million years ago. Except for you, Lily, and me, everybody who lived in that house is dead. Can't we be done with all that?"

Even as he spoke those words, El heard the hypocrisy in them. He'd gotten the switch, the fist, and the extension cord, like all the kids at the foster home. But from the day he'd learned that pulling out his guitar and singing for Mrs. Taylor meant some of his share of beatings went to Harold instead, he'd been happy to exploit the deal. Loretta hadn't been the only one to emerge from that house ready to trade anything for self-preservation.

The passing years hadn't diminished El's sense of responsibility toward Lily or his guilt for having failed her when he'd been too high and self-absorbed to protect her. Why should Harold be done with the past when El wasn't finished with it himself?

Harold said, "You've been in my way since we were kids. Even after I got Lily away from you, she talked about you every day, like you were more than another damn junkie." He leaned toward El and added, "I had to wait a long time, but this old dog's finally gettin' his day."

"You'll get that day without me. I won't climb up on that stage and help you make a fool of me, and I damn sure won't help you make a fool out of Lily."

Harold unfurled the bar towel he'd balled up in his fist and used it to wipe a shining, clean circle on the surface of the dirty table. "Do what you want. Lily's gonna be on that stage Friday night. Whether you drag your sorry ass out and let everybody see what's left of you or Lily stands there cryin' because you didn't show up doesn't matter to me. I win either way."

Lily rushed back into the room. Her hair was combed into a neat bun, and she had applied a fresh coat of makeup. "We should do 'Blues in the Night.' That was one of our good ones." Her mouth twisted, and she seemed uncertain of what she'd said. "We sang 'Blues in the Night,' didn't we?"

"That was our first song. Out in the woods," El said. "I think about that every day."

He listened as she named more dead friends she hoped might come play with them. As the "L" train thundered past outside, he understood that the leopard he'd followed here had played a mean trick on him. He would not find redemption. That big check from Forrest wouldn't fix everything. He couldn't rescue his sister. He was years too late.

Lily paced behind El's chair. "This is the best thing that has happened in ages. To tell you the truth, I've been feeling pretty low. But now I just wanna sing." She clapped her hands. "We should do 'Stagger Lee.' Wouldn't that be fun?"

She leaned down and embraced him from behind. "Friday's just the day after tomorrow. We should start rehearsing now. Okay?"

She picked up El's guitar case and shambled off toward the stage.

Using the toe of his shoe, Harold nudged El's walker toward him. "Better get to work. I can't wait for Friday night."

CHAPTER 32

Lydia's Diner in Chicago was nearly identical to Earl's All-You-Can-Eat in Plainview. The menu offerings, though double the price, were the same. Lydia had even ordered her checkered tablecloths and curtains from the same supplier her brother, Little Earl, used. When she and Richmond had planned the evening, Clarice had believed that dining with family and friends in a familiar atmosphere would calm her nerves. Now, as she chewed at her lower lip and tapped her fingers against an imaginary keyboard on the edge of her table, she understood that she'd been mistaken.

Because of the size of their party, the Plainview contingent had taken over half of the restaurant. They were divided into two long tables. Clarice and Richmond, their four children, their children's families, and Beatrice and Forrest sat at one table. At the second table, Barbara Jean and Ray, Odette and James, along with their sons, daughter, and grandkids, sat with Veronica and Clement.

Dinner began with a toast from Richmond, followed by an uncomfortably long prayer delivered by Beatrice. Clarice thought it was funny how her mother remained exactly the same under any circumstance. Beatrice was hundreds of miles away from home and seated next to a husband who'd once been her mortal enemy. Still, as if in her own dining room, she was happy to force her loved ones to sit through her admonishment that they were all hell-bound heathens before allowing them to enjoy their iceberg lettuce–and–tomato salads.

It wasn't just Beatrice who was the same. Since having agreed to return to her former home with Richmond, Clarice had been saying yes to nearly everything that had gone along with her old life. After a morning of practice, her afternoon had been spent with her mother, who'd persuaded Clarice to have her hair fried, dyed, and laid to the side, the way she'd worn it before she had declared her emancipation from all things fussy and uncomfortable. One casual remark from Richmond about looking pretty for family pictures that night had prompted Clarice to bind her body in a girdle and squeeze her feet into heels that made her want to scream with every step she took. It had been frighteningly easy to sit back and let the clock reverse.

She tried to think of something, anything, other than her journey back to her old life with Richmond and found herself ruminating on the looming concert. She thought about the sonata whose second note she had somehow managed to forget at her Plainview recital just a few weeks earlier. What would happen if she failed to remember that note in front of an audience of thousands, instead of hundreds? Would she even be able to continue? Would she collapse there, onstage, from the weight of the humiliation?

Throughout dinner, Clarice's dining companions approached her at the head of the table. They gave her hugs and kisses. They complimented her hair and outfit. They told her how excited they were and declared that they were certain a great triumph lay ahead for her. Clarice was gracious. But with every word of flattery and admiration, she felt her overpriced food perform fresh acrobatics in her stomach.

By the end of the meal, she wanted to respond to every well-wisher by shouting, "Unless you're prepared to stand up on Saturday afternoon and yell out the name of the second note of Beethoven's *Appassionata* Sonata when I need it, you should just shut the hell up!" Rather than say that, though, she favored each friend with the bright smile her mother had taught her as a child to paste onto her face in times of distress, and she looked forward to the moment when she could pry her sore feet from her torturous shoes.

BACK AT THE hotel after dinner, the group split apart. Some people headed for their rooms. Others made plans to reconvene at the pool on the lower level. A few went directly to the hotel's bar. Richmond and Clarice said good night to everyone and took the elevator to the top floor, where, courtesy of the music festival's organizers, they had a large suite with a view of the park and the stage Clarice would occupy in two days.

The moment she stepped into her hotel room, Clarice slipped off her heels and uncinched her waist. She sat on the edge of the bed, wiggled her toes, and enjoyed the sight of Richmond removing his sports jacket and unbuttoning his shirt. She couldn't imagine a day when she wouldn't want to see him pulling off his clothes. Heart pounding in her chest, she heard herself saying, "Richmond, I'm sorry, but I can't live with you again."

Richmond, his shirt open and untucked, sat down next to her on the bed. Speaking to her in his most soothing tone of voice, he said, "This is just nerves. You're tense about Saturday, so you're saying something you don't mean."

"No, I'm not. I mean, yes, I am tense. But, no, I'm not saying anything I don't mean. Not anymore. I don't want to come back to the house."

Richmond looked into her eyes and said, "I know I did wrong by you, and I know you've got a lot of reasons to still be mad at me. But for five years, I've done my best to show you I've changed. I don't know what else I can do."

"I'm not mad, and I don't want you to do anything." She placed one hand on his massive forearm. "For five years, I've been breathing free and feeling like everything in my life fit. But tonight I sat through dinner with a stupid smile stuck to my face even though my scalp hurt and I couldn't breathe in my dress and my shoes made me want to cry. If I don't stop now, I'll start telling myself that aching from head to toe feels good."

Richmond wrung his big hands, longing for a football to throw or a bat to swing. Something he understood and could control. He rotated his wedding band with his right thumb and forefinger while staring at the clock on the nightstand as its glowing blue numbers displayed the passage of one, two, and then three minutes. He said, "I think I get what you're saying. But I love you, and I want to be married."

"We *are* married. We just don't live together. Why don't we just keep things the way they are? It's working fine, isn't it?"

"It's not enough. I need a *real* marriage. What we've been doing the last few years isn't a marriage to me. I need you there when I go to bed and when I wake up. I don't want to wander around an empty house. I know it sounds crazy for me to say this, but I don't want to worry that you're with somebody else when we're not together. What we have now might be working for you, but it isn't enough for me."

Clarice thought of how, for decades, she had tried so hard to believe that she'd wanted the kind of marriage Richmond had wanted. She remembered years of lonely nights spent struggling to convince herself that what was enough for him was enough for her. Clarice reached out and draped her right arm around Richmond's shoulders. She kissed his cheek and whispered in his ear, "Oh, darling, I'm so sorry. I know exactly how you feel."

CHAPTER 33

We rode the train from our downtown hotel to the Blues Pot. The station was just a few blocks from the club, and it was an easy walk on a warm evening. I was flanked for the short journey by my sons, Eric and Jimmy. Barbara Jean and Ray strolled arm in arm ahead of us. Denise, who was and will always be a daddy's girl, followed after us, holding James's hand.

When we arrived at the club, we were surprised to see it so crowded. I recognized the two quiet drunks who had been the only patrons of the club the afternoon James and I had dropped El off. They were seated on the same two corner stools they'd been holding down on Wednesday. I wondered if they'd ever gone home. To my surprise, their names came to me. I celebrated this small victory over my often cloudy middle-aged mind by detouring slightly from the path to the table Lily had reserved for us to say hello to them. I said, "Hey, Perry. Hey, Jerome. How ya doin'?" and got a childish thrill out of their totally bewildered expressions. Then I followed my family and friends to our seats near the stage.

The candleholders on the tables were clean, the candles lit. The light from them gave the place a warm glow that fit the old-timey ambiance of the club. The stage, cleared of the cardboard liquor cartons and dusty sound equipment I'd seen two days earlier, looked surprisingly elegant. Spotlights illuminated sapphire-blue curtains that I guessed must have been there on Wednesday but hidden by the stacks of boxes. The blue drapes ringed the performing platform and gave the impression that there was an expansive backstage area.

Outside, it was a comfortable evening; inside, the Blues Pot was humid and hot. In violation of city anti-smoking laws, the mostly older patrons fired up cigarettes and cigars, whose glowing tips they kept pointed toward the ceiling to avoid scorching passersby in the packed tavern. The haze in the air was thickened by wisps of smoke rising from the stage lights, which, turned on for the first time in years, cooked through layers of cobwebs and tobacco tar.

I was glad that our children had come with us. Of course, I couldn't have kept them away if I'd tried. They each wanted to see the grandfather they'd recently heard so much about, the man who, in their mother's descriptions, had gone from Satan incarnate to sad old man in just a few weeks.

Someone said, "Hey, Odette," and I looked up to see Terry Robinson. He bent down and wrapped his arms around me, kissing me on both cheeks. I hadn't laid eyes on Terry since I'd waved good-bye to him as he'd hopped aboard a bus leaving Plainview five years earlier. He'd become more handsome. His hair was long. It extended all the way to his shoulders in a mass of thick braids. He was thin but not scrawny, as he had once been.

As James scooted his chair back to rise and greet him, Terry said, "Don't get up, Mr. Henry." (Terry had never gotten the hang of calling James by his first name, though James had asked him to years ago.) James stood, and the two of them hugged. James introduced Terry to our children. Terry had heard a lot about my kids, and vice versa, but they'd been a different generation than him and their paths had never crossed in Plainview. Terry had met Barbara Jean. The two kindred spirits started talking fashion even before Terry sat down at the table. He loved her pink-and-white striped dress. She adored his red suede espadrilles. They'd have kept it up all night if I hadn't interrupted.

I said, "Terry, when you told me you'd be coming here from work, I was kind of hoping that I'd see you in your work clothes. I was looking forward to meeting Audrey Crawford."

Terry ran his hand through his long hair and said, "To tell you the truth, Audrey's not so different from Terry anymore. You might meet her on Sunday. I'm still going back and forth about that."

I didn't say more about Sunday and the funeral; I didn't want Barbara Jean and James to start beating the "forgive and forget" drum. And there was already plenty of father-son strife floating around in the air of the Blues Pot. We ordered drinks and waited for the show to begin.

At ten minutes after nine, the room quieted as Harold Taylor walked onto the stage. He wore a rust-colored three-piece suit that had clearly been manufactured in the 1970s and a toupee that was an identical shade of red. I could almost hear the seams of his suit screaming for mercy as he did a mummy walk to keep from splitting his pants.

Harold said, "Good evening, everybody. I have the honor of introducing the greatest blues man of our time." Chuckling, he added, "He'll tell you that himself." A few people laughed, and he continued: "The famous El Walker will be joined by my wife, Lily. So put your hands together, folks. This is gonna be something you won't soon forget."

Harold departed, and El and Lily took the stage. El had forgone his walker and was using a cane, but it was clear that walking with the cane took a great amount of effort. Beads of sweat popped up across El's forehead as he slowly made his way toward his guitar, which was waiting on a stand beside two squat stools. Because of El's sluggish pace, the applause had ended well before he and Lily were seated, setting up an awkwardness that didn't bode well for the performance ahead.

El wore a baggy charcoal suit. Lily was flashier in a beaded black gown with a glittering fringe that hung down just below her knees. El began to play, and the sound system cracked and squealed, causing all of us to plug our ears with our fingers. Soon, though, the young man operating the vintage soundboard had the situation under control, and El could be heard clearly and without distortion throughout the club.

Lily began to sing. She looked frightened and confused, and her voice sounded weak and tentative. Then, after getting through one line, she and everybody else in the club realized at the same time that she had begun singing the wrong song. El was playing "Blues in the Night." Lily had started in on "St. Louis Blues."

El followed her lead and changed songs, but so did Lily. Pretty soon, they were clashing again. There were murmurs from the audience as Lily and El both stopped.

El reached out and patted Lily's hand. Then he began to play again. This time they both sang. They started out quietly, as if they still weren't quite sure what song they were performing. That lasted for just a minute or so, and soon enough they relaxed. Then, halfway through "Blues in the Night," Lily reached out and placed her hand on El's shoulder.

Later, when I described to Clarice what happened next, I would tell her that an electric current seemed to pass between the two of them. Lily found her pitch and her confidence. El's voice and his guitar became so connected that they sounded like one instrument.

Lily stood from her stool and let out a howl that bounced from every surface in the room. Then they were off. They traded verses and sang in unison. Lily arched her back and leaned against El, the two of them singing so loud that the windows vibrated.

I joined the crowd in cheering and applauding during the song. All around us, people shouted out encouragement. When the second song started and Lily dug her teeth into "St. Louis Blues" with the right accompaniment, the crowd nearly lost its mind.

I heard a familiar, brash voice holler, "Sing your song, white girl!" and turned to see Aunt Marjorie beside the stage. She was dressed in her clean Sunday overalls and a white T-shirt. She had a book of matches rolled up in one sleeve, and the tip of a fresh cigar stuck out from the breast pocket of her overalls. Aunt Marjorie swayed to the beat of the music next to Eleanor Roosevelt, who shimmied like a showgirl and waved her fox stole in the air as if she were signaling incoming aircraft. Daddy was there, too. I wanted to run up to him and say hi, but he was locked in an embrace with Mama as they danced in front of El. Mama was grinding her hips against Daddy in a manner that I could happily have gone to my grave without ever witnessing.

Lily was everything El had told me she was. The two of them together were a wonder. The frail, failing figures who had taken the stage disappeared as El and Lily made music. El's guitar playing was powerful and agile. His voice boomed with authority and passion. A confused old lady just minutes earlier, Lily became vibrant and sexy. One moment she was playful; the next she was beseeching. We fell under a spell cast by two senior citizens blasting out the blues. They might not have been louder than the "L" when it clattered by outside, but it was a sure bet that no one noticed it passing.

They sang for nearly an hour before El announced that they'd be taking a break. When they left the stage, everyone got to their feet.

James and I left our friends and family and walked outside to inhale some fresh air. Our lungs were used to a far less urban atmosphere, so what we breathed on that Chicago street barely qualified as air, much less fresh. But it felt good to be outside in the breeze.

We walked several feet away from the doorway and found a spot where we could lean against the cool stone of a shuttered bank building. As the train rushed past, James and I felt the ground tremble and watched yellow and white sparks fall from the wheels. When the last train car vanished down the tracks and only the traffic noise and the chatter of other club patrons outside for intermission competed to be heard, James spoke.

"I saw him once after he cut me. I never told you about it, but he came to see me on my fifteenth birthday."

I said, "Okay." Then I moved closer to James, knowing from the sound of his voice that he had something he needed to say and that it wasn't going to be easy for him.

"It was like a dream come true for me. He walked in the house like he'd just left the day before. I thought he was the most impressive man I'd ever seen. It was like he'd stepped out of a movie. He was all dressed up, and he claimed he'd just gotten back from California. Of course, later I understood that it being my birthday was likely just a coincidence. That would have been around the time of Forrest Payne's first wedding, so El was probably in town for that.

"He asked Mama if he could take me out in his car for a driving lesson to celebrate my birthday. She didn't want to let me go with him, but I begged until she gave in.

"It was great. He gave me my first taste of whiskey. He let me drive his car around town until I was too drunk to keep it on the road. He also gave me my first joint. I got so messed up I could hardly walk. We had to stop a couple times for me to throw up. Then I remember him half-carrying me into a strange house."

I gripped James's arm, worried about what might be coming next.

James said, "He talked to some man at the house, and then El told me, 'Happy birthday, son,' and the guy he'd talked to brought me into a room where this woman was waiting. That was my first time, on dirty sheets that smelled like sweat and perfume, with a woman who was twice my age and just as drunk as I was. When I left her room, El was in the kitchen drinking with the woman's pimp, or boyfriend, or whatever he was. He hopped up and patted me on the back, congratulating me. I was feeling kind of proud of myself, too, I guess. I was a dumb kid and she was a good-looking woman, even if she was drunk.

"I felt good until a door in the corner of the kitchen opened up and Barbara Jean walked in the room. She stopped when she saw me, and the two of us stood there staring at each other. We weren't friends, but I knew her from school. Her mother's man laughed and said, 'You can't have the young one, too, little dude.' Then Barbara Jean turned and ran out of the room.

"While El drove me back to Mama's house, I kept thinking about the way Barbara Jean had looked at me. I'd never felt that low before. The only time I've felt that bad since was after I beat that guy at the police station. When we got home, Mama saw me stumble in, and she asked what had happened. I couldn't talk to her. What was I going to say? Besides, by then I had to vomit again.

"I stayed in the bathroom for a long time, listening to Mama scream, 'What have you done to him now, Marcus?! What have you done?!'

"I'd never heard her yell like that; you remember how quiet she was. It was like I was listening to a stranger. Mama put him out right then, and neither of us ever mentioned that visit again.

"It was years before I could look Barbara Jean in the eye. Even after we got to be friends and she told me, herself, to forget about it, that half the men and boys in town had come through her house, I still couldn't erase the look she gave me in her kitchen from my head.

"When you and me got together, I was afraid to touch you, even though I'd loved you since you ran those bullies off when we were in grade school. I felt like you were this perfect thing and I was rotten. That's who my father always was to me. He was the man who made me ugly on the outside and then tried to ruin me inside, too."

I said, "I'm so sorry. I'd never have brought him in the house if I'd known that. I thought I was doing the right thing, but it was a mistake."

James said, "No, that's not what I'm getting at. What he did then and what he did when I was four years old were just the kind of dumb-ass things drug addicts do. You were right to bring him. I've had questions about him my whole life, and now I've got the main one answered."

He turned away from the elevated tracks that he'd been staring at throughout our talk. Facing me, he said, "Almost as far back as I can remember, I've been asking myself what Mama ever saw in him. I wondered what kind of fool she was to be with a man like him. I felt bad about that, like I was blaming her for the things he did. But now, I understand. She was a young girl, just a teenager, and she ran into this boy who could do what we just saw. Even if back then it was half of what he can do now, when he turned that magic on her, of course she fell in love. She didn't have a choice.

"I understand now why she never told me he was a musician and why she never played his album for me, even though that was the thing that made my father special. Mama taught me to forgive, and she knew that if I ever heard him sing and play that guitar, I'd want him in my life so bad that I'd let him get away with anything."

As I listened to James, I understood something, too. All this time, I'd thought he was just struggling to forgive El and, later, to forgive me. But James had had other things on his mind. Until that moment there on the sidewalk in Chicago, I didn't see that James had also been searching for a way to forgive his mother and forgive himself. El Walker hadn't been first or even second on James's absolution list.

Deafening screeches announced another "L" train. After that one left, James cleared his throat and said, "It's nice to finally see that my mother was no fool, you know?"

I reached out and held him tight, pressing the side of my face against his chest and listening to his heart beat. Then, leaning into each other, we walked back inside the Blues Pot to listen to El and his sister shake the walls as they belted out stories about love.

CHAPTER 34

*T*he second set at the Blues Pot was longer than the first, and afterward, none of us wanted to leave. Almost everybody in the club stuck around to congratulate El and Lily. We had to wait in line to add our voices to those of the other admirers. Several people, after overhearing that James was El's son, stopped by the table to shake James's hand, as if his father's triumph had been his as well. I was surprised to see James smile and accept the praise.

It was nearly two a.m. when we finally left the bar. I couldn't remember the last time James and I had stayed out that late. Outside, beneath the guitar-shaped sign, we made arrangements with Terry to meet him at our hotel the following afternoon and walk over to the park for Clarice's concert. We said good-bye to him as he hurried off to board the train. The rest of us piled into two taxicabs and headed downtown toward our beds.

I was surprised to catch sight of Mama on the main floor of the hotel as I stepped inside the elevator with my sleepy family. She beckoned me toward her with both hands.

Just as the doors of the elevator began to slide shut, I hopped out. Turning to James, I said, "I'll be up in just a minute." A quizzical expression came over his face, but he didn't rush out of the elevator after me. He was too tired by then and was eager to sleep.

Mama stood at the end of a long hallway that led to the lobby. As I walked closer to her, I heard familiar music emerging from the last of several sets of wide oak double doors. It was the beginning of the first piece on Clarice's recital program. I pulled open the heavy door labeled "Catalpa Ballroom" and stepped inside.

Clarice sat behind a shiny black baby grand piano. She played ten seconds or so of music, stopped, and then repeated the same bars. She did this several times as I slowly walked toward her across the cavernous room. Each repetition of the tune was a bit faster than the one before it. By the time I stood next to her, Clarice was producing a wild blur of sound.

Finally, she glanced up from the keyboard and saw me standing there. Her eyes were swollen and red. She looked as if she had aged a decade since I had seen her at dinner the previous night.

I said, "Clarice, what's going on?"

She chewed on her lower lip for a moment and then said, "Odette, I'm scared."

"It'll be okay, Clarice. You're going to play beautifully. You've been ready for this . . . no, you've been *more than ready* for this for forty years."

She shook her head. "I haven't played a decent performance in months, not in front of people at least. I don't think I know how to do it anymore. I went to the stage at the park today to rehearse, and I could barely get through the pieces. My hands shook most of the time. When they weren't shaking, I couldn't remember the notes. I've played these pieces a thousand times. I learned each one of them before I was twenty years old. But the notes were just flying out of my head.

"I hardly slept at all last night, and I've been exhausted all day. So I thought that maybe things would be better if I got some rest. But I just lay in bed listening to my heart pound. I finally gave up on sleeping and figured I'd come down here and find a piano to play. That was almost three hours ago, and it's been getting worse and worse. I can't think. I can't sleep. And I can't play.

"I keep wondering if maybe I should just go back home. I could tell everybody that I'm sick. At least that way I won't humiliate myself."

I said, "Do you want me to go get Richmond?"

Clarice made a sound that was halfway between a laugh and a wail. Then she said, "No, that definitely won't help. I don't know where he is. I'm not even sure he's still in the hotel."

My mind immediately traveled to where it had traditionally gone over the past decades whenever Clarice said that she didn't know where Richmond had wandered off to. Within seconds, I was good and mad.

Clarice must've seen the anger on my face, because she quickly added, "It's not what you're thinking. He left because I told him I won't be coming back to live with him. He packed up his things this morning, and I'm not sure where he went."

I wanted to know more, but I didn't think this was the right time to ask. I sat next to her on the bench and listened.

She said, "I made up my mind about it at dinner Thursday night, and it seemed like it wouldn't be right if I waited until after the concert to tell him, not after all he's done to help me. I would have felt like I used him or tricked him. There's been enough of that between the two of us."

"I guess you're right," I said. "But for a while there, Richmond was doing such fine work calming your nerves. It might have been worth a little bit of deception to keep him on the job a couple of extra days."

The corners of her mouth curved upward a little, but then she went back to chewing at her lip. She tapped at the keys of the piano as she spoke. "I've wanted to make music since I was five years old. Even while I was telling myself that raising the kids and being a good wife and keeping a nice home meant everything to me, I wanted to be on a stage.

I could never have said it out loud, but I thought about it every day. Now I've got it, and I'm going to fail. After all those years of telling myself that I could do it if it weren't for Mother, or if it weren't for Richmond, or if it weren't for the kids, it turns out the problem was me. Tomorrow I'm going to walk out onto that stage alone and look out at all those people in the park and fail, alone."

"You need sleep, Clarice. You'll feel better in the morning. I'll stay with you if you want."

She dragged the back of her hand beneath her eyes and wiped away tears. She said, "I'm going to play everything through one more time. Then I'll go upstairs. I'll be okay."

But I knew Clarice as well as I knew James or any of my children. There was nothing "okay" about her that night. As I pushed open the heavy door that led back out to the corridor, I heard her begin that same piece once more.

When the elevator stopped on my floor, I got out and walked down the hallway. I halted four doors before my own room and tapped on Barbara Jean's door. Her face was scrubbed clean, and she wore a peach-colored nightgown. Before she could ask why I was there, I said, "We have to do something."

MY THREE KIDS and Clarice's four, who Barbara Jean and I had summoned from their beds, were with me when I opened the door to the Catalpa Ballroom again. Our seven adult children proceeded to sit cross-legged in a circle around the piano, just the way they used to when they were small and Clarice would serenade them off to sleep at naptime.

Barbara Jean and I walked up to the piano bench and stood on either side of Clarice. Barbara Jean said, "Shame on you, Clarice. You know better than to think you're alone."

I said, "Play for the kids tonight and play for them tomorrow. You won't fail." Then, though we knew our knees would punish us for it the next day, Barbara Jean and I joined the circle on the floor around our friend.

Clarice didn't stop crying, but she took a deep breath, let it out, and played for us. Under the ballroom's glittering chandelier, she reminded herself and a ring of her most devoted fans that she was capable of creating something beautiful.

CHAPTER 35

*T*he last two patrons to leave the Blues Pot after El and Lily's performance had also been the first customers to arrive that day. "It's four in the mornin'. Y'all don't have to stop drinkin'. But you can't drink any more here," Harold said to Perry and Jerome, who sat ignoring each other atop the same corner barstools they had occupied all day.

With the place finally empty, Harold switched off the bright light above the sign over the entrance. Then he made his way around the room, wiping down the tables with a soiled towel. It wouldn't do to leave the sticky-sweet residue of cocktails to air-dry all night. That was an easy way to guarantee pests of all sorts and the extermination bills that came with them. After the tables, he cleaned the bar. There was a mountain of glassware still to be washed, but he left it in a sink full of sudsy disinfectant. He and Lily would get to that before opening time the next afternoon. Harold turned off the struggling air-conditioning unit and the ventilation fans that had inefficiently blown tobacco smoke out of the club all night.

The chore that Harold forgot was to turn off and unplug the Blues Pot's ancient sound system. It was an understandable mistake. There hadn't been a live performance there in years, so that task wasn't part of his routine. With all that Harold had on his mind, some detail was bound to slip.

The show hadn't gone at all the way he'd imagined it would. When El had shuffled into the tavern on Wednesday, Harold had thought it was a miracle. After he'd come to believe that he'd missed any opportunity for revenge against the man who had disrupted his life from boyhood onward, his lifelong enemy had been delivered to him, wounded and in a pitiful state. Harold had been given one last chance to get payback for those beatings El should have taken. He was going to watch El on that stage and have the memory of his mother calling out for El and his guitar when she was sick wiped away at last.

But the show hadn't been a humiliation for El, or a lesson for Lily. She'd been rusty and El had looked decrepit, but Harold had forgotten how brightly they could shine. That special, unnameable quality they'd had when they were together decades ago hadn't died. It had been on full display.

His chance to claim a final victory wouldn't be entirely lost, though. He could take some consolation in the money he'd made over the course of a wildly busy night. Then in the morning, he'd have the pleasure of tossing El out onto the street. That was one treat he could still enjoy. He doused the lights inside the Blues Pot, locked the door from the outside, and walked the few steps to his and Lily's home next door.

THE FIRE BEGAN just below the front right corner of the stage, in a tangle of cords running from the soundboard to the speakers. Areas of bare wire long ago stripped of insulation by gnawing mice had made contact throughout the evening, scattering hot, silver sparks in an ever-widening arc under the stage. No one saw the tiny bursts of light exploding beneath the floorboards during El and Lily's performance. But now, hours later, the sparks found purchase on a decaying cardboard box and became little licks of flame. That box contained twelve bottles of cheap liquor, as did the six boxes next to it and the fifty or so that, in flagrant violation of the fire codes, were stacked behind the blue curtains, against the surrounding walls.

IN A BEDROOM half a flight upstairs from the Blues Pot's stage, Lily spun in a slow circle. "I can't stop dancing, El. We were good, weren't we?"

"Damn good," El said. He had to speak loudly to be heard above the ceiling fan that cranked away at its highest setting in a futile attempt to force the cigarette smoke–filled air out the open window.

El sat on a low chaise lounge with cracked brown leather upholstery that crunched whenever he moved. He smiled up at her. They were both a little drunk from celebratory shots of whiskey and dizzy from lack of sleep. The sun was coming up, and they were still reliving their accomplishment.

"I can't believe all those folks came. There haven't been that many people inside this place in years. Did you see that Darius and Benny were there? If I'd known they were here in Chicago, I would have called them up and told them to bring their instruments. To tell you the truth, I'd have sworn they were both dead."

El said, "I bet they'd have said the same about us." He had his guitar on his lap, strumming as they talked. He knew that the show had contained some rough spots and that they owed a good part of the success of the evening to the novelty of such old folks just being able to make it through two long sets without keeling over. But it was wonderful to see Lily like this.

"I couldn't believe all those young folks showed up. They all knew you, El. They knew every cut on that album you made."

"Yeah, they tell me that old album keeps poppin' up on the

bootlegged-blues charts. I'd probably have me some real cash if even half the college kids who've got my record had actually paid for it."

"Doesn't matter," Lily said. "The important thing is that they know you, and they'll come see you again. I bet they never heard blues like you sang for 'em tonight. You showed 'em how it's done."

"*We* showed 'em," El corrected.

A cluster of scarves, shawls, bandannas, belts, and stoles hung over the door of a wooden wardrobe. Lily reached deep into the tangle and pulled out a blue feather boa. Wrapping it around her neck, she spun the ends of the boa in circles with her fingertips as she swayed from side to side. Tiny blue feathers floated through the air as the aged boa shed.

"You know who gave me this?"

"Who?"

"Loretta Perdue. You know what we should do? We should go back to Plainview and see Loretta. Wouldn't that be fun?" Lily caught herself then and said, "I meant to say that it was fun back then. I know Loretta's gone."

El began to play the opening of "Blues in the Night." Lily hummed along and tossed the feather boa onto the chaise next to El, where it joined a pile of scarves and shawls she had tried on and discarded during the hours they had spent together since their final set ended. This, she'd told him, was where she kept all of her old things. More often than not, she spent her nights here, among her memories.

As Lily sang, *"My mama done told me,"* she reached again into the twisted mass of accessories on the wardrobe. The item she pulled out this time was instantly familiar to El. The sheer gold-and-black leopard-spotted scarf he had given her a lifetime ago fluttered like a flag in the fan-driven air as she tugged it away from the braided jumble and draped it over her shoulders. In freeing the scarf from the mound on the wardrobe door, she upset the equilibrium of the entire heap, and everything fell to the floor. The door, which had been only slightly ajar, swung open.

Lily stopped singing and froze where she stood.

With the layers of fabric that had been obscuring it gone, the mirror on the inside of the wardrobe was exposed. Lily pushed the door open as far as it would go, so she could see both herself and El in the full-length mirror. She stared with her mouth agape, her vitality and happiness gone.

So quietly he could barely hear her, she said, "Look at us. What happened?"

"We got old, Lily."

"I don't understand. How did it happen so fast?"

El thought for a moment about how to respond, but he didn't have to answer her. He was interrupted by the sound of something shattering downstairs. In the same instant, he smelled smoke and saw thin curls of it snaking up from the floor vents, into the room.

"We've gotta get out of here," El said as he realized there was a fire below.

Lily remained transfixed by the pallid old woman in the mirror, her expression suggesting that she didn't recognize her.

"There's a fire, Lily," El said. "We've gotta get out."

She looked at him with a wide grin. "If there's a fire, Marjorie will just piss it out."

"We've gotta go, Lily," El said, louder this time. He put Ruthie back into her case and looked around, searching for his prosthesis. It was an ungainly thing that fastened to his lower leg and continued all the way up to his knee. El had stripped off the painful contraption as soon as he and Lily had entered the room. Now it lay on the floor just on the other side of where the mound of accessories from the wardrobe had fallen.

"Hand me my foot, okay?" he asked, his eyes beginning to sting.

Still moving slowly, Lily picked up the prosthesis and brought it to him. Then she walked across the room to the door that led downstairs. She opened the door and then shut it. With an unnatural calm, she said, "The smoke's pretty bad."

"Is there another way out?" El shouted as he struggled to secure his prosthetic foot.

Lily coughed several times and then came to sit next to him on the chaise. "Let's just stay here and sing. Remember when you said that to me that last night at the Pink Slipper? I got it wrong back then, but we can do it now." Lily reached for his guitar. She opened the case and said, "Please, brother, stay here and sing with me."

Smoke seeped in through the seams around the door, and they both began to cough. Maybe she was right. El hadn't planned to leave Chicago anyway, and his boy had seen the best of him now. He'd had a different plan for how he would leave things with James, but he'd gotten good at scaling back dreams. Maybe having one incredible night was enough. El looked into Lily's gray eyes, watery from tears and from the fumes filling the room around them. "Yeah, let's sing."

He took Ruthie from her. " 'Happy Heartache'?"

"Did you need to ask?"

El wiped a tear from his sister's cheek and then began to strum the strings of his guitar.

Just before the electricity cut out, the last gusts from the ceiling fan lifted the leopard scarf from Lily's shoulders. El watched as it danced in the air for a moment and then waved at him as it escaped through the open window.

CHAPTER 36

*T*he walk from Clarice's dressing room to the piano bench on the Millennium Park stage was seventy-one steps long. Down a short hallway. Across a rehearsal room. Through the wings. Onto the stage. She knew the exact number of steps because she had counted them the previous day as she'd tried to empty her mind and center herself before her rehearsal. Now, though, as she rose from her bow and sat at the piano, she couldn't remember anything between the knock on her dressing room door announcing that it was time to begin and her arrival onstage. She was aware only of her pounding heart, her trembling hands, and all the people.

They sat, clapping appreciatively, in rows of seats near the stage. They lay sipping wine atop quilts on the dark green, sloping lawn beyond the pavilion. Hundreds more stood off to the sides of the lawn, forming a human wall that seemed to stretch on for blocks. How on earth, she thought, could there be so many people?

She sat at the piano. *Breathe. In and out. Relax.* She recalled all the calming words she had repeated to herself at countless concerts, all the things she had told hundreds of jittery students. But with every deafening beat of her heart, she felt more panicked and more alone. Clarice thought again of the seventy-one steps. She imagined standing up and running that number of strides back to the safety of her dressing room.

She remembered then that just last night Odette and Barbara Jean had assured her that she was not alone. When she risked a glance to her right, she saw that she had company. Her twins, Carolyn and Carl, two years old, stared up at her from the wooden stage floor with wide, expectant eyes. Their older brothers, Ricky and Abe, were there, too, sitting cross-legged beside Odette's Jimmy, Eric, and Denise. Barbara Jean's lovely Adam completed the circle.

Clarice's heart continued to thump. But as thoughts of the crowd beyond the stage faded away, she brought her steadied hands to the keys and played for the imaginary children surrounding her. As she'd done so many times before, she entertained them with Beethoven—her first true love, her only faithful partner, her baby before she had babies.

That day in the park, it all worked. Each piece was truly hers. She took risks. She stretched tempos and arched her phrases until they nearly broke. She remembered every note. To amuse, surprise, calm, and impress the children she imagined were onstage with her, she performed the way she had, lately, been able to play only for her living room walls.

Soon it was all over. Three sonatas, three warhorses of the repertoire, performed as well as she could play them, exactly as she heard them in her head. The critics could love it or hate it, she thought. This had been her Beethoven and no one else's.

The roar from the audience when Clarice finished made the applause she'd received at the top of the concert seem like a polite smattering at a ladies' tea party. What she heard as she rose from the piano bench sounded more like a scream than an ovation. When the crowd leapt to its feet, the commotion grew even louder.

Clarice's children, the Supremes, and all of the Plainview folks were standing, waving at her from the front row. Even Veronica and her husband, Clement, stood shouting and whistling. Her grandson and granddaughter hopped and clapped alongside Odette's grandchildren. Wendell Albertson, her manager, grinned and gave her a double thumbs-up.

Richmond—who, five years earlier, had put all of this in motion by sending those recordings to Albertson without Clarice's knowledge—stood next to Beatrice, his faced buried in his hands. Odette, on Richmond's other side, patted the big man's back as he shook with sobs.

Clarice saw Terry Robinson and dozens of other current and former piano students in the audience. On some other occasion, the sight of them en masse, many of them sprouting gray hair and in the company of their adult children, would have made her feel ancient. Today, she couldn't feel anything other than a heady combination of joy, relief, pride, and gratitude.

If Clarice hadn't known better, she'd have sworn that she saw her father, Abraham Jordan, in the rear of the pavilion. He was whooping it up, whistling and leaping as high as her grandchildren, just the way he had done when he was alive.

She bowed and left the stage. When she was out of sight of the audience, she wanted to fall to her knees—in exhaustion or prayer, she wasn't quite sure which. But the festival organizer was there in the wings, clapping and saying something Clarice couldn't hear above the crowd's ovation. The organizer put her hands on Clarice's shoulders, spun her around, and pushed her back toward the piano.

As Clarice walked out for her second bow, the crowd seemed to grow even louder. The third time she returned, she was greeted by rhythmic clapping and the stamping of feet. To further cheers, Clarice sat at the piano for an encore. She turned to the audience and said, "Variations on 'The Happy Heartache Blues,' by El Walker."

Clarice had added to the arrangement since playing it at her Plainview recital. Her variations on this love song that wasn't really a love song were a little happier, slightly sadder, more insistent, and more rhapsodic now that closer study had brought her to a new understanding of the song.

The reaction to her encore was something she had never imagined. The roar from the people in the seats and on the lawn hit her with the force of thunder and kept coming. They stood again, and shock waves from the din they made repeatedly pushed against her.

Between the third and fourth times she was shoved back out toward the piano to take yet another bow, Clarice knew that she would never again be allowed to end a performance without playing that encore. She looked for El in the audience to have him take a bow with her, but she couldn't find him. *I'll thank him in Plainview tomorrow.*

She closed her eyes and listened to the applause and the cries of "Bravo!" She inhaled the aroma of summer grass and the scent of the Lake Michigan breeze, hoping to squeeze even more memories from the day. She silently thanked the invisible youngsters who danced in a circle around her, and she whispered prayers of gratitude for the Supremes who had brought the children to her when she'd needed them.

CHAPTER 37

James and I met up with Terry in the lobby of our hotel at eight-thirty on Sunday morning. Our plan, worked out at Clarice's concert the day before, was to pick up El at the Blues Pot at nine and then drive to Plainview for Wayne Robinson's funeral. The service wasn't until late that afternoon, but James said he wanted to have some extra time to play with in case we ran into traffic. I suspected, though, that James really wanted to ensure that he had an additional hour or two to play the role of the angel on Terry's shoulder in the event that Terry showed up at the hotel outfitted to take his revenge. Terry walked into the hotel wearing a conservative black suit so oversized that it nearly swallowed him up and a pair of worn but spotlessly shined oxfords. His long braids were pulled back into a tidy ponytail. With his somber expression and his backpack slung over his shoulder, he looked like a mortuary school graduate heading to his first day on the job.

I told Terry that he looked nice in his baggy suit, but part of me—the hard, unforgiving part—had hoped he would sashay in wearing the cold-eyed expression of a vengeance seeker and a floor-length, hot-pink ball gown.

At first, the Blues Pot didn't look too bad. One of the large front windows had shattered, and the sign above the door was black with soot. But as we parked across the street and walked toward the entrance to the club, which was now ringed by bright yellow caution tape, we saw that there was little left of the place we'd sat in just two days earlier. From the open doorway, I watched a car pass down the alley behind the building. With the back wall now gone, nothing blocked my view.

The blackened skeletons of chairs lay scattered across the floor. The short stairway that led up to what remained of the second-floor apartment was charred and incomplete. Oddly, the large mirror behind the bar had remained intact. It was cloudy and gray, but still able to reflect the devastation inside well enough for pedestrians on the sidewalk to see.

Terry, James, and I were still gawking at the wreckage when a clipboard-carrying man wearing an orange helmet walked out of what remained of the Blues Pot's front door. James flashed his Indiana State Police identification and then stepped forward and said something to him. The man, I later learned, was a fire investigator. He and James talked for a long time. I couldn't make out every word of what was said between them, but I heard enough to understand that although no bodies had been found, two people, Lily Taylor and El Walker, were missing. When the investigator learned that James was El's son, he added that even though the fire had burned hot because of all the alcohol in the bar, he was sure they would find any remains that might be there. He meant those words to be comforting, but some things simply can't be said in a soothing way.

James was just ending his conversation with the fire investigator when Harold Taylor appeared next to Terry and me.

Harold said, "I should've known something like this would happen. El's been waitin' all these years to steal her from me, and he finally did it."

Thinking I'd be helpful, I said, "They might not be dead. They might have gotten out before the fire." Harold gave me a look that let me know that my suggesting that El and Lily had escaped the fire and perhaps escaped him, too, was about as comforting as the fire investigator telling James that their bodies would be found. I shut my mouth.

James walked closer then and said to Harold, "I'm sorry."

Harold made a snorting sound and spat out, "Your daddy's been taking from me since the day he landed in my mother's house. The son of a bitch couldn't resist comin' back to take one last time. He's been burnin' shit down since he was a kid. That's just his nature."

Then Harold's eyes went wet and his anger dissolved. "She was all I had, and he took her." He turned and looked at the foul-smelling ruins of the club. "Now I got nothin'."

Cussing to himself, Harold walked away from us. He opened the door of the neighboring building and stepped inside, slamming it behind him.

BACK IN OUR car, James stared straight ahead as we made our way to the highway. None of us said anything for a long time. We watched out the windows as city faded into suburbs and suburbs into country. When James finally spoke, his words surprised me. He asked, "Odette, is he dead?"

"I don't know," I answered. "From what the fire investigator said—"

"No," James interrupted, "I meant, did you see him or Lily anywhere? Do you see him now?"

This was the most James and I had discussed the ghosts who visited me since he'd first learned of them, five years earlier. I instantly felt guilty for not being able to supply the answers he wanted. Just like my mother had done to poor Daddy, I had handed my husband the oddity of a wife who saw dead folks all around but couldn't give him a single benefit to go with it. "I'm sorry," I said. "I haven't seen him."

James said, "Can any of the people you talk to tell you if he's dead? I'd like to know."

"I'll ask around," I said, patting his knee.

If Terry heard any of my conversation with James, he didn't let on. Maybe he was too busy thinking about what lay ahead for him to bother with other folks' troubles. Because of the delay at the Blues Pot, we were running too late for him to be on time for his father's funeral service. As we sped south on I-65, James apologized to Terry for making him late.

"It's okay," Terry said. "I've been thinking that maybe I won't go to the cemetery, either. It's not like my family wants to see me there, no matter how I'm dressed. To tell you the truth, this 'be the bigger man' thing is tougher than I thought it would be. My head's been pounding since I pulled on these pants this morning, and this tie feels like a noose around my neck. I guess what it comes down to is that I'm not as good as you are at forgiveness, Mr. Henry." He added, "I'm working on it, though."

We'd gone about five minutes farther up the road when James slowed the car and drove onto a ramp that led to a rest area. He parked in the first available space in the lot. With his lips set in a grimace, James glared at the traffic zooming past on the highway.

When I asked if he was all right, James answered by striking the steering wheel twice with his fist and then saying, "No, I'm not all right." His fist walloped the steering wheel again.

James twisted around in his seat so that he was looking directly at Terry. "Wayne Robinson should've done better by you. Every second your father made you feel like he didn't love you was a second he failed you.

Every day he didn't beg you to come back home was a day that he failed you even worse."

James pointed a finger at Terry and said, "It doesn't matter what anybody else thinks you should do at that cemetery. You're entitled to do whatever you need to do. If it makes you feel stronger, or happier, or just prettier to show up in a damn dress, then you do it. You're owed, and it's your own business when and how you want to collect."

James settled back into his seat and watched more cars rush past on the highway. Then he said, "One more thing. Don't you worry about anybody trying to keep you away from that funeral. They won't dare."

Terry said, "I would love to see the look on Cherokee and Seville's faces if I showed up at the graveyard with a cop escorting me."

James let out a quick chuckle and said, "I wasn't talking about me. You're riding with bad-ass Odette Henry. Trust me, nobody's gonna mess with you."

"James Henry," I said, "there's not a man on this earth who knows how to sweet-talk me the way you do." I leaned over and gave him a kiss on the cheek to show him that I meant it.

Terry said, "Thanks, Mr. Henry. I appreciate what you said, and I wish I could show up there in some clothes that make me feel more like me, but I don't really have a choice anymore. I didn't bring my Audrey clothes with me." He patted his backpack. "All I've got here are T-shirts and jeans."

James gave me an odd look, and I had the feeling that he was about to ask me whether Terry could borrow something of mine. I cast a glance back at him that communicated the absurdity of this child, half a head taller and a hundred pounds lighter than me, slipping into something from my wardrobe. James seemed to grasp my message and didn't say anything more.

But just then, an opportunity presented itself. On the highway, just across a narrow band of grass from the asphalt patch where our car sat, a sleek late-model gray Mercedes-Benz barreled its way south with a beautiful black woman and a pretty white man inside. I reached into my purse for my phone.

When the Lord closes a door, somewhere He opens a window. And sometimes He opens the window to a boutique.

CHAPTER 38

Barbara Jean was ready for us when we arrived at the mansion on the corner of Plainview and Main. In addition to serving as the site for all sorts of fancy functions, the house also operated as a storage facility for thousands of items of Barbara Jean's extensive wardrobe. She welcomed Terry, James, and me into her home. In spite of the somber purpose of his visit, she couldn't help but smile at Terry with all the excitement of a six-year-old girl looking forward to forcing a game of dress-up onto her baby brother.

To Terry, who didn't need a bit of forcing, she said, "I took the liberty of choosing a couple of items I thought would look good on you."

The doorbell rang then and Ray greeted Clarice, who was carrying four boxes of shoes. I'd called Clarice during our drive home from Chicago as I'd thought about how to quickly outfit Terry for the graveside ceremony.

I had expected my conversation with Clarice to be more difficult than the one I'd had with Barbara Jean. Tell a woman that you believe a thin, twenty-one-year-old man would look good in one of her dresses, and she'll likely take it as a compliment about her slim hips. Tell her you think the same man shares her shoe size and she'll give you the stink eye.

My talk with Clarice and the shoe arrangement both turned out fine. There had been some discussion of Clarice riding home with Barbara Jean or me after what had happened between her and Richmond. But she had opted to return to Plainview with her husband early that morning. She'd been happy for the distraction of talking about shoes when I'd called her phone during that awkward journey with her unhappy spouse. She was also pleased to contribute heels to the cause. Clarice said that she had dozens of pairs she could part with now that she had chosen to prioritize comfort over fashion and had finally made peace with having big feet.

Before the fun could start, though, Barbara Jean said, "James, I have something for you." She hurried over to a round table in the center of the foyer and picked up a large, sealed manila envelope that appeared to be stuffed nearly to the point of bursting. James's name was written on the envelope in big, loopy letters. She handed it to him and said, "El asked me to give this to you."

James tilted his head sideways, and his eyebrows shot higher on his wrinkled forehead.

"He came by the hotel with Lily last night," Barbara Jean said. "What's the matter?"

James said, "We went by the Blues Pot this morning to pick him up and saw that the place was burned down. The fire investigator said El and Lily were missing. We thought they were dead."

Barbara Jean put a hand on James's arm. She said, "I'm so sorry. El never said a word about you picking him up. He must have thought I would see you before you left to get him. El and Lily are fine. They climbed out the window and down the fire escape."

"Where are they now?" James asked.

"I have no idea," Barbara Jean said. "He said they were going off together to find somewhere to sing. Then he gave me the envelope and left."

James brought his hand to his forehead and massaged his temples. "That damn old man is nothing but trouble."

Waving the envelope in the air, he added, "Thanks. We can talk about this later. You go ahead and take care of our friend here."

Barbara Jean patted James's arm again and turned her attention back to Terry. She said, "If you don't like the things I picked out for you, there are plenty more." With that, we left James and Ray and made our way toward one of Barbara Jean's massive closets.

I wasn't in the Plainview Avenue mansion very often now that Barbara Jean had moved into Ray's place, but I'd been there so many times in the past that its grandeur no longer shocked me. Terry, however, had never seen the inside of Ballard House. He stared with open-mouthed wonder as we walked through the massive home, passing rooms filled with perfectly preserved antiques and beautiful works of art. "Wow," he said every few steps.

He was even more impressed by the enormous dressing room Barbara Jean led us into. He walked around, touching the sleeves of garments and counting the pairs of shoes on display. Between gasps, Terry said, "This closet is bigger than my apartment." With a catch in his throat, he added, "Mrs. Carlson, this is a drag-queen paradise."

I've spent a substantial portion of my life hearing men stumble over themselves flattering Barbara Jean. But that compliment from Terry Robinson seemed to please her more than any praise she'd ever heard. She giggled like a little girl and insisted that he must call her Barbara Jean.

Clarice muttered out of the side of her mouth to me, "Whatever you do, don't tell him this is only the second-biggest closet in the house. If he heard that, his head might explode."

Paradise or no, we didn't have much time. I caught Barbara Jean's eye and tapped my watch.

She said, "Oh, yes, we should get to work." Then she walked to a rack in the corner and pulled down a dress. Passing the beautiful garment to Terry, she said, "Here, you can try this on behind that screen."

He read the label inside the collar aloud. Clarice and I moved in to hold him up as his knees buckled.

IT WAS MY weekend for encountering crowds. Between the packed house at the blues club for El and Lily's show, the thousands who had come to hear Clarice perform Beethoven in the park, and the hundreds of people pouring out of the automobiles that choked the winding roads of Plainview Memorial Cemetery, it seemed that no matter where I went, I couldn't avoid throngs of spectators. Wayne Robinson may not have been a popular man, but everyone I knew had heard some version or another of the threat Terry had made five years back. Curiosity and an excuse to put on your best Sunday clothes are powerful motivators in a small town. Whether they thought Terry was in the right or in the wrong, the citizens of Plainview wanted to see how the tale would end.

Because of the large number of cars, we had a long walk to the burial site. That worked to Terry's advantage. He'd wanted to be seen, and everyone there that day certainly caught his entrance. From where we parked, we had to descend a hill to reach the white tent under which the mourning party was gathered.

Thanks to Barbara Jean, Terry was a vision of glamour. She'd used the skills she'd acquired as a wash-and-set girl in the 1960s to arrange Terry's hair into a French braid. Then Barbara Jean had packed him into a form-fitting black Dior couture dress with a mesh bodice. The breeze caught the matching black silk scarf that was draped around Terry's neck, making it billow above his head like a parachute. As he carefully walked downhill in the black stiletto-heeled slingback pumps Clarice had lent him, he looked like a 1950s movie star descending from the heavens. Hundreds of eyes were fixed on Terry, and the murmurs of the crowd sounded like leaves rustling in a windstorm.

When we were nearly at the bottom of the hill, we heard someone rushing up from behind. I turned and saw Richmond Baker coming toward us. He'd gone home and climbed into his best black suit. Aside from Terry and Barbara Jean, who always looked like she was dolled up for a church service or a funeral, Richmond was the only one of us truly dressed for the occasion. He fell in next to James and said, "I want to see how this turns out, too."

A few steps farther along, Mama and Eleanor Roosevelt materialized beside me. I whispered to Mama, "What are you doing here?" Mama rolled her eyes and extended a hand at the scene in front of us. Richmond, James, and Ray, who under nearly any other circumstance could reasonably be called old-school country boys, flanked a young man in a sexy dress and stiletto pumps. They escorted him to his daddy's grave, where he might, or might not, drop his drawers and relieve himself in front of a huge crowd in the name of revenge and in honor of pretty boys in dresses everywhere. I had to agree with Mama when she said, "It's not like you see this every day."

Just as we got to the tent, two heavily tattooed men stepped away from the assembling mourners and moved in Terry's direction, as if to intercept him. One of the men looked enough like Terry that I assumed he must be his brother, Seville. Both of them approached Terry with puffed-out chests and scowls fixed on their faces. James, Ray, and Richmond stepped forward to meet them. The scarred man with the cop stare, the athletic, handsome gentleman with cold blue eyes, and the former football hero with the mile-wide chest gave the hard-eyed younger men tough-guy glares of their own, and the two sentries backed off.

I fetched a folding chair from the back of the tent and placed it at the end of the front row. Terry sat down, drawing glares from his brother, Cherokee, and Cherokee's husband, Andre. James, Ray, and Richmond stood guard at Terry's side.

After the flustered pastor said his final words and Terry's sister and brother had tossed roses onto the coffin, Wayne Robinson was lowered into the ground. Terry rose from his chair then, and the crowd grew still. He walked forward until he stood next to the open grave.

Cherokee whimpered quietly, and there was a mass inhalation of air from the spectators. Then silence fell as Terry crouched down.

He stayed there for several seconds, squatting at the edge of the hole. He scrunched his face and murmured something I couldn't hear. Then Terry reached down and picked up a handful of soil. He stood and, extending his hand out over the open grave, released the dirt in a slow stream onto the coffin.

Loud enough for everyone to hear, Terry said, "You really should have done better by me." As the people in attendance grumbled with disappointment, Terry brushed the grit off his hands with two quick swipes and walked back to his seat.

Clarice whispered, "I truly love that nail polish."

"Fire-engine red," Barbara Jean replied. "Nothing beats the classics."

Mama and Mrs. Roosevelt climbed up the hill with us after the interment. "I've got to say," Mama remarked, "I'd hoped for more. I'll have to make up something better for Marjorie when we tell her about it. Maybe I'll add some fightin'." Mrs. Roosevelt said, "Gunplay might be nice, too." Then they both vanished.

As we approached the cars, Clarice walked over to Richmond. She squeezed his hand and said, "I'm proud of you for standing by Terry like that. I don't think you could've done that a few years ago."

Richmond whispered something in her ear that made her smile. He gave Clarice a quick hug and a kiss on the forehead before waving goodbye to the rest of us and heading back to his Chrysler alone. Clarice stared after him, watching him walk away with his smooth, athletic glide, and I thought, *No, that story isn't done yet.*

Before we got into our car, Terry whispered to me, "Odette, I couldn't do it."

I patted Terry's cheek. Contrary to my nature, I found myself getting choked up. I told my young friend, "You did just fine."

CHAPTER 39

The morning after Wayne Robinson was laid to rest, I drove Terry to the bus station so he could get back to Chicago in time for his show. We were early, so we found a quiet spot inside the depot where we could sit and chat for a while. We hadn't been alone together in years, but it immediately felt like old times in the gazebo in my garden. We talked about his new life and his job at the theater. I told him I'd try to make it back to Chicago to see him perform. He said that he'd come visit Plainview again when he got the chance. I believed he might actually do it since Barbara Jean, who'd made him a gift of the Dior dress he'd worn, had told him she had other dresses she'd like to pass his way. Just the idea of walking into her closet once more had made him go weak in the knees again.

Just after the speaker crackled and announced the boarding of Terry's bus, he surprised me by asking, "Odette, do you see ghosts?"

I generally avoided telling my friends about my gift—or delusion, depending on your beliefs concerning such things. I'd never told

Barbara Jean that since her first husband, Lester, had died, I'd often seen him and their son, Adam, playing together in the garden behind her big house. I'd made no mention to Clarice of the many times I'd seen her dead father following her around, beaming with pride. I would find it torturous if someone were to tell me that people my heart ached for were nearby but couldn't be heard, seen, or touched. But there was such hope on Terry's face as he waited for my answer that I felt I had to make an exception to my rule. Also, my mama didn't raise any liars. So I said, "Yes. I do."

He said, "I wondered back when I used to hang out with you in your backyard. Sometimes when I'd come by unexpected, you'd be talking to somebody—your mother, I think. Then, when Mr. Henry asked you yesterday morning if you'd seen his father after the fire, I wondered about it again."

I said, "You've got your talents. I've got mine."

Terry leaned in close to me and whispered, "Sometimes I swear my mother is with me. I'll be watching an old movie on TV, like the two of us used to do together, and I know she's there, right beside me. Or I'll be walking down the street, or doing chores around my apartment, and, *poof,* there's Mom. Do you think she's really there?"

I said, "I can't say for sure if your mother's been coming to see you in Chicago, but I know she was with you almost all the time in Plainview after she passed. Right before you left and you were so unhappy, I doubt that she ever once let you out of her sight. It stands to reason she's still checking in." I patted his cheek. "Terry, Audrey, or both, if you were mine, I'd never stop coming to see you."

He said, "Thank you."

"I knew you were special the day we met in my backyard. What you did yesterday only showed me I was right. Since we left the cemetery, I've been thinking that if you can find a way to forgive your father after all he did, then I've got no excuse to keep holding on to the load of grievances I've made a habit of carrying. You made me want to do better. And that's saying a whole lot, because I've gotten real used to being me."

Terry furrowed his brow and leaned back in his chair. "Odette, I should probably tell you what really happened at the cemetery." He gnawed at his lower lip. "When I told you yesterday that I couldn't do what I was planning to do, I didn't mean that I'd changed my mind. I meant that I really *couldn't* do it. Like, *physically*. When I squatted down, I found out that the dress Barbara Jean gave me was so tight I couldn't get my knees apart. Next thing I knew, everybody was telling me how proud they were of me for proving I was the better man, and I couldn't admit the truth. I had every intention of pissing on that bastard, but that gorgeous dress wouldn't let me."

I laughed, picturing Barbara Jean, ever the lady, putting together an outfit for Terry with precisely that limitation in mind. I patted Terry's shoulder and said, "As long as you feel good about it, I still believe it worked out for the best." I was thinking, *I can't wait to tell this part of the story to Mama. She's gonna love it.*

A second announcement summoned passengers to Terry's bus. We exchanged hugs and kisses and promised each other that it wouldn't be long before we talked again. I waved good-bye to him as he boarded a Chicago-bound bus, on purpose this time.

WHEN I GOT back home, Denise, Jimmy, and Eric were sitting at the kitchen table with their father. They'd arrived in Plainview the previous night, along with their spouses. Denise's husband, Jimmy's wife, and Eric's partner had all been corralled into playing some sort of video game in the family room with Denise's children, Dora and William.

Denise said, "She's back, Daddy. Now you can open it." She pointed to the manila envelope El had left with Barbara Jean for James. She turned my way. "Daddy said we had to wait until you got home before we could look inside."

I resisted the urge to laugh. I had been pestering James to unseal that envelope from the moment we'd left Wayne Robinson's burial, but I'd been unable to persuade him to do it. He'd claimed that he was going to wait until the kids had left, so his attention wouldn't be diverted from enjoying their company. Our children were having none of that. And they had always been better at getting James to see things their way than I was. If they wanted that envelope opened, it was going to be opened.

James ran a butter knife beneath the flap of the envelope and reached inside. The first thing he slid out was a sheet of white paper. Standing behind him, I saw the words "My son," written in the same big, round letters that marked the envelope. Several handwritten lines were scrawled beneath that.

I pulled reading glasses from my pocketbook and passed them to James. At Denise's urging, he began to read aloud:

Dear James,

I've been trying to find words to talk to you about the past and all those things I did wrong to you and your mother. But it's like that time the Pink Slipper caught fire and everybody ran for the one door together. Every word tries to escape at the same time, and nothing gets out. So I'm writing this for you.

James paused, clearly having trouble with El's chicken scratch.

I remember every day with you. I know you won't believe me, but you were my world.

James used his index finger to slide the glasses a little farther down his nose.

I tried, but I wasn't good enough. That's the story of my life.

James stopped and said, "It's hard to read. Half the lines are scribbled over, and stuff is written sideways."

He went on:

There will never be a day when I don't look for you to come running up to me.

James stopped again, tilting the page in hopes of finding a better reading angle. "He must have been drunk when he wrote it."

Denise reached out and took the letter from her father. She said, "Daddy, it's a song." She handed it back to James. "See, these other words are rhyming lyrics that he crossed out."

James picked it up and read it again, to himself this time. Even with the reading glasses, he squinted to decipher the words. I was sure that my husband, who loves mysteries, was also trying to read the lines El had obscured beneath slashes of ink. When he finished reading, James quickly passed a finger beneath his glistening eyes and then played it off like he was just removing the glasses. His voice quavering slightly, he said, "It's not a bad little song."

He reached into the envelope again and removed a bundle of pictures bound together with a thick rubber band. He pulled the first photograph away from the stack and stared at it for a moment. It was a picture of a tall, skinny man who looked a bit like James. He wore a striped vest and a bowler hat, and by his side was a strange animal.

James turned the photo over and read the words that were written on the back in the same handwriting as the song lyrics:

Your grandfather Joe. His leopard, Raja.
If you ever see Raja, follow him.

James flipped the photograph right side up again, and Denise squealed at her brothers, "Oh, my God. This is incredible. Do you remember all those stories Daddy used to make up for us when we were little? About Joey and his leopard, Roger? I can't believe this."

Laughing, Eric picked up the picture. "I can't believe this is any kind of leopard."

Denise said, "Daddy, do you remember those stories?"

Our children's spouses came into the kitchen in a rush of conversation and giggling. Dora tugged at the right arm of her uncle Eric's partner, Greg, competing for his attention with her brother, William, who yanked on the poor man's left hand. Jimmy's wife said, "These children need feeding, and they say that Grandma Odette promised them waffles."

Denise said to James, "Do you remember those stories you used to tell us?"

Dora released Greg and ran to her grandfather. "What stories?"

"Those Joey and Roger stories I used to tell you and your brother," Denise said. "Your grandfather made them up for your uncles and me when we were little. Well, we *thought* he was making them up. It turns out Joey was your great-great-grandfather."

"He had a leopard?" William asked.

"Well, he had some kind of animal with spots on it," Denise said.

James continued to study the picture.

Denise placed a hand on her father's arm. In a tone of voice I hadn't heard from her in twenty-five years, she said, "Daddy, I want to hear a story."

Eric and Jimmy laughed at the idea of being told a children's story at their ages. But they both moved their chairs closer to their father.

Denise said, "Please tell us one for old times' sake."

I stood behind James, massaging his tight shoulders as our daughter badgered him.

Dora leaned against her grandfather's side and said, "Come on, Granddaddy."

William let go of Greg and hurried to join Dora. "I want to hear one, too," he said.

I felt the tension fall away from James's shoulders. In a hoarse voice, he began, "Once upon a time, there was a boy named Joe who had a pet leopard called Roger . . ."

My mind traveled back in time, and I pictured Daddy cheerfully humming a sorrow-filled blues song to himself as he sawed open the ceiling in my family room to give me and my children a skylight so we could see the stars. I rested my chin on my James's shoulder, and listened to the love in his voice.

It took some strength to keep from stepping away from the perfect moment in front of me to record it in the book I'd started keeping, the way Mama used to. But I managed to stay put, knowing I would get to it later.

The next time the blues comes looking for me, I'll do what you did, Mama. I'll shake my book of little miracles at it and tell it to move along, because I know how to jump for joy.

CHAPTER 40

*A*t the Club Sucre on the Rue Galande in Paris, a tall, skeletally thin young woman in a tight-fitting black tuxedo stood onstage. The red-tinted spotlight caused her platinum hair to glow pink and made the two-hundred-year-old stone walls of the club seem warm and alive.

The club was small, but nearly every seat in the place was filled, and it took the crowd some time to quiet as the woman addressed them. First in French, then in English, she said, "Ladies and gentlemen, it is my great pleasure to present to you our incredible performers this evening. She is a blues singer of the Bessie Smith and Ma Rainey tradition. He is a legendary blues guitarist and singer. Please welcome this marvelous brother-and-sister blues duo—El Walker and Lily Taylor."

People always snickered when the pale elderly woman and the white-bearded black man made their entrance after being introduced as brother and sister, and tonight was no exception. It had become a part of their routine. El, in his charcoal sharkskin suit, entered first, leaning heavily on his cane. Lily followed him, wearing a white sequined dress and a leopard-spotted scarf that matched the guitar she was carrying.

After taking their bows, El and Lily sat on the two stools at center stage. Lily handed Ruthie to him, and he connected his guitar to an amplifier cord. They thanked the audience and launched into the opening song of their set.

They began with "Blues in the Night." Three months earlier, at the start of what was supposed to have been a three-week Paris engagement, they had fallen into the habit of opening with that because singing it calmed Lily's nerves. When she became flustered, she often forgot the words to the songs they performed. So they kept the lyrics on a music stand onstage beside her to help her through her more confused days. She never forgot "Blues in the Night," though. It was a safe opener. Their regulars had come to expect that song nearly as much as they expected "The Happy Heartache Blues." They felt cheated when El and Lily didn't perform it.

The applause for their opening number died down, and Lily and El had a brief consultation about which song to sing next. " 'Every Day I Have the Blues,' " El whispered. He waited for her to dig the lyrics sheet out from the stack of pages on the music stand.

Before they could start the song, El heard the door of the club open. When he looked up, he saw the silhouettes of a tall, thin man and a much shorter, rounder woman against the light from the streetlamps outside. As the newcomers stepped in, El lifted a hand and held it flat at his brow to block out the glare from the stage lights.

Lily followed his eyes as he squinted again at the couple in back. "Yes?" she asked.

"Could be," he replied with a trembling voice.

Lily stopped sifting through the song lyrics on the stand. She reached out and placed her hand on El's shoulder as they began to sing.

Love, love, oh love, if you stay away I don't know what I'll do
How can I go on breathing without you to see me through?

I close my eyes, my love, and smile, thinking of you calling my name
But when that dream is over, you're gone and I'll never be the same

Love, love, oh love, you can treat me any way you please
Hurt me, leave me, cut me, love, I'll keep crawling back on my knees

It's you, love, only you, my love
It's been you right from the start
So come back to me and break it
Break my happy heart

Baby, baby, my baby, remember how it used to be?
No pain, no lies, just laughing and loving, sweet baby, you and me,
Can't we go back, baby, and find the joy we had at the start
Before you saw I didn't deserve you, baby, and broke my happy heart?

Yesterday's sorrow is old news, my darling, doesn't matter anymore
I'll beat my chest and beg my best for you to walk back through my door
Oh love, oh baby, oh darling, say you're willing to give us a fresh start
I'll always, always love you, after you break my happy heart

It's you, love, only you, my love
It's been you right from the very start
So come back to me and break it, love
Break my happy, happy heart

ACKNOWLEDGMENTS

Special thanks go to Barney Karpfinger for all of his help in bringing this book to life. Barney, you are a great agent and a treasured friend.

I am deeply indebted to my editor, Barbara Jones, whose talent and insight are more precious to me that I can possibly say.

I am endlessly grateful for the patience and judgment of my first reader, Claire Parins.

Peter Moore, thank you for making every day brighter.

ABOUT THE AUTHOR

EDWARD KELSEY MOORE is the author of the bestselling novel *The Supremes at Earl's All-You-Can-Eat*. His short fiction has appeared in *Indiana Review, African American Review,* and *Inkwell,* among others. His short story "Grandma and the Elusive Fifth Crucifix" was selected as an audience favorite on Chicago Public Radio's *Stories on Stage* series. A professional cellist, he lives in Chicago.